IN-BETWEEN GIRL

Book One of The Birchwood Inheritance

SHEELAGH ASTON

Published by Resolute Books

www.resolutebooks.co.uk

IN-BETWEEN GIRL

All Amish words and phrases are spelt according to the
Pennsylvania German Dictionary (Dentis book 2013).
Scripture passages are from the King James Version.
See the author's notes at the back of the book for full details.

Chapter 1

January 2024

S OFT AMBER RAYS split the pre-dawn January sky, silhouetting the factories lining the four-lane highway. The market wagon's gentle rolling lulled Hannah to sleep. Her chin tilted low and her eyelids slid down like shutters over her eyes as she tuned out of the muted thud of the draught horse's hooves on the snow's hard surface. A firm prod against her upper arm made her stir and spy the single lane roundabout ahead.

'Wake up, sleepy.' Aaron flicked the reins to signal for Blue to veer right.

She swayed as they skirted the central island and continued along the outer lane past a small corpse of birch trees by an open field buried in crisp snow where, beyond a low stone wall, a makeshift wooden cross stood.

'They should have taken it down by now. The vigil was weeks ago,' Aaron said. Hannah recalled standing ankle deep in biting snow on a sub-zero December night, teeth chattering so hard she could barely say the prayers and sing the hymns for the souls of those who had died. So many lost in the flames, all those years ago.

The wagon's boxed-in rear, filled with crates of beef and chicken, leaned to one side. Hannah gripped the wooden bench underneath her. The overhanging roof offered scant shelter from the freezing temperature. She wrapped her woollen cloak tighter around her body and stifled a yawn with a gloved hand. Biting, crisp air nipped at her cheeks and turned her breath cloudy.

Past winters had taught her that despite the protection of her bonnet's wide edges, her pale skin with its rosy undertone would appear as if she had scrubbed it with a hard brush in such weather, leaving a coarse, pinkish hue to her face.

'I'm surprised they've asked you to go in – who'd want to hire a bike or ride one in these conditions?' Aaron brushed the snow off the broad brim of his black hat, keeping the reins held tightly.

'I'm going in to serve customers coming to collect their bikes from Sol's repair shed.'

Hannah tried not to stare at Aaron's scraggy beard, typical of a newly wedded man, remembering the angelic, clean-shaven youth she had known all her life. The facial growth hid his smooth, plump jaw and full lips, belying his twenty-something years. No one called him a baby anymore.

'Sorry to get you up so early, but I do the farthest deliveries in the morning and the local ones in the afternoon. Don't we, Blue?'

The horse twitched his ears at the sound of Aaron's slow, nasal tones. Puffs of frosty air spurted out of the black gelding's nostrils as he plodded along.

'Better than walking through the snow.' Hannah rubbed her eyes, thinking of how her tiny feet would have been frozen within minutes of leaving home. She looked at the fields beyond the factories, buried under a blanket of snow. No bus could plough along the snow-filled country lane leading to her Amish home on the east side of Birchwood town, Pennsylvania. By the time she had trudged the two miles to the main road, her boots, stockings, and the hem of her dress would be soaked. It would be evening before she could return home and dry herself. Getting up before dawn was a small price to pay to avoid standing all day in damp footwear; a fate she'd already experienced twice earlier in the week. Friday had its advantages – two whole days to stay dry.

Cars sped past buggies driving into the factories' car park. Workers hurried to get inside the buildings, more for the warmth than the day's labour, Hannah suspected. A group of cloaked and bonneted women stomped their boots in the snow as they followed two middle-aged women wearing bobble hats and thick padded coats through the car park's side gate. At the other end, she spied another huddle of workers filing inside, their heads covered in broad-brim black hats, baseball caps, and woolly hats. Amish or English, all needed to earn.

From the outskirts of the town, Blue continued at a steady pace along the highway as factories gave way to retail shops, leading them to town. Over the decades, Birchwood had become the place where Amish and 'The English', as her community called everyone non-Amish, coexisted. Along the main street, the English-owned shops' night-lights pinged off amid the darkened Amish stores. Aaron flicked a rein, signalling Blue to swing left into a wide street lined with an assortment of shops and cafes. Hannah spotted English ones with their shutters down and canopies rolled up, and plain coloured Amish ones with their simple painted signage and window fronts.

'What will you do while waiting for the shop to open?' Aaron asked.

'I'll go to Izzy Stoltzfus's flat.'

'Grace's sister?' Aaron shook his head. 'They should both be married. Izzy's twenty-one, isn't she?'

'That's only two years older than Grace and me.'

'Like I said.' He grinned. The nub of his nose, red from the cold weather, glowed like a traffic light.

'Spoken like a deacon.' Hannah smiled back. Her single status seemed of great interest these days for Maemm and Grandfather at mealtimes. Time to settle down, they would say, noting which young men were 'a good catch'. Why were they so keen to see her married off? English women married later; why couldn't she? She contributed to the household by working in town. If she married, she would have to live with her husband. She might not be allowed to work, and certainly her wages would go to him or his family. Had Maemm and Grandfather thought of that? No, they were too concerned for her 'happiness'. Well, she was happy being single. They did not push her younger brother, Evan, to get married or engaged like many of his friends. Besides, she was on her Rumspringa. Nobody got engaged, let alone married, when 'running about' as the old folk referred to it. She tucked a strand of cinnamon hair back under her bonnet. 'You and Bishop Fisher would have all the single women over sixteen married off.'

'Oh, maybe not that young.' Aaron winked.

Hannah shook her head with a dry smile. She knew he jested, but his view was shared by many. A woman unmarried at twenty within her Amish community brought pity from the wedded women and sympathetic looks from the older ones. With no suitor knocking on her parlour door, they would continue. Not that she did not wish to marry; she did not want to marry just anyone. She wanted to marry the one who would make her heart dance. Meanwhile, she would pray about it and wait for her prayers to be answered.

'I shall be back later this afternoon if you want a lift home,' Aaron offered.

'Denki. But the buses should be running. I'll get off here, if I may.'

Hannah pointed to a shop with a display of hardware items in its window. Further down at the post office, a lone figure swaddled in a workwear jacket and woolly hat and scarf reached for the top bolt on a red wooden door. Aaron eased the wagon's brake lever and yanked the reins; Blue halted.

'Goot gute,' Aaron bid Hannah as she stepped down from the wagon. Her toes curled in protest within her boots as her feet sank into the snow. Bitter air stung the inside of her nose as she sniffed and glanced inside the shop at the clock on the far wall. Seven-thirty a.m.

She wrapped the flaps of her navy woollen cloak tighter, bowed her head to shelter her face from the falling snowflakes, and headed for the café opposite the cycle shop further down at the junction. The blackboard with its chalked 'open' sign was already stationed by the door. Eager to get out of the cold, she hurried past shop owners as they brushed snow from their doors. She shivered, the bitter wind slicing through the gaps of her cloak.

An elderly Amish woman, dressed head to toe in black, tottered towards Hannah, her portly body rocking from side to side as she walked by and exchanged greetings. A trail of boot and cat-paw imprints crossed each other on the snow-covered sidewalk. Hannah focused on the café with its bottle-green painted frontage. Peering at one of the large, plain windows stood a man of medium height, wearing a camel-coloured sheepskin coat and fedora hat, reading the menu. Her mouth watered and her stomach rumbled at the thought of a scrambled egg muffin or omelette. Perhaps Izzy would make one for her. Cheered by the idea, she approached the post office ahead.

'Goot meiyet.' The man with the bobble hat half-turned to her, one wet boot on a stone step as he pushed the front door open. He pulled his scarf from his mouth, his olive-skinned face breaking into a teddy-bear smile that matched the shape of his body.

'Good morning, Danny.' Hannah stopped and faced him. 'Another wintry day.'

'You bet. Twenty-five years I've been freezing my keister – pardon – body, opening up this place. Twenty-five. Colder than Brooklyn. Jeezers.'

Hannah ignored the last word, glancing up at the sign above the door: Birchwood Post Office. She could not remember a time Danny had not run the office.

A large grey car careened round the café towards them, the screech of its engine shattering the silence and deafening Hannah. Danny swung round and squinted at the vehicle, and the man by the café window spun, staring after it, his mouth dropping open. Danny slammed the post office door shut as the car sped towards them with its nearside rear window open.

Hannah whipped around, one boot slipping on the snow, her ears tingling from the sharp squeal of tires burning the tarmac road. Who on earth would be hurtling through the centre of town at this early hour? She backed away from the edge as the car approached, snow spraying from its wheels. She took a large lungful of air to steady her rapid heartbeat.

A lumpy object flew out of the rear window as the vehicle raced past. It tumbled across the sidewalk near the butcher's. Hannah scanned the empty street and ran to it, ignoring Danny's yell to stop.

A ragged-shaped object the size of a table-tennis bat lay on the ground, wrapped in an inky red-blotched cloth. Hannah stooped and picked it up. The cloth fell away from the object wrapped inside, which dropped to the ground, and Hannah froze, her mind refusing to comprehend what her eyes saw. A mass of blood and flesh. Human flesh. Her hand flew to her mouth, stifling a soundless scream.

The severed hand jerked from the force of the drop, as though prodded with a taser, and rivulets of ice ran through Hannah's veins. Wedged within its bent, claw-like fingers was a crunched-up sheet of white, blood-stained paper.

A soft wheezing followed by Danny stomping past her jolted Hannah from her daze. He bent down, tentatively tugged the scrap of paper from the hand's grasp, and unfolded it.

Scrawled across in black biro were the words: LET THIS BE A LESSON.

Chapter 2

'WAS THE VEHICLE light or dark?' The uniformed police officer barely glanced up as he jotted down Hannah's hazy recollection of the morning's grisly incident.

Hannah stared at the paper bag on the floor by the officer's feet. A man's hand, judging from the clipped nails and hair on the back, she had guessed earlier when Danny picked it up and wrapped it in the cloth. With its ridged fingers curled inwards, it resembled a chicken's clawed foot after Grandfather or her brother, Evan, had wrung its neck or cut its throat – stiff and splayed with shock and terror at its brutal death.

She pushed the image from her mind and tore her gaze from the bag, willing herself to stop trembling on the plastic chair near the post office counter as she waited to be interviewed. She accepted the numerous mugs of coffee Danny plied her with between the phone calls he made. He phoned the cycle shop to let them know where she was and why.

'Miss?' the officer prompted once more.

'She ain't gonna tell you,' Danny, who stood by her, butted in. 'You should know that. They don't help the police. Full stop.'

'Anything else you remember?' The police officer paused, pen in hand, ignoring Danny.

She rubbed her forehead, wishing the throbbing headache would go as she tried to visualise the blur that had flashed by. Grey. Four doors. That was how she remembered cars. Big or small.

'I'm telling you,' Danny interjected, 'it was a Toyota. Corolla. Dark grey like sidewalk stone.'

'Thank you, sir.' The officer paused in writing. 'Is there anything else you can tell us, miss?'

Hannah remained silent. A pang of guilt swept through her at the police officer's sigh of resignation as he snapped shut his notebook and pocketed it. How many of Bishop Fisher's sermons had she sat through on not judging others? She must do as the church commanded.

The officer slipped his pen into his top pocket. Hannah dropped her gaze. Why didn't Sol check in on her? Sam, she could understand; Sam never bothered about anything but his business. But Sol? He must have heard of the incident, if not seen the police.

'Was Sol at the shop when you rang?' She fought the fluttery sensation the question created in her chest.

Danny shook his head.

She scanned her mind for another familiar face. Her heartbeat slowed down. 'Where's Barney?' She turned to the vacant counter.

'Delivering parcels. He'll be here later.'

Kind as Danny was, she hoped Sol would come. He would give her one of his big smiles and probably crack a joke in an attempt to lighten the sombre mood and soothe her frayed nerves. Hannah wished to see one of her own people. They knew how to handle a crisis – serenely and without fuss.

'I'll drive you home. Don't worry, I've spoken to Sam.' Danny dug into his coat pocket.

Hannah raised a hand as she rose. 'No. No, thank you. I would prefer to stay and work.'

'You nuts?' Danny pocketed the keys. 'Okay. But I'll walk you down.'

A loud creak made Hannah turn to the heavy wooden doors as they swung open and banged shut.

'We're closed,' Danny barked at the stout, snowy-haired Amish man.

'Then you should have a sign on this.' He tapped on the door. 'I came to see how Hannah is.'

'Mr King.' She smiled, thankful for her wish being granted.

Mr King peered over his owlish glasses. His sole concession to the contemporary world and the weather was the black duffle coat he wore over his black suit. With rough cheeks from the cold and a silvery, bristly beard, he reminded her of Santa Claus without the red coat.

'A hand?' Mr King ruffled his beard. 'The last time something like this happened was in the early noughts – 2004, I recall, when the Leechburgs were here. They laid in wait outside the grocer's, where the florist is today. When the son opened the shop, they grabbed him and chopped off two of his fingers.' Mr King raised a hand, his index and middle finger bent. 'Right out there in full daylight. Terrible. Terrible. And that was for refusing to pay them protection money.'

Hannah shuddered.

'I'll take you home. I have my buggy.' Mr King gestured to the door.

'No. Thank you, I am fine.' Hannah adjusted her navy cloak so it covered her front and turned to Danny. 'Danny, you need to open. It's already past nine o'clock. You've been very kind. Thank you.'

A red tinge rose to his face. He wiped his nose with the back of his mutton-chop hand. 'You take care. Okay?'

Outside, the snow had melted enough for buses to trundle along the main street. Apart from the library opposite the butcher's two doors down, only the food and hardware shops were trading.

'What did you tell the police officer?' Mr King asked, falling into step with Hannah as she began to walk away from the post office in the direction of the traffic lights.

'Nothing.'

'That is wise.' He smiled kindly. 'It is not our place to judge nor assist in others being judged.'

'But they cut a man's hand off.'

'If it is God's will, they shall be punished. Leave such things to others. It is not our way to aid man's law. The Ordnung is clear.'

She pursed her lips. Wrong was wrong. Would revealing the colour of the car have been such a big sin in comparison to cutting another's hand off? No, but breaking the Ordnung rules the church taught would be. If she had given a description of the car or the men and they were tried and sentenced, then she would have participated in judgement and broken the Ordnung teaching.

'I am sure Danny gave them the information they needed.' Mr King turned to her. She halted. 'Hannah,' he said, his forehead lined with deep creases, 'you would do well to stop working in town.'

She opened her mouth to protest.

Mr King leaned in closer. 'You don't know who it was meant for.'

'Do you?'

'No. I suspect it is for one of these shops.'

Hannah took in Mr King's sombre expression. 'What does it mean? Why would someone do that?'

'It's a warning.' Mr King lowered his voice. 'One to be heeded.'

He glanced down the street past the butcher's to the florist. 'The grocer's son was in the wrong place at the wrong time. I would hate to see history repeat itself. Go home. Be safe.'

With a gentle pat-pat on her arm, he turned and strolled up the street.

The heat of the post office ebbed from her as the mushy snow chilled the soles of her feet through her boots. She kept her gaze low and steps slow as she approached the butcher's. Droplets of red marked the snow where the hand had landed. Hannah sidestepped onto the street and jumped when a car beeped its horn as it passed within inches of her. She hurried on, a drizzle touching her face. Her gaze focused ahead to the cycle shop's dual-fronted windows a few doors down on the other side of the alleyway of the florist.

'Hannah! Hannah!' A soprano voice sailed above car noises as a similarly cloaked and bonneted figure dashed across the street, oblivious to the oncoming cars. Hannah's shoulders tensed as Grace tore over to her, narrowly missing a red van. The driver shook his head in exasperation as Grace skipped onto the sidewalk. Hannah lifted a prayer of thanks for her safe arrival. Would Grace ever use the lights instead of rushing out into the road, or the stepping-stones across a brook instead of wading in or trying to jump over it? Somehow, she always made it to the other side unscathed.

'Are you okay? How dreadful for you.' Grace bounced up to her. 'I would have dropped by, but I thought you'd gone home.' Grace squashed her with a tight hug and stepped back, her face a ruby-red shade from the wintry temperature. 'What did the police say? Do they know who did it? Was it truly a man's hand? Izzy thinks it might be a spat between some local criminals – she kept going on about the Leechburgs. I hope not. The police might stop the gatherings.'

'Let's go inside, Grace.' Hannah smiled. For once, she did not mind her friend's inquisitiveness.

'I can't stop. Got to get back. I saw you walking down. Here.' From inside her cloak, Grace lifted out a paper bag. 'You must be starving. I would be, after all that drama. Here, your favourite – egg muffin and cupcake. You need the sugar. You can tell me all about it tonight.'

Grace ignored the traffic lights and dodged her way back across the street.

Hannah walked on to the cycle shop, pausing to view the florist. Mr King's words echoed in her ears. What if his guess was correct? What if the package had fallen outside the wrong shop? She looked down at her gloved hand holding the door handle and thought of the grocer's son. Another question nagged at her; one she tried to swat dead like a fly – and failed.

If Mr King was right, how safe was she?

HANNAH FLATTENED THE cardboard box and placed it on top of the pile against the window. She surveyed the two-tier rails full of cycling clothes dotted around the shop floor and the accessories on the walls. Helmets, saddles, and handlebars on the left side and gloves, maps, pedometers, and other minor items to the right. At least here few people pestered her with questions; only the customers who came to collect their bikes. All four of them.

The image of the bloody hand rolling on the ground occasionally broke through her thoughts. Each occasion brought a surge of bile to her throat, which she swallowed back down with effort. She said a prayer for the hand's owner. Whatever had caused him to lose his hand, Hannah doubted he had welcomed it.

She shivered and rubbed her hands against her upper arms to warm herself before she brushed them down the front of her charcoal cotton dress, grateful for the protection its ankle-length skirt and long sleeves gave from the fridge-like temperature. She glanced at the counter at the back of the shop, thinking of the two-bar electrical heater behind it. No one would know if she switched it on and warmed the place up...

Sol would notice. It was one of those little differences between her Amish world and his English one. Electricity – or, in her case, the lack of.

Outside, heavy, drab clouds hung in the pebble-white sky. She checked the battery-operated watch she kept in her dress pocket. Four o'clock. The bus would come at five. Through one window, she watched the swaying empty baskets hung from the doorframe of the café opposite, caught in the mid-January wind.

The café appeared warm and welcoming with its gas lamps, pine tables, and chairs lined along the windows with customers enjoying the homemade delights Grace's family sold. It is all right for some, not working and whiling the hours away in comfort.

Hannah chided herself. Envy was a sin. She should be thankful to be working.

When the traffic lights switched to red, a white transit van approached the shop. For the first time that afternoon, a rush of warmth filled her as she caught sight of the driver wrapped in a thick lumber jacket and wearing a black bowler hat with a feather sticking out of its brim. She watched as the van swung into the alley that led to the backyard. As it disappeared, a large blue lorry parked outside: another delivery. They must be lower on stock than she imagined.

Hannah went to the back of the shop and eyed the heater on the floor, plugged into a wall socket above the skirting board. Perhaps Sol would switch it on for her when he came in. Last winter she had worked at home, as she had since a girl, selling homemade preserves and vegetables by the roadside along with the children and other young women, hoping to catch the tourists passing through on their way to town. Some days she'd return home soaked, all the feeling in her fingers lost, but now that she worked at Glick's Cycles she stayed warm enough. All thanks to her friend Sol.

She thought about humming a hymn as she toyed with one ribbon hanging from her white kapp. The memory of the morning's events dampened the notion. If she did hum, she'd have to do so no louder than a bee or Sam would shout through the partition wall for her to 'shutuup'.

The door chimed. A swarthy delivery man with greasy hair and thick stubble wheeled in a trolley laden with four boxes and dumped them on the floor. After another trip to his lorry, he did the same and dropped a clipboard on the counter before he took the top two boxes of the last lot through the door marked staff. Hannah picked up the clipboard. The delivery stated four boxes. She looked over the counter and checked: six boxes plus the two he had taken in. She scribbled the four out, wrote eight next to it, and signed.

'Goodbye, Stubby,' she called after him when he returned empty-handed, swiped the signed clipboard off the counter, and headed for the door. She called him 'Stubby' because of his stubble. One corner of his mouth arched, forming a smirk. She tried not to let her annoyance show. It was the same condescending sneer the men in her village would use when they thought they knew better and she or another meet was, in their opinion, acting silly.

In the van, Stubby lit up a cigarette and, after a few puffs, drove off. Why didn't Sam let him park round the back of the shop? Then the boxes would not clutter up the shop floor. She slipped around the counter to inspect them. Why did Stubby take two boxes into the back and leave the others out here? Office consumables? After all, Sam would need paper, toners, and so on for all his admin work. Mystery solved.

The upbeat sound of country music accompanied by a tuneless whistle floated out from the corridor. She grabbed two of the boxes and backed through the staff door then looked through the office window. Sam sat behind his desk, eyes glued to the computer screen and hands tapping like a woodpecker on the keys, his body slumped in a voluminous, high-back chair, smoke rising from the cigar hanging out one side of his mouth.

Sam rarely locked the rear door during the day, with Sol wheeling bikes in and out from the repair shed in the yard. She pushed it open, dropping one box as she caught the door before it slammed shut, and eased it closed. Across the large, tarmacked space stood a wooden shed with a notice fixed on the door that read REPAIR SHOP. The white transit van was parked outside, a red Dodge next to it. She scanned the other shops' back entrances as far as the butcher's icehouse, a white aluminium shed three shops down. Deserted. Ignoring the sting of cold air and the chugging sound of a car engine, she turned to a single storey building extended beyond the shop. The storeroom.

Keys? Only Sol and Sam had keys to the storeroom. Perhaps she should have gone home with such a forgetful mind.

Hannah scrunched her eyes in frustration. So much for good deeds.

With a dejected sigh, she turned back to the exit. If her boot would not have made a noise, the temptation to kick the door would have won.

More out of habit than reason, she stared across the open parking area and froze. The boxes slid out of her grasp onto the wet tarmac. Icy air stung the back of her open mouth, stifling her gasp. There, by the icehouse with its engine running, stood a grey car. The grey car. The Toyota.

A hard thud exploded inside her as she froze. The driver raised two fingers and pointed them to his own eyes and then at her. Her eyes widened with fear. They had found her. How? The engine revved, and she willed her limbs to unlock from their immobile state. Another louder rev filled the air. The shed. She could run to it. To Sol. She tore her gaze from the car and looked at the dark, empty shed, and the slither of hope vanished. Where was Sol? Why wasn't he working in there? The exit door. She reached an arm out, fingers grasping for the handle. If she could open it...

The car sped forward; its tyres threw up wet specks of loose tarmac as it darted across the yard straight towards her, the sound of its engine roaring in her ears. Hannah commanded her legs to move, only to sense them buckling. She shut her eyes and braced for the inevitable.

A blast of warm air brushed her cheek. A strong hand gripped her upper arm and yanked her out of the car's path. The door swung shut as the car hurtled past.

The hold on her arm loosened. Hannah fought to slow down her frantic heartbeat and ease the ache of her ribs contracting in time with it. She gulped a lungful of air and let it out like a deflating balloon as she opened her eyes.

'Seems you have had quite a day, Han.'

The calm voice brought a flush of heat to her cheeks. Sol.

Chapter 3

SOL DUSTED DROPLETS of rain from his hat and pulled it so low it touched his eyebrows, the tawny-coloured feather stuck in its brim. From underneath, his long, plaited locks tumbled past his shoulders. He stood looking at her with that half smile of his. His brown eyes warmed her face faster than any heater could. She dipped her gaze.

'My advice is to forget what happened this morning. Got it?' Sol said.

'You recognise them?'

'Nope, and I don't intend to.' He pushed the door ajar, checked outside, and held it open.

'Thank you.' She rested her back against the door as he picked up the discarded boxes lying in the yard.

'You can thank me by doing what I ask.'

Hannah took the boxes.

'In, before Sam sees you.' Sol said closing the door.

As they passed the office, Sam was warbling along with the radio. He looked up and mumbled a greeting, and Sol waved Hannah on. She hurried through the staff door and, with relief, dropped the boxes on the floor and returned to her sanctuary behind the counter.

Sol counted the pile of boxes then held his little finger up. Hannah smiled, did likewise and bent hers around his. They wriggled them both, smiling at the old gesture.

'Was that the same car that threw the hand out?' he said in a low voice.

Hannah nodded.

'Take my advice, Hannah, please,' Sol said, letting go. 'Do what the church teaches for once.'

'But the police—'

'Can do their own sleuthing.'

Sol strolled over to the radiator next to Hannah and felt it. 'Hell, that's colder than an icehouse.'

'How can you think about heating at this time?'

'Because I'm freezing.'

Hannah checked her watch. Four-twenty.

'Listen, judging by the speed that car was heading at you, I doubt they'd have any qualms about hurting a woman,' Sol said.

She trembled, recalling the clawed hand.

Sol leaned over the counter and glanced past her. 'Don't know why you didn't take the day off. Did Sam make you stay?'

She shook her head; a warm current rushed through her at his attention.

'Han, I'm positive the Lord would not want you to freeze your pretty bones. Just turn the fire on.' He stroked his goatee and moved round the counter. 'It's a flick of a switch, not a gun.' He bent down and turned it on. 'Shout when you need the heating on, Han.'

'Sol, you know I'm not allowed to use mains-supplied electricity or appliances.'

Hannah kept her eyes down but registered his smile. Nobody called her Han except Sol. She felt the corners of her lips curling upwards at his concern for her, but her smile disappeared as the vibrations of boots stomping on the linoleum flooring in the corridor alerted her that her boss had emerged from his bunker.

'Hey, Sam.' Sol straightened as he changed his attention to the man coming through the door. 'You should let Hannah wear English clothes. It's too cold these days for them thin dresses of hers.'

Sam let out a hog-like grunt. 'All staff dress in Amish clothes. Better for trade.'

Sol glanced at Sam before looking down at his own black jeans and matching vest over a maroon shirt. He pointed to the radiator. 'Amish? You've got central heating. When it's on. You old tightwad.'

'Too expensive.' Sam hoisted up his belt. In one hand, he carried two parcels.

'C'mon, at least let her have a cardigan or jumper. Amish wear them all the time. It's winter, man.'

'Nope.' The response came from under a dense moustache with salt-and-pepper hairs twisted like wire coils.

Sol shot Hannah a regretful look and turned to the heap of boxes.

'Why can't I help you with taking the stock to the storeroom?' she asked.

Sol flashed a broad grin at her. 'Because it's smelly and damp. Sam would have my guts for letting you go down there, and we wouldn't wish that.'

Out of the corner of her eye, she caught a snarl half-forming on Sam's blubbery lips at his younger brother. Sol's light, breezy tone fell flat on Sam's humourless ears. Sol, tall and narrow as a pike, resembled a sparrow compared to his elder bulldog brother. Ten years separated them, but it could have been a generation in terms of personality and physique.

'Here.' Sam slid the two parcels across the countertop with his big-knuckled sausage fingers. He stabbed the smallest one. 'This is for Falcon's butcher's. The other's for the post office.' A pair of beady eyes stared out at her, half-hidden behind puffy cheeks and heavy eyebrows, as he grabbed the cloth money bag, untied it, and slapped three dollars on the counter. 'Make sure you get a receipt.'

'Yes, Mr Glick.' Hannah pulled a small purse from her dress pocket and slipped the notes inside. She ignored the churning sensation in her stomach. If it had not been so late, she would have welcomed a customer to enter and give her the chance to remind herself of the reason she worked there.

Sam thudded into the office and banged the door shut.

Hannah fought the urge to argue with Sol about helping with the stock. It would have filled the low season's slack periods, but it was not worth antagonising her employer. She reminded herself to bring in some sewing or a book to read.

Despite Sam's meanness and Sol's teasing, she enjoyed meeting and serving the customers. At home she could go days doing chores, seeing no one except on Sundays. The money came in handy. She gave some to Maemm and kept some for herself. Perhaps she should buy some woollen underclothing, if all she could wear over her dress to stay warm was a cloak.

'Need a lift home?' Sol looked at the gathering clouds. 'Looks like it's going to rain some more.'

Hannah hesitated, the 'yes' forming on her lips. Cars were electric-powered machinery, and therefore forbidden to be driven by members of her community. If you needed a lift, you asked an English neighbour or booked a cab or used a buggy. Sol might be a 'neighbour', so technically allowed to drive her, but did she have the stamina after today to face the admonishing looks and *tsk-tsks* from Grandfather for taking a lift from an unmarried *Englischer* unchaperoned?

Pewter-coloured clouds hung heavily above the roofs across the road. Fatigue nibbled at her bones. If he dropped her away from the house, she could say she walked from the bus stop at the top of the lane as always. But what if Grandfather or Evan spotted them from their workshop? Neither a male relative nor family friend, Sol may have lived Amish once, but that would carry no weight with them. She massaged the back of her neck as it tightened at the welcome she would get. Single and unchaperoned, it would be just another reason for them to argue for her to leave her job.

Trying to hide her dismay, Hannah shook her head as she retrieved her cloak from a shelf under the counter. She fastened her black bonnet over the white kapp that covered her hair and ears. The bonnet's starched material cushioned her cheeks against the hardboard frame stitched inside it. She knotted her cloak at the collar with the two ribbons sewn inside the neckline's edge, wishing it was her fleece-lined waterproof coat instead, which zipped up and stopped the cold wind nipping through the cloak's loose flaps.

Sol backstepped alongside her as she headed to the door, parcels tucked inside her cloak. 'Let me know if you change your mind.' He reached for the handle and opened the door for her.

The biting breeze that battered her body made her eyes sting. She shuddered. What she would not have given for a lift in a warm, dry car. Sol's car. But Grandfather would click his tongue in disapproval; Sol and Sam had left their community, rejecting all offers of help to live with the English.

'Hannah?' Grace's voice sailed over the traffic as she waved, standing under the café porch. Rainwater dripped from the canopy and landed on her navy-blue dress with its white apron and matching kapp. 'You still coming to mine tonight?'

'Yes, of course!' Hannah shouted back.

'Sol's picking us up!' Grace gestured to the cycle shop with a grin and disappeared inside the café.

Hannah slipped the cloak's hood up and dashed along the wet sidewalk. Friday night meant going to a gathering where Amish and English would meet with one aim: to enjoy themselves – the ideal way to end each week of early starts and house chores. Grace always housed the pre-party for the gathering held later in the evening. Hannah could imagine Grace standing in her bedroom, out of her Amish clothing, her dark hair tumbling down her back, applying lipstick to her cherry lips and mascara to her long, black eyelashes. The thought of the gathering dispelled the chill for a moment.

She hurried down the street, keeping her head bowed, and collided with a woman wearing a parka with her hands dug into its pockets, her face almost hidden under the cover of its fake-fur-edged hood. Hannah apologised, thinking longingly of her own English clothes hidden in a case under her bed.

Splashes of rain fell on her cloak, and she increased her pace to the butcher's. Her watch read four-thirty-five. If she hurried, she could catch the next bus due. Why was today full of so many challenges for her? She braced herself as she prepared to pass by the group of young Amish men standing by the buggy rail.

The horses stood quietly, tethered to the railings, each one hitched to one of the half-dozen buggies. Their owners were busy admiring one buggy's tiger-striped fur interior and the battery-powered headlights of another. Bright tape or stickers adorned some closed buggies.

The young men's loud banter dropped to a murmur over the pop music coming from inside a buggy as she approached them. Battery-operated radios were not unusual features to be found under some drivers' seats. They continued to talk, careful to avoid direct eye contact despite being aware of her, judging by the greeting from a clean-shaven, freckle-faced man. '*Vi bisht dich?*' He tipped his hat back.

'*Vell, dank.*' She recognised his face and voice but kept her eyes on the butcher's shop ahead, hoping they did not ask her about the morning's incident. If Grace knew, everybody would know.

Outside the butcher's, the darkened blotches on the snow loomed at her and she averted her eyes, sidestepped past, and turned into the alley.

'Whoa! Careful.' Aaron stared down at her from his wagon, relief covering his face as he swerved Blue around her just in time. He eyed the marks on the snow. 'You okay, Hannah? Someone told me about this morning. Terrible.'

'Yes, I'm fine, thanks, Aaron.' His frown told her he didn't believe her. 'Delivery?' She gestured to his wagon.

'Meat. Last one.' The weariness of the long day echoed in the drawn-out sentence. 'You want a ride? I'm going home.'

'Thank you, but I will get the bus with Grace.'

Aaron shrugged and flicked his reins, signalling for Blue to move.

When she entered the butcher's, she joined the orderly line behind Mr King. Rush hour, they called it.

'Is that it?' The elderly man at the front of the line took a slim package from the shop assistant and held it up with a disgruntled expression on his face. 'My, my, what is the world coming to when a pound of meat looks like a mangy dog snack?'

Hannah pursed her lips so as not to grin like Mr King.

'Elijah, stop your moaning and be grateful to the Lord for what he gives you from the land,' Mr King chided the elder Amish man between chuckles.

Old Man Elijah, as everyone called him, except not to his face, looked as though he bore the weight of the world on his shoulders and its worries on his face. He left the counter and shuffled past Hannah and Mr King to the exit, the rubber end of his walking stick squeaking with each doddery step. 'I'll be thankful for a decent meal out of these scraps.' He let out a mournful sigh.

Hannah waited her turn. No sign of the bus yet – fifteen minutes to go. Idly, she stared out of the butcher's window to the library opposite. Through its glass front, she could see people searching the bookshelves in one area, and in another young and old sat at tables, eyes glued to computers. Baseball caps and black felt hats and bonnets bowed together in silence.

When her turn came to be served, she lifted out Sam's parcel. It was no bigger than a mobile phone and lighter than a jar of flour. The shop assistant, Levi, with his bloodstained apron and net cap, held out a meat-juice-smeared hand and took the parcel. The smell made her giddy. With his bleached-blond ponytail and colourful, patterned shirt under his stained white apron, he had the physique of someone more used to the beach than a town. 'See you at Grace's,' he said to her, his gaze shifting from her to the window.

Hannah followed it and ducked her head as a grey Toyota drove slowly past. She blinked, not trusting her eyes. No, they had not deceived her. She stared blankly out as it disappeared from view. What if they had seen her? Blood pounded in her ears as chills ran down her body. What if they came after her?

'You recognised it? Was that the car from this morning?' Levi turned his gaze to her, and she lowered her own. 'Best forget, if I were you.'

If he meant it as advice, then the hard edge of his voice held no trace of Sol's softer tone of concern. Did Levi know those men? Why were they still driving around, as though nothing had happened? What were they looking for? Her? Were they waiting for her? Hannah clutched her bag and scuttled out of the butcher's. She shivered when she realised she'd stepped on the blood spots.

She hurried to the post office, keeping her gaze straight ahead. To her relief, she found it empty. Danny was behind the Perspex-screened counter, his head bald and shiny as an egg without his bobble hat. Next to him, a man her own age stood head and shoulders taller than Danny. He had the solid, healthy frame of someone used to working outdoors. His dark, tousled locks touched his shoulders.

'*Goot dawk.*' His pleasant greeting as he rubber-stamped forms made her forget the freezing weather and melted her anxiety from the butcher's.

'Barney, none of that Amish stuff here. English.' Danny wagged his pen. 'Amish when at home, English when serving. Okay?' He turned to Hannah. 'How ya doing?'

'Fine, Danny.'

'You sure?' Barney viewed her with compassion.

Danny put his pencil behind an ear and resumed checking the stamp book.

'Good afternoon, Hannah.' Barney took the parcel from her and winked.

'Good afternoon, Mr Herzberg.' Hannah fought the urge to return the gesture. Raindrops fell from her cloak as she pulled her purse from her pocket and paid for the postage.

Barney's eyes widened and his face fell. 'Mr Herzberg? So formal, Miss .' He placed his palm on his chest. Hannah felt the smile creeping across her face as he chuckled and deep laugh lines broke up his forlorn expression. His laughter drowned out the *pat-pat* of rain bouncing against the window.

Barney inquired how she was bearing up and, like she had done with everyone else, she replied in the positive, careful not to focus on the scowl on Danny's face.

'You getting the bus home?' Barney asked.

She nodded as he handed the change and receipt to her.

'I would offer you a lift... but you know how people talk. Old friends or not.' Barney's hand lingered over hers, holding onto the receipt. 'They muttered about me going English because my hair's long.'

Hannah gave him a supportive smile. Short back and sides or a pudding-bowl cut for men and long hair for women was the custom.

'That's because you behave like an English, Barney.' Danny looked up. 'You need to stop – what is it you guys say – fooling around?'

Hannah covered her mouth to hide the smile rising to her lips.

'Running about.' Barney gave a despairing shake of his head. 'Rumspringa.'

'Rumpelstiltskin?'

'No.' Hannah coughed, disguising a burst of laughter. 'Rum-spring-a.'

'Whatever.' Danny waved a hand in the air. 'Aren't you supposed to be settled down by now, Barney, according to this Rumspringa thing? You're twenty soon.'

'You sound like my daett. There is no age set. Many have by their late teens; some take longer. It's a big decision.'

'Yeah, fun or no fun.' Danny shaped his hands like a pair of scales.

'Oh, that's not so.' Hannah reined in her smile. 'It is more about lifestyle choices.'

'What'll you do, Hannah? Stay Amish or go English?' Danny asked.

Hannah paused, a heavy weight settling on her chest. As Danny knew, she was no teenager either.

'She is going to follow her instincts,' Barney said, shooting Danny a stern glare. 'Take her time and pray.'

Danny cleared his throat. 'Of course. I hope you carry on working at Glick's, if you decide to remain Amish, so we can see your pretty face from time to time. It makes a change from seeing his ugly mug every day.' His cheery smile banished the heaviness inside her. 'Are you going to take your life in your hands and ride in the wreckage he calls a car?'

'The bus will be fine.' She put the receipt in her purse. All these offers in one day. All of them, she knew, came from their concern for her after the incident in the morning, not her popularity. And she could not take any of them unless she wanted to be the number one topic of conversation for the rest of the weekend, at home or elsewhere. Did English women have to comply with such narrow-mindedness?

A journey with Sol would be spent reminiscing about childhood times when he lived Amish, and listening to music – reggae, or soft rock, as he called the songs he played. A good way to end a miserable day. Time with Barney would have given her the chance to discuss her options with an old friend and be nearer to ending her dithering. She would have welcomed either. Aaron did not count; he was a deacon. She knew his answer.

A large, thick brown envelope lay on the counter beside Barney. He slipped it underneath, then stared past her at the streaks of water drizzling down the window. 'You best hurry before it gets any worse.' He resumed stamping. '*Sel goot.*'

'Barney. English.'

A giggle escaped Hannah at Danny's playful admonishment. Barney flicked his eyes heavenward and grinned at her when she replied, '*Sel goot.*'

Outside, the youths had retreated from the rain and sat inside their buggies. People disembarked from a bus by the cycle shop. She dashed to the bus and groaned when it drove off, its huge wheels splattering water over her feet. She threw her head back in exasperation, let out a yelp of frustration through gritted teeth, and shook the edge of her cloak. She knew before she lifted the hem of her skirt, from the chilled wetness of her ankles and feet, that her stockings and shoes were soaked.

Down the opposite side of the street, another bus rambled in the other direction. Pellets of rain splashed her face, the buttonless cloak offering little shelter. She wiped her face and the welts of water filling her eyes with the back of her sleeve. Across the road, the café was still open. Her face flushed with embarrassment as she caught sight of the man with the fedora she'd seen earlier staring straight at her. His face broke into a good-natured smile as he lifted his mug, as though toasting her.

Trying not to meet his gaze, Hannah shivered and resolved to buy thermal underwear. She pondered what to do for the next twenty minutes until another bus arrived and she could go home and get out of the cold and wet. She could wait in the café, but he might try to engage her in conversation about the morning. The man sipped his drink, staring across the road. Why was he watching the cycle shop? Her neck muscles stiffened as their gazes met again. What was he still doing here in the late afternoon? How nice for him to be able to idle the day away. Hard work hurt no one, her grandfather would say as they all went about their chores at home in the evenings and at weekends. No, but a rest would do a lot of good, Hannah thought irritably as she shivered again, clasping the cloak tighter. Perhaps she should have taken the day off. It was not every day you saw a severed hand.

Dizzy, she steadied herself as the gruesome image came to her once more. She willed the bile in her mouth back down. The man placed his mug on the table and stood up, putting his coat on and peering through the window. A mysterious car, a severed hand, and a strange man. Yes, she should have taken the day off.

Hannah glanced over her shoulder to see if the cycle shop was closed. Its metal shutters were down, covering the window display. An oncoming bus approached her, its gears crunching as it rolled by; she jumped back in time to avoid the spray of water as its wheels swished through the puddle in the road. The bus's polished steel body blocked her view of the café and the man, and when it had passed, he was stepping out of the café and then strolling down the street towards some parked cars. He stopped, held up a hand, and smiled at her, the kind of smile people wore when greeting strangers for the first time; slight, pleasant, but not overly familiar. Hannah froze.

What if he was connected to those men in the Toyota? Had they found out who she was? What if he was one of them and had lain in wait for her? After all, she had witnessed them throwing the hand out of the car window. She took a step back. If she ran, he would run after her. She could not go into the shop. If she darted up the alley, she would be alone. No one would hear her if she shouted or screamed.

'Miss. Miss!' the man called, stepping off the sidewalk onto the street.

From the butcher's alley, the red Dodge appeared. *Sol.* If she could get to Sol. The lift home would be worth Grandfather's and Evan's disapproval to get away from the man. She gathered her cloak, ready to move.

'Miss Bieler.' The man glanced at the Dodge and broke into a sprint, crossing the street straight towards her, one arm reaching out. 'Hannah!'

He knew her name. He must be one of them. Heart pounding, she spun, took one step towards the alley, then snatched her foot back at the loud screech of brakes as the Dodge swung into the street, sped ahead of her, and braked to a halt. Its passenger door flew open providing her escape.

Chapter 4

'HOP IN, HAN.' Sol grinned as she jumped into the car.

'Thank you. I don't know what I would have done if you hadn't shown up,' she panted, giving him a grateful smile as she buckled up.

'Had a hunch you might miss the bus.' He winked at her. 'Even if you did blow me off earlier. Who was that guy?'

'No idea, but he called my name.'

'Really?' Sol's face darkened. 'He bugs you, you tell me. I'll deal with him.'

A rush of heat warmed her cheeks and softened her heart at his words. The cold fear that had gripped her a few minutes ago melted into a small ball of glowing warmth. She relaxed and leaned against the backrest. At least the day was ending better than it had started and her wish to travel with Sol was granted.

He softened the rebuke by holding up his little finger. Smiling, she bent hers around his and they wriggled their fingers together.

Sol laughed. 'Sorry about getting tough with you,' he said above the rev of the engine. 'Just concerned about you, Han.'

The Dodge shot off down the street. Hannah bowed her head as they passed the buggies. One thought kept filling her mind: *He waited for me.* Her stomach turned into a fluttery playground of butterflies.

'You're having quite a day, Han.'

She turned and glanced through the rear window. 'Do you think he might be involved with those who threw the hand?'

Sol pulled a face. 'Too nerdy. Probably got a thing for cute Amish girls.'

Hannah stayed silent, not sure how to respond. Sol let out a belly laugh.

Out of the town centre, the shops and factories faded away, giving way to open space. Sol thumbed at the Field of Sorrows. 'Rumour is, someone is planning to build on it. Pity. Great place for gatherings and fairs.'

'They wouldn't ever dare!' Hannah kept her gaze on the space. 'No one has ever built on the Field of Sorrows.'

'Why not? It's been decades since the fire.'

'So?'

'Solomon Glick, have you no respect for the dead?'

'Sol,' he replied.

'Solomon is a good biblical name. Your parents gave you and Sam – Samuel – them.'

'I'm English now. My name's Sol.'

Hannah leaned back in her seat. Sol. Solomon. How come it was so easy for him to choose and hard for her? Beyond the open space, barns and simple two-storey homes set back from the main road emerged with fields interspersed between the smallholdings. Sol sang along to the music blaring from the car stereo. 'Bob Marley.' He gestured to the console. 'Jamaican singer. Died in '81.'

'You like a singer who died before you were born?'

'I like the music. And he was cool for his day.' He picked up the song again; the words were few and repetitive. '*No woman, no cry.*'

'Is he the reason you braid your hair?'

'Braids?' The brightness in his eyes dimmed. 'These are *locs.*'

'You are not Black, Sol.'

He waved a dismissive hand in the air.

'No one would believe you were brought up Amish,' Hannah teased, her mood lifting as it did when with him. 'I remember you in plain clothes and a pudding-bowl haircut.'

'Like your big ox of a brother, Evan.'

Hannah chuckled.

'I ain't Amish. Sam and I are good as we are, living with the English,' he shouted above the car's roar as it tore down the highway. 'Why don't you move out? You're not baptised. Enjoy yourself. Make the folks wait. You're smart, Han. Why waste away in some drab dress and backwater village? Go English. It's not the end of the world. Then you and I could have some real fun.'

'And get into lots of trouble. Like when we were children.' She ignored the beam on his face and resisted the temptation to let out a conspiratorial giggle. 'I can't leave my family.' She twisted the ribbon hanging from her collar. 'It's different for you. You've got Sam.'

Sol wrinkled his nose.

'It would break Grandfather's and Maemm's hearts if I did. I'm not sure if they would let me visit them.'

'Your choice, Han.'

Hannah sighed. To stay Amish meant forgoing the gatherings, not dressing English, and marrying within the community. Living the simple, godly life of her people, as Maemm kept reminding her. Was she ready for such a commitment? Could she be happy with such a simple life? Despite the past few years of freedom, she could not answer either question. A decision had to be made, but not today.

'Will they catch them?' She paused, remembering. 'Whoever is responsible for this morning?'

Sol shook his head.

'Why throw it outside the butcher's?'

Another shake. 'Best put it behind you, Han. Not your problem.'

The music changed and, with it, Sol's singing. '*Should I stay or should I go?*' He attempted a grittier tone. '*Boom. Boom. Should I stay or should I go? Awh!*'

Hannah threw her head back and laughed with him.

'That's better. You're so serious these days, Hannah. What happened to the party girl of last summer? Be like Grace. Now she knows how to have fun.'

Her smile broadened at the mention of her friend. Yes, Grace knew how to enjoy herself. She always egged Hannah on so she ended up joining in. Flying over the river, hanging on to the pulley rope the boys had fixed to a zip line for all she was worth, while the other girls gasped in a mixture of admiration and horror, certain they would fall in. No other girls braved the high-wire journey. Wearing English clothes to the gatherings once Rumspringa started, dancing in a skirt that barely covered her knees and a bright blouse with the top button undone, Grace dressed in shorts and a sleeveless top.

'Remember playing *knocky-nine-doors* as kids?' Sol grinned. 'How Grace scampered out of sight faster than a hare when the owners came to the door? The expressions on their faces when they realised it was all for nothing?'

Hannah laughed. 'And the volleyball games.' She remembered how they garnered admirers as they grew from skittish girls into self-conscious adolescents. All the youths wanted to play the opposite position to Grace's. 'The young men always lived to regret it when she flung the ball hard back at them.'

At the fortnightly Sunday evening social gatherings, the Singings, Grace would encourage the rest of the girls to sing louder than the boys until their shy voices turned to excitable shrills.

'Enough of the oldies. Put some modern music on, please?' Hannah said.

He dug out his phone and handed it to her. 'Have a look. When I used to work in the factory making them motor homes, before Sam took over the cycle shop, they'd play music all day long. What do you like? Taylor Swift?' He glanced at the screen. 'Here, put that on. I like old stuff. Like I like you.'

She did not need a mirror to see the pinkish colour rising to her pale cheeks. Old or new, it never mattered, coming from him.

'You're not like most girls, Hannah. You stick to your principles.'

'You mean I'm a traditionalist. Thanks.'

'Can an Amish girl be anything else?' He didn't smile this time.

She slumped back into the seat. So, she was some backwater friend he felt sorry for. A childhood acquaintance he had outgrown. She pushed her annoyance aside, remembering how he had come to her aid. Why did he chase after her? 'Thought you might miss the bus,' he had said. If she was so lame, why wait for her? What was he playing at? Had he guessed she had feelings for him and was toying with them? She squashed the rising irritation with a stern rebuke: *Don't be so uncharitable. He's a good friend. He rescued you. Be grateful.*

Sol turned the car a sharp left and slowed as they drove along a narrow country lane that linked the Amish dwellings outside

Birchwood. On each side of the lane, wooden fences with gates hid the houses in the shadows beyond. Above them, telephone wires stretched from pole to pole along the road, but not from the homes to the poles. If you needed to talk to someone, you went to see them. The telephone lines were for the English homes.

'Levi and I'll come and fetch you at Grace's tonight,' Sol said.

'Maemm wants me to go to the games night at the Grobers'.'

'Forget it. You can do what you want at the gatherings, unlike at those stupid supervised games nights with the old folks earwigging and no booze. You've earned it after today.'

She should have protested. The games night would please Maemm, but the gathering would please Hannah more; besides, she'd promised Grace.

Sol wagged his little finger at her as he drove. She ignored the gesture. He stilled the windshield wipers as the last of the rain dwindled. 'Come on, if you're going to stay Amish, you'll have to end your Rumspringa, so make the most of it.'

'I never said I was going to be baptised.'

'You're already backsliding, Han.' Sol stared ahead.

Hannah toyed with her ribbon. Sometimes she wished he did not know her so well.

The urge to protest once more subsided. Why not? He was right. It had been, as Danny sometimes said, a pig of a day. Besides, time was running out. This would be the last winter she could spend at the shop or going to gatherings. At least Grandfather and Maemm would cease their worrying if she got baptised.

Sol reduced the car's speed as its headlights lit up the shadowy outline of a buggy plodding along the road ahead. The last drops of rain splattered on its grey canvas top. Sol steered the car well around it to allow plenty of space.

Hannah covered her face and turned away from the buggy. She might be a passenger in a car, but one driven by an ex-Amish youth would cause loose tongues and disapproving stares. Through her fingers she noted the plain black curtains, keeping the rain out and anyone inside the cabin dry. She glanced in the rearview mirror to see a bedraggled middle-aged man driving the empty buggy.

'You're allowed to ride in a car, Han. Even with an *Englischer*.' With a backwards glance to check he was clear of the horse, Sol sped down the lane.

Out of view, Hannah lifted her head and mumbled a feeble apology.

To her left, the outline of two buildings set back from the road loomed larger as they approached them. The oblong, single-storey wooden barn stood nearest the lane. Sol stopped the car by the gate in front of the path leading to the barn and a yard where the second building stood. From a downstairs window, a light shone; Maemm would be in the kitchen preparing dinner.

Hannah thanked Sol and got out, agreeing to go to the party. Sol sped off with a grin that matched her own inward smile and lightheaded mood at his happiness that she was going. Wasn't this what Rumspringa was about – having fun? She watched him roar off, listening to the creaking of the square sign lit by a battery-operated lamp hanging from the gatepost. The flimsy wood with its painted buggy and horse flapped in the evening breeze, its yellow-painted words framed with black paint reading YODER BUGGY REPAIRS. She made her way up the drive under the darkening evening sky.

She spotted the dark outline of Grandfather peering out of a window holding a large, circular object in one hand. Despite the interior propane light's shadow, she recognised the slight stoop of the man's shoulders and the shiny crown of his bare head. 'Good evening, Grandfather.' She waved at him and got one in return. She paused. She could go straight to the house and change out of her damp clothes, or pop into the barn. Grandfather lifted his head again, a tender smile softening his craggy features. Hannah strode to the barn and paused by the life-size buggy and horse cutout board illuminated by another lamp fixed to a pole. The picture helped customers avoid mistaking the house for the workshop. Behind it stood a green Volvo; at the sight of it, she sighed. Barney. She skirted around the trunk of the vehicle.

'That Sol?' The question fired from the back of the lofty barn. Further down the workbench that ran along the window, a youth wearing a tan leather apron stood, a leather strap laid out in front of him. He held a mallet in one hand and tapped it against the handle of a bradawl, the blow forcing its metal point into the leather strap.

'Yes, Evan,' Hannah replied.

'Hannah, Hannah.' Grandfather made a clicking sound as he approached her. He rested the wooden wheel he had repaired against his leg and embraced her. 'Why did you not come home? Barney told us about this morning.' Guilt consumed Hannah at his worried expression. 'Tsk, tsk, are you well?'

'Yes, Grandfather. I am well and good.'

He nodded sagely and picked up the wheel. He slotted it into a rack by the door. 'Who would do such a terrible thing?'

'Danny says the police reckon it's a local gang's spat.' Barney slouched, one arm on the work surface, by Evan.

'Why throw such a thing outside Falcon's?' Grandfather tottered back to the bench, coughing lightly.

'You missed your bus again, Hannah?' Evan continued working on the leather strap.

She shook the rain from her bonnet, giving herself time to form an answer. On the bench sat a brass lock. Grandfather handed her a tension wrench, and she inserted it into the lock hole. 'It was raining hard. Sol offered, concerned I would catch a cold.' She found the pick tool and wriggled it inside the lock, and its handle clicked loose.

Grandfather chuckled at her deftness. 'Good, good. You are swifter than Evan.'

'I heard Aaron offered to bring you home.' Evan twisted the bradawl into the leather strap, piercing a new hole.

Hannah snapped the lock's hinge shut and placed it on the bench.

'You should not encourage him.' Evan flexed the strap, inspecting his handiwork.

'Encourage him? He was being kind.'

Grandfather patted her shoulder. 'Hush now, Hannah. Your brother is merely concerned for you.'

'I have no issue with Evan being concerned, Grandfather, just the manner in which he expresses it.'

'He is your brother. One day he will be the head of this family. He has your best interests at heart.'

Hannah busied herself with her cloak, careful to keep her face from view in case it revealed her thoughts. *Head of the family, not by age but by gender.* She rolled her eyes and pushed her tongue against her cheek. Would Evan be upset if Barney had given her a lift? No. Barney was family in Evan's and Maemm's eyes. No one complained to Evan when he went off with Barney in his car. Such were the privileges of being male.

'Done.' Evan held up the strap punctured with several small pinholes. 'Good, yes?'

Grandfather took the strap and held it up under the lamp hanging from a nearby timber post. He turned it over carefully, as though it were a precious jewel. 'Yes. Very good. Like your daett. He never tore the leather when making the holes. Not even as my apprentice. One day you will teach your son how to do this, as I taught your daett and you.'

Grandfather Yoder pulled back his rounded shoulders, straightened to his full height, and tilted his head. His cotton-white hair with its copper threads rested on his shirt collar and his beard stuck out like a handle as he met her brother's gaze. He lifted his arm and patted Evan on one of his broad shoulders. '*Gott willing.*'

Hannah stopped by the horseless buggy stationed in the middle of the building and stared at her brother. Under the lamplight's glow, he resembled her father, dressed in his plain blue shirt and broadfall trousers with their large, buttoned flap in the front. Evan had the flaxen hair, pale skin, and broad, stocky frame of their father's Swiss heritage. He could have been a Viking in the past.

Evan took the strap and placed it on the surface covered in tools and half-made straps as Grandfather removed his faded, stained apron and hung it on a peg. 'It is late. Dinner will be ready soon.'

'I'll close up, Grandfather.' Evan untied his own apron as Grandfather walked stiffly out of the barn, singing an old hymn.

'You should be more careful, Hannah.' Evan turned off one of the lamps. 'He's English now. People will talk.'

'I've known him since childhood, Evan, as you and Barney have.'

'He's an *Englischer* and *Leddich*.'

'Brother Evan, are you suggesting that only married men should court me?'

A low guffaw came from Barney.

Evan scowled back at her as he lifted his black hat and coat from the pegs and put them on. 'If you needed a lift, why didn't you take up Barney's offer of one?'

Barney straightened, avoiding her glare.

'He's unmarried too.' She turned to the barn door.

'And my oldest friend.' Evan held out a hand to Barney.

Barney unzipped his duffle coat and pulled out the envelope Hannah had seen at the post office. Evan took it, slipped it inside his coat, and extinguished another lamp hanging near the door.

'What's that?' She pointed to the envelope and followed them outside.

'Nothing.' Evan might have inherited the same sky-blue eyes from their mother, but they could harden to stone when he wanted them to. From the glint of them, she knew better than to ask twice.

She darted Barney a quizzical look as they stood by the cutout bathed in shadow. He shrugged as Evan headed to the house at a brisk pace. 'He's right about Sol.' Barney held her gaze. All the afternoon's merriment had gone from his grey-green eyes.

'Why? Because he's made his choice? Isn't that what Rumspringa is about? Deciding how you want to live your life?'

He looked up in silence at the stars that pinpricked the crushed-velvet sky.

'If you are so convinced living Amish is so great, why haven't you stopped wearing English clothes and driving a car?' she asked.

Barney dug his hands into his pockets and rolled his lower jaw. 'And you? When will you stop running around, Hannah?'

Hannah smarted. 'When I am ready, Mr Herzberg.'

This time, the hurt look on his face at her formality remained. His mouth stayed clamped tight, the expression in his eyes sorrowful. Hannah chewed her lower lip.

From one coat pocket, he retrieved his car keys and stepped towards the vehicle parked behind the cutout. 'Go to the games night, Hannah.' He jangled the keys, all the softness in his face gone. 'Leave Sol to his English life.'

Chapter 5

TOASTY SMELLS FROM the kitchen's woodstove greeted Hannah when she entered the house. They filtered through the open door and made her forget the cold and Barney's stony stare.

Closing the front door, she went into the room on her right and crossed the flagstone floor to hang up her damp cloak and bonnet. She slipped off her sodden shoes and put them underneath with several pairs of women's boots, gumboots, and shoes. She glanced at the other rack with the men's coats and footwear, thinking about how in the winter, pools of water covered the floor as everyone left their outdoor clothes there to keep the place clean from dirt and the weather. The washing machine, powered by a diesel generator, hummed to a standstill.

Hannah made her way down the shamrock-green hall with its gaslights. She peeked through a half-open door. One glance at the table inside with the treadle sewing machine and several bits of material told her that Maemm had not finished the Bethlehem Star quilt on order. On a chair, two labelled brown paper parcels tied with string meant another trip to the post office to send off completed orders. Child or lap quilts, by the size of the bundles.

Her thoughts were interrupted by the peal of chimes. She turned to the wall clock opposite, its bronze face and black hands enclosed within a mahogany frame, and a wave of sadness washed over her. Simple in design, but made with love. An engagement present from Daett to Maemm. A handmade heirloom, both functional and sentimental, like so many of her family's furnishings handed down through the generations. Most of all, it was a link to him. Death had come unforeseen and unwelcomed one morning before the winter frost had thawed the ground or the cockerel crowed. Massive cardiac arrest, read the death certificate.

She sighed, lifted a prayer, and turned to the kitchen. Would someone make a clock for her with such affection one day? Did English women feel the same about an engagement ring? She would not even wear a wedding ring to mark her transition from spinster to wife.

'Hannah, thank the good Lord you are home.' Maemm stood tall and straight by the white ceramic sink under the window overlooking the yard and workshop. 'Why did you not come straight home? Would they not let you?'

'I offered to stay.' Hannah closed the door behind her. 'Working helped take my mind off things.' She hugged Maemm and kissed her cheek.

'You are safe. That is all that matters.' Maemm shuddered and returned to the sink.

She smiled, watching Maemm in her grey dress and kapp. They bore the same skin tone and delicate willowy frame. Hannah wished she had Grace's curved hips and not her narrow ones that made her resemble a leek. Though lines furrowed out from the corners of

Maemm's eyes and creased her face, she kept the vigour and figure of a woman half her age.

She started telling Maemm of the morning's events, but the meaty juices of the pie cooking persuaded her to wait until they had eaten dinner. Bad news might go down better on a full stomach.

As usual, the tap water splashed slowly into the pitcher Maemm held, with the tap half-turned. She vaguely remembered squealing with delight as a little girl the first time Maemm had turned that tap on. Father had insisted on inside plumbing, saying that with two young children and probably others, bathing, washing, and cooking would be easier for Maemm. Grandfather huffed and tsk-tsked but relented. Father would have put a phone in if not for Grandfather's Old Order Amish principles. Instead, he installed hot and cold water and a bath. A real one, with taps and a stopper. Not the galvanised tub filled with water from the stove that would be tepid by the time the hot water Maemm poured into it was cool enough for her to bathe in. Best of all, an inside toilet. No more desperate runs to the outhouse or smelly pots under the bed.

'Supper is ready. The table needs laying.' Maemm gestured to the large pine table with its nicks and stains from generations of use. It dominated the spacious kitchen, in the heart of family life.

Hannah threw a cloth over the table and laid it for supper, grateful for the light cast by the standing lamp nearby in an open cabinet connected to a propane tank. The cabinet had wheels for moving it to other downstairs rooms when needed to give additional light.

Grandfather ambled in from the rear passage that led to his room and the back door, pulling his braces over a clean shirt.

'Are you going to the games?' Maemm asked, getting the butter dish from the small refrigerator by the door. Another appliance. This time powered by gas, along with the indoor lights. How Grandfather had tsk-tsked in dismay! What was wrong, he had lamented to Daett, with the icehouse they once used for storing perishables?

Hannah set the four places in silence, knowing how Maemm would react to her not going.

'It is good to socialise. Like the Singings, it lifts the soul.' Maemm placed the pitcher in the centre of the table, the lamp's light catching her pulled-back blonde hair. 'There will be young people there too,' she said as footsteps padded down the hallway.

Hannah groaned inwardly. The Singings, where girls sat in one row across the barn facing the boys' row, all singing one hymn after another before a brief meal, allowed informal socialising. Supervised under the watchful eyes of the host family.

'She's going to the gathering at Miller's barn, Barney says,' Evan said, coming in. The toes of his damp socks marked the stone-flagged tiles. He pulled a chair up near the sink.

Trust Barney to tell Evan. Sometimes she wondered if he thought he was a second brother. Only one would speak to her the way he had outside the barn. She pushed down the bristling sensation that had stiffened her body at his parting words.

Maemm's and Grandfather's places were at each end of the table, as the elders of the family. Grandfather seated himself in the chair nearest the kitchen door, so he could get up to greet visitors. One day Evan would sit there, as their father had done.

'Barney says you're thinking of going, too.' Hannah skirted round the table to the stove.

He looked away and rested his forearms on the surface.

'It is time for you to settle, Hannah.' Maemm lifted the plate of bread rolls warming on the black stove hob and placed it on the table. 'Rumspringa is for teenagers, not a grown woman.'

'Twenty is not old,' she replied. She carried a steaming bowl of carrots and onions to the table then sat down opposite Evan.

'The longer you leave making your mind up, the harder it will be to choose.' Wearing oven gloves, Maemm carried the pie dish from the stove to the table and sat down.

For whom? Hannah ignored the wobble of anxiety in Maemm's tone.

'She wouldn't be the first in the family to go English,' Evan sniped.

Grandfather leaned back in his chair and shot him a disapproving stare. Evan lowered his gaze. Maemm's face crumpled slightly before she regained her usual serene expression.

Hannah glowered at him. Every family had their black sheep, and Maemm's sister, Ruth, was theirs. He knew better than to refer to her.

After Grandfather said grace and Maemm had served the chicken pie, Hannah focused on eating desperate to end the hollow sensation in her stomach. The crunchy pastry and hot meat in gravy slid down her throat, warming her and made her realise how famished she was. She swiftly ate another mouthful.

Grandfather poised his bare fork in midair. 'Hannah, your maemm is right. You are not a child or teenager. It is time you gave thought to your future.'

'I am, Grandfather,' Hannah replied.

'Then put them out of their worry and get baptised,' Evan cut in. 'Anyone but you, sister, would end their partying after today. The town is becoming dangerous – whoever threw that hand out of the car this morning wasn't fussy about it hitting you. According to Barney, Danny said it missed you by inches.'

'An exaggeration.' Hannah lowered her cutlery. She extended her leg under the table, her foot poised. Evan chewed, his gaze daring her, like he used to when they were children. Maemm tilted her head, and Hannah withdrew her foot. Satisfying as it might be to kick Evan, it would only serve to confirm Maemm's anxiety over her going English. Placidness and self-control were the Amish way.

'You should have come home immediately, Hannah,' Maemm chided.

Hannah studied the remaining food on her plate.

'Why change the habit of a lifetime and do what she is told?' Evan stuffed a fork load of food into his mouth.

'Oh, and you're so mature, baby brother, that you haven't even gone on your own Rumspringa—'

'I don't need to. I've made my decision.'

'And I will make mine.'

'Then make it.'

'Enough.' Grandfather's soft tone turned sharp. 'Evan, you may be Hannah's brother, but it is not for you or anyone to tell Hannah what she should do with her future. That, as you have said, Hannah, is the point of Rumspringa. Though I agree that sooner rather than later would be better.' He looked at them all. 'To join the church and live by the teachings of the *Ordnung* must be her decision and hers alone.'

'And if she decides otherwise?' Maemm asked.

Hannah counted to five. 'I am here, Maemm.'

Grandfather gazed tenderly at Maemm. 'Daughter,' he said gently, 'I remember someone who took their time, too, to decide. I worried many nights about her, but the good Lord knew what he was doing. Today she sits at my table and blesses me with her presence and her children's.'

Maemm bowed her head. Her hands trembled when she lifted her knife and fork to cut into the slice of pie on her plate.

What had happened all those years ago? Why did Ruth leave and Maemm stay?

'Hannah, perhaps you could ease your maemm's worries by agreeing to decide by Easter?'

Hannah attempted to keep the thoughtful expression on her face as her internal voice groaned. Her limbs no longer felt light and flexible but wooden and cemented. Would such pressure be put on Evan? Why did she have to make such a decision right now? Marriage. She could not marry until baptised and a member of the church. All roads for an Amish woman led to the same destination. Could she be content? Why could she not commit as others did? Was it the English way of life she wanted, or something else?

'Hannah?' Grandfather's soft tone broke her thoughts.

Maemm laid a hand on the table, just out of reach. Waiting. Without a good enough reason not to comply, Hannah tilted her head enough to indicate her agreement, and Maemm squeezed her hand.

She could only put off the inevitable so long. Easter would be in mid-April, just over three months away. Time enough to figure out a Plan B if needed. She would have to let the bishop know her intentions by late February if she was to complete the baptism preparation course held in March in time for the annual baptism service.

Grandfather huffed at her tiny nod, although the corners of his mouth arched up slightly. 'Good.'

Promise made, she slumped back into her chair as she thought about the answer they would be expecting.

Evan brushed a piece of roll over his plate, clearing up the last of the gravy and then placing his cutlery side by side. How could he be so sure about life at just eighteen? Why could she not be satisfied with hers? For once she wished for his simplicity. His certainty. The very things that irritated her now seemed so valuable. As she placed her fork and knife in the middle of her own plate, they reminded her of a curtain being drawn, hiding the unseen from view. If only she could work out what that view was, then maybe she would know the future she wanted.

When she had washed up, helped Maemm prepare breakfast for the following morning, and promised to take the parcels from the sewing room to the post office, Hannah retreated to her room. She threw her kapp on the red oakwood trunk draped with a small patchwork quilt at the end of her bed. She had made the quilt by herself. The larger rose-and-bud quilt covering her bed, with its red petals and wavy green stems, had been an eighteenth birthday present from Maemm.

Hannah unpinned her hair and fanned it out. The sensation of her hair falling over her shoulders and down her back brought a smile to her lips. Other than bathing and sleeping, it stayed scraped up. She removed her damp stockings, and from the matching oakwood tallboy by the door, she pulled out a pair of purple socks then found a small rucksack.

Headlights flashed across the window, followed by the sound of an engine cutting. Hannah paused as she returned to the bed. Barney? Had he come to persuade Evan to go out, even if it was to the games? Despite their words, she was pleased Evan had such a good friend. He needed someone to make sure he didn't grow old too soon.

A bang through the lemon painted wall told her Evan was in his room. Downstairs, Grandfather's voice rose sharply before it dropped as he greeted someone. Perhaps it was not Barney, judging by the formal tone. The bishop? Perhaps he wanted the family to host a church service, the first time since Daett had passed on? Maemm would be pleased with the honour and the signal she could come out of mourning. They would go into the kitchen; the heart, and warmest place, of their home.

She put on the socks and listened for movement downstairs. When she was certain Maemm had stayed down there, Hannah knelt by her bed, retrieved a battered, grey suitcase, and opened it. Inside were her neatly folded English clothes. Clothes that would keep her warm out in fields or an unheated barn on a cold winter's night. She stuffed a t-shirt, woollen jumper, and jeans in the rucksack. She dug deep into the case, pulled out a small, folded plastic bag and peeped inside at the plain cotton bra. The tight bodices of her Amish dresses kept everything in place, even when running, but the t-shirt and jumper would billow and flap about when she danced. Some married Amish women, she had heard, wore the contraptions. Only the married ones. Grace, as usual, had decided otherwise. 'You look like you have a pair of melons playing volleyball under your top.' The image, if not the thought of ogling eyes, was enough to settle the argument.

Hannah dug out a pair of ankle boots from the trunk and pulled them on. Rucksack fastened, she slipped on a thick, dark green waterproof hooded coat. Its big shiny buttons and fleece lining seemed at odds with the three plain cotton dresses hanging on her clothes rail.

Finally, she got a drawstring bag from her bedside cabinet and checked the contents. Money, lip gloss, and a small torch. Useful if they had to walk home in the dark. She pulled a hairband from the coat's flap pocket and tied her locks into a ponytail, ready to be loosened at Grace's. With the rucksack slung over one shoulder, she headed to the stairs. A quick glance at the strip of light under the door next to hers confirmed her suspicions about Evan. She turned to descend when the door opened behind her.

'You going, then?' Evan stood, his braces hanging from his trousers, hands in his pockets.

'Yes.'

His contemptuous look brought to mind his boorish manner at dinner. Her skin bristled like a hedgehog as she stepped back, ready to fire the retort on her lips.

It never came. Heated voices erupted from the kitchen. Hannah bent low and stared down the stairs to see the kitchen door slightly ajar. A stream of Pennsylvania Dutch in a harsh voice filled the air. Grandfather? What had upset him? Another man spoke, low and soft, quickly cut off by Maemm shushing him.

Evan leaned over the banister and cocked an ear. Another blast of Dutch.

Neither looked at each other as Hannah braced herself for another rant. After a few moments, the door clicked shut. She strained to make out words but only heard the faint murmur of inaudible voices.

'That's not Barney,' Evan said.

Hannah turned to the small window overlooking the front yard to see a car parked halfway down the drive.

'Looks like a Nissan Versa,' Evan said, looking over her shoulder. 'Must be a lost tourist.'

'Why?'

'Because they hire them.'

Hannah peered at the vehicle's navy blue hood, half-lit by the porch light. Some did get lost and knock for directions.

Evan straightened. 'Where are you off to?'

'I'm going to Grace's. You could meet us later, Evan.'

More Dutch blasted from below. Hannah recalled the smattering of Pennsylvania Dutch she had learned at school. Something about the past being the past.

'I should go down.' Evan moved back towards the stairs.

'No. Let Grandfather deal with the visitor.' Hannah passed him, placing her foot on a step and blocking his way.

The voices had dropped once more. Evan turned to his room and paused by the open door. The glow from the lamp on the handmade desk made his normally pale complexion deepen to the colour of honey. He placed a hand on the door handle. 'You say Grace is going too?'

Hannah nodded. 'Coming?'

Evan rubbed his chin. 'Maybe.' He went in, closing the door.

Hannah smiled as she trotted down to the hall. He would go. He had a reason now.

Now, to pacify Maemm, she needed to tell her she would be with Grace. Grace was sensible, Maemm believed; Grace would ensure they got back safely. Maemm's belief was founded on the demure young lady she knew, because Grace always kept her mischievous side under wraps when the adults were around.

Pleased with her plans for the night, Hannah listened outside the kitchen door. Hushed murmurs filtered through. Whatever had set the fireworks off had died down, making it safe for her to enter. She pushed the door open and stopped upon hearing the abrupt *harrumph* from Grandfather, who stood between Maemm and the other person in the room. Not Barney, the good friend come to drag Evan out, nor the bishop. Hannah's eyes widened like sunflower petals and her mouth parted as she registered the stranger. There, in the kitchen of her family home, stood the man from the café.

Chapter 6

THE STRANGER TURNED calmly to her. From behind his glasses, a pair of evergreen eyes met her astonished stare.

'*Gut'n Owed.*' She lapsed into her home tongue, betraying her shock at seeing him. What did he want? She glanced at the window. Outside was pitch black. Who else waited in the darkness? How was she going to explain his presence to Maemm and Grandfather after everything that had happened? Here he was, standing in her home, still dressed in the same clothes from the café. She fidgeted with the strap of her rucksack.

'Good evening,' he replied, his arms loose by his sides and his feet slightly apart. He understood her words. She stared at him, noting his high cheekbones and aquiline nose. His accent had none of the stilted tones of her people.

'You are going to Grace's?' Maemm, standing beside the man, eyed the bag. Hannah gave a nod, flustered by the stranger's presence.

His gaze shifted from Hannah and rested on Maemm. Grandfather stood by the stove watching them, his thin lips taut.

'This is Hannah.' Maemm did not look directly at either her or the man, but rather at the space between them.

'Hello, Hannah – again,' he said.

Maemm's eyes narrowed as she looked at her then the man. *Where was a hole when you needed one to burrow inside?*

'I was waiting for the café to open this morning when there was an incident. Your daughter is a brave young lady. Not many would have remained as calm as she did.' He moved his gaze back to Hannah. 'I'm sorry if I scared you this afternoon. I only meant to ask how you were.'

Hannah struggled with what to say. He had not been chasing her. She recalled him smiling through the café window at her and his wave on the street. She glanced at Maemm, who gave her the tiniest of nods. Relief flooded through her body. No one got past Maemm.

'I am pleased to meet you, sir,' she replied.

'Theo.' He did not offer his hand the way many English folk did. 'Theo Anderson.' He paused, checking Maemm once again. 'I came to pay my respects to your mother. Your father was a good man.'

'You knew Daett?' Hannah stopped herself stepping back. He knew her parents? Did that explain why he was here? Maybe it wasn't to do with the hand, then. If he knew Maemm and Daett, then he would not be part of whatever or whoever was behind the incident that morning. A spring of suspicion dampened her elation. 'How did you know him?' She focused on his face, searching for clues.

'I met him once when you were young.' He extended his hand palm down, hinting at the height of a small child. 'It was your maemm I knew first. When we were younger.' The words came slowly, a hint of a foreign inflection in his midwest accent.

'You're from our community?' she said, remembering how he understood her and did not shake her hand.

The half-smile widened his mouth. 'I never knew my parents. An Amish couple in Ohio adopted me and brought me up plain. They told me the note found with me outside a hospital said I was Amish. I joined the police and got posted to Birchwood before you were born. I used to go to the same gatherings as your mother and aunt.'

'You left our community?' Another leaver. Another example of life beyond these walls.

'Hannah,' Maemm chided. 'You ask too many questions.'

'Yes, and the police. I'm a lawyer these days. My job back then was to keep a low profile at those gatherings, monitoring the high jinks,' he said with a little laugh. 'Though on the whole, people behaved.'

A soft expression crept onto Maemm's face before her features tightened to a placid, polite mask. The momentary break reminded Hannah of the sad expression she would sometimes catch Maemm wearing when they talked about Daett.

'Are you attending one tonight?' He surveyed the rucksack; she avoided Maemm's frown. He glanced out of the window at the inky evening sky. 'Can I offer you a lift?'

Maemm's eyes widened. Grandfather coughed and shook his head. Hannah remained silent, wishing once more she could break the rules and avoid braving the winter's cold night.

'Hannah knows her way,' Maemm interjected before Hannah could answer. 'It is not far.'

Mr Anderson made to speak then stopped, chewing on his bottom lip. 'My apologies, Naomi. It's very dark, and there are no streetlights to guide her.'

'Evan or I can take you in the buggy if you wish, Hannah,' Grandfather wheezed, the effort changing his anxious look to one of discomfort.

63

'I'll walk. It is quicker over the fields. As Maemm says, I know the way well.' Hannah hoped her words would pacify him.

Grandfather clicked his tongue, indicating his reluctant agreement.

'Thank you, Mr Anderson, kindly,' she said.

'Theo.'

'Theo.' She echoed the unfamiliar name.

'It is getting late,' Grandfather grumbled as the wall clock in the hall chimed. Hannah slipped her arm through the loose strap of the rucksack. She checked her watch, noting the time: eight o'clock. Sol would come by Grace's at nine.

'You have somewhere to stay?' Maemm asked Theo, despite Grandfather's polite, firm hint for their guest to leave.

'Yes. I'm staying with Drummond. You remember him?'

'Of course. He occasionally drops by,' Maemm replied. Her face broke into a pleasant smile for the first time that evening.

Hannah bit her lip. Occasionally, yes, but always when Grandfather was out. How did Maemm know the police officer when the church forbade members to cooperate with them?

'He and I worked together when I was here,' Theo said. 'I live in England now.'

Grandfather fished out his watch and stared pointedly at it. Hannah edged to the door. Theo opened it for her. 'Denki,' she said.

'*Gott saykna dich.*' The blessing came stilted yet correctly pronounced.

Once again, Hannah found herself wrong-footed by their unexpected visitor. Such a personal blessing from Grandfather, Maemm, or even the bishop would have been appropriate. Elder to younger relative. Maemm to daughter. Ordinand to lay. He, a stranger, gave it to her without hesitation instead of the common *doei* or *goot nacht*. Grandfather narrowed his eyes, his brows knitting together.

Hannah lowered her head, not wishing anyone to see the deep crimson of her face, and hurried out to the front door. The fresh sting of the chilly night air on her burning cheeks dampened the flare of embarrassment at his suggestion of giving her a ride. Ignoring the wind buffeting her, she hurried past the blue sedan parked outside. The farther she headed down the path to the main road, the easier her breathing became, and the tension fled from her body. Whoever he was and whatever kind of friendship he and Maemm had had in the past, the brief encounter in the kitchen had convinced her of one thing: Grandfather did not welcome his arrival.

GAS LAMPS HUNG from a post outside Grace's home. An upper bedroom light guided Hannah to the back of the house, and laughter filtered through to her as she eased open the back door to the room Grace called the 'boyfriend parlour'. One day, Grace would entertain someone. Evan, maybe?

'Hannah!' Grace squealed in delight. Dressed in a rainbow-coloured chunky jumper, jeans, and trainers, she bounced down the wooden stairs and hugged her. Grace, whippet-like, with the exuberance of a Labrador and blessed with crystal-clear, rosy skin and round, emerald-coloured eyes.

'Here.' Grace held up her mobile phone, one corner covered in sticky tape.

Hannah ducked out of view of the screen. 'Oh, Grace, please. We are not supposed to take photographs.'

Grace huddled closer to her, holding the phone up. On the screen, Hannah caught herself and Grace. 'Smile. I'm keeping a record, so when I'm old and grey I can reminisce and remind myself of the fun times. Don't worry, I'll hide it where no-one will find it.'

Hannah shook her head.

Grace chattered as they climbed the stairs to her bedroom, which was like Hannah's own though bigger and with a view over the front, not the back. Once inside, Hannah dumped her rucksack on the single bed covered with Grace's favourite quilt of flowers sewn onto a cream background. A ragdoll was propped up against the matching pillow.

Hannah changed into her English clothes. Her loose dress was replaced by the jeans, jumper and t-shirt, and her boots with the trainers. The heavy denim rubbed against her legs, but at least its thickness would protect her from the cold night. 'Maemm's nagging again,' she muttered, pulling her cabled jumper on. Why did English people wear so many layers? The jumper hung below her waist, its cuffs pulled out of shape from nights of fiddling with it.

'So is mine.' Grace sat on the bed, zipping up a knee-high boot.

Hannah shot her a sympathetic grin and picked up the small round mirror on the bed. Vanity might be a sin, but looking like a ragdoll wasn't good either. A quick finger comb as she tried to avoid staring at her light blue, green-specked eyes assured her that her unkempt appearance after the windswept walk was now rectified.

Grace sighed as she put the second boot on and stood up. 'Is Evan coming?' She pulled on her green parka with its fur-trimmed hood.

'Aren't you going with Levi?' Hannah rolled up her discarded clothes and stuffed them into the rucksack.

'That's why I'm asking,' Grace replied. 'I don't want to upset Evan.'

Hannah paused as she applied her lip gloss.

'It's just... Levi is such fun.' Grace stared out of the window, her lips curling into a tiny smile. 'And a little dangerous.'

'And Evan isn't?'

'You know what I mean.' Grace scrunched her face up.

Hannah smudged her lips together and tried not to lick the strawberry gloss off.

'You do. Sol is the same.' Grace lowered her voice. 'It's why you like him.'

Hannah looked away. What was the harm? Better Grace ran around with Levi than Evan. Not that Evan would 'run around'. Grace had always run around full speed since she was a child. Did it not worry Grandfather and Maemm that Evan had set his sights on such a high-spirited girl? Despite Grace's habit of reining herself in when visiting them, they must know from others of Grace's antics. Time for the big-sister act – if nothing else, to warn her friend. 'Evan is my brother. Don't toy with him, Grace.'

Grace's bottom lip quivered. 'Of course not.'

Hannah yanked the toggle on the bag. 'He's still young. Eighteen. You know he has feelings for you.'

'You, big sister, are worried for him.' Grace toyed with a drawstring. 'We've known each other all our lives, Hannah. I thought you knew me better.'

Yes, she did. Too well. Rumspringa might end, but Grace would forever be Grace. 'Why not Barney? He's as much a joker as you.' Hannah threw the thought in, hoping to lift Grace's mood and assuage her own guilt over arguing.

'Barney!' Grace burst out laughing.

'Why not?'

'Oh, Hannah.' Grace shook her head as she regained her composure. 'You do go around with your eyes closed.'

As the loud beep of a horn announced Sol's arrival, Grace shot off down the stairs, bag in hand, yelling, 'Party time!' Hannah stuffed her hairbrush inside the blue rucksack's front pocket and grabbed her waterproof coat, scampering after her.

In the Dodge, Sol sneaked a peek at Hannah through the rearview mirror. 'So, no games night, eh, girls?'

'Not unless it's musical statues.' Grace took a packet of cigarettes from her parka pocket and lit one up. She gave a little cough after taking a drag. Levi, seated in the front, threw his head back and roared with laughter. Hannah tried not to wrinkle her nose at the smoke.

Grace puffed at the cigarette and stared out the window. 'I'm going to be baptised come Easter.'

The words came out rushed, and Hannah checked her friend's face, stunned.

'What else am I going to do with my life?' Grace took another drag and exhaled, the vapour forming a long, thin trail in the air.

'But you never said.' Hannah waved the smoke from her face.

'I never planned to do otherwise, and it will stop my parents from nagging me if they know. What about you?'

'Aww, Grace, I'm going to miss your pretty face and giggles.' Levi ran a hand through the mane of sandy-blond hair hanging past his shoulders.

'How long have we got to party before you start preparation classes?' Sol asked.

'Can't you party and prep?' Levi suggested.

'No,' Grace said. 'I'll stop Rumspringa in March when the classes begin before Easter.'

'What about you, Hannah?' He twisted round and fixed her with a stare.

'Still thinking, aren't you, Han?' Sol cut in. 'I'm sure you'll come round to the right decision.'

Hannah caught the wink in the mirror, and a queasy sensation bubbled up inside her stomach. Did he want her to go English for a reason? The queasiness morphed into a fluttery celebration as hope filled her before it nosedived at the thought of her family's reaction if he did.

'Hannah, I'm sorry,' Grace said in a low voice. 'I only told them this evening.'

Hannah took hold of Grace's hand and smiled at her, not wanting the tiff between them earlier to mar the evening. One of the last they would share.

Sol had retraced the road past Hannah's home and then driven them along the main road into the town centre. He swung into the alley between the butcher's and the florist, emerging at the rear of the shops. Levi jumped out and jogged to the white aluminium shed by the butcher's back wall. 'Why is Levi going into the icehouse?' Grace said, slumping back in her seat as they watched Levi unlock the door and slip inside.

'He needs to pick up something,' Sol replied, reversing the car to face the alley. The headlights caught the back entrances of the butcher's and cycle shop farther up. He had barely completed the turn when Levi reappeared, climbed into the car, turned around and dropped a small, khaki-coloured rucksack on the seat between Grace and Hannah.

'Take care of it for me, Gracie.' He blew her a kiss.

On the other side of town, Sol turned onto the narrow country road that led to the Millers'. Houses blazed with lights, cables running from telegraph poles and lighting up the rooms. The hazy, bluish glow in the distant sky told Hannah they were close to their destination.

A rabbit darted onto the road. Sol swerved and braked, and Hannah lurched forward, held back by the seatbelt. Her bag and the bag next to it fell on the floor. Grace gripped her cigarette between her fingers.

'Pesky things.' Levi looked back at the fleeing rabbit. 'You should've run it over.'

'Oh, no.' Grace's hand flew to her mouth. 'That's a sin. Killing one of God's creatures.' She opened her window and threw the cigarette out.

'Well, better it than us,' Levi retorted.

'Levi!' Grace faked a shocked expression and let a coquettish grin spread across her face.

Hannah reached down for her bag and lifted it onto her lap. 'Leave it,' Levi snapped at her when she went to lift the other bag. He half-turned in the passenger seat and glared at her.

Hannah let go of the bag, sat back, and clasped her own rucksack.

Sol shot a reproachful glare at Levi. 'Put it in the trunk next time.'

'It's got beer in it.' Levi's voice returned to its lazy drawl.

Grace gave Hannah a sidelong glance, her sunny mood evaporated. Sol switched on the stereo and filled the silence with rock music as he sped towards the growing blue haze ahead.

BY MIDNIGHT, OVER a hundred people mingled inside and outside the Millers' barn. Pop music blasted from a makeshift DJ platform with several speakers rigged up. The group threaded their way through the cars parked around the sides of the field towards the barn and dance floor with hay bales stacked around. Hannah waved at Aaron, who was standing by one of the barn's large, open wooden doors, but he was busy checking a girl's handbag.

'See? Aaron's on guard duty tonight,' Grace said.

'Well, it is his family's home. Would you want the police raiding yours for drugs or anti-social behaviour?' Hannah replied, glad no one had ever asked to hold one at hers, imagining Maemm's blunt refusal.

Grace sighed, heading to the throng on the dance floor. 'Probably checking for underage drinkers.'

'He'll be busy.' Sol, carrying a blue icebox, smirked.

Hannah knew she had Saturday to recover before Sunday, which meant church and the sedate call of Bible study, needlework, and prayer that would begin a new week. Grace had her photos to remind her of these times. Hannah would have her memories if she stayed Amish, but decisions had to be made soon; too soon. Decisions about being free. Being with Sol. If only she could figure out what she wanted…

Three-and-a-half months. Would it be enough to work it out? Going English could mean severing ties with her family and community. Where would she go? How would she live? Work? Who would help her? Hannah closed her eyes, aware of a dull throbbing around her temples. Tonight was hers, she reminded herself as they danced in a circle. She had survived facing a severed, bleeding hand in the morning and being almost flattened by a car in the afternoon. She needed to relax; to party, dance, 'hang out', as the English said. Forget about the world, all its decisions, and dance. Hannah raised her hands in the air and tuned to the fast-paced music. When a slow tune came on, Sol and Levi ambled off to get some drinks.

Despite her decision, Grace evidently intended to make the most of her time. Levi seemed happy to help, sharing his beer with her and his 'happy pills', as he called them. Hannah hoped her friend would embrace her Amish life with such enthusiasm; otherwise, it would not bode well for any suitors who came calling.

Generators supplied the indoor and outdoor lighting. Inside the barn, lamps hung from timber posts, and outside they were suspended from wire roped through the trees and poles along the outer edges of the field and yard.

Sol held a joint and, from his leather jacket, he pulled out some pills. Hannah waved them aside. By the barn, Levi stood talking to Aaron, fumbling inside his rucksack. 'Aww, come on, Hannah,' Sol teased with a winsome grin. 'In all the time I've known you, I've seen you party hard but stay clean.' He glanced over at Grace. Hannah spotted Levi approaching the dance area, the rucksack strapped on his back. 'Guess with Grace opting out of the party, it won't be long before you do, too. This could be our last time together. Last time to try all those things you're going to give up if you stay Amish.' He stared at her with those dark, dangerous eyes of his. Inciting her. 'Happy or dopey?' The overhanging lamp's glow caught the bright smile on his face.

Hannah paused. With the effects of her second tepid beer from the icebox taking hold, she thought she should probably slow down.

'Come, Hannah. Party time.' Levi slipped an arm around Grace's waist.

'See? Aaron checked you out.' Hannah took the joint from Sol, ignoring Levi's frown.

'Oh, yeah. Right little guard dog. Decoy for Sol here.' Levi laughed, taking a bottle from the box with his back to Aaron. 'Wonder if he's body-searching the girls. Now that'd be fun.'

'Levi!' Grace playfully whacked him on the chest.

'Joking.' He hugged her.

'Take it slow and long,' Sol advised, as she held the joint between her lips and inhaled. The smoke hit the rear of her throat, making her cough and sneeze simultaneously.

'Where do you get this stuff from?' Grace popped another happy pill and took a swig from Levi's bottle.

'A friend.' Sol scanned the sea of bodies in the dance area cordoned off by hay bales, which people were sitting on. Someone waved at him beyond the boundary near some cars parked by a tree. 'They help at the parties.'

'You mean they supply people who come here?' Barney appeared from the midst of the dancers and stood by Sol, Evan in tow in Amish clothes, his single concession a clean, lemon-green shirt. Like many of the others, they wore what they wanted; English or Amish clothes, it didn't matter as long as they had fun.

Hannah hastily handed the joint back to Sol and ignored the disapproving glare from Barney. Levi held Grace's hand as they danced, and she beamed, enjoying Levi's full attention, and Evan scowled.

'Be back in a second.' Sol edged away from Barney and Evan and pushed his way through the mass of dancers to the trees and cars.

'Drugs, Hannah?' Evan shook his head and swigged from his beer bottle.

'Alcohol, Evan?' Hannah countered as she watched Sol approaching the group of men in leather jackets and jeans, masked by cigarette smoke. 'What would Maemm say?'

Evan smarted and surveyed the crowd. 'Why can't we meet without all this?'

'You can.' A sudden mist swirled around her, making her light-headed. 'The Singings. Or you could meet to play those silly games at someone's house. Or volleyball.'

'In these temperatures?' Barney snorted, rubbing his hands. 'Besides, the old folks listen in to the conversations in the homes.'

'What we need is one of those youth centres.' Evan jerked his can in the direction of the road. 'Like the one the English have.'

'What? Evan, you have something good to say about the English?' She held up her palm, giggling. 'Next you'll be advocating we should have electricity, or maybe computers. Like those you use at the library.'

He did a double take at her.

'I've seen you when I go to the post office.'

'Nothing wrong in using computers – outside home,' Evan replied. 'It's for the business.'

'Of course.' Hannah smirked at him, enjoying his discomfort at her dig.

'You'll never get the idea past the bishop,' Barney protested. 'The church wouldn't allow it. And who would run it? They would insist on an elder taking charge, so we'd be swapping one thing for the same thing.'

Hannah nodded. The music filled the silence between them.

'Who was the visitor?' Evan asked.

'Changing the subject now, are we?' Hannah said.

He shot her a surly look.

'Some old acquaintance of Maemm's. He came by to pay his respects.'

'Maemm's?' Evan replied. 'Not Daett's? Strange.'

Hannah half listened, her gaze straying across the dance floor to the trees and the huddle around the tall, slim figure in the feather-brimmed hat. A shaven-headed man wearing a red bandana gripped Sol by his jacket, pushing his face so close to Sol's his hat was dislodged and fell to the ground.

Hannah moved forward and felt a rough grab of her shoulder as Evan yanked her back. 'Stay out of it,' he ordered.

It was clear Levi had no intention of rescuing his friend. *Coward*, Hannah fumed. The man pulled Sol closer, Sol's heels lifting off the ground. She would rescue him like he had her. That's what friends did. Curse Levi. She took another step, breaking away from Evan, her eyes on the animated exchange ahead.

Barney's and Evan's shouts urging her not to intervene faded as she pushed through the crowd, watching Sol struggling to free himself. The first punch landed on his face around the eye, making her wince. Why were they beating him up? Help. He needed help. She shouted into the dancing mass of people, pointing at the fight. Within seconds, half a dozen youths raced towards the commotion, bodies tumbling over hay bales. One guy slammed into a makeshift post with a lamp hanging from it; it crashed down onto a bale, igniting it.

'Fire! Fire!' A panicky shout shot into the air, galvanising others standing around to run, grab the buckets by the barn door and fill them with water from an outdoor pump. Her relief at helping Sol turned to alarm as the fire spread, separating the thugs and Sol from the rest of the partygoers. She lunged forward, the heat of the flames fanning her face.

Barney shoved his way through to her, grabbed her arm and led her across the dance area, away from the fire. In the distance sirens wailed, drawing closer with every second. Sol staggered away from the gang's flying arms and interlocked bodies, blood pouring down the side of his face. Once clear, he bolted out of the glare of the lights into the dark field where they had parked the Dodge.

If she could get to him, she could tend to his injury. Console him. An unfamiliar emotion welled up as she saw his battered face; he looked like a frightened, lost little boy. She tried to yank free from Barney as a line of flashing headlights flooded the Millers' yard.

'Hannah, come.' Barney's grip tightened around her upper arm and, with a hand on her back, he propelled her to his car. To their left, Evan hurried a panic-stricken Grace, one arm around her waist, in the same direction. Others passed them, running out of range as the police rounded up the partygoers.

Hannah's eyes darted around the chaotic scene before her. People fled in all directions and cars careened past the barn and out to the back road. Amidst the mayhem, she spotted it: the white strip on red speeding across the open yard into the light spilling from the barn's rim. As he drove past them, Sol threw her a desperate look and braked.

Their eyes locked. The passenger door flew open, and Hannah lunged forward. Barney's fingers pressed so tightly they hurt her bones. Her trainers slipped on the wet, uneven ground, aiding Barney as he yanked her away from the car. Sol revved the engine. Enraged, she fought to break free using the weight of her entire body. Barney reinforced his hold and grabbed her other arm. He spun her in front of him, blocking the way with his body, and pushed her forward. Away from the barn. Away from trouble and away from Sol.

Chapter 7

THE HARD, NARROW wooden bench caused Hannah to shift occasionally, at least helping her stay awake through the Sunday service. The headache had lasted until mid-afternoon on Saturday. An early night had accomplished little to ease her tiredness.

She surveyed the gathered congregation with all the unmarried women on one side of the barn behind the wives and widows, including Maemm, who wore black kapps and shawls to church. The men sat on the other side, a slim corridor of space separating them. In the front row, Bishop Fisher, with his thick, raven hair, towered above the two ministers and visiting clergy seated with him. All faced the far end as the bishop stood, ready to lead the service.

The sparsely filled benches near the back filled up with the younger men who straggled in last, making the most of the opportunity to remain outside to catch up with one another and watch the girls go in. Evan's head rose above the others, his wide shoulders jutting out level with the ears of the bespectacled youth on his right and the figure to his left, whose tousled head was bowed. Barney, Hannah guessed. In front of them were the married men.

She listened as attentively as she could, resisting the impulse to rub her sleepy eyes as the deacon gave the first sermon of the three-hour worship. The heat generated by over a hundred people crammed in the building supplied ample warmth to thaw out her hands from the freezing march over the frosty field. She tucked them under the folds of her cloak to keep her from fidgeting and watched the children. The toddlers played quietly with ragdolls or read. The older ones listened dutifully, as expected. They would tear around after the service, burning off their pent-up energy as she and Grace used to do. She allowed a slight smile to play on her lips, remembering from her own childhood Sundays how ravenous they would be afterwards. With so many coming from the district, everyone would contribute to the main meal prepared by the hosts.

Aaron, seated in the same row as the bishop, rose and went to the front. He cleared his throat, clasped his hands, and sang, his rich, tenor tones echoing through the silence.

Sol... was he safe? Did he escape the police and those men? What had he done to anger them? He had said they were friends. He may have been her childhood friend, yet he seemed more like a stranger these days. Did he know more about the hand and the reason behind it? He *had* warned her off.

Barney, unflappable as usual, had taken her home on the night of the fire and assured Maemm all was well, then returned to help Aaron and his family tidy up in time for the service. How very Amish. No drama. No fuss. Life goes on.

She closed her eyes. If anything had happened to Sol... She let Aaron's rich, mellow tones float over and soothe her. Tomorrow. She would see Sol tomorrow. Till then, she must be patient and appear untroubled.

She did not open her *Ausbund*, which contained the hymns she had known since childhood, as the congregation picked up the tune. The simple hymn's words calmed her mind as the voices melded together. A restfulness descended upon her. She could not describe it but knew it to be from God and those around her, encircling her with their presence and assurance. Perhaps it was time for her to choose? If she stayed, the church would continue to be a significant part of her life.

Surely God loved the English too? Was not everyone one of his children? How could going English mean going to hell, as the elders declared? Would God not love her?

An elbow nudged her. Grace's cherry-blossom smile brought her back to the present as Aaron read the scripture for the day. The anger that had provoked her to storm inside the house without a word and slam the front door when Barney had dropped her and Evan home trickled away. He had merely done what any brother in Christ would do: kept her safe.

The singing finished, Aaron read from his Bible. His tone rose and dipped as he recounted the story of the blind man seeking Jesus's healing. Blind. She had been blind to the danger the fight had put her in. She must thank Barney. Her rudeness was inexcusable. She lifted a prayer for God to forgive her behaviour and vowed to focus all her attention on worshipping, as Maemm had taught her, with sincerity and a heart for the Lord. With this aim, she devoted herself to the rest of the service.

Afterwards, replenished by the congregational meal and cleared of all chores, Hannah wandered out, tying her bonnet before burrowing her bare hands inside her cloak as the bitter cold air caught the back of her throat. She coughed as she joined Grace by a tree between the barn and house. She followed Grace's glance over her shoulder: near the barn, Barney and Evan stood talking while the children raced about.

'Your brother is strong,' Grace commented, toying with the ribbon of her white bonnet. 'He carried me off like I was a tiny lamb.'

'Barney has the grip of a vice,' Hannah grumbled. 'My arm still hurts.'

'I hope Levi is unhurt. Even if he did hotfoot it off into the fields.'

'I'm sure he is.'

'At least Evan had the decency to stay and see me home.' Grace looked at Barney and Evan again.

Hannah smiled, noting the colour rising to Grace's cheeks as Evan lifted his gaze momentarily to them. 'What about Levi?' she teased.

Grace sighed with a coy smile. 'He is fun, but Evan is a good man. He will be a good husband.'

Hannah arched an eyebrow.

'I mean, when he weds.' Grace busied herself with tying her cloak up.

'Of course.' Hannah suppressed a grin. 'I am sorry for what I said on Friday at your home.'

'As you say, he is your brother,' Grace replied, watching Evan and Barney. 'But, Hannah, I would never play with his affections. He is part of the reason I'm getting baptised.'

In the distance, Barney and Evan stood looking in their direction, and Hannah pondered. Perhaps there was a way to accomplish two things at the same time. She looped her arm through Grace's. 'Why don't we walk home, like we used to when we were younger?'

They glanced over at a group of young women chatting together in their dark capes and white bonnets. Like most of the other huddles, they stood near the buggies and horses parked on the grassy area by the path that led to the main entrance of the farm. Hannah saw a pretty girl with plaited ginger hair eyeing them, and she motioned at Grace and herself before pointing to the road. The girl nodded, turning back to her friends. Together, Hannah and Grace wandered down the pathway and tightened their cloaks around their bodies to shield them from the cold.

As she'd hoped, Hannah soon heard the crunch of gravel close behind them. She recognised the shuffle-shuffle of her younger brother's feet, and the other footsteps sounded springy and measured. A sideways peek revealed a pinkish tint on Grace's cheeks.

When they were near the end of the lane, Hannah stopped and bent as though going to tie her shoelace. Evan seized his chance, as she had hoped; he quickened his pace, overtaking her and falling in step with Grace. Barney stopped by Hannah, wearing a sheepish smile. 'Shall we walk?' he suggested, chewing a straw of hay.

They crossed the road to a gate in the stone wall bordering a field, keeping a discreet distance from Evan and Grace, close enough to see but not hear them. Hannah took a deep breath. 'I am grateful for your help on Friday evening.'

Barney chuckled. 'You were stronger than I realised.' He paused. 'You should be careful of Sol, Hannah.'

'Why? Because he prefers living as the English do?'

'No.' He took the straw out of his mouth. 'Have you ever asked why you deliver parcels to the butcher? And fetch them too?'

'It's my job to run errands.'

Barney threw her a sidelong glance and slowed down, the gap between them and the other two widening. 'You might want to ask yourself why Levi and Sol were talking to those men.'

'We should catch up with Evan and Grace.' She quickened her step. She had tried to make amends. If he wished to brush her efforts aside, so be it. The blades of grass, wet from the morning frost, dampened her ankle boots.

Barney lengthened his stride with ease to keep up with her. 'Hannah, Hannah.' He fell in step with her.

'You really do not like him.'

'I don't like what he represents.'

'There is a difference.'

'You wouldn't remember the Leechburg years.' The straw returned to his mouth. 'They were part of a gang who sold drugs to Amish youth at hops and gatherings. My second brother remembers. The friends who got hooked. The ones who...' He trailed off.

Who died? How could she have forgotten he had lost a brother?

'There were two brothers acting as the local group, working for a larger ring. Another gang from elsewhere tried to take over. All hell broke loose. That's when the grocer's son got his fingers chopped off. One of the brothers died in a shoot-out. The other turned state's evidence and disappeared. The boss man, Rafael Martinez, got imprisoned.'

'Sol wouldn't get mixed up in drug dealing.' Hannah sped up, outpacing him. What did he know about Sol other than through idle gossip? Yes, Sol had some drugs on him, but only at the gathering. Never anything that could kill someone or that he sold, and never in the shop. As Barney caught up with her, she kept her eyes ahead.

'Maybe you are right, but I suspect it's going that way again, I fear,' he sighed. 'Too many drugs at our parties. Where is it all coming from? Who's supplying it? Evan is right, we need somewhere. Somewhere safe.'

'And boring.'

Barney halted. 'Being safe is boring?' His tone matched the sadness in his eyes as he waited for an answer.

What reply could she give? She scanned the field ahead. Grace and Evan stood, heads tilted towards each other, deep in discussion. She hurried towards them.

Grace smiled as Hannah caught up. 'Evan says he's going to talk to the church officials about building a community centre.'

'We could meet and plan what to say to them.' Evan warmed to the subject with a broad grin.

'It's a great idea, Evan. We could ask some others to join us.' Grace looked admiringly at Evan, who stretched to his full height and squared his shoulders, his chest puffing out. 'When should we meet?'

'Next Friday,' Evan said.

Grace's face fell, and he frowned.

'Maybe not Friday, Evan,' Barney suggested, eyeing Grace. 'Perhaps a weeknight?'

Evan scuffed the toe of his boot in the dirt. 'Why not Friday?'

Grace curled her bottom lip. 'I have plans.'

'Another gathering? Another party?' Barney raised his eyebrows as Grace stood awkwardly, eyes on the ground.

'Why don't we all go together? We could discuss the matter while travelling there?' Evan's face took on a bright, eager look. Grace twisted her hands, unable to meet his confused expression, which morphed into a sullen scowl. '*Levi.*' He stomped the grass with a heavy boot. 'Why did you walk with me if you're going with someone else?'

'Walk with you?' Grace lifted her head sharply and stared at him. 'I thought... I thought *you* walked with me because...' She looked pointedly at Hannah and Barney.

'Whoa.' Barney raised his hands.

'Huh?' Evan gave Barney a suspicious glance.

'No,' Barney replied, staring into the distance.

Hannah glanced away and spotted a sheep watching them, twitching an ear.

Barney gave Grace a curious stare. 'It *is* Levi?'

Grace's skin deepened to a ruby shade. Evan clenched his fists and dropped his gaze, his shoulders caving. Without a word, he stormed off.

Grace shot Barney an accusing glare and hurried after Evan, her lip trembling. Evan ignored her heartfelt pleas to slow down, leaving her to trail in his wake.

Hannah rounded on Barney. 'That was cruel.'

'Not as much as you are.'

The sting of his words left her speechless.

'Don't you think your maemm has suffered enough this past year?' He put his hands on his hips. 'She'll still be wearing black next winter if you carry on like you do.'

Hannah's mouth turned dry as she caught the flash of anger crossing his features. All serious and older than his twenty years. No wonder he got on with Evan, who, Hannah sometimes believed, had been born old.

'I will make my decision when I decide to end my Rumspringa.'

'When will that be? You've been on it since sixteen. Twice longer than most.'

'What right do you have to tell me how to live?' She lifted her head but refused to meet his gaze.

'The right of a good friend,' he spat back. 'You think smoking a joint will impress Sol? You're wrong.'

'And you would know all about getting it right, wouldn't you?' She gave a vigorous shake of her head, making her hood fall onto her shoulders. 'You who run around enjoying the best of the English, including the girls?'

He took a deep breath and opened his mouth to speak.

She raised a finger at him. 'You want the best of both worlds, Barney Herzberg, with no commitment to either.'

'Sounds like someone I know.'

The urge to flatten her palm against his cheek and shake the smug attitude out of him vibrated down her arms through her hands. She gathered her skirt and turned.

'Hannah.' The rough voice softened to a tender tone. He made her name sound like a blessing. One of her boots flattened a cow pat and with it, the unintended thought. He called her name again.

She halted and spun round. 'Friend you might be, but you are no friend of mine if you persist in this. This is my life – my future you talk so glibly of. Not a car or a cow. A good friend wants their friends to be happy. Don't you want me to be happy?'

Barney staggered back, his shoulders dropping. 'I am sorry if my words hurt. I only have your best interests at heart. Friend.' He rolled his jaw in his familiar apologetic way of old. 'I lost my brother to drugs. Perhaps it's made me paranoid about them, but please consider why you are doing what you are doing. Don't define yourself by another's opinion. They should like you for you. Don't think so poorly of yourself.'

Hannah pinched her lips together as she fought against a tremble. 'Poorly of myself? For an old friend, you know me not.' She was glad he could not see her hands bunching into tight fists. 'It is because I know my worth. I will not be rushed into such an important decision, by anyone.'

He reached out to take her hand, but she smacked it away. Gathering her cloak, she ran, fuelled by anger, across the field towards the fieldstone wall and stile. She called out to Grace to wait and hurried down the rolling slope. The smooth soles of her boots slipped on the wet grass as the field dropped sharply near the wall, and something small and hard hit her toe, forcing her to stumble. With a cry, she fell backwards, one of her feet sliding from underneath her, and landed on the earth, steadying herself with an outstretched hand.

'Hannah!' Grace raced up the short incline. 'Are you hurt?'

Hannah sprang up and arranged her cloak around her, ignoring Grace's hand held out to her. 'No. I'm fine.'

Grace waved at Barney, who stood at the top of the slope, watching. Hannah flipped up her hood and fell into step with Grace as they made their way to the stile.

'Hannah?' Grace said tentatively. 'Evan. You must speak to Evan. I didn't realise how deeply he feels. I'm not ready. Not yet. When I am baptised... then. Yes?'

'You should have considered that before you encouraged him.'

Grace paled, her eyes full of tears poised to spill down her reddened cheeks.

'I'm sorry, Grace.' Hannah pushed a few strands of hair under her bonnet and scolded herself for lashing out at the wrong person.

'It should be me apologising. You spoke true. I need to sort myself out once and for all.' Grace wiped a tear. 'I would never trifle with Evan.' Another sniffle escaped her.

'Don't worry, Grace. I'll talk to him. But you must end things with Levi.' Hannah looped her arm through her friend's.

'Yes, yes. I will. Thank you. You are a good friend.' Colour returned to Grace's tear-stained cheeks.

Hannah's mind drifted back to Friday night's events. A little voice inside her questioned why she had taken the drug, and slowly, another answered. *Sol.* He made her feel vulnerable and irrational with his loopy grin egging her on. Daring her... she fell for it time after time. If Maemm knew of her behaviour, it would disappoint and pain her. Perhaps she should at least try going to the organised activities, like she used to. Things might be different with being older. Perhaps it would help her understand why she was so hesitant to commit to staying. Was it all about the freedom Sol's world seemed to offer? Whatever the outcome, it had to be made. She had promised to do so. 'Maybe we should go to the Singing next week instead?' she surprised herself by asking as they climbed over the stile.

Grace looked horrified. 'But I've promised Levi... I can't let him down. Please come with me. It will be my last one. Promise. Please? One more outing. Just the one. I promise I will tell him I am done.'

'He knows that already. You're getting baptised, remember.'

'Please. Just one more outing.'

'We almost got arrested last time. Think of the shame if we had been, Grace.'

Grace looked as wounded as a dying deer. 'Yes. Sorry.' She smoothed down her cloak. 'I just want to say goodbye properly to Levi.'

A pang of remorse filled Hannah as she watched her distraught friend shivering in the cold. What did she mean by a 'proper goodbye'? She closed her eyes, pushing away the troubling conclusion. Surely not? Once more, she found her inner voice scolding herself. It was not her friend's flightiness that worried her, but Levi's worldliness.

'After next weekend, that's it.' Grace rubbed her hands together. 'Fun becomes something else. I mean well by Evan, honestly, Hannah. It is... he is so... normal. I am sure I will come to appreciate such a quality. In due course.'

'I demand to know you are serious about Evan, Grace.' Hannah pointed a shaky finger in the direction Evan had stomped off. 'He's not a toy. You can turn a *leddich* on a sixpence if you wish. He is my brother. If you are not ready or not true in your feelings, then finish with him and be done.'

'I am, I am.' Grace placed a hand across her heart with an earnest look. 'One last time. Please, Hannah.'

What harm could it do to agree? Evan was young. He would forgive Grace and forget the dent to his pride. Levi would be a distant memory once Grace joined the church at Easter. She had a good heart. Perhaps living back in the community would calm her down and tame the impulsive side of her nature. If Hannah went to the party, she could keep an eye on Grace and Levi. Evan might need some coaxing, and her assurance that there would be no *schmunzla* would help. Still, it might impress on Grace the seriousness of her actions if she made her wait a few days for a decision. 'I'll consider it.'

She found herself on the receiving end of a hug. 'Thank you. Thank you, Hannah. You are my good friend and I, yours. Always.'

Yes, Hannah thought as she strolled with Grace. One more gathering. This time, they would not lead her astray. Why had she chosen to take the drug? Had it been the desire to please or the fear of losing him? Whichever, Hannah resolved, she had to be stronger.

Barney's words rolled around in her mind. 'Don't define yourself by another's opinion. They should like you for you.' Annoying, know-it-all Barney telling her what to do when he cantered around like an unbroken colt.

Yet, he was right. Her indecisiveness caused Maemm heartache, and she had no right as a daughter to cause her more. She had defiled herself. She had never felt the need to take drugs, but with Sol standing there, his hand outstretched, with him daring her, the desire to please him had overridden her principles. How could she live as a baptised member of the church if she did not have the strength to resist temptation or be grown up enough to come to a decision and put everyone out of their misery? She would ask for God's forgiveness and put away such foolish things, but she would need to prove to herself she could do so. There was only one way to do that. Like Daniel, she must enter the lion's den.

With a determined step, Hannah made her way with Grace across the next field. One decision filled her mind: at the next gathering, she would resist the offerings of the world beyond her own.

Chapter 8

MIDDAY THE NEXT Monday saw an influx of tourists bused in from afar descending on the town centre with its quaint shops, cafés, and Glick's Cycle Shop. A clear blue sky and unseasonably warm temperatures meant that the opportunity to cycle around the scenic surroundings of Birchwood had produced a flurry of visitors wanting to hire bikes for the afternoon. While Hannah served, Sol busied himself with replenishing the shop's goods and helping customers choose their bikes from the outdoor racks.

'Are you okay?' Hannah asked during a brief lull.

'Yep.' Sol kept his head down as he hung cycling tops on a rail.

'Sure?' She tried not to stare at the purplish, baseball-sized bruise covering his right eye and spreading across the bridge of his nose.

'I'm fine. Get on with your work. It's what you're paid to do.'

She pressed her lips together, not trusting herself to speak. Was he upset because she had not got in the car? Hadn't he seen her fighting with Barney? In silence, she tidied the pile of cycle magazines and waited for the next customer to arrive.

Stubby trudged in, wheeling his trolley loaded with boxes. Two trips of four boxes each, Hannah counted. Eight. She made a mental note to check that the stock ledger was up to date. Sol occasionally forgot to log them. But to her surprise, after Sol helped Stubby take the boxes to the storeroom, he grabbed the black hardback ledger and scribbled in it.

'Here is a map showing the route around the town for you.' Hannah handed some change and a leaflet to a middle-aged couple wearing helmets with GLICK's emblazoned on them. She opened the leaflet, pointed to the cycle shop icon, and drew their attention to some landmarks. 'And this is the Yoder Buggy Shop. A woman will show you her collection of quilts if you knock on the door. All handmade.'

A quilt sold here and there, a man's leather belt made from the leftover material used to make harnesses, all contributed to the household income. She hoped there would be a lull in the trade so she could buy lunch from Grace's family's café across the road. Grace always kept a pumpkin cinnamon roll back for her.

'Do you have a smaller fluorescent jacket?' the slim woman inquired when she tried on the large, yellow safety vest. Hannah came out from behind the counter to inspect the jackets on the rack. Medium and large sizes were displayed, but not small.

'I'll check in the storeroom. We had a delivery earlier.' She opened the stock ledger lying by the till and traced a finger down the page to the new delivery figures. Six in total. Two containing high-visibility jackets. Hannah reread the figure. *Six* boxes? 'Yes. I'll go check the sizes.' She stepped towards the staff door to find it blocked.

Sam stood in front of it. 'No. You go.' He crooked a finger at Sol, who was crouched down searching for a helmet from the bottom of a wall rack. The woman glanced from Hannah to Sol, who straightened up with a puzzled expression. Hannah fixed her eyes on the wall ahead, desperately willing the blast of heat to her cheeks to cool down and wishing, not for the first time, that Sam possessed an ounce of sensitivity.

Sam pushed his face close to Hannah's. Through tight lips and in a barely audible voice, he whispered, 'It's his job, not yours. Got it?' His black eyes bore into hers, making it clear she should not ignore his instruction. She retreated behind the counter.

When Sol returned with the smaller safety vests, one of which he gave to the woman, he scurried back to the helmets and more waiting customers. Hannah concentrated on serving. Once or twice, she attempted to catch his attention as he helped people don helmets and choose bikes. She busied herself with taking payments and checking the shelves for stock. Should she ask about the number of boxes he had entered in the book? Why had he written six when she had counted eight? Couldn't men count?

'Sol.' It took her two attempts to attract his attention during a brief break from serving half an hour later. 'I'm confused.'

'Health and safety,' came his response.

'What?'

'You're going to ask me, again, about you going in the storeroom. You can't go in there for safety reasons.' He leaned against a bike displayed near the front. 'The lighting's poor. You could trip. Boxes can fall off the shelves. Sam's scared that if you injure yourself you'll sue him.'

'Oh. I would never do that.'

'I know, Han, but he doesn't, and it's his business. He'd be liable.'

'I was confused about the recording of only six boxes arriving today.' She caught the anxiety rising in her voice and pushed it back down. 'I'm sure I saw eight?'

'Nope. Six,' Sol replied without hesitation. Whether it was the shop's lighting or his firm stare, his usually warm pupils held an icy sheen.

'Silly me.' She gazed out the window. 'I must have got distracted with serving, and miscounted.'

Sol's face softened, but his eyes remained hard. 'Why didn't you leave with me on Friday night?'

Hannah straightened the stack of leaflets. 'You saw. Barney had a hold of me.'

Sol sucked in his cheeks, making a clicking sound. 'No matter. You got home okay?'

She gave a curt yes, not sure how to respond to his truculent manner.

'Good.' He turned his back to her as the doorbell rang. He sauntered over to the two young women dressed in leggings and bomber jackets, and greeted them, all smiles and 'good day to you'. The hairs on the back of her neck prickled as he flipped from grumpy to happy.

One of the women approached her, and she pushed down the sense of failure that lodged like a stone deep within her. 'Good day.' She greeted the woman with a polite smile, like she was pulling a curtain back, wishing she had Sol's mood flip-switch. 'How can I help you?'

By one o'clock and with no lunch, Hannah's stomach rumbled in protest as the continuous stream of customers showed no sign of easing up. Sol wheeled a bike through to the repair shed while she took the helmet and jacket from an exhausted cyclist and fielded questions from browsing customers.

Amidst the bustle, two men barged in just as Sol came back. 'Where is he?' the taller one barked at him. Hannah tried not to gasp at the ragged scar under his left eye, extending to the corner of his mouth. It reminded her of a bad tear in a shirt.

They looked like they had stepped off a film set, with their expensive, shiny suits. Sol gestured to the staff door, and they weaved their way through the crowd in silence and disappeared into the back office. They reappeared after a few minutes, the taller one muttering to the shorter, tubby one with the handlebar moustache. Hannah glanced at Sol as they left. 'Business associates,' he mumbled, watching the silver-grey car parked outside the shop. 'Nice Mercedes.'

'Sol!' Sam hollered gruffly. Sol scooted through to the office and returned with two small, square parcels. He checked that the women trying on helmets were not looking. When certain, he leaned over the counter and placed the packets near Hannah. 'Sam wants you to take these to Falcon's.'

'If I go now, can I have lunch?' Hannah undid her apron and grabbed her green woollen coat from under the counter. 'I need to mail this too.' As he nodded, she picked up a brown bag; a parcelled-up quilt.

Famished, she ran to the café and waited in line as Grace served an elderly couple spoiled for choice by the authentic homemade delicacies laid out before them. Someone brushed by her. The woman, several inches taller than Hannah, halted and apologised in polite, clipped tones; she wasn't a local.

'Meet Sally,' Grace called out to Hannah. 'Our new server.' Sally flashed a half-moon smile that made her dimples deepen. Under her kapp, grey hair lined her forehead. 'Temp,' Grace mouthed to Hannah.

Hannah shifted; the shopping bag was heavy.

'Good afternoon.'

Hannah spun.

Theo grinned back at her in greeting. 'Lunch?' He gestured to a nearby table.

'Thank you, but no. I have a delivery to make.'

'Please. I am sure we will get served quickly.' He raised his head and caught Grace's attention with a hopeful smile.

'Hannah—' Grace beamed at her as she wrapped up the chosen items for the couple, '—you know Mr Anderson?'

'Family friend,' Theo replied.

'Sit down.' Grace gestured to an empty table by the window. 'The usual, Mr Anderson? Hannah, I'll bring you a sweet potato salad.'

Theo held out a chair for her and sat down opposite. 'You know each other?'

'From the cradle.'

She put the shopping bag on the floor. She knew Grace would pester her later with a barrage of questions about Theo. She had a few of her own questions, starting with why he had turned up after all these years and why Maemm had never mentioned him. She would not be able to dally over lunch because of the errands, but she might get some answers.

'Your mother still quilts?' He'd spied the bag and its contents. 'And a shop delivery?'

Hannah moved the bag under the table.

Grace came over with their orders and a jug of lemonade. As she placed the jug down, she leaned closer to Hannah. 'I need to speak to you before you go.'

'Grace, it's rude to whisper.' Hannah's face reddened.

'Sorry.'

Theo smiled and told her not to mind him. Blushing, Grace scuttled back to the serving counter.

'I gather there was a bit of trouble at the Millers'.' He took a bite of his sandwich.

Surprised, Hannah wanted to inquire how he knew, then remembered how gossip would have spread quicker than a tidal wave through the community, starting with the café. Then there was his friend Drummond.

She concentrated on her meal. The combination of the warm sweet potato and crunchy lettuce revived her after her busy morning.

'Do you run errands a lot?' he asked.

She nodded and squinted as a flash of sunlight hit her glass and blinded her. She looked out of the window and noticed Sol replacing a bike in the rack outside the shop as Levi appeared around the corner, wearing his butcher's apron, carrying a closed box. He stopped by Sol, glancing across to the café. She lowered her gaze and hoped the menu was hiding her face from view.

'The owner?' Theo gestured to Sol.

'No. He's Sol, the younger brother of the owner, Sam Glick. That's his friend, Levi, who works at the butcher's.'

A few moments passed as they ate. The sound of her own munching filled her ears. What should she say? Who are you? What do you want? She riffled through a list of questions she used to make polite conversation when serving customers. Where did he come from? That would be general and safe enough to start with. She swallowed some tomato and cleared her throat. 'Mr Anderson.'

'Theo.' He licked a finger covered in mayonnaise and wiped his hand with a napkin. 'What did you want to know?'

She hesitated, not sure if it was appropriate.

'If you are wondering why I have trace of a British accent, it's because I've lived in England for the past twenty years.'

Hannah shook her head.

'Ah, you want to know what your mother was like when she was a young girl?'

A flush of heat rose to her face at his accurate guess. She covered her embarrassment with a tiny laugh. 'I have heard some tales.'

Theo leaned back in his chair, holding the napkin in both hands, peering at thin air. 'Lovely. Bright. Cheerful. But above all, lovely.'

Across the street, Sol and Levi stood by the rack, hands in pockets, both staring at the café.

'Lovely,' Theo repeated.

Why were they staring at her and Theo? Levi turned to Sol and spoke, pointing at them.

Hannah held her salad-laden fork in midair and paused. Theo leaned forward, his face breaking into a soft smile. 'I could spill the beans, but there are none,' he whispered.

They were arguing. Levi shoved Sol, and Sol threw up an arm and pointed at the café. Levi curled his hand into a fist, frowning, and shook it in Hannah's direction.

Her fork crashed onto her half-empty plate as she bolted upright. At the clatter of steel on crockery, Theo glanced at the fork then out of the window. 'What's the matter, Hannah?'

'What do I owe you?' Hannah looked at Glick's. Levi thumbed towards them with a furious expression and stormed off. Sol stepped back from the rack; he stood directly opposite where she sat.

'What for?' Theo said.

'For the meal.' She grabbed the bag. Why did Sol seem upset with her? What had she done? He never minded her taking lunch.

'Nothing. What's the matter?' Theo rose.

Hannah pushed back the chair. 'I have to go.'

'The young man?'

'The shop's been busy. I only meant to pop out.'

Theo gave her a small smile. 'Goodbye, Hannah. Perhaps we might bump into each other another time.' He looked across the street. 'Without the guard dog.'

Despite her anxiety and rush to leave, she smiled back at him.

He extended an arm as though to bar her way when she drew level with him. 'Hannah. Be careful.' He held out a small card. 'If you ever need help, call me.'

On the card was his name and mobile phone number. She slipped it inside her pocket and hurried out. Why would he give her that? Did he regularly give strangers his contact details? Sometimes the English could be so odd.

His words stayed with her all the way down to the traffic lights. As she waited for them to change, she saw Blue clip-clopping along the street and turning into the alley next to Falcon's. Another delivery. She sneaked a fevered glance back to the shop to see Sol watching her, tight-lipped, the brim of his hat low over his eyes.

Despondent, she traipsed toward the post office to mail the quilt. What had made Levi furious? She paused by the entrance, placing one foot on the first step, and glanced at the cycle shop; Sol was at the door. The sight of him shuffling in, head bowed, filled her with a heavy sense of regret.

PARCELS DELIVERED, HANNAH returned to the shop and found a pile of flat-packed cardboard boxes propped against the front window. She peeked through the glass at the empty shop floor then saw the 'closed' sign hanging on the door. Where was Sol? Sam would have a fit if he saw the boxes lying outside. She picked up two of them and hurried into the narrow alley between Glick's and the flower shop leading to the repair shed.

She grappled with the oversized boxes, one of them half covering her face. She struggled through to the exit, and spotted Blue calmly waiting outside Falcon's back entrance, harnessed to the wagon, getting an affectionate pat from Danny heading back down to his post office. Hannah put the boxes down and leaned them against the stone wall, in half a mind to go and say hello to the big, gentle giant.

That's when Aaron and Levi emerged from the icehouse. She hastily stepped into the recess of the alley. Aaron flapped an arm dismissively at Levi, and Levi grabbed him by the shoulder and shook him, jabbing a finger at his chest. From under his apron, Levi pulled out an envelope and held it up to Aaron, who eyed it and, with a quick glance around the area, reached for the bundle and pocketed it inside his coat.

Stunned, Hannah pushed herself flat against the wall, wishing she could melt into it. Tentatively, she inched to the alley's opening and looked again. Aaron went round to the wagon's back door, opened it, and lifted out a tray of meat. He handed it to Levi, who grinned at him and carried it to the icehouse. What was so special about the meat that made Levi so pleased to get it? She turned the thought over as she stayed hidden until Aaron had driven off and Levi had gone back into the butcher's.

She carried the boxes to the large, red waste bin by the shed, skirting round the pickup parked askew in front of the bike repair shed. She quickly threw them in and slammed the lid down then turned to retrace her steps.

A shaggy-haired youth wearing ripped jeans and a biker's leather jacket came out of the repair shed, a cigarette between his lips. He dropped the cigarette on the ground, stubbed it out with a boot, and stuffed something into his jacket pocket. Sol followed, laughing, and exchanged a high five with him.

The laughter ceased when Sol spotted her. With a frosty stare, he gestured to the pickup truck and the youth got in. Hannah marched back to the alley. Halfway down, Sol caught her by the elbow and overtook her, blocking her path.

'It's you, isn't it?' Hannah wrenched her arm out of his hand. 'You've been selling at the gatherings.'

'No. No. I promise, Han.'

She stepped sideways to slip past him.

'Please, please, you've gotta believe me.' He spread his arms the width of the alley. 'I keep some for personal use. Honest.'

'Aaron? Is he in this too?'

Sol scratched his goatee. 'You've got a vivid imagination there, Han. Why Aaron?'

Hannah hesitated. She could be wrong. Perhaps Levi and Aaron had their own arrangement going?

'Hannah?' He rolled her name out with a lazy grin.

'I saw him with Levi. Levi gave him something.'

'If you were English, I'd say you've been watching too many detective shows.' The grin grew. 'Aaron is too much of a nerd.'

Hannah jerked her head to the yard. 'What about the other one?'

'He's a friend. I was helping him.'

She shot him a sceptical stare.

'Honest.' The cocky attitude vanished, a tremor running over his face.

'Sam doesn't know, does he?'

Sol shook his head so hard she worried he might bang it against the wall. 'No. No. He'd kill me.' The glass veneer that had coated his eyes melted, turning them to whipped soft chocolate. 'Please, Han, can we keep this between us? Please?'

She had promised herself not to get involved with him. That did not mean she could not keep him out of harm. It was a good thing to help someone.

'Very well, Sol. This time.'

'Oh, Han, you're an angel. Thank you. Thank you.' He lowered his arms and hugged her. A tingling sensation, like pins and needles, crept through her. She tensed her body and quashed it, remembering his surliness earlier.

'Oh, sorry.' He let go of her. 'Pardon me.' He held up his little finger, and she curled her own around, and they wriggled them together. 'Hey, why don't I take you to the gathering next Friday? It's over at the Eichers' farm. Out in the sticks. I could drive you.'

She shook his words out of her head with a resolute shake.

He flashed a broad grin at her. 'Awh, come on.'

Hannah braced herself and cemented her features. She had promised herself she would resist. Here was the first test.

Sol rolled his shoulders, letting his arms hang. 'You're mad at me, aren't you? About this morning? Han, I'm sorry. I didn't mean to be so stroppy with you.'

Cracks of warmth broke through her solid mask. She curled in her bottom lip and stood motionless.

'It's that Barney guy. He had no right to grab you like that. I know you would've got in if he hadn't got you. Sorry.'

Her cool reserve thawed to a warm stream and crumbled the mask to dust as one thought consumed her. He was mad with Barney, not her.

He held up his little finger again. She raised her own hand tentatively. *Why not?* a little voice whispered inside her head. *Besides, you planned to go with Grace.* Maemm would nag. Grandfather would tsk-tsk like a steam train. Grace's excitable face rose before her. Her friend's last hurrah before settling down. Could this be the test that would help her decide once and for all? If she followed Grace's footsteps, this would be her last outing. No more gatherings, no more Sol. Could she resist going one more time with him? Hannah sighed, knowing the answer to her question. She looped her finger around his, and the tingling turned to a butterfly glow as they wriggled them.

'Grace. She must come,' she said.

'Really?' Sol's face fell. He pushed up the brim of his hat, hunched his shoulders, and grinned. 'Oh, okay. Whatever. Glad we're friends again, Han.'

Hannah willed herself not to respond and clamped her teeth on her lower lip as he walked back up the alley with a slow, steady gait, whistling. Watching him, she could not determine whether she was pleased or not.

As she emerged from the alley, Grace rushed out of the café and dashed across the road. Hannah half closed her eyes, fearing a collision with an oncoming car speeding towards her oblivious friend.

'Hannah,' she panted, 'you left so quick. I need your help. Have you made your mind up? Will you come to the gathering this Friday? When I told Daett and Maemm I was going, they got upset. The only way I could get them to agree was to promise them it would be the last one and that I would go with you.'

Hannah searched her friend's face. Eyes wide with hope. Face flushed with excitement. Could she be a faithful wife to Evan? Why was she so determined to go?

A boulder wedged itself in the pit of her stomach as she turned the question over. It poked at her insides with the sharp stab of a bradawl as she recalled Evan's wounded expression at Grace putting Levi over him. She let out a long breath, willing the pain to ease.

Grace's face fell into pinched lines. 'You still believe I play false with Evan?' She jutted out her chin and placed her hands on her hips. 'I am merely doing what they do. They sow their oats, as they say. I want to get it out of my system so I will be a good wife, Hannah. I promise.'

The boulder shrank, giving instant relief. The honesty of her friend's words squeezed her heart into a tiny ball. She wished she had Grace's daring spirit, yet it troubled her. What precisely did Grace need to get out of her system? What was 'it'? Her infatuation with Levi? Perhaps if Grace got whatever she had out of her system, Evan might have the wife he dreamed of.

Sol. He had hugged her. The brief contact and the sensation it had brought resurfaced. He had agreed to Grace coming. Did it mean anything, or had his offer to take her been a means to pacify her because of what she had seen?

Her throat tightened at the uncharitable thought. She clasped her hands together, the skin over her knuckles stretching. Had he done it again – matched his mood to his goal to keep her on his side? She replayed the conversation of a few moments ago. How quickly he had changed from pleading to his usual manner. Too quickly. Hannah unlocked her hands.

'Hannah?' Grace's voice quivered as she waited for an answer.

Hannah closed her eyes and took in a deep lungful of air, so much it pushed her ribs outwards till they ached. She blew it out in one long gush and with it, her guilt. She had something to get out of her system too. Sol. One last evening and the chance to prove she had the will to be in command of herself and let go of him. If it helped her friend as well, that would be all to the good. 'Yes, Grace, of course I'll come.' She hugged her, firm in her resolve. 'What are friends for?'

Chapter 9

THIS TIME, THEY waited to change their clothes until Sol drove them to a gas station en route to Mellor Creek, the neighbouring town where the gathering would be. Grace insisted on doing it this way so as to not further upset her distressed parents. 'Ever since I told them I would get baptised, they've been fretting I will change my mind,' she moaned as they drove into the station. 'Honestly, I wish I'd waited until after this Friday to tell them.'

'They're worried.' Hannah recalled Maemm's anxious expression when she had left home that night.

Inside the station, Hannah and Grace headed straight for the restroom at the rear, guided by peels of laugher and exuberant voices. They made their way to the cubicles through a group of girls changing into English clothes and swapping makeup by the washbasins.

When Grace came out of her cubicle, Hannah giggled. 'You look like a carrot,' she said, applying eyeliner.

Grace laughed, held up her mobile, and took a selfie of them both.

'Grace, careful, someone might see.' Hannah checked the room, relieved they were now alone.

'And do what?'

'Tell Bishop Fisher. Then we'll all be in for a sermon on how it encourages pride as a sin.'

'Only if someone tells him.' Her friend gestured to the empty room.

Grace had swapped her usual party outfit of leggings and fleece for a baggy rust-coloured jumper dress over woollen tights and ankle boots. A black scarf enhanced the vision of autumn gold. Standing next to her, Hannah felt frumpy and boring in her jeans and cabled jumper. Grace smeared gloss around her lips and handed it to Hannah then, with a last finger comb of her hair, stuck out her tongue, laughed, and strolled out the door, Hannah following.

In the car, Grace shared a joint with Levi, passing it back and forth while Sol drove along the narrow roads. The khaki rucksack sat between Hannah and Grace. Why did they always bring it but then get nothing out of it?

'Levi, I wish you'd put that thing in the trunk,' Sol commented, looking in the rearview mirror. Levi grimaced and passed the joint to Grace once more, and she offered it to Hannah. A thin wisp of grey smoke waffled in the air from the ashy end of the roll-up. Hannah eyed it and clasped her hands. She would have to start somewhere if she was to stop her Rumspringa. Might as well start now. She shook her head, and Grace shrugged and took a drag herself.

With Sol's foot hard down on the pedal, they arrived in under half an hour at the field on the outskirts of Mellor Creek, the bass boom-boom of the rock music and the dusky glow from the lights drawing them in. Revellers danced with high energy while others huddled in groups by the bales marking out the area. Stars filled the sky, and the car's headlights and full moon gave adequate vision for Sol to park the Dodge by the entrance.

Other vehicles lined the edges of the field. Near the entrance were trestle tables laden with turntables and, at either end, massive amplifiers wobbling from the vibrations of the thundering music.

They wandered across the dance floor. Sol opened the icebox, held a beer bottle out to Hannah, and she shook her head. 'Do we have to go through this every time?' Sol groaned.

'I don't want to drink.' Hannah dug her hands in her pockets, glad of the warm jumper and jeans she wore. Grace rubbed her arms. Even with the warmth of the lights and heaving bodies, the fresh evening breeze nipped at them.

'Okay.' He lowered the bottle and pulled out a small, transparent plastic bag from his vest pocket. 'Here.' The pills resembled aspirins.

Hannah, mouth set firm, shook her head.

'Oh, come on, Hannah.' Sol pressed his lips together.

The temptation to take one niggled at her. She threw it out like a volleyball over a net. 'No.' She raised her Coke, and a wave of exhilaration surged through her. She could do this. She could control her actions like an adult should do. Like the Bible taught.

When I was a child, I spake as a child, I understood as a child, I thought as a child: but when I became a man, I put away childish things.

How odd to think about Scripture at a gathering. Why now? Was this what adulthood meant? Deciding for oneself, even if it did not please others?

'Leave Miss Goody-Two-Shoes, bud,' Levi advised Sol, holding out the pills. 'Grace?'

'It's a pill or two, not a dispensary.' Grace popped them in her mouth and took a swig of beer. 'It's my last one. I wish to have some fun.'

Hannah shot her a worried look.

A spindly youth hollered to Levi and Sol from outside the makeshift dance area. Hannah recognised him from the previous gathering: one of the gang members who'd attacked Sol. Sol's face darkened faster than a dying gaslight. The youth beckoned to him, and he rubbed his hands down his jeans, swallowing. With an unperturbed Levi, he strolled over to them, and Hannah let out a muffled sigh of relief – at least he had Levi with him tonight. 'Grace.' Hannah pulled her nearer. 'Please don't do anything foolish.'

'Like?'

'Like,' Hannah lowered her voice, 'you-know.'

Grace threw Hannah a wounded glare and turned to watch Levi. 'Why not?' She sipped from her bottle.

'Because...' Hannah struggled to find the words. Not even the decision to be baptised had tamed Grace's wild streak. Surely she would not be so rash with Levi? Why did Grace always have to go one step too far? Why did she feel more like a guardian angel than a friend these days? She pulled Grace to her and whispered in her ear, 'It's not... What about Evan? You can't marry Evan if you do.'

'Oh, Hannah, you can be sooo conservative sometimes.' Grace giggled, stepping back. 'I'm joking. Of course I'm not going to, so you needn't worry about your precious Evan.'

Relief blended with indignation poured through Hannah. She checked at Sol and Levi. Maybe she could get Sol to warn his friend off.

They stood with their backs to Hannah and Grace and their heads bent as they talked to the youth. Levi's hands dipped in and out of his rucksack. The youth reached out and enclosed Levi's outstretched hand with both of his, and Hannah caught a flash of a small plastic package, which Levi stuffed into his jeans. She recalled the shed. *Personal use*, Sol had pleaded.

'We should go.' Hannah turned.

Grace seized her by the arm. 'Hannah, stop worrying,' she yelled above the music; Sol and Levi were threading their way over. 'All I'm going to do is dance and get, as Levi says, off my face. Nothing further. Okay?'

'I think they're dealing.'

'What? Don't be stupid.' Grace waved a dismissive hand.

One night and it would be over.

Sol was next to her, grabbing her hand, and they danced to the beating drums and whiny guitar riffs. Her limbs felt stiff and disconnected to the music's rhythm despite the drum and bass thudding through the floorboards up her legs. If she could just relax.

'You okay?' Sol shouted above the din after a few songs.

'Yes,' Hannah shouted, not positive she was. Everyone else was clearly enjoying themselves. Dancing. Drinking. Laughing. From time to time, Grace would insist on snapping photos with her phone. At one point, she spotted Evan and Barney and talked Evan into taking a group photo after he refused to be included in the picture. Hannah stood one end of the haphazard line of friends, with Sol bunched up beside her; she kept her gaze low, somewhere between the ground and the phone. Evan held the phone like a hot brick and tossed it back to Grace as soon as he had taken the photo. Hannah avoided his gaze as he walked by, feeling a mixture of admiration for his stance and dismay at her failure to resist joining him. When he and Barney melted into the crowd, the urge to go with them made her half-turn in their direction. But if she left now, she would never know what she truly wanted – and there was Grace. Levi prowled around her like a panther sizing up dinner.

All around her, as the evening wore on, couples disappeared into the shadowy fringes of the field. All the goings-on left her cold. The sense of comradeship of previous gatherings seemed absent. The songs merged into a seamless wall of noise, of screaming voices and crashing beats and twangs. People around her jostled for space, dancing wildly as the night wore on. The grins on their faces grew more inert and their eyes glassy as they stared out at nothing.

Levi twirled a giggling Grace by one hand and drew her into a smoochy embrace. Her eyes shone like gems when the light caught them. How many pills had she taken? Panic rose inside Hannah. *Home.* They needed to go home. 'Grace. Grace!' She reached for her friend. 'We need to sober you up. Time to go.'

'Aww, Hannah, you're sush a good friend.' Grace turned away from Levi and draped her arms over Hannah's shoulders. 'Always lookin' out for me.'

'Careful.' Sol steadied Grace. 'Looks like the party girl got into it big time.'

'Yeah.' An excited grin spread across Levi's face. He stopped dancing and linked a hand with Grace's. 'Why don't we go for a walk? Get some air?' He pointed to a dark space beyond the bales.

Hannah gripped Grace's other arm. 'I'll take her.' She tried to sound light and breezy.

'You stay put.' The harsh tone made it clear it was not a request.

'No. You stay.' Hannah fixed him with a stoney stare and got one back.

A retching sound broke the deadlock. An undigested hot dog, beer, and whitish liquid spilled onto the grass as Grace groaned, pasty-faced. Hannah guided her to the edge of the dance area and helped her sit, then knelt and studied her friend. Pale, droopy-eyed, and limp. She propped her up, holding her forearms.

Sol came over, frowning. 'She needs to go home,' Hannah pleaded.

'Nah.' Levi shook his head tersely. 'She'll be fine.'

Grace slumped forward, only saved from landing in a heap on the floor by Hannah grabbing her shoulders. Her head lolled and her eyes closed, her chin falling on her chest. Hannah gently cupped her friend's head and lifted it. She gave one cheek a gentle tap. 'She's out cold.' She slipped her arms under Grace's and tried to pull her limp heavy body up.

Sol moved closer, staring at Grace. People ceased dancing, their attention drawn to the scene playing out in front of them.

'I don't care what you've done.' Hannah glared at Sol as she held onto Grace. 'We must get her out of here.'

Sol glanced over his shoulder at the onlookers.

'It's fine – she's had too much beer.' Levi staggered nearer, reaching out a hand. 'Gracie. Hiya, Grace, wake up!'

Hannah brushed it aside. Levi shot her a foul look and swayed.

'Let's carry her to the car.' Sol tucked an arm under Grace's armpit, and together, they struggled through the crowd towards the Dodge, Levi lurching behind them.

'We can't be seen with her,' Levi mumbled as he scrambled into the front while Sol helped Hannah drag Grace into the rear seat. Sol had the engine revving before she had slammed her own door closed. From the lurch of the car and the rapidly shifting beams of the headlights, Hannah guessed Sol was not wasting any time getting them away from the gathering. The fences and posts blurred into one as they sped towards Birchwood.

'Hospital.' Hannah studied the inert, slumped figure of her friend, and then Sol. 'She needs a hospital. Are you okay to drive?'

'Yep,' Sol slurred.

Ahead, traffic lights beamed red. When Sol didn't slow down, she prayed no cars would appear from the crossroads as he drove through and straight on.

Into the headlights loomed a patrol car.

'Damnit!' Sol thumped the wheel.

'Left.' Levi pointed to a side road illuminated by the headlights. 'I said left. Now!'

Why go left? The hospital was on the other side of town.

'Do it!' Levi snapped as the car overshot the turn.

The slam of the brakes thrust Hannah forwards. The Dodge's front end jolted; the car skidded sideways and flung her backwards, one of her feet catching the khaki rucksack.

'Sorry,' Sol shouted as he slammed the car into reverse and took the turn. The Dodge roared down the unlit lane.

Shaken, Hannah checked Grace, strapped in by her seat belt, her head resting against the small window frame. Hannah shook her. No response. Another firm shake got the same result. The wail of a siren drew nearer to them. *Wake up! Please wake up, Grace!* she screamed inside her head.

Hannah turned Grace's face to her. Blood seeped down her cheek from a cut above her right eye. She fumbled in her coat pockets, scrabbling around for a tissue. In one pocket, her fingers traced a small card, and it took her a moment to remember what it was: Theo's contact details. Fat lot of good to her now. She placed an ear to Grace's mouth. Shallow, warm breaths brushed her cheek. It reminded her of how her grandma sounded when asleep.

'Turn back.' She leaned forward, steadying Grace. 'We need to get to a hospital!'

'Shut it.' Levi exchanged a look with Sol and glanced out of the Dodge's back window. The faint wah-wah of the siren slowly increased to a piercing shrill.

Hannah followed his gaze. In the distance, the twin circular beams of the patrol car's headlights came into view, a blurred blue light above them. Sol increased his speed, and the car flew over the small humpback bridge and then sped along the narrow road, slewing round the curve. Levi stabbed a finger at the side of the road, and Sol skidded to a stop with a crunch of brakes and leaped out of the Dodge. Levi clambered out, hurried to Hannah's door and yanked it open. He grabbed her arm and hauled her out, and she stumbled at the force of his action and fell, scraping her knees.

The sound of another door slamming shut filled the air. Sol dragged Grace across the road and laid her on the strip of grass beside the road; Levi jumped back into the car. Hannah scrambled to her feet and hurried over, slumping down by Grace.

'Don't tell them we were with you. Okay?' Sol thrust his face close to Hannah's. 'Say nothing. Please. I could lose my licence. No licence, no job. Sam'll kill me.'

Grace lay sprawled on the ground, her head to one side. Her eyes were open and still. Blood seeped from her head wound.

Levi tooted the horn. 'Sol!'

'Hannah, I'm begging.'

The wah-wah of the siren grew closer.

'Go,' was all she could muster. Tears leaked from her eyes as she brushed a lock of hair from Grace's face.

'They won't arrest you. Play dumb,' Sol shouted, getting into the driver's side. Something thudded beside her as the car sped off.

Alone, she cradled Grace's head and placed an ear to her mouth. Faint rasps warmed her face.

'Grace. Wake up, Grace,' she wept as she rocked her friend, willing her to move, ignoring the siren and slamming doors of the police car.

A police officer was running over, kneeling beside her and examining Grace. 'Ed, get an ambulance,' he called, checking Grace's dull eyes. He started to administer CPR.

Swiftly, he rattled off question after question, all the while carrying out chest compressions. Dazed, Hannah answered as best she could. Trying not to shiver, she dug her freezing, stiff hands into her coat pockets to warm them. One hand curled around Theo's card.

'Ed, where the hell's the ambulance? We need the medics,' the police officer shouted.

'She's gonna need a lawyer, too,' came the reply.

Another cold shiver ripped down her spine at the tone of the second officer's voice and bit into her bones. Why a lawyer? She tore her eyes away from Grace and stared at the officer, who held up the khaki rucksack with its top pocket opened. In his other hand was an oblong parcel, like the ones she had delivered and collected so many times.

When the medics arrived, the police officers hustled her into the back of the patrol car. She wiped the condensation from the window to watch the medics tend Grace – why wasn't she responding? Why didn't they take her to the hospital?

After too long, she saw the medics wheeling the stretcher to the waiting ambulance. Grace's body was covered. With a sickening twist of her heart, Hannah realised it would not be Grace in need of a lawyer.

Chapter 10

THE CELL DOOR clanged open. Hannah stirred and woke from the fretful sleep she had succumbed to after hours lying awake on the narrow bed. She sat up, swung her legs over the side, and stood. Groggy, she wiped the thin sleepy mist from her eyes and pushed damp cinnamon strands from her face. Through the small, barred window, streaks of pale, smoky-grey sunlight broke through the dawn sky. Back home, Grandfather and Evan would be getting up to work. Maemm would finish off her quilting orders before preparing food for the next day, Sunday. A day of rest. Hannah rubbed her lower back, wishing she had managed more rest herself.

The police officers had kept Hannah in the patrol car while the quiet lane turned into a hive of activity. More officers had arrived and carried out a search of the taped-off area until the investigating officer arrived. Narrow as a wooden post and dressed in a charcoal-black suit, he looked like he'd walked out of a tailor's shop and not a police station. His polite, officious manner evaporated when she refused to give all but the barest details of what had happened. Not so much to keep her promise to Sol, but to avoid incriminating herself. The image of Grace's covered body being lifted into the ambulance kept replaying in her mind as he fired question after question. He searched her coat and rucksack. When she held her hand out for Theo's card, he unwillingly gave it back to her, and she toyed with it in her pocket like a talisman. He became more and more frustrated and, in the end, gave up. 'Back to the station, then. A few hours in a cell might give you time to develop a more helpful attitude before a conversation with the chief.'

Now, a few hours later, an officer stood in the doorway. 'You're allowed one phone call.'

Dread filled her at the thought of calling Maemm. Not that she could. The nearest neighbours who did have a phone were an elderly English couple half a mile down the lane. She would have to ask them to fetch Maemm or Grandfather and then bring them back to their house to ring the station. That would take ages, and she did not want to stay any longer than necessary. Who else could she call? Sol? Certainly not, after leaving her and Grace like discarded trash. Barney? He had a mobile, but she did not have his number. Besides, she had no wish to prove him right.

That's when she remembered Theo's card. Calling him would be quicker.

Less than half an hour later, she heard rapid footsteps on the tiled flooring outside her cell. 'Hannah?' Theo waited for a guard to unlock the door then rushed in, dressed in jeans and a grey jumper, his face etched with worry. 'Are you okay?'

Hannah did not protest when he embraced her. His solid arms calmed the clamour of unanswered questions in her head. With embarrassment, she recalled fleeing from him in the street that first day, scared he would harm her.

He insisted she have food and a wash before any interview while he called a lawyer. 'I can't practice law here in the US. If you agree, I can sit in while they interview you. My firm has an office in New York. We'll get you out.'

Grateful but puzzled at his eagerness to help her, Hannah consented to him sitting in. An officer led them to a corridor with several doors and opened one for them, ushered them in then left. Inside the small, square room with its cement-grey walls and stuffy smell, they sat at a beech-veneer table. On the table, near the wall, stood a machine with two small, clear windows and push buttons like a portable radio. 'What is that?' Hannah pointed to it.

'Recorder.' Theo pushed a button down and one of the front compartments opened. 'They put a tape in it and record the interview. For accuracy.'

Outside, someone strolled along the corridor, their chirpy whistling echoing through the walls.

'Why are you helping me? I asked you to let my family know.'

Theo tapped his pen on the table. 'They're worried and wanted you to have someone who knows the law with you. Besides, I want to find those scumbags who left you by the road.'

'And Grace's family?'

'They know.'

Hannah buried her face in her hands. Grace was dead. Dead because of her. She had wanted to go one last time instead of talking Grace out of the idea.

Maemm. Grandfather. Evan. What would they think of her? All their nightmares had come true.

The door flew open, its handle hitting the wall with a loud bang, bringing her back to the present. Drummond, the chief of police, reached the table in two purposeful long strides, his shoes slapping heavily against the laminated flooring. Without a word, he dropped a pad on the table and a pen on its blank sheet and brushed a hand over his short, steel-coloured hair. A pair of beady eyes in a face with skin rough as rock stared down at her then shifted to Theo. Behind him trailed the officer who had interviewed her the previous night.

'Theo, you are not her lawyer.' Drummond eased his quarterback-sized frame into the flimsy plastic chair. 'For the record, I am Chief Drummond, and this is Detective Holtz.' The younger officer sat down beside him, his expression gloomy as he carried out Drummond's instruction to 'do the preliminaries'.

After Holtz stated the date and location of the interview, and informed her that anything she said could be used as evidence if brought to trial and she had the right to request a lawyer, Hannah gave her name and date of birth. Theo did the same, citing himself as the 'appropriate adult'. Holtz launched into a speech about her rights and other details she half-listened to.

'You have not been formally charged, but I will tell you, young lady, you are facing possession of drugs with intent to sell,' Drummond said.

'Where's your proof?' Theo asked.

Drummond lifted a chunky hand as if poised to swat a fly, then paused and rested both hands on the table palms down. 'To be clear. The uniforms found you with a bag containing cocaine worth hundreds of dollars on the street and your fingerprints on it.'

'It wasn't hers.'

Hannah reeled. Fingerprints? She recalled a flash of headlights and a startled rabbit scurrying for its life. She had touched the rucksack then; she'd tried to pick it up.

'Did you find a phone?' Drummond asked.

'Says she doesn't own one,' Holtz replied.

Drummond raised an eyebrow at Hannah.

'You know Old Man Yoder.' Theo matched Drummond's stare. 'He'd rather burn in hell than have technology in the house.'

Hannah bit the inside of her cheeks to keep a straight face, recalling the hot water and bathroom installed at home.

Drummond raised a finger. 'One more word, Theo, and you're out. She's nineteen, old enough to be interviewed on her own.'

'Without a lawyer, you wouldn't dare.'

'Theo. You've been a good friend to me. Now be a good friend to young Hannah here and shut up.'

Theo jutted his jaw out and leaned back in his chair.

'This is not a formal interview. We haven't charged you. See, my friend has written nothing down or cautioned you, and the tape machine's off.'

Theo half turned to her, his gaze on Drummond.

'Realise why?' Drummond asked.

Hannah didn't bother to shake her head, realising it was a rhetorical question.

'Because I don't believe the package belongs to you. I mean, what were you and...' he glanced over at the detective's pad, '...Miss Stoltzfus doing at one a.m. on a deserted road halfway between Mellor Creek and Birchwood with a bag full of drugs?' He leaned closer. His voice was low, as if he was having a private conversation with her. 'You were with someone who my officers were chasing for speeding. Now, what I would like you to do, young lady, is tell me who they were.'

'And if she does?'

'Last strike, Theo.' Drummond eased back and turned his attention to Hannah. 'I'm not in the business of making promises, but I don't think you'd be facing a jail sentence.'

Theo turned to Drummond. 'Were there any other fingerprints on the package or rucksack?'

Drummond eyed his friend, a smile cracking his mouth. 'I wondered how long it would take you.'

'What you've got is circumstantial. It could belong to those whose prints are on it.'

Hannah tried to process what they were discussing. Her. But not her. Drummond wanted her to tell him about Sol and Levi.

Drummond's friendly smile disappeared. 'Now, I know helping us is not your people's thing, but I would advise you to consider doing so.'

And purge my soul? Prison. I could go to prison. Maemm... all of them... would be shamed.

If she did co-operate, what would she say? It was Levi? They would work out that Sol was there, even if Levi did not tell them himself. Sol would lose everything and go to prison. He had at least attempted to get them to the hospital. Levi. This was Levi's fault.

'You'll charge her?' Theo's question interrupted her thoughts.

'Without evidence to confirm she had nothing to do with the drugs or their selling... yes. Help, and she'd merely be a witness.'

'For cryin' out loud, Drummond. You know she's innocent.'

'Chief of police.' Drummond's face hardened.

'Apologies. Chief.' Theo shifted, his chair squeaking against the floor.

'Here's what's going to happen. You will go home to have a long, hard think, Hannah. Then we'll talk some more, with the tape running.'

The younger officer jerked his head up and looked at Drummond. 'She could make a run for it—'

'She doesn't have a passport, so can't go anywhere,' Theo butted in.

The officer's face scrunched up in puzzled lines.

'Transferred from Pittsburgh,' Drummond sighed.

'Amish people seldom have passports or social security numbers, because they've no birth certificates, which you need for one,' Theo explained.

The officer resumed his disinterested stare at his pad.

Hannah shifted and blinked. The surrealism of the occasion was fading, and the reality soaked through her numbed body, the space around her heart tightening.

'You understand, Hannah?' Drummond said.

The taut muscles in her neck strained as she forced her head up and down.

'Good.' Drummond picked up his pad and pen. 'I look forward to our next meeting. We will release you without charge, and if anyone asks why, tell them we are awaiting the coroner's report.'

Relief poured through her. 'I can go?'

Drummond nodded, getting up.

She struggled to stand, but her legs buckled and she crumpled back into the chair. Theo held her trembling body and, once again, she welcomed the embrace of this stranger.

DREARY, DAMP CLOUDS greeted them as they came out of the station in the downtown area of Birchwood, less than half a mile from the old town centre. Parked cars lined both sides of the street in front of them.

They stood under the canopy by the main entrance, harbouring from the rain. Hannah took a deep lungful of the fresh Saturday morning air, its damp chill making her cough.

Theo rested his hand on his hips, looking at the rain. 'If I am going to help you, I need you to tell me who was in that car before Drummond pressures it out of you – which he will.' In the grey morning murk, raindrops glinted like flying pins, their pit-patter filling the silence as he waited for an answer. 'Hannah, I know it is not custom for Amish to help the police with their investigations because of your belief that the church is the supreme judge and that law enforcement is intrusive, but if you don't, you will face charges. Drummond wants to break this ring. They have you at the scene with a dead girl suspected of overdosing, the drugs, and the rucksack containing them with your prints. That could lead to prison. My advice is to tell them.'

What good would it do to tell them? It would not bring Grace back. If only she had stayed firm in her resolve and not tried to be so clever as to test herself using her friend as the reason to go. That was the real crime.

Theo waited. When she did not reply, he let out a low sigh. 'My car's parked a few blocks away.' He pointed up the road. 'You stay here. I'll get it.'

He descended the steps with a light, springy motion and, watching him go, Hannah rubbed her hands and tucked them under her arms, trying to push away the muggy weariness filling her mind. She would need a clear head to answer the barrage of questions when she arrived home.

'Hey.'

Her eyes skimmed the empty sidewalk, not sure if she had imagined the sound.

'Hey, Han.'

Sol emerged from behind the building to her right. He peered around and scampered up the steps towards her, still checking. 'What did you say? Did you tell them it was me and Levi?'

Hannah stared at him, speechless. Was that all he could say? Not even a 'how are you'? 'I am fine, which is more than I can say for Grace,' she spat out at him.

A tremor crossed his face.

'They're going to charge me if I don't tell them who I was with. I could go to prison.' A bit of an exaggeration, she hoped, would prick his conscience.

'You'd break with the church teachings?'

She let the question hang in the air.

'You can't,' he snapped through gritted teeth. He stepped closer. 'Not a smart idea, Han.'

Standing so close, his tall frame towered over her and warned her she was no match for him. Maybe he had more in common with Sam than she'd realised. She forced the muscles in her face to harden and disguise her fear. He might want to scare her, but she did not have to give him the satisfaction of seeing her frightened. She pushed her shoulders back and met his gaze. 'What were you going to do with the drugs?'

Sol rolled his tongue over his upper lip, all the while keeping his eyes on the street.

She massaged her upper arm. 'Well?'

'Deliver them.' Sol moved closer still, all rabbit-eyed, a feverish look on his face.

He was involved. He and Levi were dealing. He had lied to her. Recreational use, he had said. She straightened to her full height, pushing down the mixture of anger and frustration at her own gullibility. 'Who for, Sol? Why?'

His lips quivered as he stared through the glass-panelled door. 'A friend,' he mumbled.

'Tell the police.'

'No.' He shook his head, his expression hardening.

'Grace is dead, Sol.'

Not one muscle flinched. Their childhood friend was dead. All because he and his junkie friend did not want to be caught. Raw heat erupted inside her and, in one stride, she closed in on him, catching a whiff of his smoky breath. 'Grace is dead. Doesn't that mean anything to you? It does to me. She was my friend. My best friend. How can you be so callous? She's dead because of those evil men who give you and Levi those drugs.'

'And so will I – and you – be if you tell the cops. You wouldn't wish that on your conscience, would you?'

It was a low blow, but accurate. She already had Grace's blood on her hands. She may not have given her the pill, but she did not stop her from going to the gathering or try to persuade her not to take them.

Sol squeezed her arm so hard his fingers pressed painfully to the bone. 'You say nothing. Nothing, unless you want your ox of a brother to have a buggy crash.'

A tight ball formed in her stomach. For a moment, she thought Sam had spoken. Only the quivering lip and big brown eyes reminded her Sol stood facing her with a stony expression. He would hurt Evan to save his own skin?

She glared at him. He averted his gaze, as though stung by her heat, and his shoulders sagged. 'I'm sorry, Han.'

He's terrified of them. If she told the police about him, would they get to him before those men did as he feared? He had tried to get Grace to the hospital. Levi was the one who had insisted on abandoning them and the drugs. It was him who fetched the bag from the icehouse, not Sol. Had Levi bullied Sol into dealing?

Sol leaped back as a midnight-blue Nissan approached from the direction Theo had gone. A wave of relief filled Hannah as he drove up and parked by the station. He may be a stranger in comparison to Sol, but right now, he was a friendlier face. He got out of the car and leaped up the steps two at a time, glaring at Sol. 'What are *you* doing here?'

'I heard about the arrest. I came to see if Hannah was okay,' Sol stammered.

Theo stood beside her, scepticism written all over his face. Sol took another step back, and she forced a reassuring smile at him. She could not lose another childhood friend.

'Was it you in the car?' Theo said.

Sol rattled his head with the speed of a drill. 'I gave Han and Grace, God rest her soul, a ride to the gathering. That's all. Swear.'

His boyish, innocent face made Hannah want to be sick. A million miles from the thug with his threats.

Theo switched his stare to Hannah, and Sol's eyes locked with hers. She nodded and lifted a silent prayer of repentance for her deception.

'If you're lying...' Theo raised a hand and pointed a finger at him.

'No lie.' Sol started down the steps, widening the gap between them, and shot an innocent smile at Theo. 'Take a few days off, Hannah. Sam won't mind.' Once clear of the steps and Theo's glare, he darted out of sight.

Neither spoke as they viewed the sun breaking through the clouds, streaking the darkened sky. The beauty of a new day. Hannah could take no joy or comfort from it.

She did not doubt Sol's threat, yet even as he uttered the words, she'd heard the fear in his voice. Whatever might happen to him, she did not want to be responsible for it. *Recompense to no man evil for evil. Provide things honest in the sight of all men.*

No, let God deal with Sol.

A lump lodged in her throat. She could never go back in time. All her good intentions had come undone, all her promises broken and her future in tatters. A spot of sin stained her with the blood of her friend. Why did she always let her emotions rule her head? Because of her blind selfishness, Grace was dead and Evan was in danger. How could she right this wrong?

Theo's advice washed over her, soaking her with more harsh consequences. Aiding the law to administer justice was not the only thing frowned upon. Drugs were too. Remaining silent would mean the drugs that killed Grace would continue to be sold, causing more deaths.

Doing as the English did – cooperating – meant risking harm to Evan and being punished by her own. Keeping to the Amish way would mean facing prison and her family being shamed. She was caught between two worlds.

She must choose one.

Chapter 11

GRANDFATHER WAS MEANDERING around the yard, throwing pellets on the ground for the chickens to peck at when Theo drove past the barn. They gobbled up the food, following him to the front door. As Theo parked the car he looked at them, his face creased with dark lines. Hannah noted the dashboard clock read eleven-thirty. Why could she not hear the familiar sound of hammering coming from the workshop?

Getting out, she glanced over to the barn doors, which were closed. She stared back at Grandfather and caught the pained look on his face. Without a word, he entered the house, leaving the door ajar.

In the kitchen, Maemm dropped a plate into the basin of soapy water and strode over to Hannah, wiping her bare arms on a tea towel and embracing her. The display of emotion raised Hannah's hopes for a mild admonishment she more than deserved, and humbled her.

'Maemm. Sorry.'

'Shush. You are home.' The hug tightened before Maemm let go and gave her cheek a gentle pat-pat.

'They've released her without charge.' Theo rested against the counter, his back to the window.

'Good. Yes?' Maemm searched his face.

'Yes, Naomi.' He folded his arms and explained the police's theory.

'We must visit the Stoltzfuses.' Maemm rolled down her sleeves. 'I will bake a casserole. You will make an apple pie. We shall ride over this afternoon.'

I'm fine, thank you for asking, Hannah thought, then promptly scolded herself for being so unkind, noting Maemm's strained features.

The door banged open.

'Evan, get the buggy ready for after lunch.' Maemm lifted the apron draped over a chair.

'They let you out?' Evan stood in the doorway, his eyes puffy and red. He stared at her coldly.

'Evan.' Hannah half turned, unsure how to approach him. She took a tentative step towards him.

'Go away.' He raised an arm as though shielding himself from her. 'You killed her.'

Hannah clutched the top rail of a chair as his words kicked at her like a horse's hoof.

'Evan. No.' Maemm place an hand on Hannah's shoulder.

With a long stride, Evan stood in front of Hannah, so close she could see his damp eyelashes, their ends heavy with drops of water. 'Grace went because you encouraged her, and now she's dead.'

'Evan.' Grandfather's sharp tone bounced off Evan like a volleyball on a wall.

'Why didn't you stop her? Why didn't you stop her from taking those stupid pills? This is your fault. Yours.'

'Evan, stop. This is not our way.' Maemm placed her hand on his shoulder, and Evan shrugged it away.

'Taking drugs is not our way,' he spat back through gritted teeth. 'It is the English way. Her way.' His finger jabbed at Hannah. 'You're so fond of the English. Go. You said you wanted to be one of them, so go. Better for all of us.'

Grandfather slammed his hand on the table. 'Be quiet. You talk like an *Englischer*. Remember who you are, Evan. *Gott villa* – this is God's will, not ours.' His steely look silenced the protest rising to Evan's lips. 'Leave. Open the shop. Some good, honest work may help you see more clearly and wait upon the Lord for his guidance.'

'Yes, Evan, Go. Do what Grandfather says. You are not yourself,' Maemm told him in a soft voice.

Evan's gaze stayed on Hannah, glowing with something akin to hatred mixed with deep pain.

'Do not hold it against him, Hannah,' Grandfather sighed when Evan departed. 'He is suffering, but with God's help, he will come to know the truth. Anger and hate are easier to hold onto than forgiveness. Be patient with him.'

His kindness broke the well of grief within her. Evan had the right to be angry. It was she who should seek his forgiveness. Yet she knew Grandfather spoke of their way when faced with death and tragedy. Acceptance and forgiveness were the paths to wholeness. Hatred, revenge, selfish desires, and all their related allies were to be resisted.

Throughout the night and the interview, she had fought to push the image of Grace's slumped body from her mind. Now the tears streamed down her cheeks and with them, a deep cry spilled from within. Sobs racked her body. She tried to stop them, clamping her hand over her mouth and wiping her eyes with her jumper, but they kept coming.

Firm hands held her forearms and eased her fingers from her tear-stained face. 'Hannah, you're tired, hungry, and in shock.' Grandfather's calm voice penetrated her confused mind. 'You are not to blame for Grace's death. Hear me. You are not.'

Maemm pulled a chair out, sat her down, and wrapped her arms around her.

'They breathalysed Hannah. It was negative,' Theo said. 'If you took drugs last night, it will show up in the blood test the police did.'

Hannah shook her head adamantly.

'Good. The coroner will confirm whether Grace died from an overdose or the injury to her head. We should know the preliminary findings soon. Whichever way it turns out, it had nothing to do with you.

'No, no,' Hannah said. 'I agreed to go. Evan is right.' Sol's menacing face filled her vision, and she stopped herself from saying, 'She wished to see Levi.'

She caught the troubled expression on Theo's face. Had she said too much? The Stoltzfuses were good, kindly, simple people. She doubted they knew of Levi, let alone the rest.

'Naomi.' Theo turned to Maemm. 'She should rest. Maybe it's unwise for her to visit the Stoltzfuses today?'

'I will take you,' Grandfather suggested to Maemm, resting his hand on Hannah's head.

'Yes, you need rest,' Maemm said. 'And food. You too, Theo. Where are my manners? You must be famished. I will make some breakfast. I will make the apple pie to take today. Grace liked them.' The salty smell of sizzling bacon soon filled the room, making Hannah's stomach rumble.

A while later, replenished by bacon and fried eggs with bread, Theo took his leave, promising to call when he had news.

'Now, to bed and rest.' Maemm opened a top cupboard, fetching a large ceramic mixing bowl. 'I will call you before I go.' She got a jar of flour from a tall shelf opposite the sink before fetching the sugar jar. When she saw Hannah had not moved, she let out a resigned sigh. 'Very well, help me if you wish.'

Maemm mixed the chopped shortening from the refrigerator and rubbed it into the flour and sugar to make the pastry flaky. Hannah went to the pantry and, from a wooden fruit box, picked half a dozen cooking apples. The sweetest, unblemished ones. Like Grace.

Maemm said nothing as Hannah peeled, sliced, and arranged them in a floret in the pie dish, sprinkling a tablespoon of sugar over the layer of apple slices. In silence, they worked to prepare the pie with care. Maemm hung the rolled-out pastry over the rolling pin and laid it over the sugared apples. With two fingers, Hannah crimped the edges, embedding the apple slices within the layers of pastry as a body within a coffin. Maemm cut a small incision in the centre to allow the apples to breathe as they cooked, and Hannah made four clover shapes from the leftover pastry.

A flood of memories replayed in her mind. Two little girls running through the fields to the schoolhouse. Playing hopscotch in the yard. Walking as teenagers to and from church, careful not to be too aware of the young men looking on.

They would not be each other's bridesmaids, nor would their husbands be friends. Their children would never play together. All she could offer to the family who would now struggle to live with the belief that their loved one was in a better place with God was the work of her hands as an act of contrition.

Chapter 12

ALL WEEK HANNAH waited for news. Ignoring Sol's suggestion to take time off, she had turned up for work on the Monday and discovered that news travelled even faster in town than in the outer regions. As the days went on, she took every opportunity when the shop was quiet to sneak a peek through the front window at the café. When would they release the body? Grace's body. No body meant no funeral. Already nearly a week had passed instead of the usual three days.

Maemm, always the first to know, announced at dinner on Wednesday that according to Mr King's wife, the coroner, who was sympathetic to Amish customs, had agreed to release the body on Friday, though a final decision over the cause of death was yet to be announced and the funeral would be on the next Monday.

On the day, they parked their buggy with the others, and Hannah took in the row upon row of buggies along the dirt track leading up to the Stoltzfus's dairy farm, two miles from Hannah's own home. A steady stream of people were moving inch by inch towards the large barn, and Hannah and her family, including a wan and silent Evan, fell in line.

Hannah's mind drifted back to the previous Saturday, when she and Maemm had travelled the short distance to the Stoltzfus's farm and paid their respects. Throughout the journey, the bump of the buggy's wheels along the tarmac road had sent her stomach somersaulting like a pinwheel. Everyone knew of the accident, despite no one saying anything. The passing from one world to the next called for solidarity.

Sympathetic smiles and solicitous greetings from the women to her and Maemm at the lying-in had reinforced her suspicion that the rumours of her involvement in Grace's death had become public knowledge. In the living room lay the open, simple wooden coffin with Grace laid out. Even in death, wax-pale with her copper hair brushed back from her face, she looked like one of the fairytale princesses they used to read of when young. The faint tint of discolouring above Grace's right eye bore evidence of her injury. Maemm had put her arm through Hannah's and steadied her, moved her on after one last glance at her childhood friend.

'Hannah.' She tried to form a polite smile as Grace's father took a firm hold of her trembling hands. 'You were such a good friend to our Grace. Thank you.' His sausage fingers enveloped hers, the leathery skin heating her chilled hands. *Some friend.* She had made Grace wait for her agreement to go to a gathering when she should have kept to her original refusal. If she had, none of this would be happening. She would not be here, and Grace would be still alive.

From across the crowded room of mourners, the small, waif-thin figure of Grace's maemm had watched them. In the corner near the

coffin, a small group huddled over pen and paper, talking of the funeral. Aaron sat among them with his black leather Bible open, talking softly with the relatives who would take care of arrangements for the grieving family. She moved to the group, but Maemm gave her a stern stare. They'd left an hour later with promises to bring food for the meal after the funeral.

No news from the police meant no decision about the cause of death. Theo, who visited daily, estimated it would be a week before the coroner would give a formal verdict. For now, Grace's death would be called 'The Accident'.

Now, a deep cloud of foreboding consumed Hannah as they reached the Stoltzfus's barn door. She followed the line of silent mourners into the building and sat by Maemm on a bench halfway down the right side with the other women. Evan walked through the makeshift nave towards Barney, who was seated near the front, hatless, his dark, tousled locks curled above his eyes; he was staring at her. Dressed in his black Mutza suit with its plain jacket with neither pocket, lapel, nor collar, he blended in with the older men on either side of him.

Sadness mingled with concern made Hannah shift uneasily in the tight space. In the open area at the far end, the closed coffin stood on wooden trestles. Unadorned and alone.

Throughout the service, Maemm prompted her when to stand and sit. When the congregation stood to sing after the opening prayer, Hannah mouthed the words. How could God let someone so young, so vibrant, die? Could he not have allowed her to live? What sense, what purpose was there to gain in her death?

'Sing, Hannah,' Maemm whispered, dabbing her eyes with a hanky edged in bluebell embroidery. 'It is the last thing you can do for her.'

Hannah lifted her voice in unison with the others. The hymn, "All

Things Bright and Beautiful", a favourite of Grace's, reflected her passion for life; it was all about nature and the beauty of God's creation. Bible readings describing a new heaven and a new earth interspersed the meditations and final prayers. The ninety minute service seemed to have hardly begun before a gentle nudge in the ribs from Maemm indicated it was time to leave for the burial field on the outskirts of town.

Scar pulled their closed buggy with a stately plod behind the horse-drawn hearse under the grim, grey clouds, to the open field where uniform rows of graves with matching headstones lay. Cars along the route moved to one side to allow the convoy to proceed unhindered.

To the top right of the cemetery was the Stoltzfus family plot. An open gap at the end where three of Grace's male relatives stood, shovels in hands, signalled where the brief burial service would take place. A mound of dirt, damp from the early morning shower, was piled by the hole.

On one side of the grave, Grace's parents stood, Mrs Stoltzfus leaning on the tall, solid frame of her husband, her head against his chest and her bonnet covering her face; she was wiping away a tear. Hannah kept her gaze low as the minister read out the prayers from the *Christenpflicht* book of prayer. The German words – more about celebrating life than mourning death – washed over her as she waited for him to say the words of comfort in the normal dialect of their community about how, in death, all were born to a new life in Christ to be forever one with God.

As the crowd broke their silence to say the Lord's Prayer, Hannah recited it on autopilot. The burial concluded with the benediction recited by mourners to the departed before the final leaving of the body to the earth.

'Thy will be done.' The brief sentence from the minister signalled the end.

While the men shovelled dirt over the coffin, soft weeping filled the air. No wailing or loud cries. Women dabbed their eyes with their handkerchiefs while the men pulled the brims of their hats low over their eyes. Mrs Stoltzfus raised her head. Her light-green eyes, a shade paler than Grace's rich, deep ones, found Hannah through the gap of Grandfather's and Evan's shoulders. The expression in them sent a wave of remorse through her. She brought a hanky to her eyes to block out her questioning stare. When she lowered it, Mr and Mrs Stoltzfus were walking through the crowd, which parted like the Red Sea for them, drops of rain falling on their clothes as they navigated the narrow pathway.

Hannah helped serve the assortment of food brought and prepared by neighbours far and wide. Jugs of water stood along the tables pushed together in the barn, benches pushed alongside them. Women carried large, steaming trays of potato pie from the kitchen, along with cinnamon bread and bowls of vegetables, to the serving tables down one side of the barn.

'We need more cinnamon bread, Hannah,' a plump woman in a stained apron barked.

People were hungry after the morning service. Many had long journeys to undertake. Hannah nodded and made her way to the house, through the parlour and along the narrow passage to the large kitchen.

'You should have left as you planned.'

The choked, wretched tone sounded oddly familiar, the words filtering down the passage. The door stood ajar, a honeycomb pine table and chairs visible against terracotta walls.

'May God forgive me, but I cannot help feel, if you had...'

Mrs Stoltzfus. Hannah halted, unsure of what to do. She had stumbled on a private conversation. She should leave and forget it. Who was Mrs Stoltzfus venting her grief at?

A familiar tall, willowy figure dressed in mourning clothes stepped into view. Maemm, her bonnet hiding her face, her hands twisting a blue-edged hanky.

'This would never have happened if we had remained in the old order. An unmarried woman bringing up a child.' Mrs Stoltzfus sniffed.

The words and the accompanying racking sobs almost blotted out the laboured footsteps behind Hannah. A thin, weathered hand rested lightly on her shoulder as she grappled with Mrs Stoltzfus's words. Grandfather raised a hand, as if to warn her to stay still, but Maemm heard their movements and let out a soft moan as she spotted them. Sorrow was etching her face.

Grandfather's boots clopped on the flagstone floor as he trod into the kitchen. At his appearance, Mrs Stoltzfus retrieved a hanky from her sleeve and blew her nose. Grandfather beckoned Hannah and closed the door after her.

Desperately trying to create a sense of the conversation, she searched their faces for clues. Had she misheard? Who were they talking about? Why didn't she know that such a woman lived in their village?

With his usual measured step, Grandfather drew close to Mrs Stoltzfus and rested his hands on her trembling shoulders. They stood as one, bathed in a pool of clear sunlight streaming through the window. 'I pray for God's forgiveness, Amos,' Mrs Stoltzfus whimpered. 'I speak with a devil's tongue.'

'Tsk, tsk. You speak as one filled with grief unprepared. Forgive yourself, Velda, as God forgives you.'

'She was my joy.'

'As is ours,' Grandfather soothed. 'Remember the saying, "Forgiveness is unlocking the door to set someone free and realising you were the prisoner".'

Mrs Stoltzfus inclined her head.

How many times had he recalled the proverb with a gentle wag of a finger when she or Evan became angry when younger?

The two of them were united in their bond of grief, Hannah realised. Grandfather had lost his own adopted son, Isaac, and Stefan, his son-in-law; yet he bore his sadness with lightness and acceptance of the events as a natural part of life and not the tragedy of youth in bloom snuffed out at a whim.

'Hannah did not give those drugs or drink to Grace or drive the car carelessly.'

'Who? Who did?' Mrs Stoltzfus scrunched up the hanky.

'Is that what you crave? To blame?' He lifted her chin gently. 'Revenge is not our way. Give yourself up to God's will and let go of this anger. Be at peace with yourself and others.' At these last words, he lifted his gaze to Maemm, standing still and silent.

'Of course, Amos, you are right. Please forgive my outburst.' Mrs Stoltzfus tucked her hanky inside her cuff and wiped her eyes clear of tears before she pushed a strand of hair under her kapp. 'I must attend to our guests.' With a swish of her skirt, she swept past Hannah, down the corridor, and out of the front door.

As Grandfather followed Mrs Stoltzfus out, the rowdy chatter of youths and children playing outside roused Hannah back to life.

Standing by a closed buggy, Barney and Evan faced the kitchen window, talking. When they saw her staring, Evan turned his back and Barney gave her a sad smile.

All the while Grace's maemm and Grandfather were talking, she had felt like a spectator watching a play or a film; removed from the story but captivated by it. Standing alone with Maemm now, she found herself on stage. 'What did she mean?'

'Nothing.' Maemm turned towards the door.

'I do not believe you.'

'And I do not believe you, Hannah.' Maemm whirled to face her, her usually pale face flushed. 'You know who drove the car? Who gave Grace those things that killed her? You know. Yet you do nothing.'

'You want me to help the police and purge my soul?'

'I want you to help the poor woman make sense of this. To find peace.' Maemm paused and interlocked her fingers before speaking in a calmer voice. 'You are the only one who can do it.'

'You blame me?'

'No, Hannah.' Maemm shook her head. 'Grandfather is right. Blame is not our way. But you have the means to ease their pain if you so choose.'

Maemm's shoes clattered on the flagstones as she left.

In the farmyard, some girls played hopscotch while the boys played tag. Adults mingled, talking with serious faces. Grace's maemm darted among them, offering slices of cake, smiling in return to each consoling pat of a hand or kind word. The grief-stricken woman of a few minutes ago seemed changed.

But she wasn't, Hannah knew. Mrs Stoltzfus was still a mother with a daughter to mourn. She would always want to know what happened.

How? Who? A form of living hell. She would attend the annual Sudden Death Reunion every year with others who had lost a loved one unexpectedly. With each passing year, she would count the birthdays, the life milestones, until her dying breath.

Hannah must choose. Choose between loyalty to the church or release to a grieving family.

Chapter 13

S NIPPETS OF THE funeral mixed with the events of Grace's death plagued Hannah that night, leaving her restless and afraid to succumb to sleep for fear of nightmares.

What had Grace's mother meant by saying Maemm should have left? Who was the woman with the child? Maemm? She had married Father, as should be, before Hannah and Evan were born. Why had Grandfather not rebuked Mrs Stoltzfus for suggesting such a thing, or Maemm not protested? Unmarried mothers were not common and rarely lived with their family for the shame. Maybe grief did that to some people, made them lash out at others. She should pray for Grace's Maemm, Hannah resolved, putting aside the last part of the conversation about the grieving mother blaming her for Grace's death.

Through the lemon-coloured cotton curtains, the moon threw a circle of light onto the wooden floor. Restless, she got up, wrapped a knitted shawl around her shoulders, and tweaked a curtain to look up at the dark sky. In less than an hour, the rooster would crow as threads of dawn broke through. For once, she could ignore it if she wished. Sam had given her till Wednesday off.

The moonbeams stretched the length of the yard to the chicken shed. Under the workshop door's bottom edge, a sliver of light glowed. Puzzled and unable to sleep, Hannah decided to check if Grandfather was working – he was a light sleeper and frequently started work before daybreak.

A gentle wheeze from his bedroom down the passageway confirmed he was asleep. Who was working there at this time of day? Certainly not Evan, always the last at breakfast. Hannah slipped downstairs and into the mudroom, pulled on a pair of boots, and hurried to the workshop. Inside, a lamp suspended from a hook spilled its light over the workbench where Evan sat hunched, scribbling away on paper with a thick hardback book propped open against a small box. On the floor lay several screwed-up balls of paper.

'Evan?'

He ceased writing and slapped a palm on the pad.

They had barely spoken since her return. The shattered look he wore warned her that she would do better to leave him than try making amends, yet it pained her to see him so broken. All because of her. She dropped her hand from the handle. 'What are you doing?'

'Nothing.'

Why wasn't he working on a harness or wheel?

With slow, deliberate steps, she approached him, noting the open book. Evan snapped it shut and pushed it aside.

'Why are you up so early?' she asked, halting as he scowled at her.

Evan toyed with the book.

They might be standing a foot or two apart, but the gulf could have been wide as a canyon. The crackling of the wood burner at the far end broke the heavy silence.

When he remained quiet, Hannah bowed her head and turned to

go. The scrape of Evan's stool made her pause. 'Grandfather's right. I should not have taken my anger out on you.' The words came slow and broken, barely masking the pain within that stirred her own heart.

She lifted her head and stared at his drawn face with its half-lowered eyelids and sunken cheeks. 'I'm sorry, Evan.'

He stood silently, his big-boned frame trembling, placing a hand on the bench to steady himself.

The clucking of the rooster sounded across the yard.

Hannah searched his face. 'It was her last outing.'

'I know.' His shoulders hunched. 'She told me that night. It was why I left – so she could enjoy it without me spoiling things.' He dug his hands into his pockets. 'They say she was ill at the gathering. She collapsed.'

Through the window, the first signs of daylight peeked through the canopy of the night sky.

'Who? Who deserted you? Was it Sol?'

His name rose and stuck in her throat.

'Hannah, please.' Evan slumped back on the stool in defeat when she did not reply.

She was of a mind to go when she caught sight of the title on the hardback; it looked like the ones they used to have in the schoolhouse. Lying beside it was a math book with a library sticker on its spine. 'Why are you studying, Evan?'

He tapped the pen against his palm, his eyes downcast.

'Have you been coming to the barn in the morning? I thought it was Grandfather.' She took a few steps nearer. On the bench, a brown envelope addressed to him lay open and empty. A booklet next to it read "General Education Diploma MATHEMATICS PAPER". Curious, she looked at him.

A nervous gaze replaced his usual brash, no-nonsense stare.

'Why?' She rested her fingers on the book's cover. Alongside his broad ones, hers resembled matchsticks.

Evan dropped the pen and stared at his large hands with their square palms and short fingers.

'Oh, Evan.' She hugged him. 'Why have you not said something if you are so unhappy working here?'

'Grandfather. I can't ruin his dream to hand this down the line.' He spread an arm out, taking in the workshop. 'He lost Daett, and we have no brother. There's you and Maemm to take care of.'

He had their father's sharp cheekbones and flat button nose. Everything about him reminded her of Daett. The barrelled chest. The tree-trunk legs. His teenage youthfulness was melting away as he took on an older man's yoke of responsibility. Hannah took in the workshop with its leathery smell, cluttered machinery, and hanging tools. Such a weight for a young one's shoulders.

'I want to use this.' He tapped his temple and turned his hands over. 'Not these.'

'To do what?'

A nervous smile pulled at his mouth. 'I don't know. All I know is, not this. Something else. Something where I can use my mind, my reasoning.'

'Like a teacher or doctor.'

'Doctor?' He gave a rueful shake of his blond head. 'Doubtful, given my lack of science. Teacher? Maybe. I like figures. I do the books for Grandfather.'

'A bookkeeper. Accountant. You would need to study more and gain qualifications, like the GED.'

A trace of a smile broke onto his lips.

'And Barney. He has been helping you?'

'He's acted as a courier for the distance learning materials I get. I give him my work to send back. I will take my exams soon, if I take them.'

'You must.' Hannah placed her hands on his shoulders. 'Evan, you can't live your life for other people.'

'Neither can you.'

She dropped her hands.

He closed his eyes and winced. 'I'm sorry, Hannah, but I cannot simply wipe away my feelings over Grace's death or your part in it – and don't deny it.'

She pulled him to her, but he resisted, his body stiff.

'Evan, I care for your happiness.'

'So much you encouraged Grace to behave like a wild child.' His face darkened.

Hannah fought the urge to protest. It would only infuriate him more. What could she say? If she had done what she should have done, Grace would be alive.

His shoulders deflated like a punctured balloon. 'I wish Daett were here,' he mumbled. 'I miss him so much. There is no one I can talk to like I used to with him.'

She stroked his thick, straw-coloured hair, so like their father's. If Maemm had died, what would it have been like? Who would she turn to? Who would she trust? Who would provide a female voice of wisdom when she needed it? Maemm's brother had died before either she or Evan had been born, and Father's family lived in another district.

'Grace understood,' Evan muttered, lifting his head. 'Now there doesn't seem to be any point.'

'Yes there is. Do it for yourself. Do it because you can, Evan. No one knows what future will pass for any of us.'

He hung his head. A tear fell on his shirt, and Hannah sought to find the words to comfort him. How could she help him make sense of the world when the light had gone out of it? She recalled the walk over the fields from church. How he had grasped the opportunity to please Grace. How he had become so excited about the community centre idea. How could she give him hope now? This shy, gawky youth?

'The community centre. It will need a lot of planning. You'll need to work out a budget for the building and running costs.' A rush of hope filled her. 'You could build it in memory of Grace.'

Evan lifted his gaze and gave her a sceptical look.

'Go on, build it. Build it so those of us who want to have freedom can do so safely – without drugs and drink. A place for young people, run by young people. Have your meeting with the bishop and the steering committee.'

Evan shook his head. 'No one's interested. They only want to party with drugs and alcohol before settling down or leaving.'

'Precisely. That's your argument.' She recalled Barney's words walking through the field. 'We don't have anywhere to meet and socialise other than the formal activities arranged for us by adults. When we meet, it's like a large group in someone's home. The parents get upset at the rowdiness. The gatherings in places like the Field of Sorrows, where anyone can go, English or Amish, are the only other option. The community centre could provide a safe place for our young people to meet. Especially during Rumspringa.'

Evan fell silent, blinking back the tears.

'I'll help,' Hannah offered.

'And ease your conscience.' Evan rose and packed up his books, stuffing them into a shoulder bag on the table.

She reeled back, wounded.

He turned to her. 'If you meant it, come to the meeting at the bishop's house.'

She gave an eager nod.

The growl of a car engine and the crunch of wheels called their attention. Evan glanced out of the window. 'Theo. He must have news to arrive this early,' he said.

A wave of apprehension washed over Hannah, goose pimples spreading over her arms. The engine cutting off and the slam of the car door jolted her out of her worry. She gave Evan a light peck on the cheek, pulled her shawl tighter, and started to the door.

'Did she ever speak of me?'

The question threw her into a spin. What to say? If she responded yes, he would mourn what would never be. If she replied no, he would forever feel the pang of unrequited love.

'I believe she had a fondness for you. She kept it well hidden.' She glanced back over her shoulder to see the gratitude in his eyes. Large, oval, and dark blue, so unlike her own. The ground suddenly shifted beneath her. How could she have green specks when both parents had blue eyes?

A gust of cold air rippled through her body, wiping the question from her mind as she pushed the barn door open. She glanced back at Evan. A little more encouragement and he would come round. Already she could see a thoughtful expression creeping over his mournful features.

Out in the yard, she spied Maemm hurrying from the chicken shed with a basket full of eggs. Hannah peeped through a narrow strip between the doors to view the yard. The draught reminded her that she lacked a dress; she shivered again and clutched her shawl as Maemm walked briskly to the front door, her black skirt fluttering around her slight figure.

Why had she never noticed? An image of Daett – Stefan – came to her. An older version of Evan, laughing and wiping snow from his ash-blond hair during a break from the repair shop. Evan's words about wishing their father were still alive for him to talk to haunted her. There were questions she desired answers to.

'I must talk with Maemm.' She slipped out and ran to the house, skirting Theo's car by the buggy cutout, an outlandish conclusion spinning inside her head. 'Maemm!' she shouted as her mother disappeared into the house. She bolted in and followed her into the kitchen.

'We must talk,' she blurted out, ignoring Theo at the table, checking his phone.

'There is breakfast to prepare.' Maemm placed the basket by the stove and lifted a frying pan from its hook above. She placed it on the hot plate as Evan entered. Grandfather wandered in and settled himself at the table, which was laid out for breakfast, and absently toyed with a spoon.

Mrs Stoltzfus's words tore at Hannah, try as she might to ignore them. Clawing deep into her. *Lies.* Was all she had known a lie? If not Stefan – who had brought her up – then who could it be? She cleared her throat. 'Mrs Stoltzfus...'

A fearful look clouded Maemm's eyes as they met Hannah's.

'She was telling the truth?'

Grandfather laid his spoon down with care and rose.

Theo looked up from his phone.

'It was me she was talking of, was it not?' Hannah clutched the folds of her nightdress.

Maemm stared at Grandfather, who closed his eyes, his gentle features grave, and tilted his head in a small bob. Maemm stared at the floor, her fingers twisting together like coiled rope.

Puzzled, Evan glanced from Hannah to Maemm, lips parting to speak. Grandfather held up his palm and silenced him.

Maemm swallowed noisily; the action was like a stone dropping down a deep well, and with it, Hannah's childhood.

'Why did you not marry?'

'It was not possible,' came Maemm's faint reply. 'I was young. Your... your father left. I did not know where he went.'

An inaudible grunt came from Evan's direction. Theo stood up slowly, his eyes on Maemm.

'I was not shunned because I was not baptised, and Bishop Byer was a kindly soul. He granted permission for me to stay here with Father.'

'You agreed to Maemm staying?' Evan gasped. 'But... the shame.'

'Children are a gift.' Grandfather moved closer to Maemm. 'How could I turn away one of mine?' He placed a palm against Maemm's cheek, and she kissed it, eyes brimming with gratitude.

'Well, that explains one thing.' Evan looked at Hannah, his expression turning sour. 'Even now, you're putting yourself first. As ever. You should be mourning Grace, not thinking of... *this*.'

'Shut up! You've no idea what you're talking about,' Theo snapped.

'What's it to you, English?' With a long stride, Evan squared up to Theo.

Grandfather stepped towards him. 'Evan—'

'No,' Evan snarled. 'He shows up unannounced, with this bull of a story about wanting to pay his respects. And he's still here.'

Maemm whimpered softly.

'Why?' Evan glared at Theo. 'Why turn up after all these years? Who are you? And why are you so keen to help my bastard sister?'

Theo lunged at Evan and grabbed his shirt. Maemm cried out. The force sent Evan against the wall and, with a thrust, he pushed Theo away. This time, Theo reeled backwards and crashed into the table, toppling a chair and bending double, winded. Evan towered over him. 'Who are you?' he shouted.

A haunted look crept over Theo's normally relaxed features. He darted a look at Maemm, who stood transfixed, her eyes widened.

When Theo did not reply, Evan drew back a fist, ready to punch.

Grandfather pushed between them and flung his arm out, barring him. 'Lower your fist, Evan.'

'Why? Because I am Amish?'

Grandfather placed his palm over Evan's curled fist and lowered it. 'No. Because he is Hannah's *daett*.'

Chapter 14

SEATED OPPOSITE HER, the blend of genes Hannah had inherited spoke for themselves. Maemm's build, her unblemished skin, and the blueness of her eyes sprinkled with specks of his evergreen ones. Theo's walnut-brown hair mixed with Maemm's honey blonde. At least she shared Maemm's build and nose with the curve at its tip.

Grandfather had ushered Evan out of the kitchen and marched him to the workshop, Evan talking fast, waving his arms wide and striding as Grandfather trotted to keep up. For once, Hannah understood Evan's need to vent anger. His rage at Theo had echoed her own brewing frustration at being kept in the dark. All these years she had believed Stefan Bieler to be her natural father. The man who had read stories to her by the fire as her hair dried after washing. Who had built the tallboy and chest for her bedroom and teased her when shy youths smiled at her while walking back and forth to church. All this time, Maemm had allowed her to believe a lie.

A fist gripped her heart, squeezing out all forgiving sentiments.

Heat raced through her veins. How she hated them. The deceivers. The liars.

She remembered how Grandfather always muttered to Evan when he blew up about something or other, 'This is not the way. Let leave of your temper.'

She held on tight to her resentment, so tight her jaw ached from the firm clench of her muscles.

Another tsk-tsk echoed inside as she remembered the proverb Grandfather had reminded Mrs Stoltzfus of. *In forgiving someone, you free yourself.*

Theo leaned back, one hand on the table, tapping the surface. 'As I said, we met when I was a rookie cop in 2003, working undercover at the gatherings young people went to, like today, out in the fields or at a barn.'

'When? How old were you?' She glanced at Maemm.

'Eighteen. The last year of my Rumspringa. I used to go with my sister, Ruth.'

'I was new to the area. Stationed in the next district, so people didn't know me,' Theo continued. 'Drugs were as common as today.' He paused. 'The police underestimated the scale of the trafficking going on. The dealers supplying locals, including Amish youth, were part of a bigger network. We suspected they were based in Mexico. The drugs would be transported from there and dispersed through the states they operated in. My job was to infiltrate the gang. Watch, learn, and report back.'

Hannah opened her mouth to ask what this all had to do with her.

Theo raised his finger. 'We met at a gathering. The job became secondary to me. At first, I tried to avoid getting involved. I was older. Twenty-three. It didn't seem right, but...' He tentatively moved his hand and let it hover over Maemm's. Gradually he lowered it, resting it next to Maemm's; close, but not touching. 'Someone must have worked out my identity, because I got warned by an Amish girl going out with a gang member. I had to disappear; otherwise, it would jeopardise the entire operation. So, I did. The ring got bust.'

'The Leechburgs?' The name bypassed her brain to her mouth as Barney's words came back to her.

Theo nodded. 'The Leechburgs were well-known drug dealers, but some Mafia-type family controlled the whole state's drug industry. The boss was a man named Rafael Martinez. He went to prison and died there. His sons are still around, but another person has taken over the enterprise and become the leader.'

'Has there always been drug dealing in Birchwood?'

'According to Drummond, things went quiet for a while. It started up a few years after I left. Nothing as big, but over time, it's grown. It's getting out of control. A rival gang is trying to take over, and he thinks they are doing so by selling bad drugs, which are killing people, and blaming the old gang.'

'Barney told me about the Leechburgs,' Hannah said.

Maemm lifted her gaze to her.

'He had an elder brother who died from a drug overdose,' Hannah explained.

Theo picked up the story. 'Drummond knew my whereabouts. He informed me about your birth. It was four years before it was safe for me to pass by. I didn't want to endanger any of you. When I returned, Stefan and your mother were married. Evan was a baby, you, a toddler. One happy family.'

'We have met before.' Maemm laid her hand over Theo's. 'Stefan agreed.'

Hannah turned their story over in her mind. The quietness was broken by the hallway clock's chimes. 'Would you have gone with him if you could?'

'Who knows what we would have done?' Theo said. 'Bottom line is, you had two devoted parents, a doting grandfather, and a safe home.'

'Don't excuse yourself.' The rebuke escaped before she had a chance to check herself. He stared back at her, his mouth slightly parted.

'Hannah!' A reproachful look accompanied Maemm's stern rebuke.

Hannah bit her bottom lip.

'You have wanted for nothing, and Stefan loved you as his own.' Maemm half rose, then slumped down, swaying in her seat.

'Naomi?' Theo twisted around and steadied her. 'You should rest.'

'I am fine. Just a little... overwrought.' She straightened. 'A good night's sleep is all that is needed.'

'Sure?' Theo removed his hand, but his eyes stayed on her.

A sweet smile rose on Maemm's lips, and she turned and faced Hannah. A tense silence filled the kitchen, broken by the dull hum of the refrigerator. Her gaze never wavered from Hannah's own.

'Would you have left?' Hannah shifted, grateful for the chair's solid backrest to press against and stem the mounting resentment inside her.

'Yes,' Maemm replied in a weak and tired voice. 'But I thank God for Stefan and the happiness we had. All of us.'

'Is it why Father stayed here? Why you did not live with his family as wives often do?'

Maemm lowered her head.

The stoic, proud woman she had known all her life sat bowed and bent.

The heated indignation cooled. The swell of air painfully pushing her ribs eased and loosened the vice-hold on her heart, and with it, the raw rage ebbed away. In its place grew an ache at the sight of Maemm's caved body.

'Hannah, do not make the same error I nearly did,' Maemm said, taking one of her hands. 'You seek to protect someone who should not be shielding behind you. You do it with sincerity, I do not doubt, but it is misguided.'

Hannah half opened her mouth to let the protest welling up inside escape. She pushed it down and waited.

'Your grandfather once told me "sin" stands for *selfish, individual, need*.' Maemm held a finger up at each word. 'The opposite of it is *Lieb*, love, which means *listen, overlook, value, embrace*. It is easy to mistake one for the other.'

Hannah dropped her gaze, remembering how Maemm and Theo had looked at each other, their buried emotions rising to the surface; not of love or regret, but a wistfulness for what might have been if they had thought of themselves and not others. Hannah squeezed her eyes shut, trying to stem the flow of tears rushing to them.

'I have wronged you by not telling you,' Maemm said. 'I ask for your forgiveness.'

A tear leaked out of the corner of Hannah's eye and trickled down her cheek. When as a child she had asked for Maemm's forgiveness, it came without hesitation no matter how grievous the wrongdoing. How much it had cost Maemm to do so had not crossed her mind till this moment. Could she do the same?

She pried her lips apart, ready to speak, only for a choking sound to come out and strangle her words. She squeezed Maemm's hands.

'Thank you.' Maemm lifted Hannah's hands to her mouth and kissed them. Together they sobbed, their foreheads touching, their arms embracing the other.

As the tears flowed, an inner peace grew inside Hannah. With it, she understood what Grandfather had meant when he told Mrs Stoltzfus to give herself up to God's will. To let go of her anger and be at peace. Less than an hour ago, she had been ready to rage, shout, and condemn. Now she wanted to hug those who had sacrificed their happiness for her.

Did she count Sol as one of them? What sacrifice had he made for her? When had he ever put the needs of others before himself? As Theo and Maemm did all those years ago?

She opened her eyes as a ringing sound broke the silence; Theo fished his phone out of his jacket pocket and stared at it, his face clouded.

Hannah cleared her throat. 'I have something to tell you.'

'And I, you.' Theo looked at her. 'The coroner's come back with their findings.'

Hannah linked her hands, hearing the note of gravity in his voice.

'Cause of death: drug overdose. Which means...' Theo eyed the phone as if it was a snake, '... Manslaughter.'

Chapter 15

THE WINDOWLESS INTERVIEW room still held the entombed atmosphere of her first visit. Nothing had altered, not the pewter-grey walls, not even the vinegary smell of stale sweat, despite the faint citrus odour of the air freshener above the desk. Hannah wrinkled her nose like she did when she sorted Grandfather's and Evan's work clothes to wash, their shirts splattered with salty-sweet yellow patches and their trousers musty from working with leather and wood.

Only Theo's and her clothes were different. She wore one of her working outfits, an azure-blue Amish dress and bonnet. Theo wore a black winter coat and jeans.

Drummond squeezed his large frame into a plastic chair opposite them. The same officer as before sat beside him and flipped open his notebook, clicking his ballpoint pen. On the table was a manila file and a phone in a small plastic bag.

'You took your time.'

Hannah smarted at Drummond's curt reprimand, then relaxed when she noticed his gaze locked on Theo. Under the washed-out glow of the fluorescent light, his eyes appeared hard as the studs Grandfather used to bind leather straps.

Theo rocked back in his chair and returned the iceberg stare.

'No lawyer still?'

Theo folded his arms. 'Caught up in a case in New York.'

'You can't be her lawyer, The-o.' Drummond tapped his pen on his pad. 'Conflict of interest.'

Less than two weeks ago, she didn't know of Theo's existence, let alone his connection to her. Was he even called Theo?

Theo gave a polite smile back. 'I'm here as her father.'

Despite her misgivings, his words sent a warm current through her. He threw her a reassuring grin that creased the few lines around his eyes. The eyes, Grandfather said, were the windows of a person's soul. When she looked into Theo's, she saw an invitation. *Trust me*, they seemed to implore. Could she?

Did she have any choice?

Drummond arched an eyebrow at Theo. 'Let's get on with it, shall we?'

The other officer – Holtz, that was his name, Hannah remembered – switched on the cassette machine. Once again, she recited her name and date of birth along with the others. Holtz read out her rights. Standard practice, Theo had advised her. Formalities over with, Holtz leaned over his notepad with the determination of a dog guarding his dinner.

Hannah rubbed her palms down her skirt and focused on the burly, unsmiling chief opposite her. She swept her tongue over her dry mouth.

'I need to be clear with you, Hannah. You're not being charged or arrested. Yet.' Drummond's eyes held her gaze like a tracking beam.

'You have come here of your own free will as a witness to the manslaughter of your friend Grace Stoltzfus.'

'Witness?' Theo straightened in his chair.

Drummond threw him an irritated look. 'Like I said, you're not her lawyer. You shouldn't be here.'

'Drummond, you know it is perfectly in order for an appropriate adult to sit in when you interview someone who is Amish.' Theo resumed his laid-back stance. 'To support them with police procedures.'

The two men eyeballed each other.

'I want him to be here, please.' The notion of being interviewed alone turned Hannah's stomach to stone.

'As I was saying before I was interrupted, you are a witness to what the coroner's preliminary findings cite as involuntary manslaughter. You understand what that term means, Hannah?'

Hannah gave a firm nod, not trusting herself to speak. It meant Grace's death could have been avoided. She had not received the care she needed, thanks to Levi's detour. Theo had explained it to her, along with Drummond's request for him to bring her in for questioning and what to expect.

'Please state your answer for the tape.'

Hannah took a breath. 'Yes.'

Drummond opened the file and placed a photograph in front of her. A headshot of Grace. Wax-like and lifeless, as she had been in the coffin. 'Hannah, I don't believe you're selling drugs any more than I believe in the tooth fairy. I do believe you know who was driving the car you were in.' He slid his hand into the plastic bag and withdrew the mobile phone. 'For the benefit of the recording, I am showing the witness a phone with a corner covered in tape.' He held it up to her. 'Do you recognise this phone?'

Hannah nodded.

'For the benefit of the tape, can you tell me whose it is?'

'Grace's,' she replied.

Drummond tapped the phone, and the screen displayed a photo of them all at the gathering: the one Evan had taken. 'You'll be pleased to know your blood tests came back clear.' He slipped the phone back in the bag.

'Have you interviewed the others in the photo?' Theo asked.

'Yes, and they have alibis.'

The walls closed in around her. *How? How did Sol and Levi manage that?* She toyed with her bonnet's ribbons to stem the wave of panic flowing through her.

'Now, you have a choice. You can inform me, or you can continue to protect these scumbags. Choose option one and we'll have you on the side of the state prosecution in return for a reduced sentence. Choose option two and I'll charge you with possession of a Class B drug with intent to sell, at least, or manslaughter at worst. Single ticket to jail.'

Theo jerked forward. 'That's blackmail.'

'Fact. I am merely laying out her options.'

Silence enveloped them. Hannah rubbed her eyes and fought onset drowsiness and tried to ignore stuffy warmth of the airless room that caused it.

'Can I have a few minutes with my daughter, please, chief?'

'Of course.'

When the officers left, Theo swivelled to her, his smooth forehead dented with deep creases. 'Hannah, come clean, please.'

'I can't. You know I can't.'

'You must.' He placed a hand on the table, close to hers. 'I'm sure God will forgive you this transgression if it helps shut down the ring and save lives. And more importantly, keep you out of prison.'

'I will go to prison if I do not help them?' She searched his face for reassurance, a glimmer of hope, anything, but his face was taut, the usual softness in his eyes replaced with fear.

'Definitely. With the evidence they have, the prosecution will try to tie you in with whoever you were with and the vermin they are mixed up with.'

'It's not my place to judge another. Only God can judge.'

'You're not. You're helping to find those responsible so the law can administer justice.'

'I can't be responsible for another's fate.'

'What about Grace? You feel responsible for her death.'

Hannah felt like she was being punched in the solar plexus; she curled over.

'Sorry.' Theo touched her hand. 'I know you feel bad about her death – and no, you are not responsible. Please, Hannah. I know it is a lot to ask to go against your beliefs. At least this way you get to stay with your family. Please reconsider. There is more to this than you think.'

Hannah straightened up. He was right. There *was* more to this. She recalled Mama's plea: *peace*. Bring peace to those hurting. Their fates too laid in her hands. Did she have the strength to do what her conscience required rather than the bidding of the church?

Theo pursed his lips together.

'What? What is it?' She pulled at the ribbon wrapped around her finger, making the skin turn a bruising purplish red.

'Wait here.' He got up and hurried out.

Faint voices echoed and faded outside the door. Hannah released the ribbon and laid her hands on her lap. What had she done? Not for the first time, a harsh critical voice berated her. If she could go back, persuade Grace not to go to the gathering, Grace would be alive. She would not be in this room.

If she remained silent, they would prosecute her. Her family would have to endure the trial and the shame of the inevitable sentence. Nobody within the community would ever say anything outright – it was not the Amish way – everyone would fall over themselves to be helpful, offer advice or give comfort. If she cooperated, no one would say anything. But they would know, and she would know, and her life would never be quite the same amongst them. Who would want to marry her?

Had Maemm and Grandfather not suffered enough over her birth?

A door banged down the corridor. Hannah lifted her head; the room was spinning. She closed her eyes and inhaled deeply. What was the alternative? To run away? Drummond would find her and if he didn't, Sol and his friends would. She covered her face with her hands and stifled the mixture of rage and sobs.

'Hannah?' Theo tapped her on the shoulder lightly. He handed her a coffee and she sipped then grimaced; it was laced with sugar. 'Something to keep your energy levels up,' he said with a smile.

Five minutes later, Drummond and his colleague returned. 'Hannah, I am going to tell you something.' Drummond's curt tone had softened to a fatherly one. 'You could help us catch not just those responsible for Grace's death, but also those who are killing our young people. English and Amish. The ones supplying and the ones selling.

The whole stinking lot of vipers who prey on the innocent. The ignorant. The unlucky.'

A faint ringing reverberated in the recesses of her mind. Why had this grumpy rottweiler of a detective gone all parental on her? Theo gave her an encouraging look. Drummond opened his folder again and took out two photos.

To her astonishment, they were of her. One showed her leaving the cycle shop with a carrier bag full of Maemm's quilts, on the way to the post office. The other was of her coming out of the butcher's with a white bag containing another parcel.

'You make a lot of trips to Falcon's, don't you, Hannah?'

Her stomach lurched. How many times had they watched her? Why were they watching her?

'Yes, we've been observing, and yes, if you're charged, these will be used in court. We've been watching the entire street.' Drummond tapped the last photo with a stubby finger. 'Why do you think Sam asks you to do these deliveries, Hannah? Why is it always you?'

The last morsel of moisture in her mouth evaporated.

'They have used you, young lady.'

Selfish individual need. The phrase reverberated like a ping-pong ball inside her mind. She had thought herself so important to be trusted with such errands. How could she have been so naïve?

Sol? Strange, he never once offered to go instead. Now she knew why.

'Tell them, Hannah,' Theo urged, turning to her.

The words stuck in her throat, but she dragged them out. Bit by bit, she answered their questions in hesitant sentences. Who was in the car? Where were the deliveries stored? Did she ever go into the storeroom? No, Sol got the stock when needed.

Drummond drained his plastic cup and checked his notes. 'From what I'm told, you get on well with young Sol and his friend Levi?'

Hannah shifted awkwardly. 'Sol... he was Amish.' She cleared her throat. 'We went to school together. He left when his parents died in a buggy accident when he was ten. Sol has lived with Sam ever since.'

'Did Sol get you the job at the cycle shop?'

Hannah nodded. Bored with staying at home, she would often pop into the shop when she visited town.

'Does Sam have visitors?'

She nodded her head. 'Business associates.'

Drummond let out a dry laugh and pulled out another photo. Hannah glanced at it. The taller of the two 'business associates' who had visited Sam stared back at her, his eyes cold and black like marble.

'Jorge Martinez. His father, Rafael, was the boss who we busted in 2004.' Drummond slipped the photo back. 'Is it always Levi who takes the parcels off you when you deliver them to Falcon's?'

She gave another nod. An ember of hope entered her numbed body. 'Are you going to arrest Levi?'

Drummond shook his head.

'Sol?'

He gave another shake.

'But they could be involved with the people who threw the hand out of the Toyota.'

'The Toyota?' Drummond checked his papers. 'Unrelated. Inter-rival gang spat.'

Hannah let out an exasperated sigh. If they arrested them, Evan would be safe. Sol had the means and motive to hurt him. If he'd managed to persuade someone to lie for him and Levi, arranging an accident would be simple to do.

What were the police waiting for? What would it take for them to act? They might want to play with people's lives, but she did not. Hannah squared up to the burly figure opposite her. She had no choice. One death on her conscience was too many. 'Sol threatened to hurt Evan. Last time I was here. Outside.'

Drummond leaned in closer, the smell of cigarette smoke on his breath. Foul as it was, it made a change to the stale sweat. 'To keep you quiet?'

Her jaw locked as her mouth shaped the answer. 'Yes.'

'Good. Good.' He leaned back in his chair.

'No. Bad.' Theo laid his arm over her shoulder. 'Arrest them. You've got Hannah placing them in the car.'

'Which will be taken into due consideration once we have completed our investigations,' Drummond replied.

Hannah ignored them, too frustrated with her own stupidity.

The khaki rucksack. The one they had thrown out after dumping her and Grace on the roadside. The one Levi got from the icehouse en route to the gathering. Aaron and Levi standing outside the Millers' barn, Levi fumbling inside the bag. What did he give Aaron? Drugs? Money? Why? Blades of ice ran down Hannah's back. It wasn't surprising that Levi did not want to take Grace to the hospital when the police turned up.

'Don't worry about Evan,' Theo said. 'We can get a patrol car to check on your home.'

'We? I suppose you want patrol to keep an eye out for runaway buggies too?' Drummond gave a wry shake of his head. 'Okay. Agreed. Send a message out to uniform.'

Holtz scribbled on his notepad.

'You think they are hiding drugs in the cycle storeroom?' Hannah asked, relieved at the promise.

'Possibly,' Drummond muttered.

They don't know who is behind all this. But if they did? Should I tell him about the icehouse?

Theo leaned forward, one arm resting on the table. 'You've got what you want. Now, about protection – as Hannah is no longer a suspect but a witness?'

'You have been very helpful, Hannah.' Drummond kept his gaze on her. 'Truly. I can see you want to bring those accountable for Grace's death to justice. We can do it, but we need your help.'

Theo narrowed his eyes at Drummond.

'We know about Jorge and his guys, but there's someone behind them who is organising the drugs. A boss man.' The chief waved his folder in the air. 'It's not Jorge. It might be Sam, or he could be a little fish in a big, dirty pond. We've got no concrete evidence to close the show down. The shop could be one of several locations for them to stash the drugs. Hell, could be Falcon's, the florist, or a barn out in the sticks. We don't know.'

The Millers had a barn. Hannah's mind leaped like a hare, joining dots as they popped before her eyes.

'We're working on things, but we could do with someone inside the shop. To observe. Nothing else.'

'Forget it.' Theo sprang up, sending his chair rocking.

'She's ideal.'

Theo leaned over the table. 'Are you insane? It's too dangerous. Get a female officer in.'

'It'd take months to put someone in and get the level of trust Hannah has. We don't have the time.'

'You agreed if she told you who was in the car, you'd give her protection.'

'And we will. When I have them in.'

'They've already threatened her. You are not putting my daughter in danger. She needs protection now!'

'It's not just yours in danger.' Drummond stood. 'It's everyone's. I had a fifteen-year-old boy in the morgue two weeks ago.' He snatched the file, flicked it open, and withdrew a photo. He slapped it on the table. A gangly youth with ash-blond hair and a cheeky grin, dressed in a baseball top and holding a bat, stared out at them. '*Fifteen.*'

The youth's features blurred into a smudge mixture of sunburn skin with two hazel blobs framed with mousey hair.

'You've taken this long. A few more months won't hurt,' Theo said.

'Like hell. It will harm those families who lose their children. It will hurt the friends who see their buddies die before their eyes. It will damage this community. These vermin poison the future of this community to line their greedy pockets.'

'No, Drummond. Sorry, but no.' Theo stomped towards the door.

In another life, if Maemm and Theo had left together, she might have lived as the English did. Her vision cleared to see the photo. So young. So full of life. They could have been neighbours.

'I'm not asking her to sneak around or wear a wire.' Drummond dropped his voice to a soft plea. 'Just keep her eyes and ears open. I promise I'll get her all the protection she needs if it goes to trial.'

'If whoever's in charge works out she's helping you, you'll be fishing her out of a bin.'

Drummond hoisted his belt up over his belly and let out a heavy sigh. 'Okay. It was worth a shot.'

'Yes.' She hardly recognised her own voice. It seemed disembodied from herself. A firm, rational tone.

'No, Hannah. No.' Theo reached to take hold of her, but she turned away. With a finger, she traced the youth's face. Another life cut down long before its time. Another family thrown into the abyss of grief. Another mother who would count the birthdays, never see their child grow up. Forever tormented, like Mrs Stoltzfus.

She rose from her chair, her legs wobbling and her heart pounding, whether from sitting so long or nerves did not matter. She steadied herself, pressing her fingertips against the wall. She had secured her freedom.

The youth's cheeky grin suddenly looked more like a plea. A plea for this to end. Nobody would be safe, yet she had a way to end it and give freedom to those who most needed it if she dared. A calm determination descended upon her mind. 'Yes. I will help you.'

Theo stared at her, bewildered. 'Why?'

'For the families.'

Chapter 16

'LET ME GET you a phone,' Theo insisted as they turned into the country lane that led to home, the beating rain and the rubbery squeak of his windshield wipers filling the car. 'You can call for help if things kick off.'

Hannah shook her head decisively.

'But I've seen lots of Amish youths with them in town.'

'Sol would suspect something. He knows I keep to the ways of our community.' She paused. 'Must we tell them everything? I would have thought the less Maemm and the others know the better.'

'Normally I would agree, but this way you can still go to the gatherings and work – it could be months before an arrest is made, and you said you promised to stop come Easter.'

'Please do not tell Maemm and Grandfather about Sol's threat – they will worry more than enough as it is.'

Theo sighed. 'Okay. I'd feel better if you had a phone.'

Hannah forced a smile. Anxiety etched his face, creating deep lines across his forehead and around his mouth, aging him beyond his years.

He truly cares. Her smile grew bigger and tender. 'Next you will tell me to have a gun.'

'Never. Not on Amish soil.' A faint smile appeared fleetingly.

Hannah opened the glove compartment. Empty except for some business cards and a pair of leather gloves. 'You must've carried one as a police officer.'

'Yes, back then. I'm a lawyer nowadays, remember.'

She remembered his promise to get a colleague to represent her.

'Of course. Sorry. Long day.' She stifled a yawn, noting the dashboard clock read three p.m. Interview over, she and Theo had grabbed a bite to eat and returned to the station to go through her statement. She never wanted to see or smell it again. Her dress stank of stale air.

'Drummond's going to make sure the undercover cop working at the Stoltzfus's café keeps a close eye on you. Her name's Pat Rosewood. Five foot ten, medium build, cropped grey hair – not that you will see it under her kapp. Don't approach her, though; you might blow her cover.'

Hannah recalled the tall, athletic server with the tuft of grey hair who had bumped into her the day she had lunch with Theo. 'You know her?'

'We worked together – years ago,' Theo replied. 'We could do with someone in town nearby. Can you think of anyone?'

'I'll be fine. God will protect me.'

Theo blew out his cheeks and increased the car's speed.

Later, changed and thawing out by the kitchen stove, she listened to Theo's request for Barney to leave, citing family only.

'I delivered Barney. He is like a son and brother to us.' Maemm clasped her hands and tilted her head with a firm gaze fixed on Theo, who seemed reassured.

Theo explained the plan to the others, omitting Drummond's disclosure about the police surveillance and the wider operation underway. Drummond had insisted it remain confidential. Evan listened, leaning against the sink, hands in pockets, his initial sour-faced look at Theo's arrival giving way to a thoughtful one.

'And all of this is off the record.' Theo surveyed each of them without a trace of a smile. His eyes lingered on Barney.

Seated at his usual place at the table, Grandfather ruffled his beard. 'You must do what you believe is right, Hannah. It would seem God has a plan for you, though the bishop may need persuading about you helping the police. I won't rest until I know this is over.'

'Nor I,' Evan said.

Barney gave Hannah a reassuring smile. The memory of their argument in the field made her lower her gaze.

Maemm stretched her hand across the table to Hannah. 'Are you sure? I cannot help thinking of Grace.'

'That is why I have to do this, Maemm.'

'I will pray for you. For your safety.' Maemm gave Hannah's hand a gentle squeeze.

'What if they find out? You could get hurt,' Barney said. His brow tensed, creating a deep line across the bridge of his nose. With it, she glimpsed the Barney of the field. Serious and thoughtful. The one who worried about her. *Sometimes you can be sooo blind,* Grace had teased. Was she? A flush rose to her cheeks as an oddly familiar heat simmered inside her. *Don't be silly. He is just being brotherly.*

'I'll be fine.' Touched by his concern, she gave him a bright smile despite her own fears. Good friends were a blessing. 'They want me to keep my eyes and ears open. Nothing more.'

'Why don't you have a phone?' Barney plucked his own from a coat pocket. 'Here.'

Hannah refused and explained why.

'Come to the post office if you're in trouble.' Barney held his phone up. 'I can call someone.'

'First sensible idea I've heard all day,' Theo said, tapping away on his phone.

'Evan...' Grandfather said, tilting his head at Theo.

Evan shifted from one stockinged foot to the other, not looking at anyone. He removed his hands from his pockets and coughed; Grandfather gave him an encouraging smile. 'I owe you an apology for... my outburst the other day.'

Theo paused. 'Thank you, Evan. I... I apologise for upsetting you.'

Evan's head jerked up, his eyes wide with surprise. 'Denki.'

'Denki,' Theo responded. His phone pinged, and he looked down at the screen.

'You will stay for supper?' Grandfather eased himself up as he motioned to Theo and Barney.

While Maemm and Hannah began to prepare a casserole, Theo and Grandfather disappeared into the living room and Evan settled down at the table, scribbling in a book. Occasionally, he would mutter and rip a page out before recommencing writing. Hannah half listened to Evan and Barney discussing the idea of a community centre and the meeting they would have with the bishop.

When Maemm called everyone for dinner, Hannah saw Theo go to his car carrying a large, square object wrapped in one of the small quilts used to cover the furniture. When he returned, holding his phone, he said, 'Hannah, may I take a photograph of you?'

A flurry of mixed emotions filled her. Why did he want a photo? He knew Amish people seldom allowed such a practice. At least when not on Rumspringa. 'Why?' she asked, removing her apron.

'I could say for a keepsake, but...'

'You are worried history will repeat itself?' Maemm asked.

'A passport might come in handy.' His gaze fell on Grandfather. 'With your permission?'

Grandfather returned the stare, then gave a small bob of his head with a heavy sigh.

Theo pointed to the bare wall by the dresser. 'Stand still. Don't smile. Look at me.'

Hannah concentrated on not smiling as he took the photograph. When he showed it to her, she grimaced at her solemn face and was in half a mind to ask him to take it once more, but Maemm bid everyone to the table.

'Come on, you big ox, let's get one of you.' Barney held up his phone at Evan, who was still scribbling in his pad. At first, he shook his head, but with encouragement, relented and stood for Barney to snap one.

After supper, Hannah walked Theo to his car, parked behind the buggy cut-out next to Barney's, where he opened the back door and retrieved a zippered folder, opened it, and handed it to her along with a pen. 'Sign here.'

She read her details entered in neat, clear handwriting and signed the form. 'I don't have a birth certificate or social security number to prove who I am.'

'Leave it with me. Barney is helping me sort the passports out. One perk of working in a post office.'

Hannah handed back the folder and pen.

'Your grandfather is right. You are brave, Hannah.' He dropped the folder on the rear seat and shut the car door. 'Please, don't do anything to raise their suspicions.'

'Well, your arrival has raised mine.'

Theo paused, giving her a curious stare.

'Why did you come back?' she asked.

'I figured it was time. You would be old enough, I hoped, to understand.'

Her mind went back to the police interview and his banter with Drummond. 'Is Theo your real name?'

'Shrewd guess, young lady.' He rested his arms on the doorframe. 'It has been for the past twenty-odd years.'

It was her turn to look curious.

'I can't tell you anymore, Hannah. Everything else is true.'

'What was my aunt Ruth like?' The query popped into her mind and out of her mouth, bypassing her sensibilities.

'Ruth?' Theo tapped the door. 'Why do you ask?'

Hannah paused, not sure what to say. 'I never met her. Grandfather and Maemm rarely mention her. I get the impression she is our black sheep in the family.'

Theo grinned. 'Ruth was, as they say, a free spirit, but not a black sheep.'

'Do you know why she left?'

All the softness in his face disappeared. 'That's a question for your maemm, though I doubt if she would welcome it. Best to let sleeping dogs lie.' He stared past her to the house, where Barney stood on the porch watching them. 'Looks like you've got your own guard dog there.'

'Yes, he is a good friend.'

He gave a dry smile as he climbed into the Nissan and drove off, swinging right and disappearing into the dark towards town.

Boots scuffled on the dirt behind her, and she turned to see Barney coming out of the house.. She folded her arms and resisted the impulse to stop him.

He fiddled with his hat's trim as he approached. 'I am sorry we argued, Hannah. I did not mean to upset you.'

A small smile rose to her face as the tension ebbed away. 'You were being a... good friend.' She took a little step forward.

He remained still and sombre. 'I am and always will be your friend. Please be careful.'

She got a wave and the tiniest of smiles as he got into his car and drove off.

Hannah viewed the home of her childhood. Through the kitchen window, Maemm stood at the sink, washing dishes. Grandfather wiped a plate. Above the kitchen, Evan's bedroom light shone through his curtains. Studying, she suspected. A dark, velvet-blue sky formed a backdrop behind the house, and a cool breeze warned her of the frosty night to come, yet a glowing warmth spread right through her. All around her, people cared for her. Encircled her with their love. An oasis – one she would need to sustain her in the testing times ahead as she trod between two worlds.

Chapter 17

ETTING OFF THE bus the next Wednesday, Hannah willed herself not to glance over the road to the Stoltzfus's café. Her eyes disobeyed her, and she gazed at the familiar, crimson-painted building with its empty hanging baskets. The new server walked out carrying the grey welcome board with its drawing of a white plate with a knife and fork on either side. As Grace had done each morning. The tall woman smoothed her white apron over her Amish dress. From under her kapp, the nib of a grey widow's peak poked out. Hannah averted her gaze and headed to the cycle shop.

Drummond had been clear in his instructions. She should not contact Rosewood. If they suspected she was in trouble, Rosewood would come to the shop and ask her for a pair of Shimano 100 brake levers. When Hannah pointed out that the shop did not sell them anymore, he released a knowing smile and told her that was correct. Rosewood would be able to warn her and get out fast.

She approached the shop, registering a blue convertible in the parking place normally occupied by Sol's Dodge.

'Welcome back,' Sol greeted her with a grin. 'I've missed you. Especially as I've had to do all the work.'

His greeting came easily, as if nothing had happened. So that was how he wanted it to be. Hannah gritted her teeth and tried to ignore all the uncharitable words in her mind. With a fixed smile, she waited for him to walk out from the counter, and hurried to the safety of the till. 'I am sure you coped, Sol.' She removed her cloak and set about checking the logbook with the repairs booked in and the hired bikes booked out for the day. 'Is that your car outside? The convertible?'

He grinned. Her hunch had been correct. He leaned over the counter, one eye on the staff door. 'You good, Hannah? Everything okay?'

Hannah pretended to study the open book in front of her.

'They dropped the charges?'

'Yes,' she replied. *Don't tell them anything.* Another of Drummond's instructions.

'Knew they would.'

Pursing her lips, she focused on the page.

'You're sore with me, aren't you? About Evan,' Sol said.

She didn't trust herself to speak. She held the counter's edge. What did he expect?

'I'm sorry. I panicked.' Sol kept his voice low. 'I didn't mean it. Honest. You know I'd never hurt anyone, especially you. Besides, that big ox could probably punch me into the next state.'

She wanted to believe him. For everything to return to how it was. When he issued the threat, standing staring down at her, his face hard as stone, it had seemed like someone else, not the Sol she knew. Yet he had done it. Put himself before anyone else. Even her.

She had never noticed the nicotine-yellow discolouring of his teeth. Or how close together his eyes were. She blinked away the rush of tears filling her eyes. Sol shifted under her gaze and released a lazy smile. The image of him wide-eyed and jumpy outside the station, desperate not to be noticed, reminded her of the skinny, baggy-clothed child she had known years. Somewhere underneath that easy-going, worldly manner, her childhood friend Solomon existed. A friend in need. And he was a friend. Not always a good one, she was learning. Just a friend. As she faced him, a calm reality filled her, not the usual jitterbug flutters or prickly heat to her cheeks. She looked at him standing there, waiting for some feeling to replace this calm stillness. Had she mistaken infatuation for something more? If so, what then was love? Would she recognise it if ever it came?

Lightheaded, as though she had stepped off a fairground ride, she lifted her gaze at the chime of the bell. A sheepish-looking Danny shuffled in, removing his bobble hat. She turned from Sol and greeted him. 'What brings you here?'

'Morning.' He shoved the hat in his duffle coat pocket and ambled over to her. 'Got a nephew. He's into all this cycling. Got all the gear. So, I thought I'd get him something.' He looked around the shop. 'Maybe a cycling top or a pair of shorts.'

'What size is he?' Sol stepped over to the clothes racks on the right side.

'About your build,' Danny replied.

'Medium.' Sol lifted a bright orange cycle top with long black sleeves.

'That'll do.'

Sam came in from the office and paused at the end of the counter, eyeing Hannah and Danny as Sol bagged the top.

A worried frown creased Danny's face as he paid. 'You okay, Hannah?'

'She's fine.'

'I wasn't asking you, punk.' Danny's eyes narrowed as he gave Sol an icy stare. 'This is about young Grace, God rest her soul. Terrible. Terrible.'

Hannah bowed her head in reply.

'Sam, you old miser, give Hannah here some compassionate leave?'

'I'm fine, Danny. Thank you.'

'Say, when's the last time Sam gave you a raise? Don't work her too hard...' Danny pointed a finger at Sam, '... you hear?'

When Danny had left, Sam pointed at Sol. 'You best not cause any more trouble,' he growled. 'Never pull a stunt like that again. You do, and you're on your own. Got it?'

As a shudder rippled through Sol's body, Drummond's observation of Hannah's friendship with Sol came back to her. She braced herself as Sam turned to her and said, 'You helped Sol. You did good.'

He dug a hand into his trouser pocket, pulled out a wad of cash, and placed several ten-dollar bills on the counter. 'Treat yourself. Consider it a bonus – don't expect this every time you help dumbo here out.'

Hannah stared at the bills in astonishment. He was giving her money? Sam, who kept the heating lower than a fridge in winter?

'Go on. Take it. You're a good worker, Hannah.'

She placed her hand over the bills and slid them closer. Was it a bribe to buy her silence?

Sam made for the staff door and slammed it behind him. Outside, Aaron's wagon rolled past a parked car as Blue plodded along the street. Sol let out a low, long whistle. 'What are you going to treat yourself to?' He eyed the bundle of bills with envy.

Hannah slipped the money inside one of her navy skirt's pockets. She would hide the bills in her suitcase under the bed until she decided. She doubted if Grandfather or Maemm would welcome it, given the circumstances, and lying was a sin.

'Why is Sam upset with you?' She studied him closely, waiting for the slightest reaction on his face. 'You didn't get caught.'

He glanced in the direction of the back office and made to talk before snapping his mouth shut at the bell announcing a young couple entering. 'Do your job, Hannah, and don't ask questions.' He sucked in his bottom lip, one eye on the staff door.

He's afraid of Sam. Why? The thought dropped into her consciousness, dissolving all her pent-up anger. Was Sam the boss? Drummond wanted someone on the inside. Had he told her everything? Probably not, which meant if he was right about the shop being a cover, she would have to be careful not to draw attention to herself or it could be her hand flying out a car window, or worse. Perhaps she should resign on the pretext of ending her Rumspringa. No. That wouldn't work; lots of Amish women worked in town afterwards. *Grace.* She was doing this for Grace. Stay calm and act normal.

'Sol!' Sam hollered from the office, and Sol hunched his shoulders and hurried away.

Hannah made a mental note of the conversation. At lunchtime, she would buy a notebook to take home. She would write conversations, record visitors and deliveries. Perhaps it would be a good idea to record the number of boxes, she concluded, remembering the discrepancy in the delivery in January. During the day, she would do her job as everyone had instructed. When the time came, she would be ready.

Chapter 18

RAIN SPLATTERED BARNEY's green Volvo windows as dusk replaced the last rays of daylight over the fields. Hannah pulled the flap of her cloak tight to keep out the evening's chill and stifled a yawn. She had worked three days, not five. Tomorrow would be Saturday. There would be chores to do, but she might squeeze a little longer in bed than on a workday.

'Sorry, the heating takes a while to kick in.' Barney eyed her through the rearview mirror as they drove past the Millers' farm.

'It's disrespectful to turn up at the bishop's home in a car and not a buggy,' Evan grumbled from the front passenger seat.

'Not as much as turning up like a wet weasel in your open one,' Barney replied. 'You should have got a closed buggy. Much more versatile and comfortable in bad weather.'

Evan grunted and stared out the window.

Hannah knew the source of Evan's churlish behaviour. Worry. All week he had hidden in his room, preparing for this meeting. The steering committee had agreed for representatives and the bishop to meet them this Friday to discuss the idea of a community centre, with no commitment to agreeing. Persuading them to do so was their job.

Ten minutes later, Barney parked outside an oblong house with a porch and two front doors. 'Which one?' Evan turned up his jacket collar as they walked along the garden path.

Barney pointed to the white door straight ahead. 'The other's the boyfriend door.'

How does he know which door is which? She decided not to ask, but the question nagged at her. Had he visited one of the bishop's daughters after dark, as was the custom in courtship, and left before the house awoke? The 'boyfriend' door provided privacy for the couple and a warning to those upstairs to stay where they were. Popular as it was to have them, Hannah knew any suitor of hers would have to enter via the rear kitchen door of the old farmhouse because it was built several generations ago, before the practice of installing two entrances became the norm.

Mrs Fisher, the bishop's wife, greeted them. Her welcoming smile faded when Barney stepped aside for Hannah to enter. Mrs Fisher smoothed down her starched white apron and frowned. 'They were expecting two of you.'

'We wanted representation from our sisters, and Hannah has helped us with Evan's idea.'

Barney got a polite smile as she led them to a door on the left of the hallway. A bronchial rattle-fire of coughing filtered down the hall. Through the half-open kitchen door Hannah spotted the bishop's youngest child, Abigail, half-bent and shuddering from the fit that seized her. Mrs Fisher halted and turned, blocking the girl from view.

Inside the gaslit room, three men sat on a long sofa by a roaring log fire. Hannah recognised Old Man Elijah and Mr King. Between them,

Mr Stoltzfus sat, hands clasped and resting on his thighs; her heart lurched upon seeing him. Evan had not mentioned he would attend the meeting. When she tried to catch her brother's eye with an accusing stare, he avoided her gaze. She tilted her head in greeting.

Barney gestured to a tall black dining chair, and Hannah sat down opposite Mr King, getting an affable smile. Her heart gave several rapid beats as she noticed Aaron in the corner – was he friend or foe? As deacon, he would have to follow the bishop's lead, yet they were old friends.

Once the greetings were over and Mrs Fisher had entered with a tray laden with tea, homemade pumpkin brownies, and snowball biscuits, Bishop Fisher got up from his study desk, littered with papers and books, and eased himself into the wingback armchair to the right of the sofa. He linked his hands and rested them on the small hill of his stomach. No one spoke as he closed his eyes and tilted his head down so his beard brushed his chest. Everyone followed suit and lowered their heads as he prayed.

Hannah prayed too. For Evan not to get tongue-tied or obstreperous, as he did when challenged. For Barney to keep his jokes to a minimum and be serious for a change. Lastly, for her to remember to be careful with her choice of words.

'Now, you wish to put a proposal to us.' Bishop Fisher directed his gaze at Evan and Barney. 'Have you prayed about this matter?'

'Yes, every day.' Evan bobbed his head up and down in earnest.

Bishop Fisher focused on Barney. 'I have meditated long and hard on it.' Barney sat straight-backed and without a trace of his usual cheery grin.

For all of five seconds, the mischievous voice inside Hannah teased.

The bishop's gaze moved to her. 'I have taken my brother's lead,' she responded in a demure tone.

All three men opposite dipped their heads in unison as the room fell silent. Aaron kept his eyes on the space between the sofa and the chairs. As a trainee deacon, his presence was one of observer, and later he would need to survive the bishop's grilling on what he had assessed from the meeting.

'And your proposal is?' Bishop Fisher leaned back in his armchair.

Evan explained their plan to create a place where young people could socialise alone as an alternative to the Singings or the large gatherings or going to the English part of town.

'But isn't that what Rumspringa is for?' Mr King stroked his beard. 'Doing those things you cannot do once baptised? Isn't it a time of experimentation and exploration?'

'With respect, Mr King...' Barney shifted in his seat, '... not all exploration or experimentation is good.'

Mr King raised an eyebrow.

Bishop Fisher unclasped his hands. 'I see no reason to stop young people from going to these places. They must learn to resist temptation and learn to be attentive to the Lord.'

'You will remember the Leechburg case. Many Amish died from drugs they got at gatherings,' Barney said, avoiding Mr Stoltzfus's gaze.

'And it's still happening.' Evan's well-intended words dropped like a bale of hay off a wagon. A reddish tinge rose to Mr Stoltzfus's cheeks, and Hannah lowered her gaze.

'Never happened in my day,' Old Man Elijah piped up. Up close, his head appeared to pop out from his shoulders like a wooden doll with no neck, his long beard streaked with mud-brown amidst the steel-grey and white strands. He lifted a trembling, pallid, bony finger.

'Be strong in the Lord and in his mighty power. Put on the full armour of God, so that you can take your stand against the devil's schemes.'

'Amen,' everyone said.

'Evan is right. We cannot simply bury our heads. One death is too many,' Barney said, his face grave. 'And several young people have left in recent times. I fear someone is helping them leave.'

Aaron leaned forward, arms on his legs, and glanced over to Barney. 'Choosing to stay or leave is an individual choice. We cannot make people stay if they wish to leave.'

The small furrow at the top of Barney's nose creased as the elders nodded their agreement at Aaron's words. If they didn't turn this around, they would be out of the door before the tea was cold.

'It's not only the young who are troubled about these matters.' Hannah kept her tone soft, hoping her intervention would give Evan and Barney time to think of something to say. 'It is a worrying time for families, especially parents.'

'True. The possibility of your child leaving the community is a great worry,' Mr King sighed.

Hannah glanced at Barney. The anxious expression in his eyes mirrored her own thoughts.

'With respect...' Barney cleared his throat, '... it's not totally about leaving. As recent events have shown, it's the... exposure to harmful outside influences on impressionable young people.'

Hannah smiled inwardly at his carefully chosen words.

'Hmm... knowing they are safe – but able to still 'run about' – would ease many a parent's anxiety,' Mr Stoltzfus said in a sad, reflective tone.

Hannah kept her gaze on her lap, willing Barney on.

'What's wrong with what we've got?' Old Man Elijah raised both arms. 'Parents supervise groups in their homes. We've got fine young men like Aaron here who organise games in the summer. There are the Singings. Seems to me there's more than enough choice. Those who don't want to go, don't go. Let them run off to these gatherings.'

'What do you say, Aaron?' Bishop Fisher's question hung in the air as an astonished Aaron stared at him. 'Well?'

Aaron cleared his throat loudly. Stalling for time, Hannah decided as he reached for a glass on the piano and took a sip. 'Those who wish to push the boundaries, as the English say, can do so. For those who prefer not to, we have activities. I don't see how any good can come from providing another choice. One that could do exactly what you, Barney, say we don't want – encourage people to leave our community.'

'But that's the whole point.' Evan thumped his knee with a clenched hand. 'To do the opposite and help them see how good our lives are.'

'We don't need the centre. We already have an alternative to the gatherings in the Singings and games nights,' Aaron argued back.

'Hear, hear.' Old Man Elijah beamed.

Aaron lowered his head once more and fell silent. Hannah squeezed her hands together, fighting the urge to speak. Of all the people she hoped might champion their cause, Aaron would be top of her list. Another error of judgement. First Sol. Now Aaron.

Barney sat back in his chair. 'With respect, while I have no issues with our English neighbours, we, as Amish, have always maintained that a simple life, without many of the things they take for granted, ensures a good and godly life. It is this life that keeps us close to our Lord.'

Hannah listened, tilting her head, a surprised smile tugging at her mouth as Barney shifted his focus to each of the elders, then to Aaron, till he stared directly at the bishop opposite him. 'If our young people are leaving, it is because they are either dissatisfied with what they see as the 'backwardness' of our lifestyle or want the 'freedom' of the English life. Evan is right. We need to show them that being Amish is not boring or backward.'

She bit her bottom lip, surprised at the swell of pride filling her at Barney's elegant and persuasive arguments. Thank goodness Evan had remained quiet and let Barney handle them.

Mr King curled a finger around his beard and twirled it, deep in thought. 'My understanding is, what you are suggesting is that it would be good to have an option for gatherings similar to the English ones, so those youngsters who might not wish to take part in the existing organised activities but could be susceptible to the more unsavoury side of modern life have a safer environment in which to socialise informally together.'

The temptation to get up and hug Mr King swept through Hannah. Barney's shoulders relaxed as he smiled, while Evan nodded vigorously.

'What activities will you run at this centre?' Mr King asked.

'Dances. Film nights. Volleyball, maybe roller skating,' Evan rattled off. 'Some classes – vocational, to help those who leave school but are too young to work in the factories.'

'We would carry out a survey asking young people what activities they would like to be held,' Barney explained.

Old Man Elijah's forehead creased. 'Will women go?'

All three of them dipped their heads, and Old Man Elijah harrumphed.

'How much money have you raised?' Mr King inquired.

Evan darted a look at Barney and Hannah.

'Do you know how much this venture will cost to build and run?' he probed, not unkindly.

'Not yet,' Hannah confessed. 'We wanted to wait until we had spoken to you.'

Mr King gave her a smile, which reminded her of the one Grandfather used when she was little and pretending to know more than she did.

'Who would supervise those attending?' Bishop Fisher asked.

'Er, well, we were going to encourage those attending to help run the centre and its activities. People like Aaron.' Barney's hopeful smile sailed across the room in Aaron's direction. Aaron seemed more interested in picking at a loose thread on his trousers.

'Competitive sports breed competition and pride,' Old Man Elijah muttered, shaking a finger, 'and there is plenty of work for the younger ones at home or farming.'

'Agreed.' Bishop Fisher raised a hand.

Hannah shot Barney a worried expression. They were losing the advantage his speech had gained. As though reading her thoughts, Barney stared helplessly back.

'As I have said,' Bishop Fisher said, 'Rumspringa is time for our young to learn to resist temptation, just as our Lord did in the desert. It is part of becoming adult. It seems to me that you merely wish to prevent them from learning this with your idea.' He held up a hand at Evan, who had opened his mouth to speak. 'I fear there are more fundamental matters to address than organising a volleyball game.'

He raised a finger and ticked off each question he fired at them. Did they have the money to fund the construction of the centre? Where would they build it? Did they have drawings of the building for them to see? Who would fund the running costs and help maintain it? How would they ensure activities planned didn't encourage competitiveness? What measures would they take to ensure no inappropriate behaviour occurred between the young boys and girls?

Each question weighed on the idea like a slab of stone, flattening it under their heaviness. Evan's cheeks turned from a light flush to brick red. Hannah darted a warning glance at Barney, who kept an eagle eye on him.

An uneasy silence fell when the bishop finished speaking.

'They are good questions, Bishop,' Barney said in a slow, serious tone. 'Perhaps we could do some more research? Come back with some plans and costs?'

Well done, Barney. Buy us time.

Evan gripped his knees, turning his knuckles white.

The bishop shook his head, one hand rubbing his chin. Old Man Elijah gave a dismissive sigh.

'I can see the merit of you coming back to us with evidence of the need or a coherent plan of action and some money behind it,' Mr King said, lifting his shoulders slightly. 'I have to say, there is much to be argued for things staying as they are, given the range of leisure opportunities already available.'

'I'm sorry.' The bishop's grave tone matched his expression. 'What you are asking could lead to a breeding ground of competitiveness with all those sports. Too much investment of time and energy to set up and run, on top of all the existing activities we hold, which by your own admission you see continuing. I've heard of these centres the English have. Far too much freedom permitted.' He sighed. 'There will be no community centre. That is our decision.'

Evan flung an arm out. 'But—'

'That is our decision, Evan Bieler.' Bishop Fisher leaned forward. 'If you want to do something on your own, pray. Pray for them to have the strength to resist the evil of the world and be obedient to the Lord.'

'Amen.' This time, neither Hannah nor the others joined in.

'And you...' Bishop Fisher gestured to Barney, '... have you decided on your future, young man? Do you intend to be baptised this Easter?'

Barney stood up slowly, taking his hat from the chair's spindle top. 'I will meditate upon it, Bishop, long and hard.'

Hannah turned swiftly away from the others and hid the bemused grin that burst across her face. They may not have left with what they desired, but thanks to Barney's swift thinking and reasoning, they had at least put up a good argument. One they might still be able to return to, despite the bishop's objections, especially if the drugs gang were exposed. They could use it as evidence of the 'harmful influences' Mr King had referred to.

The rain had turned to a drizzle when they left. Hannah sidestepped a puddle on the path by the gate.

A violent wobble vibrated through the Volvo as Evan slammed the front door shut, a deep scowl etched on his beet-red face. 'Patronising—'

'Evan.' Barney thumbed to the backseat, where Hannah sat. Evan banged his fist on the dashboard.

'Easy.'

'I wanted something for Grace. For her to be remembered by.' Hannah flinched at the pain in Evan's words. 'They made us look like idiots.'

'No, we made ourselves look like idiots.' Barney turned the ignition on and the wipers screeched across the windscreen, mirroring

Hannah's own sense of frustration. 'We went in there with pipe dreams and no plan.'

Should she compliment him? It would have been worse and the meeting shorter if he had not put such a good argument across. 'You spoke well.'

Barney mumbled a half-hearted thankyou back.

Evan whacked his palm against the dashboard again. Hannah tried to imagine the look on Barney's face at his precious car being treated so brutally.

'Pity about Aaron,' Barney remarked. 'Was counting on him.'

'Snake in the grass,' Evan spat out.

'That's because...' Hannah stopped herself from saying what she thought. Of course Aaron would be against it. If the young went to the centre rather than the gatherings where the drugs were sold, he'd lose out. *If he is involved in the gang.*

'Because what?' Barney glanced at her in the mirror.

'He wouldn't want to upset the bishop or elders.'

'Weasel,' Evan grumbled.

For once, she agreed with Evan. Aaron delivered meat to the butcher's several times a week. Meat was stored in the icehouse. He and Levi had just come out of the icehouse when Levi gave him the envelope. What was in it? Money? What for? How easy would it be for Aaron to fetch and deliver without being noticed? What if they stored other things in the icehouse besides meat?

'You okay, Hannah?' Barney's voice broke her thoughts. 'Don't fret. We'll come up with a plan.'

Did Barney know something? Hannah looked out of the window, her eyes trailing the dim outline of the fields against the backdrop of the falling evening sky. She replayed the conversation in her head. The expressions on the men's faces. Mr Stoltzfus, quiet and withdrawn. Old Man Elijah, all doom and gloom. The bishop, pragmatic. Mr King – only he had understood why the centre was important. The what and the how they could work out, but unless others understood why, it would be hard to convince people of its viability. If they could make others see the need for it, perhaps Evan's wish would come true.

'What about a petition?' she suggested.

Evan threw her a look of contempt.

'Not a bad idea,' Barney mused. 'What did you have in mind?'

'If we get enough people to support the idea, the committee will have to reconsider.'

'What's the point?' Evan snapped.

'The point is Grace.'

Evan twisted round violently.

'Come on, not in the car.' Barney's alarmed glance worried Hannah.

'How come you're all of a sudden concerned for Grace now that she's dead?' Evan said.

'Evan, settle down!' Barney shouted. The Volvo swerved as it rounded a corner. The rain was increasing again; it splattered onto the windscreen faster than the wipers could keep up with.

The swerve threw Hannah sideways. 'You're not the only one who misses her, Evan. She was my best friend.'

'Well, you should have thought about that before you killed her.' Evan lunged at her. Hannah gasped as he caught Barney's face side on and the car lurched off the road.

She spotted the iron gate in the headlights as the Volvo careered towards it. She clamped her eyes shut and braced for impact.

She catapulted forward. The seat belt snapped against her, and she slammed back into the seat.

It took her a moment to accept she was still alive. Still in one piece, still in the back of Barney's car.

'Hannah?' Barney groaned as he clambered out, cold air sweeping in. A second blast, closer and colder, stole her breath as he opened her door. 'Are you hurt?'

'No,' she slurred, dazed.

Barney leant over her, unbuckling her belt and helping her out. Groggy and a little unsteady on her feet, she glanced around.

'Evan?' She stared at the front of the car. The passenger door hung open, blood on its handle and on the dashboard. She staggered round to the hood and stared frantically ahead. 'Where's he gone?'

Barney stared down the pitch-black wet lane. 'Wait. I've got a torch.' He fetched a large yellow torch from the trunk. 'It's battery operated.'

'I didn't think the Holy Spirit powered it.' Hannah scanned the lit section of tarmac ahead.

A zigzag trail of blood droplets dotted the surface. They followed them for a couple of hundred feet before the torch's glare fell on a dark, hunched figure kneeling in the middle of the lane. The retching sound and smell of half-digested food mixed with liquid made Hannah's nose wrinkle.

When he had stopped vomiting, he sat back on his heels and turned to them, his face a ghoulish grey-green and damp from tears. Hannah waited for Barney to step forward and comfort his friend. When he remained still, she glared at him, only to receive a nudge in the ribs. 'He's your brother, big sis.'

Sometimes she could throttle Barney. Deep down, she knew he spoke the truth. Evan was her little brother. Half a foot taller and several feet broader, with his simple view of life. Black was black and white was white. Grey was not something he either understood or cared for. Grief? What colour was grief to him?

With tentative steps, she approached him and slowly, she crouched by him and gazed into his eyes; bewildered, diluted with tears and filled with pain. He stared blankly at her. His usually firm jaw and hard features had taken on a slack, blank expression. Blood matted his bangs. She pushed his hair back to see a deep cut above his hairline.

'Why? Why didn't you stop her?' he asked as she retrieved a hanky from her pocket and pressed it against the wound.

'Evan...' Barney's words floated over them, '... you know she tried to get Grace to the hospital. Grace's death is not her fault. Hold on to that.'

A low sound, like a pitiful whimper, escaped Evan. He crunched up into a ball and rocked back and forth. She dropped the hanky, slipped an arm around his back, and held him. He lifted his head to face her, tears rolling down his sodden face. 'She told me,' he stammered between gasps of air, 'that after her baptism, she'd walk with me.' Another deep, wrenching sob. 'She was all I wanted. All.' His fingers squeezed her arm as though hanging onto a lifeboat. 'Help me, Hannah. Help me, sister.'

'I'm here. I'm here.'

She strained to hear what he was trying to say between his muffled sobs. 'I'm sorry. I'm so sorry.'

She kissed his forehead and brushed some strands of damp hair aside. Their tears mingled. United in their grief and their love. As she knelt there, Hannah realised how much she had missed those around her in her quest to find her own life. What kind of life would hers be without her family? Without her boneheaded younger brother? All this time, she had thought only of herself. In her wake, others lay injured. Walking wounded surrounded her. Mr and Mrs Stoltzfus. Grandfather, Maemm, and Theo. Evan.

Cradling Evan's crumpled figure, Hannah remembered the interview and her agreement to help the police. She had told Theo the families were the reason. Now she had another reason. Something she knew would sustain her, whatever befell her. It was not just Grace's and the other young people's families who needed to find peace, but the whole of Birchwood.

Chapter 19

February 2024

AS HANNAH RODE the bus into work over the next couple of weeks, she noticed the damp starkness of January giving way to February with its overcast early morning clouds which cleared to brighter days. The brightness and slightly warmer temperatures faded with the daylight, and her bones ached with cold as evening descended and darkness shrouded the world once more. She longed to see the fields green and full of lambs sprinting about.

She had changed her woollen cloak for a buttoned raincoat reserved for the above-zero mornings and wet showers February brought. A shawl sufficed during the day in the shop. Each evening, she would write snippets of conversations and the number of boxes Stubby delivered. She carried on with her deliveries to Falcon's, her awareness of their true purpose making her anxious to complete the task quickly. She invariably bumped into someone during the trips. She monitored the icehouse, using her lunch break to walk down the back lane, along the open space behind the row of shops. In her notebook, she jotted down Aaron's deliveries when she spotted his wagon outside the butcher's. She did a similar walk after work, noting the quiet times and the lack of security cameras. Recording everything she saw.

With each week, Friday evenings came, and with them, Sol. He would park his convertible halfway up the lane and wait for her. When he dropped her off, he would cruise the car with the lights off and stop a few feet from the driveway. Once, such covert actions would have sent her into a dizzy spin of excitement, but nowadays relief swept through her as she walked up the driveway lit by the familiar solitary porch lamp. Being free from whatever had held her in awe of him gave her the stamina to be in his company and gather what information she could from their outings.

'Do you have to go, Hannah?' Maemm asked the next Friday, standing in the kitchen doorway as Hannah descended the stairs in jeans and a hoodie. 'Those jeans are far too tight.'

A pang of guilt pricked Hannah's heart at the anxious way Maemm nibbled her bottom lip and twisted the towel in her hands. 'It will not be forever, Maemm.'

'You have decided?' The tone of hopefulness was unmistakable.

Hannah shook her head. 'But I will, as we agreed, and I promise you will know first.'

'The bishop will need to know soon. The baptism classes will start in March,' Maemm said.

Hannah looked away. The chimes of the wall clock striking nine p.m. allowed her to remain silent – no one ever spoke over them; Stefan had always insisted they stop and listen.

'And young Sol,' Maemm sighed. 'I do not trust him. There are rumours about him and Sam.'

'You have nothing to fear, Maemm. He gives people lifts.' She didn't look up to see Maemm's reaction; she knew neither of them believed her answer.

He had threatened her. He had put his own needs before hers and Grace's. He could not be trusted. Whatever she had felt for him had withered like a weed in the hot sun. Going with him was a means to gathering information. Information she could pass on to Drummond.

She closed the door, buttoned her coat, and walked down the road at a leisurely pace, half listening for the rev of his car. The scruffy urchin she had known as a child kept coming back to her and, with it, a nagging desire to see the good in him. An old memory came to her: Sol riding his rickety bike at breakneck speed from the schoolhouse to avoid the bigger boys chasing him down. The one who always escaped.

What if he wanted out? If he wanted to escape and live his own life? With friends like Levi and a bully of a brother, what chance did he have? Had his threat been born out of fear of what Sam might do rather than of getting caught? If it was, could she abandon him? A friend in need, so the saying went. She stopped. Yes, that was all he was. A childhood friend. Like Barney. Only she knew which one she should trust.

If only the police would act. No matter how much information she passed on to Theo for Drummond, it was never enough for the police to make a move. She asked herself if she was wasting her time. Evidence. Hard evidence, Theo kept telling her. They needed to discover where the drugs were stored. She reasoned that hanging out with Sol might be the way to get it.

Tonight, she and Sol did not have far to travel. Just to the outskirts of town, to the Field of Sorrows. When she glanced over to it, she noticed the cross had gone. 'Shame it didn't work out,' Sol remarked, parking the convertible on the roadside. 'Some utopia.'

'Utopia?'

'It means ideal. Paradise.' He paused, holding the door open. 'In the early eighties, some English guy and a local Amish decided to set up the commune here, believing they could get the English and Amish to live together rather than side by side. They were trying to create a utopia.'

'And several members died in a fire, including the English man and his girlfriend.' Hannah stared at the field surrounded by forest. 'I remember Grandfather telling us it was the biggest loss of life at Birchwood, hence the annual vigil.'

'Caused by a fight after locals came to find out if the hippies had stolen cattle and chickens. Some things never change,' Sol sighed.

'What happened to the Amish man?'

'No idea. Ran off, according to gossip.'

Hannah remained silent. She thought of the shops and how the owners and shoppers mingled among them day after day. It was a meeting point of sorts, she supposed. Live and let live seemed to be the motto of the town.

Bunting and gaslights hung from trees lining the field's edges, and loud music blared out from the upper end as they strolled through the latch gate carrying their rucksacks with refreshments. Soft drinks and snacks in hers, beer in Sol's. They made their way through the groups milling around to the dance area. Previously, the sight of chatting, laughing partygoers and the sound of rock music would have filled her with excitement. Tonight, it served as a reminder of all that could go wrong. Sol popped pills but did not offer her any. Aware of the silence between them, Hannah searched her mind for small talk, gazing at the couples mingling.

'So, are we dating?' The question torpedoed out of her mouth before she could think, and she scrunched her eyes shut. Why did she say that?

Sol stopped dead and stared blankly at her.

'Well, we keep going to these gatherings.'

Perhaps it was not such a stupid question after all. The scales may have fallen from her eyes, but she needed Sol to believe nothing had changed. That she was still infatuated with him, in the hope he would not suspect her.

To their right, sitting on the grass, a couple appeared to be glued by the lips, arms entwined.

'No, Hannah. We are not dating.' Sol scratched his goatee and cocked his hat back. 'We're friends, like always.'

'Oh.'

He pointed to the couple. 'That's dating – English style.'

A flame of heat rose to Hannah's cheeks. She averted her gaze as the opening chords to a heavy metal song boomed across the field.

What was she doing here? Sober and clean while others got drunk and high? *Grace*, came the answer. *You are here for Grace and the others.* The thought calmed her, giving her strength. If only she could find some evidence. Something that would make Drummond end the uncertainty of the past weeks.

'You okay, Han?' Sol peered at her, his warm eyes half closed. 'I didn't mean to upset you. You and me friends?'

She lifted her right hand, little finger raised. With a grin, Sol grasped it and wriggled it with his own.

They hit the dance floor with a vengeance. It helped while away the time, and she could scout around, noting things to jot down in her pad when home. Sobriety had its advantages. As the hours passed, the gaslights glowed more brightly, giving a ghostly glow to the space. A glassy-eyed Amish youth staggered towards them and high-fived Sol. 'You got stuff?' he asked, falling into step with them.

Sol shook his head. The youth pulled his hand from a pocket and opened it. In his palm, he held a small plastic bag with a pink pill no bigger than an aspirin. 'You should try this. Want some? The best.'

Again, Sol refused, and Hannah with him. The youth wandered off to a group past the bales stacked around the dance area.

'Why didn't you give him some of yours?' Hannah asked, unfastening her rucksack and getting a can of Coke.

'Told you I only have it for private use.' He flipped the lid off his beer bottle, his face darkening. She followed his gaze to a huddle by some bales farther up.

'I see Levi's still dealing.' She watched Levi, head bent, long hair falling over his collar, surrounded by several younger men and girls. Nearby, a bullish, crew-cropped man stood watching the goings-on. 'Looks like he found a new partner.'

'Who cares?' Sol dropped his pack on the ground by a bale and held out a hand to her. 'Come on, friend. Let's party some more.'

She did her best to join in. She danced and laughed at Sol's antics and jokes. When another dancer bumped into her, she masked her irritation with a smile at their clumsiness. Midnight came and went. As she jostled among the bodies surrounding her, the fresh evening air grew pungent with the smell of sweat and smoke.

Another wasted evening, she concluded, glancing at her watch. Two a.m. She was about to suggest calling it a night when someone crashed into her. The Amish youth fell to his knees, retching. She leaned over him. One whiff of the stench of something strong and acidic mixed with undigested food made her stomach muscles flex and heave in protest. Sol dragged her off as the youth moaned and collapsed on his side. His body twitched and twisted, coiling snake-like on the ground. 'He's dying!' a girl shrilled.

'Nah, just a bad trip,' a calm male voice chipped in.

'Someone help him!'

Sol knelt and examined the youth's sweaty, pale face.

Another retching sound filled Hannah's ears. A petite girl nearby bent over, clutching her stomach.

'We've gotta get out of here.' Sol grabbed her hand and the bags and pushed through the crowd. As they reached the nearest gap between the bales, he cursed as a man with bleached-blond hair barged into him: Levi, bolting out to the road. Sol dragged Hannah towards the woods, away from the commotion, away from the lights.

All around them, bodies writhed on the ground; dozens of them. Their cries and moans filled the air as they rolled on the grass while others scattered in all directions. 'We have to help.' Hannah yanked her hand free from Sol's hold.

'And get arrested? Don't be stupid.' Sol gestured towards the flashing lights and sirens approaching from the direction of the road. 'This isn't food poisoning. Trust me.'

The convoy of police cars and ambulances drew alongside the fields. Partygoers dispersed in all directions, a small group running past them and into the woods.

'Police!' an authoritative voice bellowed through a speaker. 'Stop. Police.'

'Han!' Sol shouted.

A girl in a crop top and shorts, screaming hysterically, ran towards them. Two uniforms caught her and manhandled her to the vans. Without a second glance, Hannah dashed to the trees in Sol's wake, her eyes struggling to adjust to the diminishing light. The new moon's beams splintered through the dense foliage. She concentrated on the flash of Sol's watch glinting in the air as he raced in front, his arms wide, weaving his way into the depths. Dank air hit the back of her dry throat as she panted hard to keep up with him. A stitch seared through her left side. Ahead, Sol disappeared, and Hannah skidded to a stop and spun around, panic filling her as she searched for him in the dark.

Sol's shout came from her right, and she stumbled down a bank towards him; he reached out and pulled her down beside him, a finger on his lips. Her rapid heartbeat thudded in her ears as they listened for the snap of twigs and watched for the glow of torches. By the time she regained control of her breathing, the sirens had stopped, along with the music.

'What's happened? How did they get ill?' Hannah hissed at Sol as he rummaged in his bag, aided by a little moonlight.

He lifted a small pill bottle and a bag with a dry, grass-like substance, then sprang up and threw them into the clump of bushes nearby. 'Dud gear. My guess is someone sold it at the gathering.'

'Levi?' A picture of him deep in conversation with the huddled group came to her.

'I don't know, and I'm not hanging around to find out. Let's get you home.'

They threaded through the woods parallel to the main road till they reached the roundabout linking the Amish side with the town centre. A streetlamp lit the sidewalk ahead, and Hannah gave an inward sigh of relief. On the other side of the roundabout was the mile-long road to the lane leading home.

Her legs had turned to logs, heavy and stiff. The mile seemed never-ending as they trudged along the roadside. Maemm would be beside herself. Hannah stuffed her icy hands into her hoodie's pouch.

'Wait up.' Sol barred her way, gazing ahead. The blood drained from Hannah's face as she followed his stare. A sedan idled at a junction, waiting for an oncoming vehicle to pass. *The Toyota.* A violent jerk shot through her, and she steadied herself, locking her gaze on the vehicle. What was it doing here?

The Toyota edged forward, the driver checking both ways, his blond locks tossing from side to side. *Levi.* Sol groaned. Levi spotted them, frowning, and Hannah stepped back, her body half shielded by Sol's.

The car door swung open, and Levi jumped out, reaching behind his back. The headlights of the other vehicle swept over the Toyota, confirming its colouring and Hannah's fears. Levi swung round and dropped his arms to his sides, facing the approaching car.

'Put your hood up,' Sol ordered, 'and keep your head down.'

Instinctively, Hannah did the opposite and stared straight into the beam, which blinded her. She blinked frantically to dispel the black spots blocking her vision. After a few seconds, she recognised it to be a patrol car by its white body and dark stripes.

It pulled to a stop, and Levi retreated to the Toyota as two uniformed officers got out. 'You're up early,' one of them commented with a curious expression.

Hannah rubbed her eyes, trying to rid herself of the spots.

'Been in town.' Sol flashed a good-natured grin.

'The gathering?'

Hannah blinked once more and froze. There stood the officers who had arrested her the night of Grace's death. Nearest to her stood the one who had cuffed her. This time, she noticed he wore a gun holstered in his belt.

'No. For a pizza.' Sol kept his voice light and polite.

The officer shifted his gaze to Hannah. 'At two in the morning?'

The other officer came round the front of the car. 'Bags. Both of you.'

Hannah spotted the Toyota reversing into the shadows.

'Several young people are in the hospital,' the first officer said, checking both rucksacks in turn. 'Having their stomachs pumped of whatever they took. Nasty.'

An eerie sense of being watched crept through Hannah, and she gazed past the patrol car. Across the road, the Toyota nudged forward enough for her to see Levi... and another man. The bullish guy from earlier. A tightness wrapped itself around her chest and squeezed hard.

The officer turned and gave a backward glance at the Toyota. 'Friends of yours?'

They shook their heads.

The officer turned his attention back to them. 'Miss, would you like a lift home?'

Hannah made to speak. 'I—'

'That's so kind of you, officer,' Sol broke in, all smiles. 'I'd be mighty pleased if you gave my friend here a lift. In fact, it'd be the saving of me. Her brother will have my hide for keeping her out so late.'

Sol beckoned Hannah to the car, and she slipped inside, grateful for its warmth and security and for Sol's quick thinking. What if she had been on her own? What if the police had not turned up? She shuddered.

'You'd best get in too, young man.' The officer looked at the Toyota as he held open the door. Hannah moved along the backseat for Sol, and the familiar odd flutters rose inside her as he brushed his arm against her.

As the patrol car drove off and passed the Toyota, Hannah saw Levi sullenly glaring at her. The image of his sharp-boned face with its tight-jawed snarl stayed with her all the way home. She bit her lip to prevent herself from smiling as hope surged through her body. She had not wasted her lunchtime walkabouts. Her attending the gatherings had not been in vain. It had been Levi who had given Grace the pill that caused her to become ill. Levi who had sold drugs at the Field of Sorrows. She riffled through her memories: dropping by the icehouse so Levi could get some 'beer', Aaron and Levi talking outside it.

She knew where the vital evidence Drummond needed was.

Chapter 20

AFTER WORK THE following Monday, Hannah sat in the café, sipping her milky coffee at a leisurely pace while she waited for Falcon's to close along with the other shops. Most stayed open until six o'clock, hoping to catch office and factory staff going home. All except Glick's. Rain or shine, at five o'clock the window shutters came down.

'Hannah, we close at six,' Izzy announced from behind the counter, pointing to the large clock on the wall opposite Hannah's table. Five minutes to six. Sally, the temp, whom Hannah knew to be Officer Rosewood, was stacking the chairs onto the other tables, ready to sweep the floor. She drained her cup and put her hands into the pockets of her coat. Her fingers curled around the objects nestled inside. The previous evening, she had waited until all the shops were closed and the backyards deserted before inspecting the icehouse door's padlock. She had been around Evan and Grandfather long enough to know breaking a padlock required a few basic tools and deft hands, not brawn. A tension wrench and a straightened-out paper clip would be sufficient and easy to find lying about in the workshop or house.

She headed for the café door. Mr Falcon, grandson of the original butcher, was climbing into the closed buggy with 'Falcon's' on its side. Hannah bid the server goodbye and stepped out into the twilight.

She headed to the crossroads. With no cars in sight, she strolled over to the other side to avoid detection by Izzy and the server. She scouted the street for anyone watching and, confident no one could see her, darted down the narrow side alley out of sight of the street. At the other end, she halted and scanned the open backyards. Empty. Despite knowing there were none, she still scanned the roofs for CCTV. Amish retailers' believed in human goodness and Sam was too mean to spend money. Glancing both ways in case someone appeared, she sprinted to the icehouse and pulled the tools from her pocket. She inserted the tension wrench into the padlock, slipped the paper clip in above the wrench, and pushed it down the barrel. A few wriggles with a firm grip on the wrench and a bit of serious prayer, and the lock yielded. Later, she would pray for forgiveness.

Inside, shelves lined the side and back walls, stacked with large slabs of ice. Above them, meat hooks were screwed into the beams. Noting there was no lighting, she lifted a toolbox near the door and wedged it so the door was ajar enough to let in moonlight for her to see the fresh meat packed among blocks of ice. A heavy, sweet smell filled the shed.

She sniffed closer. Sickly sweet. Not the bloody juices she had expected. In between each set of ice blocks, chunks of meat lay piled on top of each other while legs and carcasses hung from the hooks. She shivered, not sure if it was the gruesome sight or the freezing temperature that made her bones shake.

Starting on the left side of the door, Hannah searched the gaps.

Cautiously, she lifted the chunks of frozen meat or pushed aside those
hanging to inspect the area behind and below. Nothing. She turned her
attention to the back wall shelving, covered from top to bottom by
plastic sheeting. She grabbed a small stepladder and mounted it,
reaching the top shelf and flinging the sheet back. It slipped to the
floor. Nearby was an assortment of objects: a thermostat, a siphon
tube, some long-handled spoons, a rolled-up cable, and a large metal
pot. She got down and viewed the rest. A row of two-gallon buckets
with lids and large bottles with dark brown liquid fermenting stood on
the floor. To her right, wedged behind one of the plastic buckets, stood
a small black briefcase. She pulled it out. A combination lock held the
two spring locks; she tried a couple of combinations, to no avail.

She fished out the paper clip and picked the locks. One by one, they
yielded, and she flipped the lid open. Inside lay a stamp machine,
passport-size photos, and two bundles held together with a rubber
band. An assortment of passports, birth certificates, and a thick roll of
dollars. No drugs. But Levi had collected the rucksack with drugs from
the icehouse. They had to be here some place.

Hannah sat back, taking in the scene. Another pungent whiff of the
rich, sweet, meaty smell filled her senses. '*Barley*?' The word slipped
out before she realised the shed had darkened.

A rough hand clamped over her mouth as her arm was forced
behind her back. 'Scream and I will hurt you,' Levi whispered in her
ear.

He hoisted her up and pushed her flat against the shelving. She
winced as the upper shelf smacked her chest. 'Beer. You're selling beer.'

He spun her around and gripped her upper arms.

'Levi, I promise I won't say anything. It's just beer.'

'You're right, you won't. You shouldn't have opened the case,

Hannah.' His eyes glinted hard as steel. 'You know how cold it gets in here? Especially at night? If you're not dead by morning, you'll be suffering from hypothermia.' He grabbed a length of rope lying on a shelf and tied her wrists together. Holding the cord, he yanked it as he stepped away from the shelving, forcing her to stagger forward. 'Everyone's gone home, Hannah. No one will know till morning. When I arrive tomorrow, if you're still alive, we'll go for a drive. Either way, you'll be history. Problem. Solution.'

Hannah pulled away from him, but he merely yanked the rope tighter, forcing her towards him.

'My family, they'll search for me.' Even as the words left her, Hannah knew how pathetic they sounded. It would be too late by then. Her ribs crushed the air out of her, leaving a heavy weight inside.

'As they do for lots of young Amish who vanish...' Levi sneered, '... but are never found or reported to the police, thankfully. They'll search, but they won't find you. Dead or alive. Everyone knows you people leave to go English, and what with Grace dead, I doubt if it would surprise anyone you'd fled – being involved with her death.'

A stab of remorse mixed with a maddening frustration welled up inside her. The urge to kick him would have won if it hadn't been for her need to maintain her balance.

With one hand, he shoved her backwards into a row of hanging carcasses and prodded her until she stood under a metal hook suspended from a beam. He picked up the cord and looped it over the hook, then he pulled the dangling end, taking up the slack. Hannah's arms rose till she stood with her shoes just scraping the floor.

'Passports. You're selling forged passports and birth certificates.'

'You'd be amazed at how much your kind will pay for them. Especially the young, the unhappily married, or the hustler who needs to get out fast,' he replied, stepping behind her, taking the excess part of the rope with him. She felt a jolt as he gave it a tug, and a sharp pain pulled at her shoulder muscles as he tied the cord around a wall hook several times.

All her arguments against him leaving her to freeze to death had bounced off him. What could make him reconsider? Give her time to figure a way out? Drugs. He sold drugs. Sam. The parcels. 'The dealers you work for. Do they know about this?' She jerked her head to the case with the fake passports. He ceased winding the rope for a moment. It gave her the answer, even though she could not see him. 'They don't know what you are doing. They're not getting any profit from it. I wonder what they would do if they found out?'

Levi stepped out from behind her. 'And they are not going to. Not from you.' He snapped the case shut and pushed it into its hiding place, covering it with the sheet. He sauntered to the door and stopped by the toolbox.

'You are right, not from me.' Her mind raced, throwing the single thought like a spear at him. 'From you.'

He halted and turned, letting out a snigger.

'If I disappear, it will get reported to the police and they will investigate.'

He took a step back towards her, the smug look gone.

'Theo, the English man, my... uncle, he used to be a police officer. He'll report it.'

'So?'

From the depths of her mind, Hannah scrambled for the hook she needed. 'They'll draw attention to the shops. Whoever you work for won't like that. The police already suspect there's a connection.'

In one step, Levi reached her and grabbed her face, squeezing her cheeks, forcing her jaw open.

'They kept asking me about the parcels I bring to the butchers.'

'What did you tell them?'

'Nothing.' Pain burned through her cheekbones as he pressed harder. 'Honest.'

Levi loosened his grip. She gasped and flexed her jaw to ease the pain. 'If they think I have been carrying for whoever you work for, then I disappear...'

He dropped his hand and stepped back, eyeing her as though mulling her words over. Was it enough? Would he think again?

He cocked his head to one side, the perplexed expression gone and, in its place, a bullish smile. 'Nice try, Hannah. You really think you're that important. Seems to me I will do people a favour getting rid of the weak link.'

He turned and retraced his steps. Fear tinged with frustration blazed through her. She kicked out, making her whole body writhe. '*You're* the weak link. They'll work it out. The police will know you killed me and why, Levi, and it will be more than your pathetic side business they'll be wanting to interview you about. What will those men do when they find out all the police attention was because of you wanting to keep your little secret? What do you think they will feel about you when they have so much to lose? At least my death will be quick.'

Levi hunched down by the toolbox and retrieved a brand-new padlock. As he straightened, she caught his face lit by the early evening moonlight, his smooth brow marked with a crease. Hope tensed her body then turned to lead when he stepped outside and, with a bang, the door shut, plunging her into darkness.

In the blackness, a helpless sob escaped her. All her brave words, threats, taunts had failed. She wriggled and twisted round to the wall. Her eyes slowly adjusted to the eerie light created by the shiny, wet surfaces of the ice blocks. Levi had wrapped the cord several times around the hook with the end tucked in the loops.

Icy air hit the back of her throat. Hours would pass before anyone would come. She stretched her feet so her toes reached the floor, trying to steady her body. The less exertion, the more energy she could conserve. A burning sensation spread from her shoulders along the underside of her upper arms as the weight of her body strained them. The rope cut into the thin layer of flesh covering her wrists.

Frustration, anger, and self-pity seethed inside her. What good was knowing who might have killed Grace when she could not tell anyone? This was not how she envisaged dying. Young, single, in an icehouse. Would anyone believe Levi's lies? She had accidentally got locked in? Maybe he intended to come and remove all traces of evidence in the morning – including her body.

Cold bit her bones. All warmth and feeling ebbed out of her hands. Her eyelids grew heavy as her breath's icy vapours faded. What was it people got when too cold? Think, Hannah. Stay awake. Hypo-something. Hypothermia. H-Y-P-O.

The rattle and click of the padlock and the brief pale flash of evening light through the door snapped Hannah out of her drowsy state. She blinked, focusing her gaze on the solid shape in front of her. *Levi.*

He stood watching her shiver, the chatter of her teeth filling the icehouse.

He reached inside his fleece jacket and pulled out a Swiss Army Knife. He didn't bother to catch or support her as he cut the rope and she dropped, her knees crashing against the stone floor. He grabbed her tied hands and cut them free. She rubbed her arms frantically to revitalise them, willing warmth into her body. 'Why?' she stammered.

'I'm not a killer. I had no choice that night. It was either Grace or me.' He stared down at her. 'And, I don't want to end up being mincemeat.' He bent down and grabbed one of her hands and inspected the red marks around her wrist. 'They're superficial. Keep them covered.' He let go and lifted her chin. 'You so much as squeak a word about this and you'll be dead meat too, and not by me. Take my advice, steer clear of the two men who visit Sam. Got it?'

Her shiver increased to violent trembles as she looked at him twirling his blade.

She scrambled up blindly and stretched out a hand for something to steady herself on, letting out a small scream as she touched a slab of cold meat. Levi's snigger rang in her ears as she groped her way out of the icehouse and fled into the darkened yard, grateful for its cover.

The purr of a well-oiled car engine and crunch of wheels made her slow down. She glanced over her shoulder and saw a Mercedes approaching from further down the back street; it was identical to the one that had parked outside the shop. She froze. Was it the two men who visited? Too relieved to be free, she dismissed the urge to stop to find out.

The icehouse door banged shut. Behind her, Levi's boots smacked against the tarmac. Had he changed his mind? She fought the crippling fear that threatened to paralyse her. Ahead, the faint shape of the alley opening loomed. She glanced over her shoulder and saw Levi by the icehouse, his knife blade glinting in the moonlight. She shot across the unlit yard to the alley, searching for a glimmer of the main street lighting, and her boot hit a paved stone, knocking her off balance and throwing her towards the ground.

Instead of falling, she collided with a soft, warm body. Firm, gentle hands enfolded her. Faint with relief, Hannah buried her face against her rescuer's chest, tears spilling down her cheeks. A few seconds later, she broke away and looked up at the Amish apparition in front of her. There, through the blur of her tears, stood the café's temporary server.

THE WOMAN PLACED the steaming mug of hot chocolate on the table in front of Hannah and sat down opposite. Hannah cradled it, letting the heat thaw her hands.

'I saw you slipping into the alley. My name is Pat Rosewood.' She had hustled Hannah into the café using her key. A nervous Izzy had peeped over the banister when they entered and retreated, satisfied with Pat's tale of needing to discuss buying a bike for a relative with Hannah.

'How did you know where I was?' Hannah asked, plucking a marshmallow from the mountain Pat had topped her drink with. In her mouth, it melted, releasing its sugary coating.

'It wasn't hard to figure out what you were doing. What did you find?'

'How do you know I found anything?' Hannah stammered as she inspected her wrists. The angry, red welts throbbed as if her skin had been scorched with a branding iron.

'Because you wouldn't have been strung up like a hare otherwise.'

'You saw me?'

Pat nodded. 'And Levi loafing around. Then going back in. Which is why I didn't come and get you straight away.'

Hannah pulled her coat sleeves down over her wrists. 'He's selling bootleg alcohol and fake passports. The passports are for Amish who want to leave.'

'We've been aware of Levi helping your people to leave for a while.'

Hannah gave her arms a vigorous rub, willing the icy blood in her veins to warm up. 'He also works for the drugs ring you are after.'

'How do you figure that?' Pat said.

'He gave Grace the bad drugs. The night she died, we stopped on the way to the gathering at the Millers' barn for him to go to the icehouse and get the rucksack with the drugs in it.'

'The one the police picked up when you were arrested?'

Hannah nodded. 'And he was dealing in the field where everyone got sick. I saw several of the people he sold to get ill.'

'Coincidence?'

'I didn't see anyone else dealing.'

'Because they are more discreet.' Pat sipped her drink. 'Believe me, he's not alone.'

'Will Drummond arrest Levi?' Hannah asked.

'Not for me to say,' Pat said. 'That's for Drummond to decide. Levi's going to be spooked by your snooping around.'

Hannah smarted at her put-down.

'We can't pull off a good, old-fashioned break in and seize some of this stuff because he will think you've grassed him up and will come after you. And this time, I doubt if he will entertain any thought of letting you go. We must leave things as they are – for now.' Pat took a marshmallow from her drink and ate it.

'I've told you what is happening.'

'No, you've given us a piece of the jigsaw we're piecing together.'

'So, Levi gets off for trying to kill me?'

'No.' Pat gave her a terse stare. 'When the police are done, they'll arrest and charge him.'

'*If* you arrest him.' Levi's snarling face filled her vision and sent a tremor through her whole body.

'Trust me. We don't know what we don't know and, at the moment, that's not a lot.' Pat drained her mug and placed it on the table. 'One thing I do know is if we pull him in, we might as well put an ad in the paper for whoever is masterminding this entire operation.'

'Don't tell me you need more evidence.'

Pat gave a reluctant nod. 'Hard evidence. All we have is circumstantial.'

'I'll get it – I can help you.'

'Not anymore.'

Hannah threw her hands up in exasperation. 'Why?'

'Because you've blown your cover.'

Chapter 21

A FTER THE CRASH, a subdued Evan went about his work during the day and holed up in his bedroom at night. Occasionally, Barney visited, and afterwards Hannah would make him a hot drink and sit with him a while.

He turned up the evening after her failed break in, as she was thinking about how she would have frozen to death in the icehouse had her desperate words not penetrated Levi's skin of self-preservation. Only that had saved her, not any shred of humanity within him. The thought sent chills through her, despite sitting close to the heated stove. She thought of the Mercedes. Whoever those men were, Levi's warning was clear. Were they the ones he worked for, or the rival gang Drummond had referred to as being responsible for the severed hand? Why did they appear? Had they seen her?

As she and Barney sat on opposite sides of the stove, Hannah longed to unburden herself. With his usual calm, pragmatic manner, Barney would assess the whole situation and, united, they might make sense of what to do next. If the drugs were not kept in the icehouse, where were they?

'You're worrying about the police. What will they do?' He sipped from his mug.

No. She could not tell him. Too many people had suffered because of her selfishness. She carried on sewing a button on a work shirt of Evan's as Barney drank.

'Have you decided, Hannah?' Barney stretched his legs out and crossed them at the ankles. He leaned back in the chair as he warmed himself.

Hannah shook her head. 'And you?'

Barney let out a long, low sigh and placed his empty mug on the stovetop. 'Danny's offered me the lease of the post office. He has no family here. He wants me to take it over.'

'Will you?' Hannah paused in her sewing.

Barney turned his hands over, looking at them. 'I prefer working with my hands.'

'It would be a good living.'

He tilted his head, concurring.

'He's young to retire.' Hannah toyed with the needle. 'Late Forties?'

'Don't know how he can afford it. The post office is doing well, but not that well. He's single. Seldom takes a holiday and is so tight, he squeaks.'

A light giggle escaped Hannah as she threaded the needle through the button. Danny had no family. Barney knew how to run the business. 'Why not take him up on the offer? You're no farmer, Barney.'

'I know, but... stuck indoors all day? Pen pushing?' He made a face. 'And you, Hannah? You like working in town?'

She concentrated on stitching.

'You could still work there. More women are working after baptism.'

'If their families or husbands allow it.'

'Hmm.' Barney folded his legs and peered out of the window. 'A good husband would. If it made his wife content. "Happy wife, happy life", my daett says.'

'Not all think like you.'

The standing lamp dimmed, its light flickering over Barney's face. Yes, he would make a good husband for someone one day. Her needle pierced the shirt and pricked one of her fingers, and she sucked on it, pushing all thoughts of marriage aside.

'Did Grace love Evan?' he asked.

Button attached, Hannah knotted the thread and bit on it. 'Why do you ask?' She swirled the contents of her half-full mug, hoping for clues about how best to answer his question.

'She seemed pretty keen on Levi.'

The statement hung like an unpleasant smell in the room. 'I believe she could see a future with Evan, unlike with Levi.'

Barney held her gaze. The clock in the hallway chimed eight times.

Please don't push this, Barney, a little voice pleaded inside her. *Let sleeping dogs lie.*

'Evan is like a brother to me.' He lowered his head. 'Maybe now he will come to terms with her death and be free to be truly happy.'

Hannah closed her eyes, not trusting herself to speak. He knew the truth. Grace would never have made Evan happy.

After he had left, she lay in bed with the eiderdown tucked under her chin to keep out the chilly evening breeze. With a start, she sat, clasping the blanket tight to her body, dazed by the odd thought that came to her. For the first time in all the years she had known Barney, she wished she knew who he lived his life for these days.

Chapter 22

BY FRIDAY, SHE was glad to shut the shop door, knowing she had two complete days away from the town. Levi had maintained his distance, though his looks were mean whenever she passed the butcher's or saw him in the street.

Drummond, as predicted, refused to continue to use her as a source of information, much to everybody's relief but her own. Undeterred, she decided to continue to go to the gatherings and keep making her daily notes. To help Levi believe he had scared her into silence, she had let it be known this would be her last summer working at Glick's on the pretext of preparing for the Amish way of life for good.

When she entered the kitchen dressed to go out, Maemm's strained expression as she sat sewing the child's log-cabin patchwork on her lap made Hannah wish she could stay and spend the evening quilting like old times.

The kitchen door opened behind her, and Evan ambled in. Hannah did a double take. Gone were the plain clothes he normally wore. She marvelled at the tall, athletic figure dressed in belted blue jeans and a blue shirt under a woollen navy jacket. Only his straw-blond hair stayed the same, although the layers thinning out the thick mop around his ears and the back of his neck softened the pudding bowl's razor-sharp edges. She inspected him with a dry smile.

Evan shuffled, burying his hands in the jacket pockets. 'Barney suggested it might help me blend in. So we can be on hand if you need us.'

'But I'm no longer helping the police,' Hannah said.

'Sister, trouble follows you like a hungry dog,' he replied.

Maemm's face lit up with gratitude. Hannah pursed her lips to prevent the grin pulling at them. Somewhere deep inside, a warm swell of tenderness filled her.

Evan tugged the collar of his shirt and scratched his neck.

'Thank you, little big brother.'

She got a gruff 'okay' back.

The night turned out uneventful. Levi was nowhere to be seen, and Sol kept his distance, seeing Barney and Evan with her.

When they returned after midnight, Maemm and Theo were talking in the kitchen. She waited until everyone had gone to bed and crept downstairs, still dressed, carrying her notebook. 'I need to talk to you,' she whispered to Theo, who was heading to the front door.

'And I you, young lady.' Theo let go of the door handle and retraced his steps to the kitchen, placing his cap on the table.

Hannah lit the gas lamp, reducing the glow to form a small circle on the table, and sat down. He stared down at her, his face expressionless. 'What in the world were you doing poking around the icehouse?' He kept his agitated voice low and sat down opposite her. 'Never do that again, Hannah.'

'But I said I would help.' Hannah placed the notebook between them.

'Yes, by using your eyes and ears.' Theo leaned into the pool of light. 'Not playing detective. Your maemm would fry me alive if anything happened to you.'

'But it all fits. The clues were there.' Hannah showed Theo her notes.

Theo barely glanced at them. 'All Levi is doing, as Drummond has told you, is bootlegging and forging passports for young Amish, not for international terrorists or criminals.'

She bit her lip, resisting the urge to snap back.

'What about those who were hospitalised and had their stomachs pumped after the gathering at the Field of Sorrows? What if it happens again?'

'Patience, Hannah.' He thumbed through the book.

She watched him flick through the pages, stopping to read at various points. Would they be sitting having this conversation if she had found drugs there?

'Leave it to the professionals. Keep your head down. Your cover's blown. Don't attract attention. If Levi does change his mind and mentions you to his bosses, they'll keep a close watch on you.' Theo handed the book back to her.

'You think he will?'

'No, otherwise he's going to have a hard time explaining why he let you go.'

'When will the police do something?'

'All in good time.' Theo fiddled with his hat.

Hannah eyed him. 'You know something. What has Drummond told you?'

'Nothing.'

'But you're his friend.'

'Friend, not colleague,' Theo said. 'He won't tell me, or anyone, anything that might jeopardise his investigation.'

'So why did he tell us all those things when I was interviewed last time?'

'To gain your cooperation.' He leant back, shaking his head. 'And you fell for it.'

An unpleasant taste filled her mouth. A pawn in a game of cat and mouse.

'Your notes will be useful when the time comes,' he said, tapping the book gently.

'If.'

'When,' Theo said. 'Given what you found, it's certain the drugs are stashed in the area.'

'The cycle shop?' she ventured. A guarded look crossed Theo's face, and she matched his stare. 'What about the deliveries to the cycle shop? You could put drugs inside the boxes.'

Theo blew out a heavy sigh. 'Highway patrol has stopped and searched the delivery van. Nothing.'

'Unlucky?'

He arched an eyebrow.

'But Drummond thought I delivered drugs to Falcon's.'

'Unwittingly,' Theo said.

'Then the drugs must be on the shop's premises.'

'Not necessarily.'

'Why doesn't Drummond get a search warrant? Then you'll have the evidence you need.'

'Like I said, he's not sharing his plans.' Theo sighed. 'And rightly so.'

She cradled the book in her hands and resisted the temptation to throw it in the dying embers of the stove's firebox.

'Hannah,' Theo said softly, 'they are selling drugs all over the place. Good and bad drugs. Birchwood is one of several towns with dealers working. To be honest, even if Sam does keep some there, whoever is behind the operation will find another place. I know Drummond – he wants to get the key operators. To cut the supply. That's why he's not rushing in.' He picked up his hat. 'When he is ready, he will make his move. Meanwhile, you serve customers and continue jotting down your observations. Nothing more.'

Hannah stroked the book. What was the point of writing all those silly bits and pieces? Without hard evidence of the drugs being stored on the premises, the book itself would never bring those responsible for Grace's death and all the other senseless deaths to justice. She owed it to their loved ones. To the Stoltzfus family.

Would these faceless people ever be held accountable for the misery they had caused? The thought of not knowing gnawed at her insides, accompanied by another equally painful realisation. Theo was right. Maemm would be heartbroken if something befell her. She must put aside her impatience and let the police handle this. What else could she do?

Chapter 23

THROUGHOUT THE NEXT week, Hannah kept her head low. She stopped writing in her notebook at night, despite Theo's assurances that the information would be useful. Useful for what? With no sign of progress, she doubted history would repeat itself with any arrests, as had happened with the Leechburgs. She took the notebook with her to work, not wanting its contents to be discovered by anyone at home.

On Wednesday afternoon, Sol disappeared into the repair shed to work on two bikes to be collected at the weekend. Hannah busied herself reviewing the stock on the floor. They would need more cycling shorts and were down to the last speedometer. During a quiet spell, she rummaged under the counter and found the stock ledger. One box of shorts and another of parts, including speedometers, were in the storeroom. She would have to wait for Sol to come back and ask him to fetch them. She picked up a clothing catalogue lying near the till; beautiful, healthy people in bright lycra smiled up at her. She went back to the ledger and noted the last delivery date, scanning the figures in the itemised stock columns. From her bag under the counter, she retrieved her notebook and compared her own numbers of the previous week's deliveries to those entered in the ledger. Two boxes less than her totals. A familiar discrepancy, she noted dryly.

She shoved the notebook under the counter as the familiar van pulled up, closely followed by the silver-grey Mercedes with blacked-out windows and shiny hubcaps. She resumed her station by the till, staring through one of the front windows.

Stubby jumped out of the van. The two suits, this time in sunglasses, marched in and straight through to the office. Their appearance catapulted her heart hard against her rib cage, and blood pounded in her ears. Had they come for her?

The staff door banged open. To her immense relief, the men reappeared with Sam.

Stubby wheeled his trolley in, stacked high with boxes. The short man fired a sentence or two in Spanish at Sam who, in his crumpled suit, stayed quiet for once, his eyebrows knitted together tightly. 'Is Sol out back?' he asked as he turned to go back the way he came. 'I'll go give him my keys.' From his belt, he unclipped a bunch of keys.

The taller man laid a hand on Sam's shoulder and squeezed so hard Hannah could see his finger sinking into Sam's flesh. He held out his free hand. 'Keys.'

Sam's hand shook so hard the keys jangled as he gave them to the man.

'You give to Sol.' To her astonishment, the man threw the set of keys at her, and she caught them by one key's long stem.

'Take the boxes to the store,' the taller man ordered Stubby.

Stubby held out the clipboard, and Sam scribbled on it. The trolley wheels squeaked as Stubby, to her surprised, wheeled all four boxes into the back. Why did he not leave some on the shop floor as normal?

'Tell Sol he needs to lock up,' Sam grunted at her as the men marched him through the front door. Hannah watched through the window as the taller of the two shoved him into the back of the Mercedes. Giddy with relief, she let out a long, slow sigh and hastily straightened as Stubby returned and followed them.

Hannah stared down at the keys, a deep foreboding filling her. Sam had looked like a fox snared by huntsmen. She thought of alerting Sol but ditched the idea based on his record of going in the other direction of trouble. Barney? Theo? They would tell her to wait. Do nothing.

The keys weighed heavily in her hand. Evidence. Hard evidence to make a move, Pat Rosewood had said. What if the boxes were filled with drugs? A plan formed in her mind. She dropped the keys on the counter, grabbed the notebook and ledger again, and flicked back to the first entry in her notebook, finding the corresponding delivery in the ledger. She examined the next page and the one after that till she came to the previous week. None of the figures matched. Each time, she'd recorded more boxes than Sol had entered.

With Sam gone and Sol occupied, this might be her only chance.

What about Sam? It was her duty to help someone in need. Her hand hovered over the keys. Evidence. Hard evidence, and she could get it – if she could get to the storeroom undetected.

She stepped around the counter and crossed the shop floor, fumbling with the keys, searching for the one she knew from watching Sol lock up would secure the front door. She flipped the small notice with the shop's opening times over to CLOSED and hurried to the staff door.

To the left inside the corridor, the office door stood ajar. The desk inside the small, square room was littered with mugs, cigar butts in an overflowing ashtray, and a desktop computer. Through the window, she could see a filing cabinet next to the desk and a small trolley holding a printer. She hurried in and behind the desk, and pulled the drawers out. Papers, pens, bills. Old catalogues. She tried to open the filing cabinet. Locked. Why? She thought about trying to lever it open but decided if it did hold some drugs, there couldn't be much in there; the rest would be in the storeroom.

She rushed down the passage to the exit, pushed it open and peeped outside. The yard was clear. The repair shed door was shut, and through the small plastic screen window, Sol stood with his back to her, headphones on, working. She lifted a quick prayer and slipped down the back wall towards the storeroom.

She fought to regain command of her fingers, which had turned to jelly, and identify a key from the bunch she held. It took two attempts. The key with the longest stem slotted in the keyhole and turned. Opening the door wide enough for her slender frame to pass through, she darted inside and was plunged into pitch blackness as she closed it. She fumbled about for the light switch and paused. Could she turn it on? The bishop's face rose in front of her, his finger wagging firmly. *Get a grip,* a small voice reasoned. *You need light.* True, Hannah told herself, and it was for good reason. Her hand found something small and solid by the door. She flicked the switch and prayed for forgiveness.

She took in the layout. Shelving units stood on either side, rising a good foot above her own medium height but narrow enough for her to reach to the back. Beyond them, an assortment of large, oblong cardboard boxes labelled with GIANT, DAWES, and other brand names containing bikes for assembly stood with cycle racks and stands.

Sol would go into the shop soon; she had to be quick. She focused her attention on the shelving. Sol invariably checked the stock when he stored it after a delivery; the boxes he'd left loosely sealed were easy to pry open, peek into, and shut without undoing the flaps. She found a small ladder leaning against the unit on the far side and checked the boxes on the top shelf. Brake levers, pedal clips, seats. One by one, she searched the shelves, front and back, and found more stock. Handlebars, lights, bags, pedals, bells.

With frayed nerves from searching, she turned her attention to the bigger boxes and tried to lift the nearest one from its resting place, wedged against another. It was too heavy to contain anything but a bike. She pushed the ladder up to the remaining unit and inspected the boxes on the top shelf. Helmets, jackets, shoes. She got to the second-to-last shelf and, pulling open a box, spied cycling shorts packed inside.

A blaze of daylight suddenly fell, blinding her for a second, before a dark, solid mass blocked the doorway. 'What're you doing here?'

At Sol's sharp voice, Hannah wobbled on the ladder, one hand inside the box while the other gripped a rail. 'Shorts.' She held up a pair sealed in its plastic wrapping. 'We're low in the shop.'

'Out! Get down and out! Now.'

In a swift movement, Sol stepped to the ladder and grabbed her arm. She jumped down before losing her balance, still holding the shorts. Holding her tightly, he marched her out, switching off the light and banging the door closed.

Had he worked it out? Had Sam come back? The questions raced through her mind. She stumbled to keep up as he thundered to the exit door. Instead of going into the shop, he dragged her into the side alley and, once clear, he spun round, his fingers digging into her flesh. 'What in hell's name were you up to, Han? If Sam knew, he'd go ballistic.'

She held up the shorts weakly.

'Don't. I mean, don't ever, ever go in there.' Beads of sweat covered his face as he spoke.

'Why?'

'Never mind why.' He let go of her.

'You're frightened of Sam, and those men? The ones who drive the Mercedes?' She saw the wave of fear sweeping over his face.

He took her by the shoulders. 'Listen, I'm trying my best to protect you, Han, but you aren't helping.'

'Grace died because of them.'

'Shush.' He placed a finger to his lips. 'Will you quit your hollering? Those men who came in and took Sam – they're the ones to worry about. And if they get wind of you sniffing about...' His hands shook as he held her. 'Han, you did me a big favour with the police, and I've tried to do the same for you with those guys. They thought you told the cops about me and Levi, but I told them you didn't.'

He still cares. A little surge of hope filled her. If he still cared, he was worth trying to save.

'Han, Han, are you listening?' Sol's voice broke her thoughts. 'If they've taken Sam out for a chat, it means they're worried, and when those guys are worried, it's not good news.'

A chill ran down her spine. Just what had she got herself into? Had Levi told his boss about her? Did they believe Sol?

She stepped back. 'How did you know about them coming for Sam?'

'Stubby texted. We talk.' Sol wiped his face with the back of his hand. 'Oh, hell.' He grabbed her hand and headed back to the yard; she heard it before she saw it. The Mercedes. 'Keys.'

She passed them to him.

'Get inside.'

He pushed the exit door open, shoved her in and slammed it shut behind them. She raced down the corridor, and he overtook her, stumbling through the staff door. She dashed into the shop, stuffing the shorts under the counter as he unlocked the door, swinging the small card back to OPEN. By the till lay the stock ledger and, to her horror, on top of it, her notebook.

'Cops. Filth.' Sam barged in, spitting the words, the two men following. The bell was muffled by the door hitting a bike nearby. 'Second bust in two weeks. Who's feeding them info?'

Hannah kept her shaking hands below the counter and twisted her dress to help her stay calm. The book. If they had found the book...

The shorter of the two men cast Sol, who stood by the door, a distrustful glance.

'No way.' Sam clamped a cigar between his teeth. 'Not him.'

A tall, well-built Amish woman pushed the door open. Recognising her, Hannah instinctively opened her mouth.

'We're closed,' Sam barked.

'But I want a brake lever,' she demanded as Hannah clamped her mouth shut and swallowed her greeting.

The three men turned to Pat Rosewood, who stood patiently in the doorway. 'For my son.'

Hannah grabbed the ledger and her notebook, using the distraction to slide them under the counter. Quickly, she released the till drawer with its loud zing to appear busy. Sam threw her an irritated stare, and she summoned what she hoped passed for an apology to her face.

'Sorry.' Sol stepped in front of Rosewood, his back to the others. 'Not a good time, ma'am.'

'But I need a pair of Shimano GS 100 brake levers.'

A sledgehammer thumped against Hannah's heart. The code. The code to get out fast.

Sol glanced at the display of bike parts. 'We don't sell them.'

'But you're a cycle shop.' Pat pointed to the shop floor.

'They're obsolete.' Sol held the door open for her. 'Try eBay.'

With a tut-tut, she swished out of the shop. Sol locked it, flipping the OPEN sign over to CLOSED.

Hannah shuddered, an icy hand clutching her heart.

'Someone's gotta be snitching.' Sam chomped on his cigar, pacing the floor while the suits stood silent.

Hannah kept her head low as she rolled up all the dollar bills, twisted a rubber band over them and bent to place them inside the cloth money bag under the till, moving the spare bags over the books as she did so. She hoped none of them noticed her hands shaking. She scooped up a handful of coin bags and placed them on the counter. She would offer to bank the money; that would be a good enough excuse to leave.

All the while, the taller man watched her. He ran his fingers through the charcoal hair combed back from his olive-skinned face, his raven eyes preying on her like a hawk's. Sol followed his stare. The man didn't so much look at her, but through her. She tried to count a growing pile of cents before it toppled under her fingers, and inside, her mouth turned to wallpaper.

'Her.' The man flicked a ringed finger in her direction, a thick gold chain jangling on his wrist. 'She was in the car with you?' He held his gaze on her as he waited for Sol to answer.

Over the roar of her heartbeat in her ears, she heard Sol reply, 'Yes, but Jorge, like I told Sam, she said nothing. Nothing.'

The man tilted his head. His scar was clearly visible.

'She's just a stupid Amish girl,' Sam grunted.

An indignant retort flew to her lips. With an effort, she swallowed it down. Stupid was good. Stupid might save her.

Jorge rolled his eyes and peered at her, and she dipped her gaze. At a measured pace, he approached the counter. She took the pile of coins and placed them in the bag, sealing it.

He turned to Sol. 'Bring her to the office.'

She placed her hands flat on the counter to steady herself.

'What? Her?' Sol held his hands up. 'No. Jorge, you're wasting your time.'

'Bring her,' Jorge barked as he shoved through the staff door, followed by the others.

Sol swore. Hannah stayed silent. He held out his arm and beckoned her.

Her pulse thumped in her ears as he guided her through the door. With shaky legs, she walked as sedately as she could, ignoring the deadweight lodged in her stomach. The hollow thud of the door against the wall made her flinch.

In the office, the man Sol had called Jorge leaned on the desk, facing her. He reached inside his jacket, pulled out a cigarette, and lit it. The burnt, woody smell wafted under her nose, its acrid scent making her want to sneeze. She resisted the reflex to inhale and instead parted her lips and exhaled slowly.

'You're Naomi's Yoder's daughter?' He spoke the words in a lazy, nasal drawl.

Through another puff of smoke, she saw Sol gave her a slow blink. A warning not to ask the question that begged itself. How he knew her mother was not important right now. Surviving was.

'Yes.' She pressed her arms against her body to steady the tremors, frantically trying to summon up some plausible reason.

'You have a phone?'

Hannah shook her head.

He glanced at Sol. 'She yours?'

'She's Amish, for cryin' out loud,' Sol replied. 'Let her go.'

Jorge ignored him and returned his gaze to her. 'You helped the police?'

'No. Amish do not "help" the police.' She dug her elbows harder into her sides.

'Some do. What did you tell the police?'

For a moment, her jaw locked. No words came out, though she could hear them in her head.

'That... that I and my friend got a lift with two youths we met at the gathering.'

'You went with two strangers?'

Dear Lord, what now?

Another stream of smoke, this time directly into her face. 'What, a stupid Amish girl like you?'

There was that word again. Stupid. Hannah curled her bottom lip in, lowered her eyes, and prayed she appeared as stupid as she attempted to look. 'They were English.'

'Oh, I see.' He broke into a sleazy smile. 'You like English guys, huh?'

God, help me. She kept her head down. At least they had not asked about the icehouse.

The vice grip on her lower face, together with the yank upwards, knocked her off balance. 'You think I'm stupid?' He thrust his face into hers, the scar an angry, pulsating deep red. Cologne and smoke smothered her senses. 'I think you aren't so dim.'

If she could have swallowed, she would have, but a desert had replaced the inside of her mouth.

'Sam here tells me you're smart. It's why he hired you, Stupid.' He leaned his face closer still and exhaled. The blast of smoke stung her eyes. He lifted a hand to her face and ran a finger over the hair visible below her kapp. 'I knew a stupid Amish girl once. Only she wasn't as stupid as I thought.'

He lowered his finger to her cheek and pressed. 'Why did you go into the icehouse?'

Hannah flinched. *'They're the ones to worry about,'* Sol had whimpered to her.

'We saw you.'

And Levi. What had he said to them?

She willed her muscles to stiffen and block the tremors of fear that seized her as she searched frantically for an excuse. Something that would convince him.

'Why did you go there?' He pressed her cheeks harder.

Levi had let her go. If she revealed to them that he supplied fake passports and bootleg beer, he would know who had told. He would come after her if they did not get to him first. Not a risk she wanted to take.

An idea came to mind, not so far from the truth. 'Some Amish young have left the community. I heard Levi was the one to go to if you wanted to disappear. They said he had contacts.' Jorge's bemused stare turned to steel. 'I remembered the icehouse. We had to go to it one time, before a gathering. He often works late.' She glanced over at Sol.

Jorge kept his eyes on her. 'True?'

'Yeah,' came Sol's faint reply. 'That's what Levi said. So, you want to leave?'

Despite his grip, she managed a nod.

Jorge let go, and she rolled her jaw. He flicked his gaze to Sol. 'You believe her?'

'Yes.'

Jorge arched an eyebrow and flashed a smug smile. 'Check her,' he snapped.

Sol's face crumbled. 'For what?'

'Wire. Bug. Phone.'

Sol's face paled. Hannah retreated a step, the full implication of the order dawning on her.

Jorge made way for the other man, who removed his hands from his pockets as he came and stood before her, leering at her, and raised his hands, broad as table tennis paddles and thick as posts. One hand had fingers stained yellow.

Over his shoulder, Sam's eyes widened in horror, and he shrivelled as Jorge shot him a menacing glare.

'Hands up, girl,' Shorty sneered.

'Do it,' Sol whimpered, standing still, his arms by his sides and his head lowered so the brim of his hat hid his face.

As she fanned her arms out, Hannah understood why Sol was averting his gaze. She fought the overwhelming desire to slap the violating hands away as the odious creature's fingers crawled over her body. Instinct told her not to. Instead, she clenched her teeth and willed herself to stand perfectly still. Grace. This was all for Grace.

'Maybe I should check underneath?'

At his chuckle, she forced her eyes open. Sam sat, unlit cigar in hand, looking nowhere in particular. Sol kept his position, his fists clenched, knuckles pushing through skin. Good. A sense of satisfaction wavered within her at his discomfort.

'You say nothing.' Jorge's hawk eyes bore into her as he stubbed his cigarette out in the ashtray. 'Go.'

The calmness that had held her through the ordeal stayed as she straightened her kapp and walked out of the office into the shop and collected her bag, bonnet and coat. When she reached the door, she remembered they had locked it. For one dreadful second, she panicked and twisted the doorknob, venting her frustration as it rattled. She would have to go back. Then she remembered the key kept in the till for the odd occasion she had to lock up.

She unlocked the door and put the key through the letterbox. Clutching her bag, fingers digging into its coarse material, she hurried down the street. Past the flower shop where the owner carried bunches to his van for delivery. Past Falcon's and the empty meat trays in the window. Past people walking by her in both directions as they went about their business.

Whether it was familiarity with the route or simply the desire to see a face she knew, she found herself outside the post office. Empty, apart from an elderly woman standing at the counter. She tumbled in, sniffling, barely registering Danny's face crumpling as he rushed up to her. A minty whiff of his chewing gum hit her. She searched the shop with its racks of leaflets, forms, and envelopes. Where was he?

'Hannah?'

At the sound of Barney's voice, full of concern, the last of her resilience evaporated, and she sobbed, grateful for the reassuring embrace he offered.

Chapter 24

B ARNEY DROVE HER home in silence, leaving her free to concentrate on ridding herself of all the evidence of the afternoon's trauma. Along the highway, she focused on slowing her breathing, cooling her red, weepy eyes with her hanky, and letting the wind fan her face through the open passenger window.

The car turned into the lane towards home. 'Stop. Please stop.'

Barney sighed and pulled over onto the grassy edge by the stone wall, and cut the engine. 'Did he threaten you?'

Hannah checked her appearance in the mirror. Her cheeks had paled to their natural peach-pink tone, and a pinkish hue coated the whites of her eyes. She shoved a lock of hair back under her kapp.

'You must tell Theo.' His grip on the steering wheel tightened, making his tanned skin pale around his knuckles.

'No.'

'Yes.' Barney faced her. He placed one hand on the back of her seat and the other on the wheel. His grey-specked green eyes glinted at her as his eyebrows drew close with concern. 'I'm not one for violence. It's not our way, but—'

'Our way?'

'The Amish way.'

She gave a despairing shake of her head.

A ringing sound broke the silence. Puzzled, she glanced around as Barney pulled his phone from his inside pocket. 'Theo. Yes, she's with me—'

Hannah snatched the phone from him. 'Hello?' She listened as Theo explained that Pat had contacted him. 'I'm fine. Fine. They let me go. It was Sam they wanted to talk to. Yes, they knew about the icehouse.' Quickly, she summarised the scene in the office, leaving out the body search.

Barney gawked at her, open mouthed.

'Barney's driving me home. We are nearly there. Please don't worry.' She handed the phone to Barney.

'You didn't tell him about them searching you. He should know. Drummond too, and Evan.'

Hannah gave an adamant shake of her head.

'I may not believe in revenge, but I believe in accountability, and they are accountable for what they did.'

'And shall you hold Theo or Evan accountable for what I fear they might do?'

He cleared his throat.

Hannah twisted the hanky in her hand. 'Let the police take care of them. That's their job.'

'And Sol. This is his fault.'

'He is our friend.'

'Yours. Not mine,' Barney replied. 'He's a dealer.'

'And as much a victim as those he sells to.'

'Hannah, I lo—' Barney stopped and stared out of the window, biting on a fingernail.

Hannah held her breath. What had he meant to say?

She lifted a hand and let it hover over his. He leaned his head against his headrest, and she dropped her hand back onto her lap.

'Hannah, I like that you are such a loyal friend. It is a fine quality, but it is misplaced. You cannot trust him. Surely you can see that after everything he has done to you?'

She wanted to argue with him, waiting for the rise of anger and indignation at his uncharitable opinion, but nothing stirred within her. Sol's own fecklessness had given weight to Barney's words.

'What will you do?' he asked, breaking the silence.

'Nothing.'

He stared at her in astonishment. 'You can't carry on working there. Not after this. Hannah, it's too dangerous. You must stop before you get hurt.'

His voice was calm, even gentle, with a hint of worry.

A small rush of warmth seeped through her. Weeks of taut nerves unravelled like plucked stitches from a quilt.

'I can't stop now. If I do...' she squeezed her eyes shut. '... everything will be for nothing.'

Barney started to protest. She cut him off, raising the palm of her hand. He gave an exasperated sigh and gripped the steering wheel.

'Barney, you say you're my friend. I need you to be one now.'

His eyes brightened. 'Always.'

A horse-drawn closed buggy with a grey top rumbled up to them. With a quick, polite bob of his head, the driver gave them a courteous greeting as he passed. Hannah recognised the yellow cross painted on the side and the man with the wide-brimmed hat driving. The bishop.

'Oh, great,' Barney groaned. 'I'll have to marry you now.'

The absurd remark sent her into a fit of giggles. The sound lifted her spirits, evaporating some of the oppressive weight she had carried out of the shop.

'You're not wrong about Amish young getting help to leave...' Barney paused, reaching for the ignition. 'A fake passport or birth certificate would be a help in getting a social security number.'

'It's Levi helping them.'

Barney tapped the wheel, a thoughtful look on his face. 'Did they believe you? Jorge and his thug?'

A shiver ran down her spine at the memory of Jorge's stony stare. 'He didn't question it.' She covered her mouth to stop from blurting out the next question in her mind. Why would Levi tell Jorge about his enterprise? Still the cold stare filled her vision. She shut her eyes and willed the image to disappear. When she opened them, she gazed out of the window and soaked up the shoots of grass sprouting up along the stone wall.

'I have an old bike in need of fixing.' Barney turned the ignition on. 'Maybe I'll pop in to get some parts. Would that be okay?'

The suggestion soothed her fraught nerves. He wished to support her, and she needed to see a friendly face in a hostile place. It was not ideal, but the tactical agreement brought Barney's silence and her time.

The afternoon's events had confirmed what she suspected. Sol's agitation at discovering her in the storeroom and the men's thuggish behaviour bore out his assertion of how dangerous they were. Was Jorge the leader, or did he report back to a faceless boss? There was only one way to bring the peace and closure she had sworn to achieve and so far failed: to obtain undeniable proof of their guilt. Why else would Jorge and his brother visit the cycle shop so much if it was not a storage space for drugs? If only Sol had not found her. Every time she got close, her plans were thwarted. They would watch her like hawks. Any attempt to sneak in and complete her search would be blocked. She was so close – the knowledge of it rattled around her body like balls inside a revolving tombola drum.

The storeroom held the vital evidence needed to put them all away. The key to unlocking it lay with Sol.

Chapter 25

PUSHING THE SHOP door open, Hannah's pulse increased from a jittery bounce to a flat-out gallop; a horse pulling a buggy so recklessly fast it would topple the vehicle.

Her appearance brought Sam out of his office. He toyed with a half-smoked cigar and viewed her as though seeing a ghost. 'You came back?'

Hannah hung her coat up.

Sam stuffed the cigar in his mouth. 'Good girl.' He dug a hand into his jacket pocket and pulled out his leather wallet. Sol watched from the corner, arching his eyebrows. Sam placed three ten-dollar bills on the counter. 'Call it compensation. For... yesterday.'

Without another word, he slunk off to the office. Hannah picked up the money as if taking a dirty rag and stuffed it inside her bag under the counter. More money to donate to some worthy cause.

Sol busied himself putting out the bikes for hire. When he had finished, he brought some boxes from the storeroom and refilled the racks low on merchandise while she served the customers. The morning crawled by. She occupied herself by flicking through the latest clothing catalogue, willing the clock's hour hand to inch to midday and lunchtime. A cool drink and a sandwich would revive her. Sol could take over, whether he liked it or not. Bracing herself, she flattened her apron and prepared to speak.

The bell's ring made them both gaze at the door.

'Good day.' Barney entered as if he were strolling into the kitchen at home. He walked up to her, removing his hat, his eyes on her, and handed her a poster. Her heart lurched at the heading which read "Singing for Grace".

She noted the request for everyone to attend. 'But it's not a church Sunday? Singing is generally on a church Sunday.'

'It's a special one Bishop Fisher has agreed to in memory of Grace,' Barney explained. 'He's sent a message to all the families so they can pray for the event when they worship at home. The Stoltzfuses want all the young people to attend. I'm asking the shops and cafés to put the poster up. Even Danny agreed. Will you put it up and come?'

Sol hollered to Sam through the door and waited for a response; Hannah heard a vague grunt. 'Yeah. He says okay.'

She offered to post it up in the window.

'What can I get you?' Sol said to Barney, edging to the counter and eyeing an open box.

'A saddle, please.'

'You drive. Why do you need a bike?' Sol rested an arm on the box.

'I have an old bike.' Barney addressed Hannah as he spoke. 'I'm fixing it for my nephew, Lucas.'

'What kind of bike?' Sol asked.

'A bike. Two wheels, handlebars. Two pedals with brakes.'

Sol jutted out his chin. Barney rocked on his heels, his gaze on Hannah.

'The old boneshaker you used to ride as a child?' she said.

'I'll get it.' Sol straightened. 'Anything else? Brake blocks? Tyres?'

Barney pulled out a worn brake block from a coat pocket and placed it on the counter, and Sol looked at it. 'They come in pairs.'

'Then I will need two pairs.'

They stood facing each other. Barney's calm presence strengthened her resolve. His laid-back manner she had once taken as a sign of laziness masked a quiet solidity. The tweak of the corner of his mouth made her want to smile back, but she resisted, aware of Sol's sullen gaze.

When Barney had left, Sol hovered by the counter. 'You seeing him?'

She ignored him and returned to the clothing catalogue, quietly pleased that Barney's appearance had rattled him.

He shuffled closer and leaned into her. 'Look, I'm sorry. All right? About yesterday.'

The padded shorts and tie-dyed top looked cool and sporty on the blonde model in the photo. Hannah tried to imagine what she might look like in such attire.

'Maybe now you'll get what I'm tryin' to say to you.'

Over the page, a tanned man with muscular thighs straddled a silver road bike in the middle of an open highway.

'Han? Hannah!'

The mountains and the sea-blue sky behind Mr Muscle looked stunning.

'Let me take you home. I gotta talk to you.'

He shrank back when she replied with a frosty stare.

'It's important.'

She recalled Barney on his old boneshaker. Tousled curls in the wind with his head back, laughing, eyes filled with mischief. Twelve years old, pedalling for all his worth down the slope to the river.

She stared at Sol, hunched with his arms folded across his chest, hands tucked under his armpits. She knew it was wrong to gain satisfaction from seeing another in distress; she would make sure she prayed for forgiveness, but right then and there, a small ball of pleasure rolled around inside her.

Then Sol spoke the words that catapulted her to the present and into the fray of her mission.

'I know what you were looking for.'

IF THE MORNING had crawled by, the afternoon passed with the speed of a slug. Now she sat in the passenger seat of Sol's new metallic blue convertible, passing a familiar figure sifting through a bundle of letters outside the post office. Unsure whether Barney had seen her, Hannah hoped he did not follow them home.

Off the highway, Sol slowed down, parked up near the same spot Barney had, and got out of the car. He climbed the stile in the wall and walked a few feet into the field, beckoning her to follow. The stile posed no problem for her in a long dress, thanks to the many years of scampering around the fields.

Sol paced a short stretch of grass, hands on his hips, waiting for her. Behind him, the last rays of sunset trailed gold across the hilly horizon. 'The gear. The drugs Grace took.' He kept pacing. 'I didn't give it to her. Levi did.'

'I know. I was there, remember?'

'Sam. He only sells clean gear.' Sol stroked his goatee anxiously.

'So, the shop is a cover?'

'What?' He stepped forward, his boot sinking into something smelly and squishy. 'Hell.' He stomped a foot on the grass. 'You were hunting for them. The drugs.' He pushed his face closer to hers. 'Why? What have I done to you?'

She held his gaze and waited, imagining a weasel standing before her. Too spent for anger, she let her head dip. 'Grace.'

Sol stared at her, his face drawn and pale. 'Hannah, you got to believe me.'

'Where did Levi get them?'

'I don't know.' He gave a little gulp. 'He brought the stuff in the bag he threw out of the Dodge. I was supposed to take it to Sam. That's the way it works. I collect and deliver. My guess is, there's a gang wanting to muscle in on the patch. One way is giving the existing dealers bad stuff to turn trade to them instead.'

'You made me do it. Fetch and carry.'

'Sam insisted.' He averted his eyes, his shoulders dropping like a scolded child. 'Said it would be safer.'

'Who for? You?' She felt her body shaking with rage. How did she ever consider him to be her heart's desire? 'You left me by the roadside with my dead friend and a bag full of drugs. You used my friendship to save your own skin. You threatened to have my brother killed. You stood there yesterday and watched what they did without a word. You coward.'

With each accusation, he shrank till his head hung low and his back hunched over. 'I'm sorry. I'm sorry.'

Selfish individual need, Maemm had called sin, and here was a prime example. How stupid and naïve she had been. Had he only got her the job to provide Sam with a delivery person?

He lifted his head enough to raise his gaze to her. Here was the urchin, and with it, the old tug of war: save him or scorn him.

Calm down. Get control of yourself. Unlock the key. That's what matters. Use him like he used you. With effort she stepped back and curled her hands into balls so as not to give in to the temptation to touch him. 'Why did those men at the Millers' fight with you?' It was a long shot, but worth the push, she hoped.

'There's always someone from outside the area trying to take over. Jorge and his men take care of them. They're the muscle of the operation. They work for whoever's overseeing things. It's them who deal with anyone who is a threat.'

The memory of the previous day haunted her. It made her skin go clammy and her stomach churn inside her, cooling the anger of a few moments ago.

A bloody image rose before her eyes. 'The severed hand. Was it them?'

He wiped his nose on the back of his hand. 'No. Not Jorge. The other gang, I suppose. Like a warning shot, that they meant business.'

'Who was it meant for?'

'Dunno and don't care. I want out. It's all going south.' He rubbed his sweaty, snotty hand down his jeans. 'I'm sick of it. All of it.' He paced again before stopping. 'There's a delivery coming in next weekend from our regular suppliers. I'm supposed to deliver gear to our dealers, collect their money, and get it to Sam.'

'You do hide drugs at the shop.'

'Forget the drugs. Forget the whole stinking mess. Listen to me: the merchandise comes in from outside the area. A barn here, a lockup shop there. English. Amish. Wherever makes a suitable cover; but with all the leaks, it's coming to us now.'

Hannah's heart somersaulted. Any minute, he was going to ask her the question.

'That's why Jorge and his brother came yesterday. They're convinced there's an informer.'

Why was he telling her all this? Why incriminate himself? There could be only one reason. He knew she had helped the police.

In the distance, the field merged with the darkening horizon. The nearest building was her home. A faint whistle of early spring breeze grazed her ear. She hoped it would be quick, whatever method he chose to kill her.

He curled his hands into fists. Was he going to beat the information out of her? She took a hold of her skirt, ready to lift the hem and run.

Sol gripped hold of her upper arms. The sensation of his trembling fingers rippled through her skin. Tracks of salt water dribbled down his face, and she steeled herself against the tender rush of emotion.

'Come with me, Han. Levi and me, we're leaving once I got the money. We can go anywhere you want. Anywhere, and start a new life. One of our own. Not Amish. Not English. You and me.'

She gawked at him in astonishment. 'Leave?'

'Yesterday made me realise how much you mean to me.'

'But you said...' She stared at him. All she could see was panic and fear etched on his face. Was this another lie, to ensure she did not reveal his plan? Would he desert her once safe?

'I don't want to live like this. Not anymore.' He straightened, dropping his hands. 'Come with me. There's enough money from the delivery I'm about to get to see us through for a good while. And I can get a job.'

Fireworks exploded in her brain. She raised her hands towards him, her mind racing. The very thing she had once dreamt of had come true.

What if they did go? She paused, hands in midair, turning the question over. Leave? Now, when she had the means to bring peace to the Stoltzfuses, to her family, to herself?

What if it all goes wrong? What if he deserts you once more? a little voice whispered back. *What next? You can never come back. Never. Another family in mourning for a loved one.*

The notion tore like a remnant of cloth ripped in two inside her. Caught once more between the two worlds she had flittered to and from all her life. Never settling, never committing to either.

Beads of sweat covered his forehead. A tatty dreadlock or two hung down over his shoulders. Who was he? Sol or Solomon? Even the way he spoke sounded out of kilter with either Amish or English manner of speech. He might not know who he was, but she knew her identity.

'Han?' He searched her face. 'I need you to come with me.'

The panic in his voice confirmed the nagging doubt in her mind. Why so desperate to leave? Why did he need her to go? Not *want*.

'They will find out who it is. The informer.' He shook her, more firmly this time; his rings dug into her flesh.

She wrenched herself free. 'No.'

'But I've just spilled my guts to you.'

'I won't say anything, Sol.'

He shot her an incredulous look, shaking his head.

'I said nothing about you driving, and I won't say anything about your plans.'

'See, you do feel for me.'

'Did. You killed it. All of it.' She lifted her chin.

He staggered back and searched her face. 'How can I trust you?'

'Because I don't want your blood on my hands.'

He scratched his goatee and considered her words, shifting this way and that.

She stepped away from him, her eyes on the road, searching for a car or buggy approaching. 'If you stay, I can vouch for you.'

He snorted.

'You could be free of Sam and the others if you go to the police.'

'I thought you'd understand, Han,' he simpered. 'You, of all people. I thought you wanted to be with me. Seems not.'

'I understand you perfectly.' She sighed. 'Do what you always do when things get tough – run. That's your answer to everything. It always will be.'

If he stayed, he had a chance. Slim, but a chance.

He stopped his little shuffle dance. 'Last chance, Han.'

She did not bother to shake her head this time but stood still, her eyes dry, though a swell of hot tears burned behind them.

'Guess this is goodbye, then.'

She stared back at him and then gave a firm nod.

He strode back towards the stile, shoulders low and head bowed. Halfway, he stopped and turned to her. 'I won't be there to protect you anymore, Han.'

You never did. The words formed on her lips, but she wiped them away. 'I have a protector, thank you.' She gazed at him, noting how weak his chin was under the goatee and how ferret-like his thin body.

With another shrug, he turned and vaulted the stile and marched over to the convertible.

Her knees buckled under her as tension fled, turning her legs to jelly. With several quick gasps, she forced air into her body to steady the shaking.

So much for romance, she mused, retracing her steps to the stile. The thought seemed at odds with the gravity of the conversation, yet the stark reality of Sol's plan, his false declaration and her own stupidity for once believing he cared for her sent a bolt of irritation through her. There was only one person Sol cared about. Himself. He would leave for good. She would report everything to Drummond as she had planned, but not this. They would have enough evidence to arrest Sam and the dealers without Sol and the money he collected. He deserved his second chance.

A well of pity filled her as she approached the car and peered at him. Let him live his life in the shadows. *God be with you.* She blessed him silently, turned from the car, and traipsed down the lane towards home and those who truly loved her.

The crunch of tires spraying loose dirt on the bank as the convertible reversed and roared away filled her with sorrow. The scruffy child who had tagged along with Evan and Barney, the youth who lived under his brother's shadow, would forever be running. Running from those men. Running from Sam. But most of all, running from himself. *God be with you,* she repeated, despite the doubt such protection might save her friend from the inevitable end waiting for him.

HANNAH DRAGGED HERSELF along the unlit lane. A nice stroll home with clean, fresh air to blow away the stench of the world would help her calm down and digest Sol's words. Despite the dark, she'd soon be home; in the distance she spotted the familiar post with its painted board swaying in the wind.

The screech of tires on the tarmac made her jump over to the grass edge. She spun to see Barney's Volvo jerking to a halt, the passenger door swinging out and barring her way. 'Get in,' Barney ordered. The car lurched down the lane as she sat down, the force of the wind slamming the door closed on her. 'I hope you had a good reason for being with that rodent,' he remarked tersely.

Hannah did not reply. She stared at the sheep wandering about the fields.

Instead of driving up the path to the house, Barney stopped by the post, the Volvo's engine idling. 'You're playing a dangerous game, Hannah.' He stared out of the window. 'What are you up to?'

She remained silent.

'I fear for you, and not only for your physical safety...'

She turned her head to him.

'... but your soul.'

A chill slithered down her.

'You've changed. You're so distant these days.'

She bit her lip, pained at the sadness in his tone and on his face. *Dear Lord, am I losing the only real friend I have?* Was sharing the burden with him a mistake? What if he got hurt? It would be her fault for dragging him into this mess when all he wanted to do was help her. *Lieb*, love: listen, overlook, value, embrace. The opposite of sin, Maemm had said. On Barney's anxious face, she read all these qualities. In the familiar deep furrow on his brow, the creases around his eyes, and the pulled-in bottom lip. Her heart twisted. 'I want to get this over with. I must speak to Theo.'

Barney revved the engine, released the brake, and swung the car through the entrance and up the lane, the darkening sky casting shadows of the white railings in its headlights.

Hannah relaxed back in the seat and allowed herself a sigh of relief. She had what she needed to bring the wretched mess to an end. With Sol's confirmation, Drummond would be able to get his hard evidence and arrest those responsible for Grace's death, and she could return to her life. It would soon be over. Peace would come.

Chapter 26

Late February 2024

H ANNAH CLAMPED THE pillow over her ears to block out the screech of the cockerel. She kept her eyes shut, not wanting to greet the morning, knowing it would bring another day working at the shop. Her only consolation was that it was Friday. The tightness inside her stomach added to her sense of dread.

She rolled onto her back, pressed her hands against her chest, and prayed for protection. Unable to put off the inevitable, she rose and got dressed, one question in her mind. Would this be the day Sol would confess to Sam that she knew everything?

Five days. One hundred and twenty hours, she had worked out on the bus one morning the previous week. Sol steered clear of her, which suited her. He worked in the repair shed, took extra-long lunch breaks, and found excuses to stay out of the shop as much as possible. Sam didn't seem to notice or care. He rushed through the front door so frequently she wondered whether they should put a revolving one in.

On Thursday afternoon, Barney had strolled in and waited patiently to be served. This time he wanted a mudguard and a new chain. She served him with a polite hello and goodbye. Aware of Sol wheeling a repaired bike through the shop, Barney had inclined his head to her, ignored Sol, paid for the items, and left. His visits comforted her and strengthened her resolve to see things through.

Friday proved busy, with a dry clear sky and weekenders arriving to stay at the nearby B and Bs and hotels. The last-minute rush of returning hired bikes meant she was late cashing up.

'Sam, why don't you let Han help tomorrow so I can get these repairs done?' Sol pointed to the parked bikes outside, muddy from their excursions.

'Nope.' Sam chewed on his ever-present unlit cigar as Hannah placed the final money in the cloth bag, tied it, and gave it to him. 'Don't come in tomorrow.'

'But it will be busy,' Sol said. 'I can't serve and mend them at the same time.'

Hannah reached for her cloak.

'Yeah, you can. It's not full season,' Sam stated, staring at Hannah. 'You do as I say. Got it?'

Hannah didn't know whether to be relieved. With nerves tauter than fabric in a wooden sewing loop with fear over Sol breaking his silence and the effort of pretending nothing had occurred between them, she was longing for everything to be normal.

'You hear me?' Sam barked. 'Get.'

She grabbed her belongings and headed for the door before he caught her anxious expression. Given Sol's confession, the delivery must be due. Would Drummond act?

For the first Friday evening in weeks, she stayed in. They cooked brownies, prepared dinner for the next day and laughed about old times. Later, they warmed themselves by the stove sewing patchwork squares for a quilt. She counted the hourly chimes from the hallway clock. Seven, eight… nine. She paused, needle mid-stitch. Nine o'clock. The time Sol generally collected her.

'Are you not going out tonight?' Maemm inquired.

Despite the light tone, Hannah caught the underlying worry in Maemm's question. She shook her head. 'I thought I might go to the Singing in memory of Grace on Sunday evening.'

A slow smile appeared on Maemm's face, and she hummed a hymn. It occurred to Hannah she had not heard Maemm's gentle, floating melodies filling the house for a good while. How many weekends over the past few years had she gone and left Maemm to sit alone? Maemm's humming lulled her into a dreamland, the sound soothing her as she sat, eyes closed, listening like she did as a child. Seated there by the stove, she forgot her present troubles and found a harbour of peace to anchor herself to.

Light showers peppered Saturday. Evan and Grandfather spent the day in the workshop, coming in solely for lunch. As she helped Maemm with chores, Hannah peeked out of the windows at the passing cars and buggies. Every time a car drove past, a cold, hard lump wedged itself in the pit of her stomach. She wished for once that she had accepted Theo's offer of a phone. She could have rung him to find out if her guess was correct.

In the evening, she helped Maemm tidy up her sewing room. Afterwards, Maemm settled down at the table and wrote a letter with the aid of the portable lamp by her armchair.

'Who are you writing to?' Hannah paused at the door, watching her.

'An old friend,' Maemm replied, writing on a cream-coloured sheet from her writing pad. An envelope lay beside it.

Hannah went into the living room and stood in front of the bookcase with its assorted books of different shapes and sizes. On the second shelf from the top a bulky, oversized book jutted out from the others. The family Bible Grandfather had mysteriously lent to Theo. He must have returned it during one of his frequent visits.

Hannah lifted it from the shelf and sat down in a comfy armchair, resting it on her lap and opening it in the middle, where the pages contained the Yoder family tree. Several generations spanned the pages. Evan's name had a line joining with Stefan's and Maemm's. To one side of Maemm's name, she found hers. A single line connected it with Maemm.

A shadow fell over her.

'I should ask your grandfather to put Theo's name in it.' Maemm stood by her, looking at the open pages.

Hannah moved her finger to another name along from Maemm's. Ruth Yoder, born on the same day.

'Twins.' Hannah gasped in surprise. 'You were twins?'

'Yes.' Maemm perched on the armrest.

Why had she never noticed that before on the rare occasion Grandfather had shown her the Bible as a child?

'Why did she leave?'

'She got involved with the wrong man.' Maemm paused, staring at Ruth's name. 'It was she who warned Theo that his true identity was known.'

Hannah felt her jaw slackening at the news.

'Ruth had to leave. If they had found out she told him...' Maemm pressed her lips together, stifling a sob. 'I miss her. She was brave. Like you.'

'Where did she go?' Hannah read the name again.

Maemm remained silent for a moment. 'She is safe. That is all that matters. That is all I want for you, Hannah.'

When Maemm stroked her hair, all worries and fears of recent weeks disappeared. She was just a little girl staying up with Maemm once more.

Sunday, as Hannah had reminded Barney, was a "non-church day", but families still gathered to say prayers and read the Bible together after breakfast. The day brought sunshine and a strong breeze that rattled the windows and doors like a thief trying to get in. Hannah busied herself helping Maemm with packing quilts for mailing and cutting out material for new orders. After supper, she settled down to work on binding a wedding quilt for a couple getting married at Easter. If her hands were busy, they could not tremble, but keeping her mind from churning over the *what ifs* proved harder. What if Jorge was watching? What if Sol told Sam?

The chug-chug of an engine sounded outside, and her hand wobbled as she stitched the border to the body of the quilt. Grandfather's voice greeting Theo caused her to lower her head and concentrate on her work.

'This is where you are hiding.' Theo's cheery smile belied his pained expression. 'And you, Naomi? How are you today?'

The tenderness in his voice surprised Hannah.

A faint rose tint bloomed on Maemm's pale face. 'Fine, Theo, thank you.' Maemm rose, putting aside a shirt. 'Would you like supper? We have ham, vegetables, and rolls.'

'Thank you.'

Hannah placed her work down too and followed them into the kitchen, where Evan sat hunched over a book.

'Have you news?' she blurted out.

Theo shook his head. 'I just wanted some company.' He spoke to no one in particular, but she guessed he sensed her question as to why he had appeared if not to update them. Maemm hummed softly as she gathered the food for Theo.

'What are you reading?' Theo asked Evan.

Evan snapped the book closed.

Theo peered at the book's cover. '*Catcher in the Rye*. You like reading?'

'Some.' At Evan's guarded tone, Theo looked away.

'I'm leaving for the Stoltzfus's,' Evan announced, getting up and going to the door, the book tucked under his arm. His heavy footsteps, even without boots, resounded through the hallway.

Theo closed the door behind him. 'Drummond will contact me when the operation is over,' he said in a low voice.

Hannah fetched some milk from the refrigerator to make coffee.

'Grace had such a beautiful voice,' Maemm sighed.

Hannah smiled, remembering how she used to listen to Grace's angelic soprano in church and her more wild voice accompanying rock songs in Sol's Dodge on the way to the gatherings or in her bedroom while getting ready to go out.

'Hannah is going with Evan to the Singing for Grace.' Maemm placed the food on the table with cutlery.

Hannah sighed. She had forgotten expressing her intention to go. Theo's announcement had changed her mind. Could she wriggle out of it to stay with Theo and wait for the news?

'Good idea. It will give you an alibi.'

Hannah paused, pouring the milk into his mug.

'You may as well know. Drummond and his men are going to arrest

Sam and the others tonight. There's been a delivery, so they know the drugs are there.'

'He told you. Why?' She lowered the milk container, careful not to spill its contents.

Theo paused, lifting a forkful of ham to his mouth. 'We had words. I was worried about you.'

Evan reappeared, booted and with his threadbare jacket on.

'Evan, take care of your sister.' Maemm's voice wobbled with emotion.

Evan glanced from Theo to Maemm, trying to read the subtext of their conversation. He let out a heavy sigh. 'Yes.'

Hannah did not have the energy to argue. Torn between wanting to honour her friend or to wait, the Singing won.

While Evan drove the buggy, Hannah's heart lurched as she considered going to the farm with no Grace there. How would Mrs Stoltzfus greet her? They had not met since the funeral. She let the pop music from the battery-operated radio wash over her as Scar clip-clopped his way up the hill, skirting around the fields. Near the top, before they came to the T-junction, the roofs of the Stoltzfus's farmhouse and barn were visible. Evan urged Scar on, but the horse ignored him and plodded on in his usual unhurried manner. 'Have you and Barney argued?'

'No.'

'He's mighty grumpy these days.'

Hannah picked at a loose thread on her cuff and busied herself with snapping it off as the buggy bumped over a pothole, making her grateful for the padded red cushion Evan had attached to the hard wooden seat. Conservative Evan might be, but he still appreciated some modern-day comforts. At least it was not an artificial leopard- or tiger-skin covering, like some more fashion-conscious *leddich* might use.

'Hannah.' He pulled on Scar's right rein to direct the way. 'I am sorry for how I have treated you of late.'

She patted his arm and got a small, grateful smile back.

He nudged her side. 'You say a prayer for me, please.'

She looked at him, confused.

'I have my higher education exam this week.'

Hannah reproached herself for forgetting about his studies in all the events of the past weeks. In the distance, cars and buggies turned into the farm's entrance. 'Of course. When is it?'

'Monday. In town.'

'What are you going to tell Grandfather?'

'I've got to collect some wood for harnesses and wheels, and I've told him I will visit you. Which I will do after the exams. Will you help me?'

'Oh, you want me to cover for you?'

He gave a swift nod. 'Pray for me, Hannah.'

'To pass the exam?'

'No.' Evan flicked the reins, his gaze straight ahead. 'For courage to do what is right. Like you have done.'

His words occupied her mind as they arrived and parked alongside other buggies and wagons in the field near the barn. Youths loitered about the yard, while the young women gathered in groups outside the outbuildings. Steadily, everyone trickled in and settled down on the benches. Hannah took her seat with the women while Evan joined the men. Each group faced the other with tables running down between them. A soft glow of light from the lamps on the tables and hanging from the surrounding beams gave the building a cosy campfire feel.

As she waited for the Singing to begin, a trio of young men straggled in late and stood behind the seated ones. Among them was Barney, who positioned himself near the barn door. His profile looked familiar, yet strange. The nose straighter and stronger, his jaw squarer than she recalled. His usually smooth face was covered with stubble. Where had the skinny child with the corkscrew mop and infectious smile gone?

After the welcome by Mr Stoltzfus, a lone male voice struck up. Aaron Miller. She recognised the slight dip in his tenor voice as he sang the low notes. The youths joined in the second verse of "Jesus, My Shepherd". By verse three, the women joined in. Blending into one voice. One soul. The hymns came one after another.

Mr Stoltzfus called his young son, Noah, to the front. 'Noah, you lead us now.'

The eight-year-old with the same dark hair and enormous eyes as his mourned-for sister flapped his mouth open and shut. Taking his cue from his father, he began to sing "What a Friend We Have in Jesus". The assembled group of over a hundred picked up the tune and joined in, the youths increasing the speed of the song, a kind of game they liked to play, some banging their fists on the table. The girls kept tempo to the tune. Towards the end, the youths slowed and all sang the final verse in unison.

Laughter erupted at the good-natured frolics. Hannah giggled as she listened to the next hymn, "Stand Up, Stand Up for Jesus". She gazed at the joy on the faces of those gathered and felt a little bit of it herself. The soulful sincerity of their singing, their voices rising in unison in the communal activity, arose from an inner place of peace – just like Maemm's humming.

Was this why Maemm had stayed all these years? She could have left with or without Theo. She would have had good reason to do so, despite the kind bishop or Grandfather's protection. Something must have held her here. Something that gave her the strength to withstand the stares and gossip. Would it be the same for her? She made a mental note to find time to speak to Maemm.

'You should be singing, Hannah,' the girl next to her whispered. 'Where's your brother? I can't see him. I'm sure he was sitting on the second bench.'

Hannah searched the row of youths seated opposite, noticing the laughter and shouts from outside. 'He must be playing volleyball,' she replied with a wink at the girl, who blushed. Over the two hours, young men and girls had kept slipping out to play games or talk before being ushered in for the last round of hymns.

She checked her watch. Ten-thirty. The delivery must have arrived at the shop. She had held her promise and said nothing of Sol's plan when she spoke to Drummond on Friday. Would Sol finally come to his senses and cooperate with the police? What if he escaped? Then her efforts to save him would be wasted. He would never find peace. Never stop running. She prayed Drummond would arrest those responsible. All of them. Only then would everyone be safe.

If Sol escaped, where would he go? She chided herself. He had made his choice and she hers. Hannah surveyed the room. How would they react if they knew she had been helping the police? Law-abiding as her people were, and amicable as relations were with the law, they dealt with their own disputes internally and kept out of the courts. Would they understand or think that she had done so to clear her conscience?

Another prayer. Another request for help.

The peace of the previous hour disappeared, leaving her empty and restless for news. As unobtrusively as possible, she tiptoed out of the barn and into the courtyard. Outside by the entrance, she bid greetings to Mrs Stoltzfus, who was sitting on a hay bale chatting with some older women.

Taking a deep lungful of chilly evening air, Hannah strolled past the Stoltzfus's unlit home fronted by a small garden with a path leading to the porch, surrounded by a low-level stone wall with a wooden gate. For a moment, she was a child, swinging on the gate, feet wedged between the wooden planks, hands gripping the tops. Grace pushing it to and fro, laughing. She ran her fingers over the gate; it barely reached her waist.

She turned and bumped into Aaron. She sidestepped to go around him.

'I'm told you got locked in the icehouse, Hannah.' He stared down at her, making full use of his height, all traces of the angelic singer gone. 'You should be more careful. You might not be so fortunate if you were to be so careless again.'

She stood tall, her gaze level with the nib of his nose, ready to speak, but he turned, voices drawing his gaze to the barn as those inside spilled out into the yard. He hurried away, heading to a group of youths in the huddle of bodies.

Hannah stared along the winding lane down to the road, letting her jangled nerves settle. She traced the trees and hedging of the fields opposite, her gaze dipping and weaving across the evening sky, returning to the lane with its open entrance. At first, she thought the man staggering up the path was a latecomer. As he stumbled into the light, she caught her breath and narrowed her eyes. His golden locks glinted as he zig-zagged along the path, clutching his arm, which was swaddled in stained cloth.

Hannah glanced over at Evan, standing with some of the others with his hands on his hips. Barney was next to him, wearing a disdainful look as though smelling a rancid stink. Evan broke away from the group. 'What's *he* doing here?'

By the time she had registered that the stains on the cloth were blood, Levi had reached the yard, his shirt and jeans splattered in mud. Droplets of sweat dribbled down a swollen, purplish cheek. With effort, he stopped in front of Hannah. 'Help me. You got to help me. It's all gone wrong.' He swayed and pressed his wounded hand to his chest. 'They were waiting. Sol got away.'

'Then find a hole to bury yourself in,' Evan hissed as Mrs Stoltzfus came striding towards them, Aaron in her wake. 'We'll even dig it for you, friend.'

Hannah studied her brother. The Viking heritage said it all. Brawn before brain.

'Please, I need shelter,' Levi said, cradling his arm, his eyes damp and overly bright. 'I let you go.' His arm seemed shorter than the other one, even with the bandage.

'What is the meaning of this?' Mrs Stoltzfus demanded. 'Why are you preventing this young man from joining in?'

Evan and Barney both shifted uncomfortably, avoiding her gaze. Aaron stared stone-faced at Levi.

Mrs Stoltzfus took hold of Levi's arm and with two fingers lifted the edge of the cloth, releasing the pungent smell Hannah recalled from the icehouse. Raw bloody meat. Mrs Stoltzfus looked away. 'Oh, good Lord.'

'Please, you've got to help me. If they find me—'

'Who? The police?' Hannah asked, trying to tear her gaze from the stump end of the arm.

'No.'

A trickle of ice slithered down her spine.

'They saw me and you,' Levi whimpered. 'Please... you're Amish. You help people.'

Evan thrusted his face into Levi's. 'Like you helped ours?'

'Enough.' Mrs Stoltzfus pushed her diminutive frame between the two, pushing them apart. 'This man needs first aid, if not a doctor.' She beckoned to Aaron and another man nearby. 'Take him into the barn.'

The two men grabbed him more roughly than needed and marched him to the barn, leaving a direct view to the bottom of the lane. Hannah blinked and strained her eyes as a grey sedan cruised by.

Barney followed her gaze.

The trickle morphed into a violent shiver, draining all warmth from her face. 'I must go.'

'No.' Barney blocked her path with an outstretched arm.

'I must.' She gestured to the crowd mingling outside the barn. 'They could get hurt.'

Barney whirled round to the men and young people watching. 'Get the women and children in the barn. Aaron, Lucas, take some of the others and go search the rear of the house, the orchard. Evan, search the front end, stables and sheds, then come back here. The rest of you with me – we need to protect the barn.'

One hand on her back, he steered her to the barn, ignoring her protests. When she stumbled inside and heard the doors slam shut and the bar shunted across, she covered her face. What had she done? What if they came after her or Levi? Would the police realise? Would they care?

Mrs Stoltzfus, with two other women, tended to a feverish Levi stretched out on a bench. The rest looked on, silent and unsmiling. Some held children close. A young girl around Evan's age, thin, pasty and dotted with freckles, pulled at the hem of her cardigan sleeve, glaring at Hannah. 'What's *she* doing here?' the girl asked.

The silence answered the question in its lack of defence for Hannah. No finger pointing or snide comments, just a quiet consensus humming in the air. They were trapped inside the barn because of her. This was her fault. If she had not meddled, let the police deal with things, they would not be in danger.

Levi let out a high-pitched howl of pain as Mrs Stoltzfus pressed a clean piece of wadding against the stump where his hand used to be.

Whoever drove past must have seen her and Levi. Two occasions seen together. Too coincidental.

She turned to the doors and, placing her palms on the old wood, stared out through the tiny gap between them. Bodies shifted across her vision. Barney, now, directing a copper-haired youth to the lane. She banged on the doors. It was her they wanted.

'Hannah,' Mrs Stoltzfus said. 'Come away from the door. Stand with the others.'

'I must leave. This is my fault.'

'Fault, fault.' Mrs Stoltzfus got up from the bench. 'It is not your place to judge, young lady.'

'But you have seen what these men are capable of.'

'The very reason you should stay!' Mrs Stoltzfus gestured at the girl still picking at her sleeve. 'Leah, go stand by the door, and you, Izzy.'

Hannah lifted her head, restraining herself from uttering English words no Amish would say. What if they broke in?

She scoured the barn for objects. Hymn books, cutlery, pots and pans stacked. 'We should defend ourselves. Here.' She picked up a pot from a long table laden with piles of crockery and held it out to Leah.

'And we will, with the Lord's help. Sing, ladies.' At Mrs Stoltzfus's order, the front row of women straightened up. A soprano voice rose amongst them: *The Lord's my Shepherd*...

A screech of tyres and brakes drowned the hymn's words.

Hannah rushed back to the door, pushing Leah and the others aside. She raised the pot high as the bar rattled loose. It might not be a hammer, but a hard, quick blow to the head would stun her opponent long enough for her to escape.

Shielding her eyes from the blaze of light, she swung the pot forward and swiped thin air.

A hand grabbed her forearm, and another wrenched the pot from her. Black dots danced, blotting her vision. She pulled back, using her weight to anchor herself.

'Stop fighting.' She stopped dead, recognising Barney's voice. Rubbing her eyes, she peered through the open doors. A familiar Nissan stood in the yard. Theo flung open the passenger door. 'Get in.'

'But...'

'Now, Hannah!'

She turned to the barn.

Barney pointed to the car. 'You want to save them? Go.'

'Levi came,' Evan said to Theo, bending down to the window as Hannah got in and buckled up. 'Blubbering about things going wrong.'

'You best come too, Evan.' Theo said.

Evan shook his head. 'No. They may come for Hannah. I'll help out here. Get her to safety.'

Hannah half-wound the car window up. 'Levi. He needs a doctor.'

Barney glanced around and pulled out his mobile from inside his jacket. 'I'll call an ambulance. Now go.'

Theo sped away quickly. 'I'm taking you home. Then we must

leave.' The stone wall along the lane blurred into a blank grey canvas in the headlights as he careened left at the junction and down the hill.

'Leave?'

'Someone tipped Jorge and his boss off that Sol and Levi planned to take the money and run. The delivery guy.'

'Stubby?'

'He's a cop. Turns out he's on the gang's payroll. Drummond didn't know. Thankfully he's kept the circle of information about the case to a few trusted people, so Stubby didn't know about you or tonight's swoop. Sol told him he planned to leave and how, believing he was legit. The slimeball snitched on him. They were waiting for Sol and Levi along with the police at the drop-off. All hell broke loose, and Sol got away.'

'What's it got to do with me?'

'Drummond went in with his men. They arrested some of the people involved in the drugs operation, but not Jorge, his brother, or Mr Big. According to Stubby's version, Sol said you were going to leave with him. That makes you the number one candidate he'll run to for help.'

'But I'm not.'

'You matter to Sol. They'll use you as bait.'

'Not anymore.'

'He knows who the head guy is. He's a dead man walking.'

'Sam?'

'He's disappeared.'

What if it was Jorge? His sneering face in the office filled her mind as the car raced down the hill and the Stoltzfus's barn faded out of sight.

Maemm was waiting in the hallway when they hurried in. In the low gaslight, the lines on her face were deeper, making her look older than Hannah had ever known. A suitcase stood by her feet. Grandfather was by the stairs, a hand on the balustrade.

'Any sign of Sam?' Theo glanced back out of the door. Grandfather shook his head.

'I have packed clothes, your Bible, and *Ausbund*. Here.' Maemm thrust a thick envelope into Hannah's hand. 'Money. You will need it.'

'I cannot leave you.'

'You must.' Maemm held the suitcase out to her.

'Come on, we don't have time.' Theo took the case and grabbed Hannah's hand.

'But where?'

'England.'

Hannah's feet were welded to the floor. 'No.'

'Yes.' He turned to Maemm. 'Where's *your* suitcase?'

'I'm staying.' Maemm lowered her gaze.

Theo's face fell. 'Naomi. They could hurt you. Hurt you all.'

Maemm shook her head and held up a hand. 'My place is here. It has always been here, Gabriel.'

A gasp of breath, like someone had landed a punch in his stomach, escaped Theo. He moved to Maemm, his arms out to her, glancing over her shoulder to where Grandfather stood. Grandfather lowered his head and looked away. Theo tenderly held Maemm's hand, wrapping both of his around, and brought it to his lips. It lasted a few seconds, yet time appeared to stand still as they embraced. A sniff broke the silence. His or hers, Hannah could not tell.

'Go via Drummond if you need me. He'll look out for you all.' Theo fished a brown envelope from his inside pocket and handed it to Maemm. 'If you need it.'

Maemm nodded.

Theo cleared his throat. 'I have your passport, Hannah.'

'I can't just go,' she pleaded, staring at Maemm and Grandfather.

Theo silenced her with a raised palm. 'They won't stop. They will work it out, Hannah. All of it. They'll hunt you down and kill you. Like they tried to with me. Like they will if they get hold of Sol.'

Tears spilled over Maemm's eyelashes and down her cheeks. 'Go.'

Hannah hugged her, storing away the imprint of her warm body. 'Sorry.'

Maemm stroked her cheek. 'God go with you, daughter.'

A pair of bony arms embraced her, and she barely heard the blessing Grandfather whispered as she hugged him back. The blessing given to one who is leaving.

This could not be happening. No one had told her this be the result of her trying to right a wrong, to help the police find and stop those who supplied the drugs that killed Grace and many others. Being torn apart from her family was not part of the deal. Why hadn't she considered the consequences? Impulsive and strong-willed, came the answer. Selfish individual need.

In the car she wiped her eyes, replaying the brief conversation. With one hand on the wheel, Theo dug into his outer pocket and held out a passport.

Inside, staring back at her, was the photo he had taken on his phone.

'You have one for Evan too?'

'I texted Barney and asked him to take one of Evan. Less obvious.' He changed gears, and the car jerked as it ascended the hill. 'It's in the envelope I gave your mother.'

'Does Maemm have one?'

'Yes. I got her one when we met. We had planned to leave. She's kept it valid – just in case. Because you don't have birth certificates or social security numbers, the government allows Amish people to present the family Bible and get a letter from the bishop to prove citizenship.'

The recollection of Theo walking to his car with a wrapped book-shaped object came to her. The Bible. She wondered again why he had turned up after so many years. 'She contacted you, didn't she?'

The jigsaw pieces of time slotted into place. It was a moment before he returned a slow, awkward tilt of his head. 'She was worried about you. There were rumours going around.'

'Rumours?' She remembered Maemm's relief at her staying in. One question still niggled at her. 'Why did she not leave with you?'

Theo remained silent. Slowly the answer came to her.

'She stayed so you could leave unhindered?'

Another regretful nod.

'What about Ruth?'

'She got away.'

In the distance, mist clouded the starless skyline. As they approached the hilltop, she saw billows of smoky clouds mushrooming in the sky. 'Stop. Stop!' She pulled the door handle; it was locked. 'Fire!' Embers leaped and flickered across the horizon.

There was only one building sited on the hill. Hannah shook with horror.

The Stoltzfus's barn.

Chapter 27

'WE HAVE TO help.' She pulled the handle again, willing it to budge. The locking system held it firm. She bashed the door. 'Let me out.'

'No.' Theo veered left to the T-junction.

'But Evan!' she banged on the window.

'I'll call the emergency services.' He fumbled for his phone.

A clanging sound filled the air as a bell tolled. The fire must have taken hold for someone to send the age-old Amish distress signal. For miles around, its sound would summon people. Out of the darkness, two horse-drawn wagons rumbled towards them, their battery lights blinding Hannah as they passed.

'I have to stay.' She rattled the handle. 'You go.'

Indecision creased his face. Frantic screams and shouts came from the direction of the farm. With a rueful toss of his head, he released the brakes and steered to the right.

They abandoned the car halfway up the lane, seeing it blocked with people running, carrying buckets to the burning barn. The wah-wah of a siren echoed through the air. Glancing back down the lane, Hannah caught the flashing lights of a fire engine arriving. People formed a line from the well to the barn, relaying buckets of water. Several youths stumbled out of the barn, carrying furniture. Away from the fire, Mrs Stoltzfus and the older women tended to the injured, including Levi, wrapped in blankets and quilts and seated on hay bales. Near them, makeshift tables made from planks of wood on bales were laden with refreshments, first-aid equipment, and an urn.

Hannah tore up to Mrs Stoltzfus. 'Evan. Have you seen Evan?'

Mrs Stoltzfus pointed to the barn's entrance.

Hannah made to run, but Theo grabbed her arms and held her tight. 'Let go!' She wriggled and fought, but he maintained his grip.

A young man emerged, carrying a coughing girl with clothes smeared in grey smoke. Her kapp had fallen off and her long, copper hair fell about her shoulders. 'Evan!' Hannah rushed forward as her brother lowered the girl tenderly. Two other girls took hold of her and led her to a bench.

Evan rocked back on his heels as Hannah crashed against him and hugged him. 'What are you doing here?'

'I saw the fire.'

Firefighters carried hoses ran into the barn while others sprayed the outside area. The water chain carried on, all working to get the fire extinguished. 'What happened?' Theo stared at the sight before them.

'We were having some snacks when someone noticed the smoke coming from the bales under the rear window. Looks like it was set alight deliberately.'

'And I can guess who by,' Theo muttered.

'Is this something to do with you?' Evan eyed Theo with suspicion. Neither Hannah nor Theo returned his gaze. 'Have the police arrested those drug dealers?'

'No. The ringleaders escaped,' Theo said.

Evan's face paled. 'I must go home.' He hollered for Barney, who broke from the chain and rushed towards them. 'I need your car, friend.'

'We have to leave,' Theo urged, as Evan and Barney sprinted towards the mass of parked buggies and cars.

Hannah gave a firm shake of her head. 'No. There are people injured. I can't leave them.'

'We must.'

'What is wrong with you?' she snapped.

'I don't want to end up hanging from a tree or taking a swim in the river.'

'Fine. You go. I am staying,'

'If they find you—' His voice trembled.

'If, if!' she snapped back. The muscles in her neck strained as she berated him. From her deepest being, a hot, raw anger burst up and out into the air. 'Always if. That's how you live your life. If this. If that. Well, not me. You want to run? Go. Leave the mess for others to clean up. Again.'

If he tried to reply, she did not hear as she marched over to help the injured.

When her racing pulse and the heat burning under her skin had subsided, she saw him standing in the chain.

As she sat on a bale with a solitary lamp beside her, wrapping a bandage over a young man's burnt hand, a hand on her shoulder made her jump. Mrs Stoltzfus stared at her. 'You came back to help.' The older woman glanced in Theo's direction. 'Thank you.'

Hannah fastened the bandage at the ends, careful to keep her face from view.

'Brr.' Mrs Stoltzfus shivered. 'It is getting cold. We will need more blankets and quilts for those in shock.'

'Would you like me to get some?' Hannah rose and smoothed down her dress, stained with blood and charcoal dust.

'In the house.'

Hannah picked up the lamp and made her way to the stone house with its plain wooden door. That's when she spotted a group of familiar figures walking towards the hub of activity and into the glow of light.

'Maemm!' Hannah raced to her.

'We came as soon as we heard the bell. We bumped into Evan; I have explained everything to him,' Maemm said. 'Now I must see what help I can be to Velda.'

Grandfather and Evan went off to join the chain, and Hannah returned to her task. She knew the layout of the house from years of sleepovers and visits. Walking about in the semi-darkness did not hinder her. She climbed the stairs towards the spare room with its wooden chest filled with quilts. She had helped get them when Grace had overnight visitors.

At the top of the landing, she paused outside Grace's door, then pushed it ajar and stepped inside. The lights outside shone through the open curtains. She stared around, a lump in her throat. The single bed with Grace's favourite quilt. Her rag doll propped up on the bedside cabinet. The clothes rail with her dresses and coats in a neat line. All as if she would walk in at any moment. By her dresser, with its trinket box and hairbrush, stood a battered brown suitcase Hannah knew contained the jeans, tops, and dresses Grace had worn to gatherings.

She swallowed, retraced her steps and closed the door. To touch anything seemed disrespectful. The ghosts of the past occupied the room with their memories.

She went across the landing to the opposite room and came out with an armful of quilts. The glow from her lamp dimmed; the oil must be low. No matter, she knew the house well enough not to come to any harm. With care, she descended the stairs. Her feet had barely touched the hall floor when a hand clamped over her mouth and cold steel pressed against her temple.

She dropped the lamp and the quilts.

Theo's fears had come true. One of them had found her.

She tensed, waiting for the puff of cigar smoke, pressing her lips together to avoid coughing. Instead, her nose twitched at the whiff of mint; the sucking sound of someone chewing on gum grated on her ears. Slivers of ice ran through her veins.

Then a thunderclap of horror exploded inside her as she realised who held the gun.

Chapter 28

HIS HAND PRESSED against her back and shoved her down the hallway. The hollow thud of her boots echoed in the silent house as she stumbled towards the kitchen door.

Another forceful shove. This time into the kitchen.

Hannah spun. The thin-lipped mouth moved like a cow's chewing the cud, the clicking sound of the gum filling the room. 'Thought I was someone else, didn't ya? Sam?'

Danny kicked the door shut and levelled the gun at her. He reached out and pushed her roughly, jerking her arms behind her back and tying a rope tight around her wrists. She kicked out and hit something solid. A chair toppled over.

'Seems you're not so bright after all.' Danny swung her round to face him, grabbing her by the throat. He pressed the gun against her forehead. 'Where's the double-crossing thieving runt Sol?' he demanded.

Hannah searched for something to say.

'Where is he?' He jabbed the gun harder.

Her eyes screwed up as a small ball of pain formed where barrel met bone. 'I don't know.'

'Liar.' Danny curled his fingers tighter, digging into her throat, crushing her windpipe. A gurgling sound escaped her as she fought for air. 'You're his pet friend. He'd come running to you.'

A strip of faint light from the yard's lamp spilled through the kitchen window. 'I haven't seen him.' The table's edge pressed into her lower back.

'Liar, liar,' Danny chimed. 'Stubby told me all about his and Levi's plan to leave. He'll come looking for you just as sure as daylight follows night.'

'You... flatter me,' she rasped, forcing the words out. He squeezed tighter. She surprised herself at her rejoinder. What else could she say to buy time till someone noticed? 'Why not send one of your thugs? Why take such a risk and come yourself?'

'Ah, now that is a good question. It's personal. You see, Hannah, I know Sol's not the only one snitching. The little incident at the icehouse confirmed it. And after all I've done for you.'

Exactly what he had done for her would have to wait. But in the wake of the fire's chaos, would anyone notice? She twisted her head to try and see out of the window. People were mingling freely. Talking. Drinking tea, coffee. Comforting one another. If she could break off... shout...

Mrs Stoltzfus stood talking to Mr King, glancing towards the house. When would the older woman realise she had not returned?

If she could somehow get to the window...

Danny pulled the safety catch back. Hannah clenched her teeth, muting the scream in her head.

'Tell me. Where is he?'

His brusque voice focused her mind on the present. *Time.* She needed to buy time. 'I don't know.'

'I'll find him, and when I do, I'm going to hang him from a butcher's hook,' he sneered.

She stepped sideways, closer to the sink. Danny yanked her back, looking past her to the window. 'Nice try.'

'They worked for you? Sol and Sam?' What was it Drummond had said? He wanted Mr Big, the person running the whole drugs ring. Not Sam.

He gave a deep, throaty laugh. '*Did*. Sam changed allegiance. I thought the severed hand would scare him silly. Seems Jorge scared him more.'

The image of the rolling hand, its blood spotting the snow, filled her mind. 'Jorge?'

'Yeah, sorry about the little frisk-down.' His face broke into a leer. 'Never did have any manners. Ungrateful scum. Sol won't be alone hanging from a hook when I get a hold of my dear cousin.'

'Your cousin?'

'Yes, Hannah. My cousin,' he replied, his voice laced with syrup. 'I was brought up in Brooklyn but born in Matamoros, Mexico.'

'Jorge brought the bad... gear in.'

'Oh, you can join dots too. Smart. Pity. I prefer my women dumb. Fewer arguments.'

Time. If she could keep him talking. 'He wants to take over? His men gave Levi the bad drugs?'

Danny's lip curled back in a tight, ugly grin, his gaze fixed on her.

'You arranged the hand? It was your men in the Toyota,' she said.

'Like I said, I needed to scare them. The old folk's story about the two fingers seemed appropriate. Thought I'd go one step further.'

'Jorge's setting up his own gang.'

'Time's up, detective.' He pressed harder against her windpipe. She squeezed her eyes closed as the gun dug deeper into the flesh of her temple.

The loud bang of the front door sent her heart pummelling against her rib cage. 'Hannah! Hannah!' Evan hollered from the hallway.

Danny pushed her aside and in one long stride reached the kitchen door, pulling it open, the gun raised.

She threw herself side-on at Danny, knocking him off balance so he slammed into the pine dresser before he could shoot. She breathed a sigh of relief as Evan backed through the front door and slammed it shut; good. He had the sense to go and not play the hero.

Danny steadied himself, lifted the butt of the gun, and whacked it against her cheekbone. Pain exploded inside her head.

Fingers like talons wrapped themselves tight around her neck. 'Now, for the last time, where is Sol?' Spittle fell on her cheek as he pushed his face into hers. 'Don't give me that innocent look. I know you're no stupid Amish girl, and I'm no mug.'

Her knees buckled, and she forced herself to freeze them, leaning against the table for support.

'You and your snooping. Sucking up to dumbass Sol. I thought Sam giving you money might shut you up. Sol told you what was happening, didn't he, huh?' He pressed the gun to her forehead. 'I could hand you over to Jorge and his boys. Before I deal with them. They'd make sure you squeal. Tell me where the runt is, and maybe I'll shoot you instead. Believe me, it'll be better for you.'

'They'll hear the gunshot if you shoot me.'

He eased his finger off the trigger. 'See, you ain't so dumb.' He gave her a sardonic grin.

She risked a glance out of the window and saw a small group heading out of view while others stood huddled close. One or two glanced in the house's direction. Hope surged inside her. 'I have no idea where he is, but... I can guess where he might be.'

'Where?' Danny eased his grip.

Hannah gulped a lungful of air. 'There's a buggy house out the back.'

Danny let go of her throat. He yanked her around, jabbed the gun between her shoulder blades, and clamped a hand on her shoulder. 'Move. Back door.'

The beam from the yard provided enough light for her to navigate around furniture, to the archway to the rear passage. As she passed the window, she saw a stringy row of people forming, facing the house.

He shoved her along the stone-tiled passage through the parlour, past the utility room with its coats and boots, and to the back door. 'Open it. Nice and slow.' The gun dug into her spine. He untied her hands, and she rubbed her wrists and, with a trembling hand, opened the door and stepped out onto the porch.

The line greeted them. Arms by their sides, they stood in silence. Two men stood at each end, holding lamps; the glow lit the three steps down from the porch.

'What the hell?' Danny snapped. 'What are they doing?'

When she did not reply, he nudged her forward and down the steps. Impassive faces watched them.

'Move!' Danny shouted at them.

'They won't.' She wanted to laugh. Here he was with his gun, stumped by unarmed men and women. How ridiculous. How wonderful! How Amish.

'I said, move!' Danny waved the gun.

Distracted by her thoughts, she did not realise he had moved the gun away from her until the gunshot's snap-crack sound filled the air. A stout woman yelped and jumped, but quickly resumed her place, unhurt.

The man to the far left lifted his lamp high, lighting Danny's face. 'I would suggest you let young Hannah go. You seem troubled, my friend. Why don't we talk?'

The reply came with a stream of profanity. In normal circumstances, Hannah would have blushed in shame at such language. He fired another shot, this time into the ground near the group. The woman who had jumped stayed still and bowed her head.

Danny gripped the back of Hannah's neck and backed up the steps, pulling her with him. Her feet stumbled as he dragged her back into the house.

Inside the kitchen, he steered her to the window. Outside, another line had formed, stretching across the front of the house, with everyone facing the kitchen. Some held lamps. Others held hands as if forming an unbroken chain. Maemm and Grandfather stood in the centre.

Danny shifted his hand to her upper arm. With the butt of the gun, he smashed one of the windowpanes and fired another shot. Hannah's heart sank as she heard a pitiful scream like the bleating of a frightened lamb. Leah, the girl Evan had carried, fainted, and crumpled to the ground. Next to her, an ash-faced Aaron jumped back out of range of the shot. The two youths on either side tucked their arms under hers, hoisted her up, and resumed their position.

A word Hannah seldom thought of, and never spoke, rose in her mind. She prayed for God's forgiveness, then she realised he had more important matters on his mind, like getting her out of this hellish mess.

Danny yanked her out of sight of the window, twisting her around to face him. 'You tell them to let you through. Got it?' Sweat dribbled down his face.

The little ray of hope that had ignited in her out the back grew as they approached the front door. They would not harm Danny, but neither would they let him leave.

The gun. What if he shot someone?

'We are coming out.' She kept her tone as calm as possible so as not to alarm those outside. Danny held the door ajar.

It took her a moment to adjust to the fairy-like halo around the lamps, their gasoline fumes mingling with the fresh evening air.

She stumbled along the neat path bordered by small stones. The line at the bottom stretched from one side of the house to the other across the front garden; in some places people stood behind those in front. The men and women who had stood by the back porch were among those facing her and Danny. Beyond them, the firefighters were still hosing the barn down; black smoke snaked into the sky. To the far left, Barney stood fiddling with his hat, the anxious expression etched on his face making him appear much older than his years. She ran her gaze along the row. All wore similar pained looks. To the right, a brooding Evan stood, also holding his hat; from the tilt of his head and tight line of his mouth, she knew a volcano was brewing. Next to him was Theo, grim-faced. Behind them, several police officers hovered, staring at the house.

Her boots crunched the pebbles as Danny nudged her down the path. When they reached the end, he ordered her to stop, keeping the gun pressed against her shoulder. 'Move,' he barked. The line remained solid. 'Move it, damn it!'

A stocky officer wearing a bulletproof vest stepped forward. 'Now, calm down and let the woman go, then we can talk.'

Danny yelled back, 'No police. I said no police.'

Theo broke ranks and motioned to the officer to remain silent. The space he left quickly filled as those nearest closed the gap. He took a cautious step into the no-man's-land between the line and Danny and Hannah. 'You're surrounded. Drop the gun and let Hannah go.'

He got a short, two-word reply.

Some older men, including Grandfather, shook their heads sadly. Hannah smiled inwardly, knowing what they were thinking. Why make life hard for yourself when you could sit down and talk things through?

Danny pushed the gun under her chin, forcing her to tilt her head up. 'I said move.'

At the cold feel of the metal, she quivered.

The line of men and women regarded each other in dismay.

Theo raised his hands at Danny. 'They won't let you pass.'

'What the hell is this?' Danny frowned at the ragged line.

'Civic arrest, Amish-style,' Theo replied dryly.

'I've got the gun.' Danny pushed it deeper into Hannah's neck, and pain spread through her throat as it butted her jawbone.

Theo gestured at the line. 'They've got the patience of Job.'

'They don't move, I'll shoot her.'

The human barrier stayed in place.

Hannah twisted her head, trying to read Danny's expression. The sweat on his face and the nervous twitch of his eyelids made her wonder how sure of himself he really was. 'He will.' Her words came out faint and strained.

Danny's finger hovered over the trigger. 'I'll count to three. One...'

'Now!' Barney lifted his hand.

Danny tore the gun from her throat and pointed it into the crowd as two hats sailed into the air from each end, spinning like frisbees. Danny fired.

Theo dashed towards them.

Danny lowered his arm, swinging the gun to the right, and fired again.

The snap-crack burst into the air. Theo staggered a pace or two before he halted and stood perfectly still then dropped to his knees and slumped to the ground.

A woman screamed. Maemm?

Get up, get up, Hannah willed him. *Get up, please.* When he did not move, a cold numbness filled her, like the kind when out too long in the winter snow, paralysing her desire to run to him and shake him awake. He had to be alive – they had only just met! There were years to catch up on, memories to create. She willed him to get up. To move. Instead, he lay face down and still. This was all her fault. Another life lost because of her.

A stunned silence froze the air. The line resembled statues, their collective gaze on the body sprawled between her and them. Light-headed, she swayed like a cornstalk in a field. The cold seemed to bite into her bones, turning her body limp. She took a lungful of air, trying to gather enough strength to stay upright. When would it be over? She wanted these good people to go home to their beds and their loved ones.

Some men removed their hats as they stared at the inert body. Grandfather held a weeping Maemm, her face buried in his shoulder. The women bowed their heads in prayer. Mr King edged forward.

'Stop,' Danny ordered.

Mr King glanced at Barney, who waved him back to the line.

Several lines deep had formed now, with more firefighters and uniformed police. She scouted to see if Drummond was among them. Why didn't they do something? Why were they standing back? They were trained to deal with situations like this, surely?

'Now you know I am serious.' Danny hid behind her, the gun at her head once more; she trembled.

The police officer who had addressed Danny before stepped forward, his arms loose by his sides. 'Back-up's on the way. Best put the gun down and let her go. No one else needs to get hurt.'

No one else needs to get hurt. Theo was dead. Hannah stared at the officer in disbelief.

Danny spat on the ground.

She moved her gaze to the row before her, the community that had gathered to help a neighbour save a barn and found themselves in a hostage situation. The banana moon's beams partly lit a small clump of trees to her right, their branches swaying in the night breeze. A fleeting shadow shimmered through them. A fox?

It was a good place to die. Among God's creation, with her people near. Silently, she asked for courage. She knew she would need to do this one last act of penance for her actions.

'This time, she gets it.' Danny's hoarse voice broke the hush of silence.

Hannah braced herself. If she kicked, would he panic like before and shoot wide and hit someone? She already had two deaths on her conscience. There would not be a third. She was the nearest target. She hoped it would be quick.

'*No.*'

A short, barrel-chested man and a plump woman parted, and a

rangy, thin figure walked into view. 'Well, well, if it ain't the little runt,' Danny snickered.

Sol didn't reply as he stepped tentatively into the open area, stopping near Theo's body. 'Let Hannah go,' he said in a quiet, firm voice.

'Now, why would I want to do that, punk?'

'Because she's not the informer. I am. It's over.' Sol glanced towards the trees to his left. 'There are armed officers out there. Snipers. The only reason they haven't fired is because of the others.' Sol thumbed back to the crowd.

'You're lying.'

Out of the corner of Hannah's eye, she caught Drummond squeezing his way to the front, his eyes falling on Theo's body and his face turning ash.

Sol bent over, picked up the black hat on the ground and, with a swift movement, threw it into the air. All eyes followed it. A gunshot cracked the air, with a flash streaking across the night sky from the direction of the trees. The hat landed a few inches from Evan's feet, and he picked it up and wriggled a finger through the hole in the crown, staring mournfully at it.

Danny tugged Hannah left and right as he checked the darkness beyond the line.

'I never told Hannah when the drugs were coming in, only that it would be on the weekend,' Sol said, stepping forward slowly, the sharp snap of a twig breaking under his boot sending shock waves through Hannah's body.

Danny held the gun out, pointing level with Sol's chest. Whether the gun shook from fear or rage, Hannah could not tell.

Sol remained perfectly still, out of reach of the gun but not its bullet.

'Why? I took care of you and Sam,' Danny thundered.

'You took care of yourself. You pimped us out. Made us dealers. Killers,' Sol roared back. 'People have died because of us, and for what?'

'You're dead. Dead,' Danny yelled. 'You ruined everything. Everything I've built these past twenty years.'

'Let her go!'

'This is what you came back for?' Danny yanked Hannah around. His fingers squashed her cheeks so much her teeth ached. He pressed the gun against her forehead again. As she spun, she spotted Drummond shifting along the line till he was level with Sol, one hand inside his jacket.

Hannah's eyes met Danny's. In their reflection, she saw her stark, pale face. She squeezed her eyes shut and waited for the inevitable click of the trigger.

Something broad and solid slammed into her, lifting her off her feet and sending her flying backwards onto the ground. She landed with a thud on the damp grass. A gunshot exploded overhead. She covered her ears to black out its firecracker snap and rocked to and fro. Tears tumbled down her face as she fought to regain control of her rapid, shallow breathing.

'Hannah. Hannah?' a gentle voice called.

A scream leapt to her mouth and came out as a whimper. Someone was cradling her as she sat in a heap on the ground. Too frightened to open her eyes, she raised a hand and felt soft, velvet, china-boned fingers clasping hold. 'Maemm!' She threw her arms around her mother's neck.

'You are safe. It is over.' Maemm wiped Hannah's tear-stained face with a hanky.

Hannah grappled to still her shaking limbs, all the while keeping her eyes shut. A blanket fell over her shoulders, and she sat hunched, propped up by Maemm. She pulled it tight, grateful for its warmth.

When she had regained some sense of self-control, but still cocooned in her darkened world, she asked, 'Sol?'

'Wounded but alive.'

She bolted upright. She must have misheard. Only one person she knew spoke with a transatlantic twang. She inched her eyes open, and her gaze fell on a pair of tan boots and blue jeans.

Theo looked down at her with a sheepish grin.

Hannah tipped her head and stared at him, her mouth flapping open.

He unzipped his jacket to reveal a bulletproof vest. It was more compact and lighter than the thick, heavy ones the uniformed officers wore.

'You... you hit the ground.'

'We knew Danny had a gun, and Evan saw enough to tell us it was a handgun.' Theo examined his jacket; it had a ragged hole in one side. 'We heard him fire two shots out the back and one through the kitchen at young Aaron and Leah. Then another at the hats and one at me. That left one remaining. Thanks to Sol it wasn't you on the receiving end.'

Two medics wheeled a stretcher by; Sol lay covered in a blanket, strapped in.

'How did Sol know Danny was here?' Hannah said.

Theo shrugged.

The stretcher headed towards a waiting ambulance parked on the lane. Hannah clasped the blanket closer and, with an unsteady wobble, stood and stumbled after Sol. Two officers approached a police car idling nearby, leading a subdued, handcuffed Danny, and put him in the back.

'He's Mr Big,' she said.

'Yes.' Theo fell into step beside her.

'All these years, I thought he was a funny old man.'

'He covered his tracks well.' Theo watched the police car drive down the lane. 'When we learned Jorge had set up his own gang, Drummond did some digging. He found out about Jorge's connection to Danny, and everything made sense. It wasn't hard to trace Danny's family origins and history.'

Levi, cradling his bandaged arm, climbed into another ambulance.

Theo smiled. 'He will be charged, as promised, with forgery for supplying fake passports to the Amish. Drummond doesn't know who was helping them, though.'

A name came to mind. Hannah pushed it to one side.

Sol flashed her a weak, loopy smile, motioning for the medics to stop as Drummond joined them. Drummond eyed Theo. 'That's not a regulation vest.'

'Got it online from a security wholesaler,' Theo replied.

Drummond arched an eyebrow.

Hannah stared at the thick pad taped over Sol's collarbone. 'He's got a shoulder wound, but it will heal up fine,' Theo assured her.

Sol lifted a hand to her. 'You weren't the one informing. I was,' he said in a groggy voice.

'No, that's not true.' She leaned over and took his hand.

Sol glanced at Drummond. 'Tell her.'

The chief thumbed his belt. 'He's been working for us for months.

Feeding us information about the setup here and elsewhere. Names. Places.'

'I wanted out. It was a friend's hand thrown out the window on Danny's orders. The guy you saw visiting me in the repair shop was his brother. Helping the police was the only way out.' Sol screwed up his face in pain. 'I'm sorry. I never meant for you to get caught up in it. I had to throw you out of the car the night Grace died.'

'Why?' Hannah caught the exchange of glances between Sol and Drummond.

'We were tailing them,' Drummond said as Sol took a gulp of oxygen from the mask over his mouth. 'The patrol officers were expected to pick both of them up and interview them, giving Sol here a cover to update us, and release them, confiscating the gear. Unfortunately, the officers didn't get close enough in time to pull you all over and get Grace help.'

'Levi didn't know about me working for the cops,' Sol said, pulling the mask away. 'He knew Grace was in a bad way, but hospital was the last place he wanted to go. I dumped you both, hoping the police would pick you up. The bag too.'

'But you accused me of dealing,' Hannah said to Drummond, who avoided her stare. 'Another cover?'

He tilted his head.

'We need to go. He's losing blood.' The medic placed the mask over Sol's waxy face.

Sol squeezed her hand. 'You were right. Running wasn't the answer. When I heard the bell I knew I had to come back. Make it right with you, then I heard Danny had you. My fault again.' He paused. 'I know I have no right to ask for your forgiveness, but...'

She looked at the drawn, pale face and remembered how angry he had been at her going into the storeroom. How he had prevented her every time she tried to go there. His threat outside the police station. All his actions, which she had believed were meant to stop her from finding out the truth, he had done to protect her. She had come so close to costing him his life. All this time he had put her safety first.

'There is nothing to forgive.' She looped her little finger around his in the old, familiar gesture of the cherished friend of childhood memories. Once she had hoped for more; for him to make her heart dance. Maybe in time they could be friends again. Just friends, nothing more. 'God be with you,' she whispered.

Drummond stepped back and motioned for Hannah to do the same. Still processing Sol's revelation, she watched the ambulance join the stream of cars and buggies making their way home.

Theo searched her face as she turned over Sol's confession in her mind. A question nagged at her. 'Why was I arrested?'

'No choice.' Drummond lowered his gaze. 'They found you with a dead girl and drugs. If we had done nothing, it would have seemed odd.'

'But if Sol was your informant inside the shop, why did you need me?' she blurted, not sure whether she was angry or relieved.

Drummond sighed. 'Truth be told, I wasn't sure of young Sol. You were my insurance policy.'

'And I asked Drummond to offer you a deal as a favour to me.' It was Theo's turn to look apologetic. 'To help you with your case, should it ever go to trial.'

The first interview. She recalled Theo leaving her to fetch some drinks.

'Except we didn't figure on you going all detective on us,' Drummond explained. 'You were supposed to observe, stay out of trouble, and be a reliable state witness. Sol came and told me he'd found you in the storeroom and about Jorge's visit.' Drummond rubbed his eyes and stifled a yawn. 'Luckily for you, we've got enough evidence to charge Danny and close the drug ring. So, you are now a witness for the prosecution.'

'With a good lawyer, you'll be fine,' Theo said.

'What about Jorge?' The idea of him free sent a chill down her spine.

'We're working cross-state to find him and his brother Miguel.' Drummond's craggy face broke into a broad grin. 'Hopefully, they'll be six feet under. Less paperwork.'

Theo gave a small laugh.

Hannah shuddered.

'What about whoever was helping Levi with the passports?' she asked.

'I'm sure Levi will tell us. His sort always does. They don't like to fly solo when caught.' Drummond gave a rueful grin and headed back to the open area where the standoff had taken place, now taped off by uniformed officers.

Hannah studied Theo's sea-green eyes, noting his concerned expression. A lump rose in her throat. 'You saved me from Danny.'

'Sort of. Sol charged at him. I grabbed you. Team effort.' He broke into a bashful grin.

A deep swell of tenderness engulfed her as she returned his smile. Tears pricked her eyes, blurring her vision, but not before she had hugged him tight. 'Thank you, Daett.'

Chapter 29

THE STOLTZFUSES HAD a new barn raised within the week. It became obvious to those who returned the next day to help clear the debris that what remained of the old one would require extensive work. It was quicker to pull it down and build a new one.

After Hannah had provided the police with her statement, she had gone to help over the two days it took to build the barn once the cemented foundation had been laid. With the other women, she cooked meals, served drinks to the builders, and kept the area tidy. At other times, she chatted with the women as they sat sewing a wedding quilt for a couple to be married in a few weeks.

Grandfather closed his workshop and, with Evan and Barney, sawed and hammered along with the others. To her delight, Theo came too, lugging wood from the wagons, bringing supplies for the carpenters to customise to different lengths, and inserting joints into them. Sometimes she saw Mr King surrounded by a huddle of men, including Grandfather and Mr Stoltzfus, pencil and pad in hand. Occasionally, they would call for Evan or Barney to join them; those two occupied themselves with trying to persuade people to sign their petition for the community centre during breaks.

On Friday afternoon, a service of blessing was held for the new barn, the dusty smell of newly cut wood and oily varnish hanging in the air despite extensive cleaning. Bishop Fisher declared at the end that the Stoltzfuses would host the church service on Sunday. A murmur of approval rippled through the assembled crowd. It was a fitting acknowledgement of all the suffering the family had endured over the past few weeks.

Hannah tried not to allow the flash of hurt and shame his words brought to her. The honour of holding the church service would be a mark of support to the Stoltzfuses. They, Hannah agreed, deserved it more than anyone.

On occasion, she had caught Mrs Stoltzfus staring at her with a troubled expression. 'Why does she stare at me like I am a bad smell?' she commented to Maemm. 'If she does not want me here, all she has to do is say so.'

'Be patient with her,' Maemm replied, sweeping the back porch. 'She will be reconciled to herself in God's time.'

Hannah, with everyone else, went to the Sunday service held in the Stoltzfus's new barn. The benches numbed her as usual, the singing uplifted her, and the odd smile from Maemm, who broke from tradition to sit by her, sustained her through the lengthy worship. A sense of peace mingled with relief rested on her as the last notes faded.

Bishop Fisher was heading for the side entrance when Mr Stoltzfus rose from one of the front benches. 'May I, by your leave, say something?'

Bishop Fisher stopped, sighed, and waved a hand in acknowledgement.

Mr Stoltzfus stepped out from the row and cleared his throat. In one hand, he held the pad Hannah had seen him with during the week. 'You know I am a man of few words.' A good-natured murmur of laughter rippled through the barn. Bishop Fisher grimaced, looked at his watch, and gave an irritated nod.

'Bishop, recently two young men came to us with a young lady. They spoke of wanting to create a place for our young ones to socialise without the temptations of the world and as an alternative to the Singings. We rejected the idea.' He paused with a heavy sigh, adjusting his steel-rimmed glasses. 'I beg their forgiveness. We were too hasty, too quick to dismiss and slow to wait for God's wisdom to discern the proposal fully.'

The bishop jerked his head up.

'Barney Herzberg. Evan Bieler. Come out here, if you will.' Mr Stoltzfus beckoned them.

Barney and Evan rose as one and hurried to the front.

'I want you to explain to everyone here your idea.'

'Moses...' Bishop Fisher wagged a finger at Mr Stoltzfus, '... this is highly irregular. If you want a members' meeting, you must ask the steering committee for permission and give notice.'

Mr Stoltzfus ran a hand over his brown beard, dulled by a film of dusty grey. 'Of course, Bishop, you are correct.' He gazed out at the congregation. 'Committee members, may I hold a meeting here to discuss the proposal put forward by these young men, Barney and Evan, to set up a community centre for our young people?'

'Not everyone is here,' Bishop Fisher protested.

'Begging your pardon, Bishop, but we are.' Mr King stood and with him, all the other members. 'Permission granted,' Mr King said. 'And due notice is given. Continue, Mr Stoltzfus, if you please.'

Hannah bit her lip so as not to giggle. She glanced sideways at Maemm, whose lips were curling slightly.

'Very well, but the young and those not baptised must leave,' Bishop Fisher ordered.

Mr Stoltzfus raised his hand as people started to get up. 'I beg your indulgence, Bishop. As this matter concerns our young, including those who have yet to join our church, I request they stay.'

'All in favour?' Mr King boomed.

This time, Hannah wedged her tongue between her teeth to suppress the urge to chuckle.

Barney and Evan explained everything as they had done to the committee. As they talked, the barn door opened and banged shut, and Theo and Drummond entered. A uniformed police officer stationed himself by the door.

'And we have the support of the local police.' Evan gestured for them to come forward. 'Mr Anderson has offered for his firm to undertake all the legal work needed to get things up and running.'

'What sort of activities will there be?' asked a youth near the back.

'No music or dancing, I hope,' came a disapproving female voice.

'Only appropriate activities, like, er...' Evan faltered, a panicky glaze crossing his face.

'Sewing!' Hannah suggested.

Barney grinned. 'Yes, sewing.'

Maemm rose. 'If I may speak?'

'Why not?' The bishop threw up his hands.

'Many within our community run their own businesses. We have to keep the books – something I am sure some younger members might appreciate learning before they set themselves up. It would help to save a lot of mistakes in the early stages. As many of us know from experience.'

A few uh-huhs and amens endorsed Maemm's words.

'Will the English be allowed to come?' a young man in a side row said, glancing up hopefully.

'No,' Barney said. 'The community centre will be for our people only. If young people wish to mix with English, they can do so elsewhere.'

'Can we have a book club?' a flaxen-haired girl two benches in front of Hannah said.

'Films?' someone else said.

Evan and Barney nodded.

'Will this mean the end of Rumspringa?' another youth piped up.

'No, it's simply to provide another option,' Evan replied.

'What about games?' a young teenage girl shouted.

'Yes,' Barney answered. 'But we don't want to encourage any competitiveness. The purpose is to have fun and meet others.'

Hannah smiled at Barney's pre-emptive move, remembering how the objection had been raised during their ill-fated meeting at the bishop's home.

'As I asked at the meeting, how will this centre be run?' Bishop Fisher demanded. 'Who will supervise the activities?'

Barney turned to the bishop, all smiles. 'Some of the young people have agreed to help. We will open initially on Friday and Saturday evenings.'

'Rather in a building than my home,' a small, grey-haired lady on the opposite bench to Mr King piped up. 'I hold our young very dear, but with twenty of them stomping about the house, it can get rowdy and untidy. And the mess. Oh, the mess.'

Mr King looked hopefully at the lady. 'Would you be willing to help get a cleaning gang together, Sarah?'

'Consider it done.'

'Now, in case you are wondering, as you did before, Bishop, how we are going to build this centre...' Mr Stoltzfus held up his pad, '... some of us have worked out the design and cost. Though more donations would be welcome.'

Hannah heard several *I wills* from the congregation.

When they had died down, Aaron Miller shuffled off his bench and ambled towards the front, holding a small manilla envelope. 'Bishop, I'm afraid you will need to find a new deacon.'

Bishop Fisher's brow creased into deep lines.

'I am not worthy to serve this community, for I have sinned. I earnestly beg God and the church for sincere patience with me, and from now on, I will carry more concern and care with the Lord's help.' He held out the envelope to Evan. 'For your centre.'

Hannah strained to see as her brother took the envelope in silence.

Aaron coughed. 'I confess I passed on falsified passports and social security cards to our young people so they could leave without permission or blessing. This is the money I earned from my sinning. All of it.'

Hannah had expected uproar, but only sighs and pardons came from those listening.

With one long stride, Bishop Fisher was standing before a cowed Aaron. 'Aaron Miller. We give thanks that you have seen the error of your ways and for your act of atonement.' He placed a hand on the young man's shoulder. 'We will meditate on your future and seek God's will.'

A faint 'thankyou' left Aaron's lips before he returned to his seat.

'Did you give Evan Sam's money?' Maemm whispered to Hannah, and she nodded, remembering how Evan's speechless hug had crushed the air out of her lungs.

Mr King stretched out his arm to those gathered. 'And, as we were saying, we will build it. Moses has a list – though we'd welcome some more volunteers.'

Several hands went up in all directions, including Hannah's, Maemm's, and Grandfather's.

A middle-aged bearded man stood up. 'We don't need this community centre. We've got homes for the young to go to, and there's the church and Singings. If they want to run about, if they must experience the outside world, there are the gatherings.'

'Hear, hear!' Old Man Elijah cheered from the middle of the men's side.

'Not everyone wants to attend gatherings or the Singings during Rumspringa.'

Hannah had not meant to speak. At the sound of her own voice, her cheeks burned and several heads turned to her, including those at the front. Maemm gave her an encouraging smile.

'Miss Bieler is right.' Barney gazed at her over the other women's heads. 'Some wish, as is the point of Rumspringa, to experience the outside world in order to be able to make their minds up about whether they wish to continue living within our community, but as recent times have shown, some unwittingly get hurt or worse, through no fault of their own, before they can make that decision. We only wish to provide an option for those who may feel less confident about leaving home, even for a short while. Equally, we wish to help those young people see the value of being part of our community and living Amish.'

A light, feathery sensation fluttered through Hannah as she listened to Barney's calm, measured voice, turning the rhythm of her heart into a little jig that beat against her ears in the thoughtful hush that fell.

'Abolish Rumspringa!' Old Man Elijah shouted.

A woman gave a tiny yelp as his words shattered the silence.

'Never.' Grandfather eased himself up. 'You, Elijah, know how important Rumspringa is – remember, it is time for our young to learn about themselves. The opportunity should be there for all.'

Mr King laughed. 'Amos, you used to disappear for weeks, then turn up all haggard with a bag of washing and tall stories.'

'They weren't tall stories, King.' Grandfather broke into a good-natured smile. His eyes rested on Evan. 'It was by going away that I discovered my true self.'

With a disquieted expression, Evan stared back at Grandfather.

Hannah lifted her hand. 'If I may?'

Mr Stoltzfus's face broke into a genial smile.

Hannah stood up. 'All we are asking for is a safe place to meet on our own and socialise without the dangers some gatherings can present, as Mr Herzberg has stated.'

A tinge of red rose to Barney's face as Evan nudged him playfully.

A low rumble of agreement rippled through the congregation, mingled with murmuring. 'The English. It's their fault,' someone complained as Hannah sat down.

'No,' another retorted.

Hannah looked around but could not identify the speakers.

Drummond moved to the front and introduced himself. 'English parents are as concerned as you are about the dangers their youngsters are exposed to. Recently, I visited a family to tell them their fifteen-year-old boy had died from a drug overdose. You're not the only ones, believe me.'

Hannah noted the number of people nodding.

'But they have arrested those responsible for the drugs,' a baggy-suited man reasoned.

'And we have indicted several young people from your community for possession of drugs,' Drummond replied.

'So, the matter is dealt with,' Old Man Elijah said.

The room fell silent before a puzzled buzz spread around the congregation. Barney whispered to Drummond.

'Not quite.' Drummond tugged at one of his ears. 'Even if those indicted give up using drugs, the government can still charge them for up to five years afterwards if they are caught using them or storing them.'

A blabber of voices erupted at his words. 'What? Outrageous.' 'Why don't they forgive them?' 'Five years? Ridiculous.'

'Order, order.' Bishop Fisher fanned his hands to calm the agitated congregation.

'There's something else you should know.' Theo stepped forward and stood beside Drummond. 'There is a law called the Fortitude Law. It means if drug use takes place in your homes or business premises, even if it is not you using or storing them, many of you who run your businesses from home could be unfortunate victims.'

'Seems to me we do need this community centre after all. Not for drug taking but, as young Barney says, to provide a safe space,' Mr King remarked, shaking his head. His comment fell on a stony silence while everyone absorbed Theo's information.

'More serious is the harm drugs can have on an individual and community – as we have witnessed.' Drummond signalled to the officer at the door. 'There's someone who can testify to this.'

All heads turned at the squeak of the barn door as Sol entered, handcuffed to another officer. He shuffled along the narrow gap between the men and women, head down, staring at the floor, his right arm in a sling.

'Why is he handcuffed?' Maemm whispered to Hannah, frowning. 'He helped the police.'

'In return for a lighter sentence,' Hannah replied, her gaze following Sol. 'He still broke the law.'

When Sol reached the front, Drummond touched his shoulder. 'You know this young man. He is one of you.'

'Was,' someone sniped. An audible shush chided them.

'Go on, Sol.' Drummond took a step back.

'Most of you know me—' Sol stopped, his gaze sweeping over the sea of faces in front of him.

'He's Adam and Rachel Glick's youngest son.' Hannah recognised Mrs Stoltzfus's crisp tones.

'Drugs don't respect any community,' Sol continued. 'They destroy lives. I know I've ruined a good many, including some belonging to this community.'

Several young people lowered their heads.

'There's nothing wrong with Rumspringa or the gatherings. It's just that some people see it as an opportunity to make money out of selling the stuff. Like I did.'

Peering over everyone's heads, all Hannah could see was the little boy she knew from school. Scrawny and picked on by the older ones.

'Not everyone is as brave as Hannah.'

All eyes rested on her. She closed her eyes, wishing she could be invisible and not the centre of attention. When she opened them, smiles greeted her. 'Maemm?'

'I may have mentioned it was you who tried to get Grace to the hospital,' Maemm whispered, patting her hand.

'Or clever as Evan here...' Sol gave her brother an encouraging smile, '... coming up with this centre where you can keep drugs out and people safe. I wish I'd had somewhere like that to go to. Maybe I wouldn't have ended up as I have.' He lifted his cuffed hand. 'I know I have to leave the community. I have broken the *Ordnung,* God's law. I have broken the law of the land.' He led the officer to the women's side and stood in front of Mrs Stoltzfus. 'I want you to know I am truly sorry about Grace. It's not enough. It will never be enough, but it is all I can offer you.'

Tears pricked Hannah's eyes; Maemm dabbed her own and passed the damp hanky to her. In the hushed silence, she could hear the birds outside and the neighs of the horses harnessed to the buggies.

Mrs Stoltzfus rose and faced Sol.

Hannah steeled herself. What could she have to say to him?

The petite, black-clad woman stepped out and stood beside Sol, her pallid face still etched with deep grief. A lump formed in Hannah's throat, glimpsing the beauty of Mrs Stoltzfus's youth in her fine-boned profile and button-shaped lips. An older Grace. One that would never be.

As Mr Stoltzfus joined his wife, she raised her hands, gently placed them on Sol's shoulders, and moved him to face her. She brushed his cheek and then kissed him. Sol dropped his head, took her hand, and kissed it. If he thanked her, it got lost in the sighs and murmurs of approval spreading around the place. It was Hannah's turn to pass the hanky back to Maemm to use. She may not have saved him, but at least he would have a chance to live his own life once he had served his sentence. She made a mental note to ask Drummond to keep her informed. A wave of deep sadness washed over her. He was so alone, no family. No friends. Perhaps she could visit him, be a friendly face to him.

'We will write to your lawyer to say we bear no ill will and believe others led you astray,' Mr Stoltzfus told Sol. 'It may help.'

Instead of going back to her seat, Mrs Stoltzfus walked steadily down the gap between the benches, her ramrod-straight figure turning heads. Her eyes scanned the women's side of the congregation till her gaze landed on Hannah and Maemm.

Hannah straightened. Whatever she had to say, she resolved she would not answer back.

'Naomi.'

Maemm kept her gaze down.

'Please.' Mrs Stoltzfus gestured to her to stand. Maemm rose and slipped past a young girl in a grey dress and white smock.

'Your daughter is a brave young woman. You have brought her up righteously.'

Though she did not move, Hannah knew from the manner Maemm twisted the hanky that the words were not the ones she had expected.

'I spoke unkindly to you once. I ask for your forgiveness today, if I may.'

'Of course, Velda.' Maemm placed her hand on Mrs Stoltzfus's arm. 'You were grieving.'

'No. I was at war with God. My soul was not at peace. It is now.'

Grandfather's words came back to Hannah. The proverb.

Forgiveness is unlocking the door to set someone free and realising you were the prisoner.

Mrs Stoltzfus met her eyes, a wisdom beyond the world shining in them. They were both released from their cell of guilt and pain.

Mr King stood and surveyed the congregation. 'I believe we have heard enough—'

'Yes, quite enough,' Bishop Fisher interrupted. 'We can discuss it at the next steering committee.'

'We don't need to, Bishop,' Mr King said. 'The committee is present. We have sought the views of our community, as is our way, so I say, let's vote. All in favour?' He raised his own hand.

A sea of hands shot up like stems of barleycorn.

'Carried!' Mr King shouted to cheers of delight.

'Question.' One of the young men held his hand up, glancing nervously at Evan and the others. 'Where will we build this centre?'

'That, my friend,' Evan replied with a broad smile, 'has already been decided.'

Chapter 30

ORD SPREAD OVER the course of the following week. They came from every corner of the district. Buggies and cars filled the Millers' yard and fields, and English and Amish worked side by side with one purpose in mind. Wagons lined the lane at the bottom of the farmstead, loaded with timber, generators, and items for the centre's interior. A steady line of people went from the Millers' home across the lane to the opposite field, a field Hannah had wandered through with Grace countless times after services, family get-togethers, and Singings. It was far enough away for the activities held to not disturb the Millers, but close enough for them to monitor the centre when not in use.

Where one small wooden stile had stood, a sizeable gap had been made with a gate large enough for cars and buggies to drive through, a smaller side gate for walkers next to it. The men formed into three teams. One to create a path from the road to the centre. Another to hammer posts in the ground and nail fences around the land the Millers had donated. The rest worked to build and assemble the frame, making the most of the increasing daylight of the final days of

February. Next, cladding and wooden coverings were nailed to timber frames and generators installed for the kitchen and toilets. Partitions for small meeting rooms around the sides of the centre were built, leaving a large communal space in the middle.

Hannah helped the other women with the usual chores. Drummond turned up with some of his men to help paint walls and doors, ready for the next and final day where everyone, including the women, carried desks, chairs, fixtures, and fittings into the building.

Hannah walked from the farm to the new entrance, the pale winter sun warming her skin. As each person emerged after their last task, groups formed outside, some in conversation, others simply waiting. When all had assembled, the bishop blessed the centre and prayed before they sang "Abide with Me".

So familiar was the song that no one needed hymn books. The words came to Hannah without effort or thought, the song's soulful theme bringing a lump to her throat, making her stumble over the final line of the second verse. All this time, Maemm and Grandfather had waited patiently for her to make up her mind. And Barney? Had he been waiting patiently for her? Dared she hope, after all her rebuffs and wilful determination to get answers to Grace's senseless death, that her chance for more than friendship had passed?

When I was a child, I thought like a child...

Now was the time to put away childish whims and wishes. Her future beckoned. What it would be, she knew she would have to wait patiently to be revealed. The suitcase with her English clothes would remain under her bed. A reminder. If she studied hard, she could be baptised at Easter.

During the last chorus, Mr King climbed a ladder by the front doors, a hammer in one hand and nails in his mouth. When the singing had stopped, Evan handed him a simple wooden board, which he nailed over the entrance. The name given to the place a young girl had strolled through, laughing, catching blades of grass with her fingertips. The decision had been unanimous. There above the door, in simple, bold black letters trimmed with yellow edging, were the words THE GRACE CENTRE.

A hollow silence fell as everyone stared at it.

A lone female voice struck up, 'Amazing Grace...'

Others followed soulfully, their hearts in their voices.

Through moist eyes, Hannah stared at the sign. Tears rolled down her cheeks, then sobs broke out; both of which she had withheld since the funeral. Tears of sadness for the friend who would be imprisoned. Tears of grief for the loss of a beloved friend. Most of all, tears of thankfulness for the love that surrounded her. The knowledge of where she belonged was no longer straddled between two worlds. Once, she had believed one was better than the other, when in reality both held light and darkness. Both had led her to a place of peace and reconciliation, and in that place came the freedom to live her life as intended.

Chapter 31

March 2024

THE SADNESS IN his eyes told her the time had come. 'You're leaving.'

With heavy steps, Theo walked from his Nissan to the porch where she stood. His faint smile matched the sorrow in his eyes. Above them, rain-packed clouds floated in a drab sky. Puddles of water from an early morning shower dotted the yard's surface. 'But not alone.' He gestured to the house as Maemm and Grandfather came out. Instead of her usual black dress, Maemm wore a light blue one. Had she changed her mind?

Maemm took hold of Hannah's hand. 'It is not I who is leaving.' she said with a secretive smile. 'My place is here.'

Theo gave her a resigned nod, his eyes still melancholy. 'Take care of your mother, Hannah.'

Hannah linked her arm through Maemm's. 'Of course.'

A solitary figure passed underneath the board and strolled up the path toward the house, carrying a suitcase. The young man, dressed in a plain blue shirt and grey trousers, looked oddly familiar, but she couldn't make out his face at this distance.

'May God go with you.' Grandfather offered his hand to Theo. 'There is always a place at our table for you.'

'Thank you,' Theo replied in a gruff voice, shaking Grandfather's hand. 'Ready?' he called in the house's direction.

Hannah turned to see Evan coming out. Gone were his usual clothes, replaced by jeans, a buttoned shirt under a green fleece jacket with a passport poking out of one side pocket and trainers. He held his hat in one hand, a small patch covering the bullet hole, and carried a bag in the other.

'Evan?' Hannah gasped in bewilderment.

He handed his bag to Theo, who put it in the trunk.

'You're the one leaving?' Her eyes widened in surprise.

Evan shifted uneasily from foot to foot, his eyes darting around.

'Is this what you meant when you asked me to pray for you to make the right decision?'

A wave of pain crossed Evan's face. 'Grace's death made me realise I was hiding from the world, not ignoring it. I need time to discover who I am, and I can't do it here.'

'Theo has agreed Evan can stay with him in England,' Maemm explained. 'I look forward to reading his letters.' She turned to Evan. 'Maybe you can study while you are abroad?'

Evan stared at her, his mouth dropping open.

Maemm held up a hand, smiling. 'Do you think I do not know my son?' She embraced him and kissed his cheek. 'You must do what God calls you to do, Evan.'

He went to Grandfather and stood before him with his head bowed.

'*Gott segan eich.*' Grandfather rested a hand on Evan's head, his eyes closed. A calm, prayerful expression filled his face. After a moment or two, he dropped the hand to Evan's shoulder and gave it a gentle pat-pat along with a soft tsk-tsk, whispering in Evan's ear.

'Naomi...' Theo faced Hannah and her mother, '... you should tell Hannah. You will need support.'

Maemm hushed him, her gaze darting from Grandfather to Evan, still whispering together.

'She's not well.'

Blood drained from Hannah's face. She touched Maemm's arm. 'What ails you?'

Maemm patted her hand. 'I am fine. Just some tests. Now, hush to both of you.'

'But—'

'Shush, I will explain later.'

'Hold her to that, Hannah,' Theo muttered.

Maemm handed Theo a cream-coloured envelope, which he slipped into his pocket. 'I'll post it on the way.'

Maemm thanked him and lowered her head. Another loved one leaving her. Hannah sighed inwardly.

Where had she seen the envelope previously? The question niggled at her for a second before the answer came. The letter Maemm had written in her sewing room. Who was it to?

As though reading her thoughts, Maemm placed a finger to her lips and glanced over at Grandfather. 'He does not know?' Hannah whispered.

Maemm shook her head. 'It broke his heart when Ruth left. We have stayed in contact.'

'You know where she is?' Hannah glanced at Evan and Grandfather, still talking.

'Shush. Say nothing. I am worried. She had not written since before Christmas or replied to my last letter. Most unusual.' Maemm smoothed down her dress as they strolled over to them.

'Who will help run the workshop?' Hannah kept her voice calm and bright, her mind coming to terms with Maemm's revelation.

'Barney's young nephew,' Evan replied. 'Barney's been fixing Lucas's old bike so he can get here.'

Grandfather stroked his beard, gazing down the drive as the young man with the suitcase entered the yard. *Barney*. She could see him properly now. Tousled hair and wearing his usual affable grin. She shook her head in astonishment at his appearance. 'You're wearing Amish clothes.'

'Almost.' He pulled back the strip of material covering the shirt's buttons. Hannah giggled. He placed the suitcase on the ground by Evan. 'You might need something more stylish when you date those English girls.'

Despite his cheeks reddening, Evan laughed and held out his hat to Barney. 'Keep it warm for me, friend.'

'Where is your car?' Hannah said.

Barney smiled. 'Sold it to a traveller crossing America.'

'I understand you have returned to your family home.' Maemm wore another secretive smile.

A giddiness overcame Hannah as Barney put Evan's hat on his head. 'I realised there is more for me here than out there.' His gaze met hers, his meaning slowly penetrating her brain, the warmth rising to her cheeks. The giddiness melted. In its place, a tender glow of understanding filled her.

LATE AFTERNOON, AFTER Theo and Evan had left, she wandered down the path with Barney. Standing side by side by the railings, they watched the tangerine sunset sinking and spreading across the horizon. The trees, outlined against the skyline, moved slightly in the gentle breeze. He listened as she shared her concerns over Maemm's health. When Grandfather retired, she would sit Maemm down and find out exactly what was wrong with her. When she remonstrated with herself for not noticing anything amiss, he simply encouraged her to be there now she knew. Good advice, as usual, she reflected, staring at the fading light.

Barney reached into his pocket, pulled out an oblong envelope, and handed it to her.

Intrigued, Hannah opened it and read the contents. 'You've taken over the shop. The cycle shop?'

'Leased the premises. Glick's Cycles is shut down. The police confiscated all Sam's and Danny's worldly goods, including their businesses. The shop is owned by some real estate company.'

'What are you going to do with it?' She handed the envelope back to him, but he did not take it.

'Tourists like to cycle around here. I like to build and repair things.' He stared down at the envelope. 'Not so good at paperwork. Keeping books and things.' He pushed his tongue against one cheek, making a funny shape on the side of his face. 'I might need a partner. Someone who could work in the shop and help me with the paperwork. That kind of thing.'

A warm, tingling current flowed through Hannah. 'Partner? Business partner?'

Barney swallowed. 'Kind of.'

The clip-clop of a horse's hooves approached.

'More a lifetime partner,' Barney said faintly.

'Oh, that kind of partner.' The faint beat of a jig stirred somewhere around her heart.

He leaned against the rail, facing the road. The grey-topped, closed buggy with the yellow cross on its side rolled by. 'Good evening,' boomed a rich baritone voice; the driver, well wrapped up.

They returned the greeting and watched the buggy disappear down the lane.

A memory emerged in her mind, and she pressed her lips together to keep the giggles in. The one of them sitting in Barney's car as the bishop clip-clopped by with a curious glance at them parked on the roadside all alone. She struggled not to give in and avoided Barney's quizzical stare for fear of him remembering too, in case she had misunderstood his meaning.

He inched a little closer, so his face filled her vision. A nervous smile played on his lips, and she fought to suppress her own only to fail and unleash a half-moon smile across her face as she gazed at him. His eyes sparkled as bright as his grin. He straightened, and the odd glowing sensation grew in the depths of her.

'Well?' His tone had a slight quiver in it. 'Shall I make a clock for you, Miss Bieler, before the bishop passes us a third time?'

'Yes, Mr Herzberg, I believe you should,' she replied as she placed her hands in his.

The End

Notes on Amish Words, Customs and Names

Glossary of Amish words and phrases

The Amish words and phrases used throughout Hannah's story are Pennsylvania Dutch. The Amish language is essentially spoken language developing from the Dutch and German languages used by the first Amish settlers. Over time more than one spelling for words and phrases have developed. For example: mother/mum can be Maemm/mater/mama. Good morning: goot melyet/gude mariye. As the story is located in Pennsylvania, I have used *The Pennsylvania German Dictionary* by D. Miller (Deitsh Book, 2013). The spellings are the same found in the Pennsylvanian German Bible.

Amish Word	English
Maemm	Mother or mum
Denki	Thank you/thanks
Goot gute	Have a good day
Goot meiyet	Good morning

Goot dawk	Good day
Gut n Owed	Good evening. (Theo says this. 'Good' is spelt differently, as he was brought up in Ohio.)
Vi bisht dich?	How are you?
Sei Goot	Be good
Daett	Father/Dad
Dawdi	Grandfather
Englischer	Non-Amish person
Leddich	Unmarried man
Gott saykna dich	God bless you
Goot nacht	Good night
Gott villa	God's will

Customs, Beliefs and Traditions

Rumspringa – A time when adolescents are allowed to experience the wider world before they decide whether to be baptised and live as Amish. Usually starts from 16+. Often called 'running about'.

The Ordnung – Written and unwritten rules of the Amish upheld by the Church. Most know them by heart. They may differ from district to district.

Christenpflicht– Amish prayer book.

The Ausbund – Amish hymn book.

Kapp – Headcovers are very important as they denote the marital status of both men and women. A kapp is a prayer cap always worn by women except at night. On a day-to-day basis the same coloured kapp is worn by all women. In most cases this is a white kapp. In some communities married woman may wear a black kapp on their wedding day and when attending church or worship services. However, colours used can differ from community to community (i.e. the colours can be reversed for married and single women in different communities). On the advice of my Amish friends, I have chosen to have Hannah wear a white kapp as a single woman and the married women to wear black ones.

Names – Biblical names are common for Amish people, and several are used amongst most Amish communities, especially the Old Order and New Order (which Birchwood is a mix of), such as Hannah and Aaron. I have used less well-known names such as Evan, Velda, and Sol to avoid similar sounding names.

Bible Quotes – Hannah would have been familiar with the Pennsylvania German Bible. There is no direct English translation of this. The most comparable Bible is the Lutheran Bible because it is the one that many German Bibles are founded upon. The closest English translation is the King James Version. It is this version I have used.

Author's Notes and Acknowledgements

FOR MANY YEARS I lived in a town populated by two different faith communities in the north west of England. In 2019, I had the privilege of spending two weeks doing not much else but listening to the stories of volunteers who came to help the BBC's "DIY SOS" team convert the church hall belonging to the church where I was vicar into supportive accommodation for the local Blackburn homeless charity Nightsafe. A vision the church and charity had begun working on in 2018. The diverse workforce became united in their cause yet retained their identities. Muslim volunteers took time out to hold daily prayers. Sunday services were held. Food and Rovers FC provided a common bond. This was just one case where I saw unity and diversity go hand in hand over the years. I also encountered many who struggled with knowing who they were, where they belonged as citizens or members of a faith community. These experiences as a minister and former community worker living in mixed cultural communities raised the question at the heart of Hannah's story. What does co-existence really mean? Parallel lives or integration? Is it possible for two communities to converge on some matters but respect the differences that exist between them? It is the overarching theme throughout the series. Hannah finds she must go against her own people's reluctance to work with the police to free her town from the crime that affects both communities. In doing so, she learns that darkness and good exists within each. The dilemma of choosing what to embrace and what to let go will continue in the next instalment of The Birchwood Inheritance series.

They say writing is a solitary business, but there are many I am enormously grateful to for their invaluable patience, knowledge, and wisdom.

Despite researching the Amish, there is no substitute for firsthand knowledge. I am deeply indebted to Rachel Garwood of the Mission to Amish People Project based in Ohio, and Dee Yoder, author of Amish and Mennonite fiction, for keeping me right on all things Amish. However, as this is a work of fiction, I have taken some liberties, i.e Evan's hot-headedness turning physical. Any inaccuracies are mine.

Inspiration for some of the story came from Rumspringa: To Be or Not to Be Amish, by Tom Shachtman (2006), and The Amish Way: Patient Faith in a Perilous World by Kraybill, Nolt & Weaver-Zercher (2010), particularly the community centre idea and the Leechburg drugs case. Thanks to Lyndon Smith and his team from Consulting Cops for their advice on law enforcement procedures in the USA. (www.consultingcops.com)

Thanks to members of ChristianWriters.com who gave me feedback on early drafts. To Terrie and Kate for their spot-on assessments of the MS. Thanks to Liz Carter (Capstone Publishing Services) for working her magic on the final edit, formatting and book cover. To everyone at Resolute Books for all your support, good humour, and encouragement to publish this series.

Last of all, a huge thanks to my family, who have quietly championed me over the years to pursue my dream.

And to you dear reader, thank you for taking the time to read In-Between Girl.

Sheelagh

If you have enjoyed reading this book, please leave a review and let others know about it on either your own social platforms or book review sites. Thank you.

About The Author

SHEELAGH IS A freelance writer living in the northeast of England with her black Labrador who takes her for long walks and is chief adviser for all things writing. With failed A-levels and a flunked secretarial course (not a good career choice for a dyslexic person with severe loss of sight), she worked as a community worker and for the last 20 years as a parish vicar. In late 2024, she retired and became a freelance writer. To find out more about Sheelagh and subscribe for updates on future instalments of The Birchwood Inheritance series at: www.sheelaghaston.com.

About Resolute Books

We are an independent press representing a
consortium of experienced authors,
professional editors and talented designers
producing engaging and inspiring books of the
highest quality for readers everywhere. We
produce books in a number of genres including
historical fiction, crime suspense, young adult
dystopia, memoir, Cold War thrillers, poetry,
and even Jane Austen fan fiction!

Find out more at resolutebooks.co.uk

for the joy of reading

Printed in Dunstable, United Kingdom